BRAZEN
DECEIT

ROBERT F. LACKEY

ROBERT F. LACKEY

Heron Oaks, Murrells Inlet, SC
Copyright © 2018 Robert F. Lackey
Heron Oaks

ISBN-13: 978-0692063149
ISBN-10: 0692063145

Other Pulaski books by Robert F. Lackey:
Pulaski's Canal – ISBN: 0692625267
Blood on the Chesapeake – ISBN 0692688676
Raven's Risk – ISBN 0692831320
Kingdoms in the Marsh – ISBN 0692831355

As Pug Greenwood:
Bim and Them   ISBN: 0692569561
Tooey's Crossroads ISBN: 0692566198
Tooey's Crossroads II ISBN: 0692628134
On The Way To Alice ISBN: 069291417X

ROBERT F. LACKEY

DEDICATION

To my sons
Alexander Berl Lackey
and
Brandon Robert Lackey,
and to my daughter-in-law
Caitlin Sisson Lackey.
I am proud of you.

- Robert F. Lackey

ROBERT F. LACKEY

ACKNOWLEDGEMENTS

*No book can make its way to print without the hard
work of many people.
I wish to acknowledge the valuable assistance of
stalwart beta readers
and thank each of them for their contributions:*

James Cameron of Havre de Grace, Maryland

Judee Cooper of Edgewood, Maryland

Linda Cross of Avenue, Maryland

Kathy Cullum of Havre de Grace, Maryland

Lori English of Las Cruces, New Mexico

John Gross of Newark, Delaware

Jeanne Hawtin of Havre de Grace, Maryland

Joseph King of Laurel, Maryland

Christine McKay of Callaway, Maryland

Buddy Quade of Columbia, Maryland

Marian Stokel of Leonardtown, Maryland

Mike Webb of Newport News, Virginia

Lynn Whitt of Elkton, Maryland,

who aided significantly in finalizing this manuscript.

*Reverend David Beaubien, St. Aloysius Gonzaga Church
Leonardtown, Maryland*

*Copy Editor, Jennifer Cosham
Mount Airy, Maryland*

*The supportive members of the Surfside Writers Group,
Surfside Beach, South Carolina*

FURTHER ACKNOWLEDGEMENTS

I offer my appreciation and recognition for the wonderful generosity of

The Susquehanna Museum at the Lock House, Havre de Grace, Maryland

The Havre de Grace Maritime Museum, Havre de Grace, Maryland

The Friends of Concord Point Lighthouse, Inc. , Havre de Grace, Maryland

The Chesapeake Bay Maritime Museum and the St. Michaels Museum, St. Michaels, Maryland

Mr. Robert McAlister, Director of the South Carolina Maritime Museum, Georgetown, South Carolina

Leonardtown, Maryland, home of my childhood memories

Mayor of Leonardtown, Dan Burris, for your kind reception and generous gift:
'A Most Convenient Place – Leonardtown'

Executive Director of Saint Mary's County Historical Society, Susan Wolfe, along with the very helpful Frankie Tippett, and the wonderful staff at Tudor Hall.

Karen and Ed Garono, Owners of the historic Sawyer Building (C.1840), for the private tour during its renovation. I used this memory as the Newkirk Hotel.

And that exquisite gem at the head of the Chesapeake Bay:
Havre de Grace

BRAZEN DECEIT

ROBERT F. LACKEY

BRAZEN

DECEIT

x

September 23rd, 1847. Waccamaw River, South Carolina

Ben Pulaski gripped the rail as the small steamboat turned from the river into the murky entrance canal to Palmetto Haven Plantation. The air was a sultry reminder of the lingering summers that hung oppressive over the rice plantations. The musky scent of swamps mixed with the smell of burning coal wafting over the deck, pretending to be a breeze as the steamboat shoved its way forward. The land near the canal edge was truly low country. The soil was barely above water and permanently saturated, little more than black mud held together by the acres of reeds. Ben absently tapped his boot against the small crate placed by his feet. It contained the final personal effects of Herbert Binterfield, a conniving man he once threatened to kill but was murdered instead by the man's own business partner.

Ben smiled around his pipe stem, releasing a muted chuckle. He muttered to himself, "Stabbed by his wife's lover."

He hated this chore, almost as much as he once hated Herbert, but he had agreed to do it in spite of himself. He had sailed his schooner *Raven* down from Havre de Grace for another load of Carolina Gold rice in Georgetown and intended to abandon the crate on the wharf. He wished to leave it for someone else, anyone else. The harbormaster made an unusual grand gesture to assist him in delivering it, and Ben was too near the plantation to refuse the chore. Now he reluctantly escorted Herbert's effects to the man's widow, Lydia, the name emblazoned on the stern of the very steamboat he rode.

In just a few years, Lydia had managed to gain

ownership of the plantation stretching out on either side of the entrance canal. He drew on his pipe, letting the blue smoke rush past his beard, frowned and shook his head at his memory of her. He could not deny her beauty, but she was sullen and spiteful when he had delivered her here in '44, fulfilling another obligation. That one was to her brother. No one else in her family would have her as an equal. Ben was hopeful she would rot away in the marshes, but she thrived.

Spanish moss hung like funeral shrouds from the gnarled live oak trees growing along the banks leading to the manor house in the distance. In manicured spaces between the trees, at odds with their world, pale marble statues of Greek women holding grapes or flowers stared out at him with empty chiseled eyes. The marsh beyond the canal was still lush green, stroked with buff-colored reeds and spotted with brilliant white egrets. The rice fields were laid out beyond in ten-acre fields marching into the distance, surrounded by the low mounds that mastered their water. The mansion sat like an alabaster castle nestled among shade trees at the bend in the canal. Decorative white columns, supporting nothing, marched along the edges of an intricate brick pathway from the dock up to the mansion entrance.

The heavy doors of the mansion flew open, and two white-coated slaves dashed down the walkway to the dock, greeting them with hurried bows and picking up the crate. Ben tasted the acid in his mouth and drew on his pipe to flush it away, then forced himself to follow them into the domain of Lydia Binterfield, once more. Driven from Maryland, her white half-brother exiled her to the lusting hands of her uncle in South Carolina, who had soon died of a wound delivered by Ben himself.

The servants picked up the crate and escorted Ben into the mansion parlor where the box was placed gently on the floor in the middle of the room. The slaves backed away and vanished into the hallway. Lydia Binterfield sat in the great chair once favored by her Uncle Jeremiah, her hands draped over its padded arms, a cut-glass brandy cordial sitting on the small table nearby. Looking like the subject of an Italian painting, she seemed never to age, nor suffer lines on her face from her notorious rage. Standing behind her chair was her new Plantation Manager, Horatio Cuttingham, an Englishman once imported by Jeremiah as master of his private steamboat. The very same Cuttingham who once tried to drown Ben for sport, only allowing him to breathe so his master could kill Ben himself.

Ben glared at Cuttingham. "I haven't forgotten you," he said, "One day we will settle accounts."

Lydia smiled at Ben, but the smile did not reach her violet eyes.

She motioned with her hand toward another man seated in a nearby chair. The man stood and stepped toward Ben.

"I am William Postell..."

"I know who you are," Ben said.

"...Sheriff of Georgetown County. Benjamin Pulaski, you are under arrest for the murder of Jeremiah Williamson."

Two men stepped from the hallway and took Ben by his arms and pulled them behind his back. The sheriff slipped manacles around Ben's wrists as he struggled.

"What the hell is this?" Ben yelled. "Get your hands off me! Postell, you were there! It was a duel!"

"You are charged with goading a feeble man into a duel, Pulaski."

"You were part of it!" yelled Ben, twisting between the deputies, trying to charge toward the sheriff. "You were there! You know damned well that is a lie! Williamson demanded it!"

The deputies pulled him from the room. Postell bowed toward Lydia and followed his men. Cuttingham approached the crate and called for the slaves to pick it up.

"Where would you like this, madam?" he asked Lydia.

"Burn it," she said, but hesitated and sighed. "No. Wait. Have one of the servants take it up to my room. Might as well look into it."

Near sundown, Sheriff Postell stood outside Ben Pulaski's jail cell in Georgetown.

"Mr. Pulaski, just make the best of it tonight. You'll

be in front of the judge as soon as he allows it in the morning. I promise you all this will be resolved before lunch tomorrow."

Ben stood with his back to Postell and did not answer. He was still standing there after Postell left as darkness filled the cell. His heartbeat pounded in his skull; his breath came shallow and tense. He pumped his fingers into fists, crushing, crushing.

Five miles north of Havre de Grace, Maryland, in the little canal village of Lapidum, Sonja Pulaski wiped the remaining tears from her eyes so she could see her older son.

"Oh, Isaac!"

She pulled him tightly to her, letting the tears fall again and slip onto his dusty Army uniform.

"Are you hurt?" she said into his shoulder.

He held her out so he could look into her face.

"No, Ma. Not a scratch. We won! We took Mexico City! They are finished."

"I...I just read that in the *Whig*. And...now, you are here!"

"I came with two other officers to deliver General Scott's initial report to the President..."

"To the President?"

She looked at him with wide reddened eyes. He released a boyish smile, and he was once again ten years old, showing her the big fish he had caught.

"I just stood there, while the Colonel and Major spoke, but President Polk nodded to me."

Sonja's chest swelled, and she pulled him into another hug.

"I am a captain, now, Ma," he said into her curls, noticing her hair, still golden, but with random strands of gray.

Sonja pushed herself away so she could examine his uniform, and smiled up into his eyes.

"Come. Sit down. I will fix us some coffee," she said.

As Isaac sat down, he asked, "Have you heard from Aaron? Do you know where he is?"

"Your brother is in California," she said over her shoulder as she pumped water into the coffee pot.

"California? What is he doing there?"

She turned from the counter and pushed loose curls up her forehead with the back of her hand.

"He didn't say, Isaac. It was a short letter. He said he was well, and not to worry about him...."

"Well, at least we know that much. I was worried of much worse. After Maggie...and little Sarah, both died. Wife and daughter lost..."

Sonja held up her hand to him and turned away, halting his words, looking out the back window at nothing. Small shoes charged across the wooden floor in the front room, coming in from the porch.

"Isaac!" Alisha screamed and threw herself onto his lap, her muddy fingers streaking reddish brown on his uniform coat.

"Hello, little sister," he said, hugging her. He tussled her yellow curls and smiled into her blue eyes. "Is this what you looked like, Ma? When you were a girl?"

"Mud and all, son." She smiled as she said it.

Someone knocked several raps at the front door.

"Oh, that must be Catherine Price. We were talking when you came up the path..." Sonja gave a faint laugh. "Oh no, in the excitement, I forgot all about her."

Sonja quick-stepped through the front room. "Catherine, I am so sorry...Oh, hello," she said to an unknown woman standing before the open doorway.

The woman stood sternly erect with dark eyes that almost matched her black dress. Deep pox scars speckled her cheeks.

"Are you Mrs. Pulaski?"

"Yes. Yes, I am..."

"I am Ramona Tatum. I am told you have my sister buried here?"

"Yes...in the back field, under a tree. We did not know she had any..."

"And I understand you have taken in my sister's daughter?"

"Well, I have my daughter, now. My daughter. She was rescued by Rachel..."

"She is my niece, and I am here to take her home," Ramona said.

Sonja stood in silence, her mouth open, gripping her hands into fists.

"She is my daughter," Sonja said. "I gave birth to her!"

"Her mother was Rachel Tatum," Ramona said through gritted teeth.

Alisha came into the front room with Isaac behind her.

"Who are you?" Alisha asked.

Isaac stood over Alisha, resting his hands on her shoulders and frowning at the woman.

"I am your mother's sister, Mos, your Aunt Ramona. And I am here to take you home with me," she said, locking her eyes with Sonja's, "...where you belong."

Alisha stepped next to Sonja and took her hand in a tight grip. "Sonja is my momma," she said to the stranger.

Sonja held tightly to Alisha and glared at Ramona. "Alisha is my daughter. I gave birth to her. She was swept from my arms by the ice flood when she was an infant."

Ramona frowned and opened her mouth to speak, but Sonja cut her off.

"Rachel found her and kept her on Shad Island and told Alisha she was her mother. Rachel admitted all of it to me on her death bed, while Hattie and I tried to save her life. Alisha is my daughter, and you will never take her."

"That girl is my sister's daughter, and I will have her where she belongs."

"She is where she belongs," Sonja said, then slammed the front door in Ramona's face.

Hours later, Ramona Tatum barged into the Havre de Grace office of Lester Watkins, Esquire. Watkins looked up and sighed, setting aside the letter he was preparing for Lydia Binterfield.

"I was hoping to get a letter on the afternoon steamer to Baltimore, but the prospects of that are dwindling.

May I help you, madam?"

"My niece has been kidnapped and is being held against her will by a canal woman!"

Watkins adjusted his spectacles. "Madam, you should go see the deputy sheriff at once! Has this just happened?"

"I need an attorney. This crime has been going on for some time. The woman has my sister buried in her back field!"

"What! Oh, dear," he said. "Surely Deputy Mattingly is the man to see. He rose from his desk and reached for his hat. "Do you believe she was murdered? How old is your niece? This is terrible. I will show you to his office..."

"N-No, sir. My sister died of consumption. Her daughter was taken in by the canal woman, who now claims to be the girl's mother."

Watkins frowned as he sat down.

"How old is your niece?"

"Well, seven or eight, maybe ten..., I had never seen her until today...my sister referred to her as 'Mos' in her letter."

Watkins motioned to the chair in front of his desk. "I think, madam, you should give me more information before we take any action."

He pulled a few sheets of loose paper from his file cabinet, placed them on his ink blotter, and plucked a steel-tipped pen from its holder. He dipped the tip into the ink bottle, cleared his throat, and held his pen over the paper.

"Now, what is your sister's name?"

"Rachel Tatum."

"Your niece's name? Mos Tatum, I assume. Is that short for some other name?"

"I...I don't know. Rachel only named her Mos."

"And your sister died of consumption recently?"

"Two or three months ago, maybe four..."

"And, what is your name, Mrs...?"

"Miss. Ramona Tatum."

Watkins dipped the pen in ink. "Mrs. Tatum was your sister-in-law?"

"No. We were sisters. Neither of us married."

"Oh...so..."

Ramona had fire in her eyes as she emphasized each word. "My. Sister. Had. A. Daughter. That daughter is my niece. I am her only living relative. My niece is being held by a woman without my permission."

"Well, Mrs., I mean Miss Tatum, it shouldn't be much trouble getting your niece back into your custody. Where is she staying?"

"In a village a few miles north of this town. I believe it is called Lapidum."

He wrote more notes. Without looking up, he asked, "Do you know the name of the woman holding your niece?"

"Pulaski. Sonja Pulaski."

Watkins placed his pen back in its holder and leaned back in his chair, lacing his fingers together over his stomach. "Sonja Pulaski? Trim woman, thick yellow curls, bright blue eyes, oval face?"

"Yes, that is what she looks like."

"Mmm. And your niece? Also blonde curls and bright blue eyes? Called 'Alisha' by Mrs. Pulaski?"

"Yes. And I want my niece out of that house."

Ramona pulled paper money from her purse and counted out fifty dollars on his desk.

"You will handle this for me?" she asked.

Watkin's eyes grew wide, and he exhaled through his teeth.

"Yes," he said then sighed.

Inside the office of the defunct Tidewater Bank and Trust Company in Havre de Grace, Maryland, the inventory of its contents continued under the contentious scrutiny of three men. One man was Deputy Sheriff Lyle Mattingly, investigating the murder of the last owner, James Williamson. Another man was Jason Williamson, the younger brother of that previous owner, and claiming ownership of the bank. The third man was Lester Watkins, the lawyer representing the estate of the original bank owner, Herbert Binterfield, for his survivor, Mrs. Lydia Binterfield.

"The only item Mrs. Binterfield has specifically claimed is this large mahogany desk," the lawyer said, standing in the rear of the office tapping the desk.

"Have it, Mr. Watkins," Mattingly said.

"You two are free to do what you will with the rest, but mind you, Mr. Williamson," Watkins said, pointing his finger at Jason. "Lydia Binterfield has a legal claim to twenty-five percent of all value realized from properties and financial accounts."

Mattingly sighed and shook his head. "What the hell does the woman want with that desk? It has the blood stains of two dead men on it! Her husband and her brother."

"Half-brother," Jason said. "Lydia was of my father, but not of my mother."

The lawyer raised his finger. "That, sir, is unproven and scandalous. Mrs. Binterfield holds signed papers from her uncle – your uncle – stating he was present at her birth from white parents – your parents."

"Uncle Jeremiah was a drunkard," Jason said.

"Be that as it may..." Watkins began.

"Enough," said Mattingly. "Get on with your damned

inventory, but nothing leaves until I say so."

One of the two bank clerks kept by Jason to assist with the inventory approached him.

"Ledgers are missing, sir," he said handing Jason a list. "Many of the day journals for the last two years are not here. That covers both the management by Samuel Briscoe and James Williamson."

The other clerk came out of the massive vault holding another list. "Three named ledgers are missing in here, sir. The Bs, Ps, and Ws."

"Damn," Jason said. "The Ws include both James' account and my father's original investment."

Watkins frowned. "And the Bs hold both the Binterfields...and Briscoe."

Mattingly chuckled, "Oh yes, Sam Briscoe. The man who killed Herbert. And the P's include the Pulaskis. Those three ledgers probably hold the accounts for everyone we might suspect."

"Total up the named accounts you do have," Watkins said to the clerk, snapping his fingers. "And balance it against the cash and property value. Twenty-five percent of that will belong to Mrs. Binterfield."

Jason scowled at Watkins.

"Not until I release this building and Judge Jessup has ruled on the estate," Mattingly said. "It will be Christmas by then, gentlemen, or later. Get comfortable with this."

Jason and Watkins both glared at Mattingly.

"I will need to meet with Ben Pulaski about this," Mattingly said.

Watkins extended his hand toward the front door. "Then, by all means, go do that, Sheriff."

"Can't. He's in South Carolina on business. Not sure when he will be back here."

The mechanical clock across the street rang six times in the falling darkness.

"Time for my supper," Mattingly said and ushered everyone out of the building, locking the doors behind them.

The others made their way toward the town center. Mattingly turned down Oyster Street toward the basin for the Susquehanna and Tidewater Canal, crossing the swing bridge near the lockhouse. He ambled north along the towpath, a long finger of dirt, rocks and cypress logs poked brazenly between the canal basin and the Susquehanna River. He paused to take in the fresh air off the river slapped at the towpath, still angry over the water stolen from her to fill the basin. Behind him, the sun set over the hill above town, barren except for old rotting stumps of trees cut years ago for firewood. He slipped his hands into his pockets, jingling the few coins there, and watched reflections of emerging stars dance on the surface of the water.

"Damned confusing day," he muttered to the river.

The next morning, Ben sat up on his bunk bed in the Georgetown jail when Sheriff Postell arrived. Ben glared at him through the bars of his cell. The sheriff hummed to himself as he unlocked the cell door, and motioned for Ben to step out.

"God damn it, Sheriff," Ben said.

"No," the sheriff snapped. "You will not utter such profanities in my presence. Kindly contain your protests until we have had our coffee and breakfast."

Ben blinked his eyes and followed the sheriff into the front office. The room was already warm from the morning sunshine. A blue calico cloth covered a tray on the desk. Next to it was a metal coffee pot with vapor drifting up from the spout. Two chairs stood on opposite sides of the desk. Ben inhaled deeply, savoring the aroma of cooked food and fresh coffee.

"Please sit, Captain Pulaski," Postell said as he uncovered the tray. "One of my few treats afforded me by the county is breakfast from the corner tavern. Let us eat, and then I promise to answer all your questions and complaints."

Ben displayed a momentary scowl, but let it slip away and settled into his chair.

"Do you eat grits, Captain?" the sheriff asked.

Ben released a sequestered smile. "Oh yes, Sheriff. My wife is from North Carolina. She cooks that often."

"Please call me William. May I call you Benjamin?"

"Ben." He answered with a frown.

Postell waved away Ben's concern. "We eat it with shrimp, here. A little salt and pepper and lots of butter. Coffee, sir?"

Ben blew out his breath his anger and gave the breakfast his full attention.

When serving bowls and plates were empty and the second cup of coffee sat before each man, Postell cleared his throat.

"Ben, there are times that I need to portray different, even contradictory, intentions for the same act...."

Ben returned to his frown, leaning over the desk and opened his mouth to speak.

"Please, Ben. Hear me out."

Ben relaxed back in his chair, folding his arms across his chest.

"Ben, we have three audiences for our conundrum." Postell tapped his thumb with his first finger. "We need to satisfy the needs of one of the largest plantations in the county, which is now owned by a woman who has the romantic attention of powerful local men." He tapped with his second finger. "We also have a no-nonsense judge who is a serious advocate of our essential slave culture, and the honor of southern gentlemen, as he sees it." He tapped with his third finger. "And lastly, we have a local business community that is itself growing in money power, and wishes no harm to come to trade with the north, specifically our rice trade with the north."

"I am not from the north..."

"Yes, yes, yes." Postell patted the air in front of Ben, pushing away the correction with his hand. "Maryland is a southern state and a slave state, but for us, it is 'farther north,' and it buys more like northern states. It buys our rice."

"So?"

"So, you seem to be at the crux of all three needs."

"And how does that justify you lying about my involvement in a duel?"

"It doesn't."

"But, last night..."

"Last night, I played to one audience by bringing you here. This morning, we need to address the second in such a way that will allow me to please the third."

Ben gave Postell his full attention.

Postell smiled. "I only locked you up for the benefit of Palmetto Haven. In a more quiet circumstance, we will tell the judge the truth this morning, and most likely by noon you will be on your way back to your ship and then on to your not-northern Maryland – with our rice."

Postell pulled a pocket watch from his vest.

"Let us go see Judge Allston in his chambers, Ben," he said.

Moments later Ben and Postell stood before the judge's desk. In a corner chair, Dr. Daniel Tucker sat reading a newspaper, holding it at an angle to catch the morning sunlight through the nearby window. They waited in silence while the judge mumbled through the documents he read at his desk. He raised his head and turned to Postell.

"Sheriff, if you were a witness to Mr. Williamson's challenge and say they were equally involved, and Dr. Tucker here bears witness to statements by Mr. Williamson to the same effect, why are you taking up my time with this?"

"Well, your honor–"

"Why did you even bring him to jail?"

"I had a charge by a prominent member of the community, sir. I thought it best to resolve the legal charge in your honor's presence, not just out of hand."

The judge grunted and turned to Ben.

"You Pulaski?"

"Yes, your honor."

"This all true?" the judge said, tapping the papers.

"I don't know, your honor. I haven't read it."

The judge lifted the papers and pointed them at Ben. "What should these statements say?"

Ben took in a deep breath.

"That I was forced into a duel against my will, your honor. That Jeremiah Williamson fired first and drew blood. That I stood my ground and shot second, aiming not to kill. That we were both treated by the same doctor.

Williamson died, and I did not."

The judge locked eyes with Ben a long moment.

"We don't approve of dueling in this state, sir, but neither do we interfere with affairs of honor," he said, then turned to Postell. "Both men had a fair opportunity to fire?"

"Yes, your honor."

The judge cleared his throat. "I find no evidence that a willful act occurred warranting a trial." He turned to Dr. Tucker. "Thank you, Daniel. I look forward to seeing you again at the luncheon."

"You may go, Sheriff," the judge said to Postell.

The judge gave his attention to another document on his desk. He dipped his pen into the inkwell and wrote his findings, ignoring Postell and Ben. Postell motioned his head toward the door, then led Ben out.

Moments later, Ben strode along Front Street making his way to the docks and the gangplank of his ship. The schooner *Raven* occupied 130 feet of dockside, reflections from the water painted serpentine lines dancing along her hunter green hull. She sat low in the water, her belly already filled with rice barrels for buyers farther north. The low white cabin roofs near her bow and stern glistened in the sunshine, squat bookends for her two masts. His half-brother, Edward Leonard, first mate of the *Raven*, met him as Ben stepped on deck.

"Did you have an enjoyable evening at the plantation, Ben?"

"No Eddie. As a matter of fact, I did not. I spent the night in a jail not far from here."

"In jail? What? How? Why?"

Ben waved him away as he headed toward his cabin at the stern. "It is resolved now. More tricks by Lydia Binterfield. Damn the woman," he said over his shoulder. "But, at least I was served breakfast by the sheriff."

Edward stood open-mouthed as Ben walked away, then shrugged his shoulders and returned to his work.

Moments later, shed of the new suit he had worn to Palmetto Haven, Ben returned on deck in canvas trousers and cotton shirt under his blue captain's coat.

Edward brought him the cargo ledger with a receipt slipped between the pages.

"Rice and indigo all aboard."

"Thank you, Eddie."

"You don't think we're sitting too low, do you, Ben?"

"No. I looked at the ship's trim as I came aboard. She looks right and her keel is still well above the bottom. Why do you ask, Eddie?"

"Well, remember we replaced the rocks in her ballast last year with that old cannon from Hughes Ironworks in Havre de Grace..."

"Yes?"

"Well, rocks are easy to throw out to lighten the ship if we take on more cargo, but that cannon was a monster to get below."

"It will do fine where it is, Eddie. The *Raven* is a light ship, she calls for more ballast than most. And Hughes never got paid for that cannon after the last war with Britain, so we got it for a pittance. I promise we won't put any more in her than she can safely take."

Edward continued to frown.

"What else, Eddie?"

Edward tapped the edge of the ledger. "The receipt doesn't show the indigo, just 'quantity of rice and other cargo.'"

Ben nodded. "They don't want to show they're shipping indigo."

"Why?"

"Federal tariff. They try to avoid it down here. Been doing it since the '20s. They don't care to write down any more than they have to." Ben slapped his arm gently. "Sometimes I think you worry too much, Eddie, but then I remind myself that is what a good first mate is supposed to do."

Ben scanned the deck, picking at his trimmed beard, black like his hair, then lowered his voice.

"Any other cargo not on the receipt?"

Edward smiled, pushing his freckled cheeks up toward his eyes. "Do you recall the slave from Mansfield Plantation who wouldn't go last year, because he could not leave his family behind?"

"Yes."

"We received seven special barrels of rice yesterday evening," he said, keeping his smile. "Him, his wife and all six of their children."

"That's eight people, Eddie. You said seven barrels?"

"The momma took the youngest with her to keep him quiet."

"How long have they been in the barrels?"

"We took them out last night, Ben. But we're making sure they stay down in the hold until we leave."

Ben's attention settled on a young white man in quality clothes, leaning against a building across the street from the pier. The man had his arms folded and dangled his hat from his exposed hand. As soon as they were in direct eye contact, the young man nodded, put on his hat and ambled away.

"Please see that they do," Ben said. "I want the steamer to tow us through the channels this afternoon, so we can sail out of Winyah Bay this evening."

"Stop him! Stop him!"

The shout came from a nearby street leading to the docks.

A slender black man dashed down the street with two white men close behind him. As the white men drew close to the runner, reaching out to grab him, the runner dodged to the side and ran along the docks in front of the *Raven*. The larger of the two white men stopped and drew out his pistol, aiming it at the fleeing black man.

"I'll shoot you, George!" he yelled.

Ben dropped the ledger and ran down the gangplank, tackling the runaway. Ben and the runner tumbled over the planks just as the younger pursuer reached them.

The older pursuer kept his pistol trained on the runaway and stepped closer to him.

"Damn you, George! I warned you what I'd do if you ever tried to run again."

He punched the gun barrel against George's head.

George spat the words. "G'wown. Do it."

"Pa, don't shoot him," the younger white man pleaded, shaking the loose manacles he carried. "I can train him..."

"Shut up Matthew, I've had it with this nigger," the owner said, cocking the hammer.

Ben stood and placed his hand on the angry man's arm.

"Sir," Ben said. "You do not want to do that."

The man turned his eyes toward Ben, keeping the pistol in place, his reddened face twisted in rage.

"Who the hell asked you? He is my property, and I'm going to put him down."

"That would be a terrible waste of your money, sir," Ben said.

"Take your hand off my arm. He ain't worth a damn penny, mister. Can't get him to do anything unless I got another one watching him every minute."

Ben kept his hand in place, locking eyes with the man and showing a smile. "Consider passing him along to someone else at a profit."

"No one around here would have him."

"Sir, I can easily get you four hundred dollars for him in Charleston, less my commission, of course."

"You a trader?"

"Yes sir, I am. Licensed in all the slave states, from Delaware to Texas. And I have a standing account in Charleston."

The man kept the barrel tip against George's head and turned to his son. "Chain his ankles, Matthew. And this time make sure you lock'em right."

"I can take him on consignment, Mr..." Ben waited for the man to give his name.

"Dunkin. Joshua Dunkin," the man said.

"Joshua, I'm Ben Pulaski. Let me take him on consignment, and I will bring you your money on my return to Georgetown."

Some of the *Raven*'s crew stood at the railing overlooking the commotion on the dock. Ben turned to them.

"Alistair," Ben said to one of the crew, "come down here and help this black up on deck."

Ben turned to Joshua. "Joshua, come up on deck with me and we can sign the papers so I can represent you at the Charleston auctions."

Joshua drew the gun back from George's head, eased the hammer onto the nipple and slid the pistol into his belt.

"Four hundred dollars, you said?"

"Less commission, sir," Ben answered.

"And what will be your commission?" Joshua asked.

"Twenty percent, sir. Eighty dollars. That will still get you three hundred and twenty dollars and shed yourself of a bothersome slave."

"Well, it's more than I paid for him. Should have known not to buy a young buck on the cheap. It was too good to be true."

"Very well," Ben said. "Let's go to my cabin and sign the papers. Do you like rum, Joshua? I have some excellent Jamaican rum on board."

Joshua smiled broadly and followed Ben up the gangplank and down into his cabin.

Minutes later the two men stepped up onto the deck and strolled toward the portal chatting amiably. Joshua folded his consignment document and slipped it into his coat pocket. At the head of the gangplank, they shook hands. Ben stood near the portal as Joshua returned to the dock and slipped his arm over his son's shoulders as they walked away.

Edward handed Ben the dropped ledger, looking deep into Ben's eyes. "Sometimes you are too bold by far, brother."

A breeze played with Edward's sandy colored hair, another trait from his mother, a woman Ben's father once knew.

Ben released a ragged sigh. "Couldn't stand there and watch Dunkin shoot that man…"

"He might have shot you, instead."

Ben shrugged his shoulders. "But he didn't. I need to go down and see how angry our new passenger is."

He stepped down onto the landing in front of the door to the captain's cabin, then down into the ship's hold. Rice powder floated in the air, scented with the aroma of frying meat and baking bread coming from the galley. The rice barrels filled all free spaces on either side of the narrow passageway that ran the center length of the hold, except where it went around the two masts. The cramped space above the barrels, too low to take another stack, was turned into lounging and sleeping areas for the runaway passengers. Planking laid over the barrels and covered by straw-filled canvas pads served as beds.

Not much room, Ben thought, *but it'll get them away.*

George sat on the hold's deck with his back against the galley partition and both ankles wrapped with shackles. He scowled as Ben approached. Ben settled on the bench of the narrow mess table nearby, perched between walls of rice barrels.

"If you will look over your left shoulder," Ben said, "you will see a small loop of twine hanging from a hook."

George twisted his head to see the hook.

"So," he said. "Git it yo'sef."

"At the end of the twine is a key, George, to those manacles."

George reached up and fingered the key, then eyed Ben.

"It's your choice, George. You're welcome to keep them on, but I think you would be more comfortable without them."

"You gonna sell me in Charleston. Bet that key don't work."

"No and yes," Ben said. "No, I'm not going to sell you in Charleston. You and I are going to cheat Joshua. When I come back to Georgetown, it will be my sad duty to tell him you jumped off my ship into Winyah Bay and drowned."

George glared in silence.

"And yes," Ben said, "that key does work. No one stays in chains on this ship except for the occasional show."

George remained silent.

Ben turned toward the slim galley entrance. "Warren, would you please set a full plate for George?"

Warren stuck his head into the doorway. "Already fixed it, Cap'n." Then he stepped over to the table and placed a mound of biscuits and bacon beside Ben.

"You will have to come over here to eat, George.

Everyone on the *Raven* sits at the table."

The sun settled low over the western shore of Winyah Bay as the *Raven*'s sails popped free of their ties and grabbed the evening land breeze. Her two masts leaned away from the push of the wind, but the tilt of the deck was still kind to the new passengers.

Ben and Edward stood side by side at the tandem wheels on either side of the binnacle that made the fore and aft schooner unique. The windward wheel always had a clear view unobstructed by sails. The low roof of the captain's cabin at the stern and crew quarters at the bow gave them excellent views in all directions. The ship sailed through the mouth of the bay under a clear sky and onto the long rollers of the Atlantic Ocean. Once settled into the new rhythm, Ben signaled to Edward and released his grip on the wheel, leaving it to his brother to steer, and then stepped closer to him.

"We will head due east a while, Eddie, until we're out of sight from the lighthouse. Then we'll come back into the bay later."

Edward smiled. "I thought I saw that fellah across the street signal to you."

"I hope you were the only one who did," Ben said with a brief frown. "People willing to risk themselves to free slaves are a rarity down here. I would not want that young man compromised."

"Any idea how many slaves we are coming back for?" Edward asked.

"No, Eddie, but we'll take on any that come out to us."

Edward whistled to two crewmen standing near the bow. Alistair and Daniel trotted back to the wheels.

"We're going back tonight to pick up some more passengers," Edward said. "Make sure the rope ladder is at the ready."

21

Alistair walked away speaking over his shoulder, "I'll tell Warren and Wyatt, and the passengers we already got."

Daniel, the *Raven*'s only black crew member, stayed near the wheel.

"It never crossed my mind that I would wind up working on a slaver around the deep south, and then stealing them north."

Ben smiled. "It used to be a slaver. Now it's a cargo vessel, and sometimes we take on special passengers. Just make sure we're alone before you speak of it, Daniel."

"Alistair said that you killed the captain and crew and took this ship, then set the slaves on it free."

Ben stared into his face a brief moment. The yellow light from the lantern above the binnacle tinted Daniel's brown eyes.

"That is a cold summary of the results. I did kill some of the crew. Their stains on this deck haunt me still. They had kidnapped my wife, but it was my friend Simon Bond that took off the head of their captain. And it was a dozen deputies that attacked this ship and freed the slaves on it. One of those that helped the deputies was also a good friend of mine who died for his effort."

Ben took a step away from the wheel, then turned to address Daniel again. "Tomorrow, examine the stain on the deck near your quarters, you will see the initials A.T. carved in the middle of it. That stain is where another good friend died, keeping this ship in our hands, letting us continue to do what we do."

"Adam Tuttle," Daniel said.

Ben placed his hand on Daniel's shoulder. "I am glad Alistair told you his name. He was a friend since my childhood, and crewed with my father. He is still sorely missed."

Ben walked away toward the aft ladderway. "I need to explain our actions to our passengers."

They continued their course another hour, making sure anyone gazing out from the North Island Lighthouse would see the *Raven* take that direction. Any knowledgeable observer would assume she would head east to avoid the shoals, and then turn south for her run to Charleston.

Just over the horizon from the North Island Lighthouse, under a bright silver moon, Ben called out to shift the sails as he spun his wheel, turning the *Raven* back toward Winyah Bay. Well after midnight, the *Raven* slipped quietly toward a sandy beach at the southern tip of North Island, a mile south of the lighthouse. They lowered sails, secured the stern anchor with a heavy line and let it out by hand in the shallow water to keep the *Raven*'s keel from running aground. Then Edward ordered the bow anchor slowly lowered into the water to keep them parallel to the shore. All lanterns were out, except an enclosed signal lantern held by Edward. The shoreline was a smoky pearl slash across the belly of the steel darkness before them.

Near the bow, two large storage boxes bolted to the deck were unlocked and their ends opened. The crew rolled out the small cannon hidden there, pushing them to ports in the railing, their barrels sticking out over water.

Daniel whispered to Alistair, "What are those for?"

"Hopefully nothing, but if our passengers have been found out, there could be many angry men shooting at them and us."

A light showed from the shore, then quickly vanished.

"Wait," Ben whispered, counting to ten.

The light on shore showed three more times.

"Now, Eddie," Ben said. "Three flashes."

"I know," Edward muttered.

Moments later there was the echo of an oar dropped in a boat. Ben gritted his teeth and pressed his lips into a snarl. The crew tensed, staring into the darkness, listening for any sound from the trees to tell them they were discovered. Then, there was a small splash near the ship, no louder than a hungry fish feeding, and a lantern showed briefly nearby. Daniel used a boat hook to stop the rowboat from thumping into the side of the ship. Alistair used another boat hook to pull the boat to the rope ladder.

Two men, a woman, and three children scampered on

board. They stood frozen in place for an instant.

"You are safe," Ben whispered.

One of the runaways released a ragged breath. A hand reached out in the moonlight and grabbed Ben's arm.

"Thank you," a man said.

Ben laid his hand on the man's shoulder. "I will speak with you later," Ben said. "Daniel, take them below."

The man leaned back over the rail and whispered toward the rowboat.

"We safe," he said, and the boat pulled away.

Edward and Alistair raised the mainsail into the land breeze to push them away from shore, and then Ben dashed to help the others raise the anchors. Then Wyatt joined those at the sails while Ben took the wheel to steer the ship back out into the Atlantic.

At sunrise, the *Raven* had run all the easterly distance she needed to make her turn safely northward. Once on a steady course with only gentle rocking, Ben allowed a fire in the galley's enclosed brick and iron stove. Warren had mastered the unique stove, designed with pan clamps to enable cooking even while underway. By ten o'clock everyone had eaten, and the coffee pot was empty a second time.

Ben stood at the doorway to the galley explaining to the passengers the next steps in their journey.

"We will sail up into the Chesapeake Bay," he said. "That is a big bay between Virginia and Maryland, so we will still be in slave territory. That means if we are boarded, you must behave as slaves going to market, and do whatever the boarders say. In the middle of the bay, we will meet with a passenger steamer. You will get on that boat, and it will take you to another. The third will take you up a long canal into another bay, called Delaware Bay.

"That's freedom, right?" George asked.

"No," Ben said. "Delaware is a slave state too. But at the northern end of the Delaware Bay is the Delaware River which flows down from Philadelphia. When you near Philadelphia, on that side of the river is Pennsylvania, a free state. On the other shore will be New Jersey, another free state. There you will be free, and other people will help you on your way to a place where you can find work and live on your own. You may stay in Pennsylvania, or go on to New York, or even Canada. It will be up to you, then."

"Thank you, Lord," one of the women cried.

"I'll believe when I see it," said George.

Four days later, after fighting crosswinds that tried to shove the *Raven* farther out into the Atlantic, Ben focused his eyeglass on the bold black and white stripes of the Cape Henry Lighthouse. He faced Edward and nodded in agreement.

"We have arrived, Eddie, Let's take her East-nor'east for Hampton Roads."

Edward relieved Alistair at the windward wheel and sent him to direct all the passengers to go below decks to hide from view.

"If I go back down there I'll be pukin my guts out," George said.

"We'll be in calmer waters shortly, George," Alistair said, then raised his voice so Edward would hear him. "Maybe the first mate will let you stay near the forward ladderway, 'til we're in smoother waters."

Edward smiled and nodded his head to Alistair. George perched himself on the cowling around the upper deck edge of the ladderway, dangling his feet in the opening.

Daniel approached Edward. "Sir, George worked on coastal luggers and canal scows a while, before he was sold to Georgetown. Said his captain was sorry to lose him, but he had a debt to pay."

Edward kept his attention on the approaching headland of Cape Henry. "And?"

"And, maybe he could help haul sails and such on deck until we meet the steamer."

"Here, take the wheel, Daniel. Keep her a point north of due east, while I speak with the Captain."

As soon as Daniel took a firm grip on the spokes, Edward walked toward the bow where Ben continued to watch the shore with his glass.

"Daniel says George there could help us with the sails.

Says he knows how, and none of the others care to clean up after him again."

Ben chuckled. "Let him stay up on deck. Have him work with Wyatt. They're closest in age."

Soon after entering the mouth of the bay, the wind dropped, and the water lost most of its waves. The wind moderated even more as they sailed. The westerly wind they had fought for days was nearly gone, and their forward way fell off quickly. Ben called to hoist more sails until all fair weather sails were in the rigging clawing the air for a breeze to keep them going.

While creeping along at little more than two knots, a huge steamboat charged past them at five times their speed and making no effort to spare the *Raven* from its wake. Wyatt was high up the ratlines of the foremast clearing a knot in one of the flying jib lines when the wake struck. The deck tilted dramatically, leaning the masts over the water. Wyatt lost his footing but managed to keep a bear hug around the upper foremast. Instantly, the wake passed under their hull, and the ship righted with a snap that pulled Wyatt loose from his grip. The motion sent him flying away from the *Raven* and into the choppy waters created by the steamboat side wheels.

"Man overboard!" yelled Ben. "Throw him a float. Wear ship!"

Wyatt flew into the water then struggled to the surface.

"Can't swim," he yelled.

Daniel and Alistair ran to the railing, one with a float and line, the other with a line only. Both tossed them out toward Wyatt, but the lines did not reach him, and the ship continued to move slowly away from him even as it turned. George shoved them aside.

"Out the damned way," George growled as he hurled himself into the water.

George went down in the water like a returning fish, not surfacing until he was forty feet away from the ship. Panic entered Wyatt's voice as he fought to keep his head above water. His words gargled through swallowed water that was already splashing into his lungs. George kept his head low in the water, breathing on his side as he swam, pushing the water behind him with long powerful strokes. He shoved himself four feet along with each stroke. George grabbed the line to the float, cramming it between his teeth. He struck out faster toward Wyatt. Wyatt gurgled and coughed, gagging. His head slipped beneath the water. He raised his hand from below, grabbing for air and went down.

George made it to the spot. He plunged his head down, flipping his feet high into the air, following Wyatt down. The crew watched as the float's line snaked down into the water. Yard after yard of the line went under the surface. The churning waves washed away the bubbles where Wyatt had struggled. In the distance, the steamboat shrieked its whistle and began a laborious full turn to come back. All sails on the *Raven* were loosed and allowed to hang limp. All eyes from the *Raven* fixed on the spot where the two men went down.

Halfway between the spot and the *Raven*, the water erupted as George burst to the surface with Wyatt under his arm. George rolled onto his back and pulled Wyatt on his chest. George kicked with powerful legs as he beat Wyatt's chest with his fists, moving them closer to the ship. As they neared the ship, Wyatt began to cough and sputter.

Hands reached down from the railing to take Wyatt's arms and lift him up onto the deck. Wyatt continued to cough and vomit water.

"Thank you," he rasped in a coarse whisper, rolling on his side and continuing to cough.

Ben ran to the railing to help the others pull George back in, but he was not there. Frantically they looked around the edges of the ship, but could not find him.

"There," Daniel yelled, pointing away from the ship.

Twenty yards away from the ship, beyond the spot where Wyatt fell in, George swam leisurely on his back. He yelled back to the crew.

"They never let me have a swim, and I loves ta swim."

Alistair moved to the bow and waved to the steamer, then pointed north.

"You coming back?" Ben yelled at George.

"In a bit," George said.

Ben chuckled as he turned to Edward. He motioned toward the nearby shore to their east.

"Let's raise enough sail to get us out of the main channel and anchor there for the night. Let the passengers be free on the deck. Pass out fishhooks and string. I'm in the mood for some fried fish."

In the distance, the steamboat made a complete circle and continued north.

It was another hour before George climbed aboard, smiling. The *Raven* had anchored in the shallows.

"Thank you, George," Ben said.

"We eatin?"

Ben motioned toward the ladderway and George followed the aroma down to the galley. A half mile north, a sailboat launched from shore with a man standing at the bow holding a rifle in the afternoon sunlight.

Lapidum, Maryland

Isaac was in his civilian clothes and gathering firewood near the barn when a man in a dark suit rode up the Pulaski lane from Stafford Road. The setting sun threw long shadows across the lane and speckled the rider with flashing patches of sunlight as he came. Isaac stepped in front of the man's horse.

"What do you need, mister?" Isaac asked over the bundle of split wood in his arms.

The man tipped his hat. "Hello. I am Lester Watkins, Esquire. Is this the Pulaski place?"

"It is. I am Captain Isaac Pulaski. What do you need, sir?"

"I guess I need to speak with your wife, Mrs. Pulaski."

Isaac smiled. "Mrs. Pulaski is my mother. Follow me up to the house. There is a place in front of the porch where you can tie your horse."

Watkins followed Isaac up the slope to the porch. As he got down and tied his horse, Isaac took the load of wood into the house, leaving the front door open. He paused as he walked around the horse, gazing between the two massive oak trees sitting in the front yard like giant sentinels. Down the slope still deep green with grass, the canal crossed the view going south. On the opposite side of the canal, the towpath he had just ridden along was framed from behind by the Susquehanna River. Rowboats were floating in the current with only a single person in each. Four fishing poles stuck out over each side with lines from each angling down into the water. The boats' appearance suggested giant water spiders.

"What do you need, Mr. Watkins?" Sonja asked. Her hands were in fists, resting on her hips.

"I need to speak with you, madam..."

"About what?"

"Well, may I come in, or sit on the porch at least?"

"No. I can hear you fine from here. What do you want?"

"Mrs. Pulaski, I represent Miss Ramona Tatum..."

"I expected so. Say what you need to say, then go."

Watkins' horse shivered his haunch to drive away a fly. He cleared his throat.

"Miss Tatum has made some insinuations that I feel we must discuss before we consider any legal action."

"Alisha is my daughter. I told all this to that woman. Alisha was still an infant when the ice gorge pulled her from my arms on Pearl Lane in Havre de Grace. Rachel Tatum found her when we could not. Rachel raised her as her own daughter, but then confessed the truth to me before she died."

"Mmm. I am told you have Rachel Tatum buried on this property. Can you tell me why?"

"She died a watch-mistress on a fishing island belonging to others. She could not be buried there. She had nowhere else to go and no one else to mourn her that anyone knew. I had her buried here because she was the only person Alisha knew as a relative...A girl should know where her family is buried."

"So you agree that Rachel was Alisha's family?" he asked.

"No. I agree that Alisha was told that and she believed it."

"May I see the girl?" Watkins asked.

Sonja blew out her breath and turned toward the door. "Alisha, honey, come out on the porch, please."

Across the canal, Deputy Sheriff Lyle Mattingly rode along the towpath heading south. He waved to the house as he passed. Sonja waved back.

"Yes, Momma?" Alisha said as she stepped onto the porch.

She moved beside Sonja and took her mother's hand. Except for the clothes they wore, Alisha was like a miniature statue of Sonja. Each had the same golden curls, the high forehead, and the brilliant blue eyes.

Watkins blinked. "Well, there indeed is a striking

similarity between you and the child.

"Two peas in a pod," Isaac said from the doorway.

Mr. Watkins said nothing else. He tipped his hat to Sonja, then mounted his horse and trotted away.

Sonja was turning with Alisha to re-enter that house when Lyle walked his horse into the front yard. The horse nickered. Sonja turned back to face the yard.

"Lyle," she said in greeting.

"Sonja," he said. He released a heavy sigh as he got down off his horse.

Sonja's shoulders dropped, and she blew out her breath, locking eyes with him.

"What is it, Lyle?"

"Was Lester Watkins talking to you about Ramona Tatum?" he asked.

Sonja folded her arms and shifted her stance. "What else?"

He cleared his throat and coughed. "She filed a complaint saying you murdered her sister and stole her sister's daughter."

"That's a damned lie," Isaac said, placing his hand on Sonja's shoulder.

"I don't doubt it, Isaac," Lyle said. "But she's got a baptismal registry with the local Catholic church, listing Moses Regina Tatum, born February 1840, as the daughter of Rachel Tatum, widow, resident of Shad Island."

Sonja stamped her foot. "The gall of that woman!" She balled one hand into a fist and shook it at Lyle. She folded her arms and marched to the north edge of the front porch, then punched her fisted hands onto her hips and stood there in cold silence a brief moment. Sonja spun around and faced south, then paced toward the southern edge of the porch. Isaac offered his hand and opened his mouth to speak as she approached the doorway, but his mother snapped her palm up in front of his face and continued her march. At the farthest edge, Sonja halted and folded her arms again, then stamped her foot and spun around facing Isaac.

"Isaac," she called.

"Yes, ma'am."

"Go fetch your father's rum bottle...and two glasses...no, three."

Sonja returned to the center of the porch and faced Lyle. "Get up here."

"Yes ma'am," he said.

Moments later, Sonja had managed to settle into one of the chairs and blew out her breath. Isaac sat nearby sipping his rum.

"What else does that...that, woman say, Lyle."

Lyle waved away the question with his glass. "All you have to do is show something from your own church's registry, or something from the courthouse that Alisha is your child, and this mess is over."

She lowered her head. "We never did that. I was waiting for warmer weather to take her to church for her baptism. I don't think there are any records of Alisha's birth."

Lyle finished his drink and set it on the little table next to his chair. He sighed and shook his head, then pulled out a small notepad.

"Were there any witnesses to Rachel Tatum's death?"

"Me, Ben, Edward – his brother...

"Edward Pulaski?"

"No. Leonard. Edward is his half-brother. Then, there was Hattie and Cephus."

"Mmm," Lyle said. "Well, Hattie and Cephus can't testify. They're black folk. You and Ben can't because you benefitted from the demise..."

Sonja fired glaring eyes at Lyle.

"...so to speak," Lyle added. "But Edward being Ben's family, I'm not sure. Sonja, I don't know why Miss Tatum is so set to have that child, but you need to get a good lawyer, right away."

The next morning Sonja tied her horse in front of the First National Bank on Washington Street and was the first visitor to the upstairs office of George Milton, Esquire. She entered wearing the canvas trousers she had adopted since sailing with Ben on the *Raven*, preferring them to dresses when she rode a horse.

"Oh, why would someone want to do such a thing,

Sonja?" George asked after hearing a summary of Sonja's concerns.

Sonja's eyebrows wrinkled in a frown and tears slipped out of the corner of her eyes.

"I don't know why, George, but Lyle Mattingly said that woman has a baptismal registration from the Catholic Church, naming Rachel Tatum as her mother."

"You say an attorney had visited you only minutes before Mattingly arrived. Do you recall his name?"

"Lester Watkins," she said.

"Well, Lester is not a bad fellow, although he does chase legal problems for the wealthy among us far more often than the poorer."

Sonja placed her hand on the desk.

"I will not give up my daughter, George. I will not."

He reached across the desk and patted her hand.

"We are nowhere near to such a thing happening, Sonja. First I will speak to Lester, then Lyle, and then have a look at the baptismal registration myself. Allow me a few days to do that, and then we can talk about this again. Alright?"

"Can we not write a document now and sign it, saying Alisha is my daughter?"

"I wish it was that easy, Sonja, but it would be dated today and could not challenge her baptismal record," George said.

"Well then, what about Doctor Harper? He saw Alisha the day after she was born. And, and, Martha Johnson, my God how could I forget her? Martha Johnson was the midwife for Alisha's birth. She could sign a paper. And Doctor Harper could sign a paper. Wouldn't that be enough?"

George released a long slow breath and gave her a kind smile.

"Alisha was barely a month old when she was swept away," he said." Those papers could prove that you delivered a baby...a...baby, but they could not prove that your infant is now Alisha. I must investigate this further."

Sonja bowed her head while George made a series of notes, then he stood as Sonja left his office. Sonja mounted her horse and pointed him toward the canal basin. Then she let her thoughts wander, and her horse find its way along Washington Street. When she neared Bourbon Street, she turned her horse toward the piers and Market Street, where she stopped in front of the new General Goods Store. Even though it had been there over four years, most people she knew still called it the 'new' store. The front door was set back from the boardwalk, creating display space in the windows on either side, filled with the owner's latest merchandise. Catherine Price had mentioned the new dolls that graced the front window. Catherine's daughter Patty, Alisha's closest friend, could speak of little else since she saw them. Sonja stood before the front windows admiring the dolls.

"If you think buying one of those will keep Mos under your spell, you are mistaken, Mrs. Pulaski."

Sonja spun around to face Ramona Tatum, standing next to Nadja Lister, the undertaker's wife.

"Stay away from me," Sonja said, "and stay away from my daughter."

"She is not your daughter, and the sooner we get that proven, the sooner I can take her home with me."

"Stay the hell away from my daughter and me," Sonja said, stepping close to Ramona's face.

"Really, Mrs. Pulaski," Nadja said. "How can you be so rude to this poor woman? She has lost her only sister and grieves for her. She is concerned for her sister's daughter."

"I have been to see a lawyer," Ramona said, "...and the sheriff. They will sort this out and rescue my niece."

Sonja leaned almost nose to nose with Ramona.

"Yes. They've already visited me," Sonja said. "And I just came from my lawyer's office. We will stop you from this insanity."

"See here, Mrs. Pulaski–" Nadja said.

Sonja turned toward Nadja and poked a finger hard onto her chest.

"You shut the hell up, Nadja."

Nadja took a step backward.

"You hit me," she said.

"Nonsense," Sonja said. " If I had hit you, you would

be sitting in the street."

Several men and women had gathered close by watching the argument.

Nadja glared at Sonja and grabbed Ramona's arm.

"Come along, dear, we shouldn't have to tolerate anything from this person."

Nadja raised her voice for the audience. "She used to be a house servant in town, and they discharged her for poor behavior."

Ramona and Sonja locked eyes as Nadja pulled Ramona back.

Ice settled into Ramona's eyes.

"I am having Rachel's body removed and sent home."

"Fine," Sonja said. "Just leave the hole open for yourself."

"Hah! She threatened us," Nadja said.

"Just her," Sonja said as she started to turn away.

The two women marched away together. Sonja blew out her breath and turned toward her horse, where a man stood handing her the reins."

"Not the kind of display you need to have, Mrs. Pulaski," said Deputy Sheriff Lyle Mattingly, as she snatched the reins from his hand.

As she settled into her saddle, Lyle handed her a folded paper.

"It's a bill from the owner of Shad Island, and the company-owned house Mrs. Tatum stayed in as watch woman."

Sonja flipped open the page with one hand and held it, so the sun highlighted the words.

"Fifteen dollars? For what?"

Lyle cleared his throat. "Breaking into the emergency supply crate on his island and theft of company supplies."

"We were trying to keep Rachel Tatum alive."

Sonja crumpled the paper and punched it into her shirt pocket.

"Great. Just great," she said and trotted the horse away.

Eastern Shore of the Chesapeake Bay

"Ahoy *Raven*." The voice drifted from the east.

Ben stood amidships with Edward, Wyatt, and Daniel as a forty-foot fishing sloop approached. The man standing in the bow held a rifle, and four other armed men sat on benches.

"What business do you have with my ship?" Ben asked.

"You are in Northampton County shallows, and I am sheriff of this county. What business do you have here?"

"Just anchoring for the night and having supper."

The sheriff peered among the men near Ben, then exchanged words with a deputy next to him. The deputy stood and looked up at Ben, then spoke quietly to the sheriff.

"I will speak with the captain," the sheriff said.

"I am the captain," Ben said. "What the hell do you want?"

"Where is Hoagg?"

"Dead, now back away," Ben said.

"I am Sheriff William Scarborough. Who are you?"

"Benjamin Pulaski. You may be the sheriff or maybe not, but armed men approaching my ship make me nervous. I have cannon aboard and will use them. State your business or back away." He turned to Edward. "Bring up my pistols."

"We lost slaves, Pulaski, last time *Raven* came here. Hoagg was a pirate and that ship is the location of his crimes."

Ben folded his arms. "Yes he was, but as I said he is a dead pirate now. This ship is mine."

"I have a warrant for the arrest of the *Raven*'s captain and crew for theft of several slaves. We saw several blacks milling about your deck. We also saw that big one try to escape by swimming away. I aim to board your ship to ensure none of them came from here."

Ben turned away, tapping Alistair and pointing at the storage locker holding the starboard cannon. Edward arrived with Ben's pistols, with his own stuck in his belt. Ben made a show of slipping his pistols in his belt as he faced the sheriff.

"You do not have permission to come aboard my ship. You are a stranger to me that has come out from shore with a boat of armed men. You say you are a sheriff, but I have no proof of that. I tell you again, back away.

Alistair and Daniel rolled out the cannon to the railing. Murmuring bubbled among the deputies sitting in the boat, one of them shaking his head emphatically 'no.'

The sheriff exchanged several short comments with the deputies. The man at the tiller snapped a line to swing out the sail into the wind. The boat moved away from the *Raven* and returned to shore, where the deputies quickly left the boat to climb the little dock there and walked away. The one who had identified himself as the sheriff stood on the dock, shaking his fist toward Ben.

"Do you think he was actually their sheriff?" Edward asked.

"Don't know, but I think we convinced him to leave us be," Ben said.

The following morning with the faintest light of dawn climbing into a sky fat with gray clouds, a voice bellowed across *Raven's* decks.

"Ahoy *Raven*. Stand by to be boarded!"

Ben jumped from his swinging bed, pulled on his trousers and dashed barefoot up on deck. He was joined by Wyatt and George, as others were coming on deck. Near the side of the *Raven* was a seventy-foot revenue cutter with her two gun ports open showing brass cannon already run out.

"This is the Virginia Cutter *McLane*," the captain yelled through his speaking trumpet. "Stand by to be boarded, or we will fire on you."

Standing beside the cutter's captain was Sheriff William Scarborough.

The captain and his crew appeared to be dressed in similar uniforms, but not uniforms of the U.S. Navy. No American flag flew from the rigging, only the flag of Virginia.

"Who the hell are you?" yelled Ben.

"We are the party preparing to board you. Do you accept, sir?"

Ben blew out his breath and turned to Edward as he approached. "Get all the passengers up on their pallets. Shackle all you can, but make sure one of them has the key."

"I'll go with him, Cap'n, and hold the key," George said.

Ben nodded at George and turned back to the cutter. "Come ahead, damn you."

The cutter's crew pulled their rowboat up to the portal, and four men climbed down into it. Within a minute they came alongside the *Raven* and began climbing up the side ladder.

With the sheriff was a uniformed officer who addressed Ben.

"Are you the ship's captain?"

"Yes. Benjamin Pulaski," he said through gritted teeth.

The officer gave Ben a quick salute. "Lieutenant Comey, sir, cutter *McLane*. What is your cargo?"

Ben gave the officer a cold glance, then shook his head. After a moment of silence, he addressed the officer "Why have you boarded my ship?"

"The cutter *McLane* is charged with maintaining the safety of Virginia shipping, its shores, and its property. Your ship is identified in the theft of numerous slaves." The officer pointed to the sheriff. "Sheriff Scarborough here informed us he had attempted to verify your business yesterday and you threatened to fire on him with..." He stopped speaking and glanced around the deck. "He said you have cannon." Then he looked toward the sheriff with his eyebrows raised.

Ben sighed heavily. "In the crates at the bow."

The Lieutenant turned toward them and tilted his head. "Interesting," he muttered, then returned his attention to the sheriff. "Very well, Sheriff, you may perform your duty."

"The hold is this way," Ben said.

The sheriff and the Lieutenant walked slowly through the center aisle of the hold. Twice, the sheriff addressed some of the slaves lying on top of the barrels.

"Where are you from, boy?"

"South Carolina," each said with an obvious deep south accent.

When the sheriff neared the galley, George was sitting on the flooring with shackles on his ankles. "This is the one I saw trying to swim away yesterday."

"I likes to swim," George said.

"He smelled like shit, and we threw him overboard to rinse off," Ben said. "We kept a line on him to make sure we didn't lose him."

"You have papers?" the sheriff asked Ben.

Ben motioned toward the stern. "In my cabin."

In the captain's cabin Ben opened his desk, withdrawing the cargo papers from Palmetto Haven and his consignment from Joshua Dunkin.

The sheriff glanced at the consignment document then paused as he read the Cargo manifest from Palmetto Haven.

"All this says is 'rice and other cargo.'"

"They are concerned with the federal tariffs down there. Their people loaded the slaves themselves," Ben said.

Scarborough returned the document and sighed. "Now, why the hell didn't you just do this yesterday?"

"Most places I go, the sheriff has a badge of his office pinned to this coat. You were just a man with a rifle."

Scarborough pulled open his coat displaying a badge on his waistcoat.

"Now, why the hell didn't you just do that yesterday?" Ben asked.

Lieutenant Comey chuckled and slapped the sheriff gently on his shoulder.

"I believe we are done here, Sheriff."

As the men walked back up on deck, Ben spoke to the Lieutenant. "Since when does Virginia have its own revenue service?"

"Oh, no, sir. We don't," he said. "The *McLane* did use to be a revenue cutter, but Virginia bought her in '40 for shipping enforcement here in the Hampton Roads area. We just happened to be moored up the coast at Cape Charles Town yesterday evening, when the sheriff galloped up in a lather."

The sheriff's back stiffened, and he did not turn to face either the Lieutenant or Ben.

As they neared the portal, the Lieutenant turned and pointed at the crates bolted to the deck near the bow.

"What do you have in there?"

"Brass six-pounder in each crate," Ben said.

"Wouldn't match our nines, but a respectable deterrent."

They shook hands; then the Lieutenant climbed down into the cutter's boat. Edward stepped beside Ben as the boat rowed to the cutter.

"Do we have any trouble?" he asked.

"Just a misunderstanding, as it turns out," Ben said. "But if he had a warrant for the Captain of the *Raven*, there may be other towns that hold ill will toward this ship because of Hoagg's treachery."

Seconds later George stood next to Ben. "Maybe I believe, you," he said, then walked to the bow.

"Where's the key?" Edward asked George.

"In my pocket," he said.

Ben turned to Edward. "Let's get the ship ready to sail, Eddie."

By three o'clock that afternoon, the *Raven* dropped anchor near Pooles Island in a thundering downpour. The water was disturbed with low chop, which gave the ship a subtle twisting motion. Once both bow and stern anchors were secure, crew and passengers scurried below deck to dry off. Within minutes the first passenger was overwhelmed with vomiting. All available ship buckets were brought to the hold, as others suffered similar fates in what had become a corkscrew motion of side to side, bow to stern, and erratic yawing.

"We will not see a steamer out in this weather," Ben said to Edward.

The rain continued throughout most of the next day and into that night. Finally, on the third day, the clouds broke away, the sun shouldered its way through, and the bay waters calmed. The steamship *Columbia* arrived just after noon. With well-practiced efficiency, the steamship crew tied on to the *Raven* and shoved a gangplank across the short span between them. The *Raven's* fourteen special passengers lined up at the portal to make their way across. Ben and Edward stood next to the gangplank wishing them a safe journey. Their faces showed a mixed array of emotions from anxiety to exhilaration. An elderly Amish man with wispy gray hair drooping from under his hat, took each of them by the hand as they stepped onto the steamer. George was last in line. As he came to Ben, he stopped and extended his hand to him.

George spoke with a softened voice as they shook hands.

"You a good white man, Cap'n Ben."

"There are many more where you travel, George."

George smiled. "I'll believe when I see it," he said.

The steamship captain leaned out of the wheelhouse with his speaking trumpet.

"Don't know who or what will come next time, but it won't be me or this ship. We've done this enough."

Ben eyed the captain. "Can't blame him," Ben said to Edward. "He risks his position with each trip."

The steam whistle shrilled three quick notes, then the gangplank was yanked back onto the steamer, and the sidewheels began to churn.

Ben turned to the crew. "Get her ready for Baltimore. We should be docking in about four hours unless the breeze dies. Then we spend the night there."

Edward was sullen while the other crew members smiled and chatted with each other.

Ben patted his shoulder. "Tomorrow we will sail to Annapolis, Eddie. I know you look forward to seeing Mrs. Leonard."

September 30th, 1847. Lapidum, Maryland

In the middle of the night, Sonja heard Alisha crying and noticed candlelight seeping in under her bedroom door. She got out of bed and threw a blanket around her shoulders as she followed the cries. Alisha was curled up in Isaac's lap with her head on his shoulder.

"Alisha," Sonja said, "What is the matter, honey?"

Alisha's eyes were reddened and her eyelashes matted with tears.

"I don't want that woman to take me away, Momma."

Sonja knelt beside her and stroked her head.

"We won't let that happen, Alisha. You are my daughter, and no one will ever take you away from me."

"I had a bad dream," Alisha said. "She came into the house and tied you up and then she came into my room and said I had to leave right now." She released a torrent of sobs.

Isaac stood, letting Sonja take Alisha into her arms and sit with her.

"Let me know if I can do anything, Ma," Isaac said heading for his room, then turned back to Sonja. "I need to leave at sunrise."

Sonja released a sad smile and nodded her head, then gave her attention to Alisha. Sonja held her close, and they sat together without talking as Isaac closed his door. Soon they were all asleep again.

Sonja felt a man's hand on her shoulder.

"Ben?" she said, opening her eyes and letting in the dawn light.

She was still in the chair holding Alisha. Alisha stirred in her arms.

"Ma, it's Isaac," he said. "I'm going to ride down to Havre de Grace on one of our barges. The *Osprey* is in the holding pond above the lock."

Alisha frowned. "No. Don't go, Isaac."

Isaac tweaked her nose. "Got to, Punkin. I need to be in Baltimore this evening."

Alisha slid down to her feet as Sonja stood up.

"Let me make you some breakfast, son."

"No ma. They've got coffee going in the barge cabin. I already took my bag over there. Just came back to tell you good-bye."

Sonja wrapped him in a tight hug and spoke into his shoulder. "You be careful, and come home as soon as you can, Isaac."

"It will be easy duty, Ma. Captain Lee is making Fort Carroll up to snuff. I'll just be keeping track of materiel, troop strength, and correspondence."

Alisha wrapped her arms around Isaac's waist.

"I wish you would let me fix you breakfast," Sonja said.

"I'm fine, Ma."

The three walked together out onto the front porch. The cool morning air was scented with autumn and laced with a wispy aroma of coffee floating up from the canal. The *Osprey*, tied nose-to-tail in tandem with the *Turtle* ahead, had already passed through the lock. They sat waiting against the little dock at the lower edge of the front slope that Isaac had built when he was a boy. David Booker waved from the *Osprey*'s tiller. The tow rope dipped from the bow of the *Turtle* into the canal waters and climbed up to the towpath across the canal seventy feet farther down, to the waiting mules and young boy tending them.

Isaac kissed his mother on her cheek, gave a gentle yank to one of Alisha's unruly pigtails, straightened his Army tunic, and walked down the slope. As he passed between the massive twin oaks that stood as sentinels between the canal and the Pulaski home, he turned and gave Sonja another wave. The sun was still low behind the hillside on the opposite shore of the Susquehanna River. The sky above the trees turning amber kissed with rose-tinted gold.

The barges *Osprey* and *Turtle* were just entering the canal basin near the lockhouse as Ben climbed up from the *Raven's* rowboat mounting the dock on the lower edge of town. The sun was well up over Perryville on the far side of the river. He stretched in the cool air, then made his way to the Newkirk Hotel on Washington Street. The folded note in his pocket from Anthony Renowitz delivered to him in Baltimore had simply given the name of the hotel and its address. Anthony was always frugal with his words in messages passed among his contacts, and never signed them, rarely even with initials or a symbol.

The building had been named the Slater Hotel when Ben returned home in '41. He had passed the hotel then, following his adolescent son Isaac up St. Clair Street, going home at last after three years held prisoner in China; to a home that no longer existed. The view of the hotel ahead of him faded in the haze of his memories: bad news; lost home; lost daughter; lost life.

Ben forced the memories away and focused on the building before him. He crossed Washington Street and approached the hotel on the corner. Its brick walls still shined in the morning sunlight, and its huge matched chimneys on each end lifted wood smoke into the cool morning air four stories above. He entered the central doors into a lobby of polished wood floors and carved wood walls reaching up to a high ceiling. Shiny brass spittoons and healthy potted plants decorated the rooms. To the left was a narrow carpeted sitting room where a well-dressed lady sat with a gentleman. To the right more doors opened into a decorated dining room where cut glass and silver sparkled from the tablecloths. Ahead, next to wide stairs leading to the upper floors, was a highly polished mahogany desk staffed by a clerk in a dark green jacket.

"Good morning, sir," he said. "May I help you?"

The words were polite, but the tone was almost resentful.

Ben approached the desk.

"I am here at the request of Mr. Anthony Renowitz."

The clerk's face lit up like a child on Christmas

morning.

"Yes, of course, you must be Captain Pulaski?"

"Yes."

The clerk stepped quickly around the desk and motioned for Ben to follow him up the stairs.

Ben did not move. "The rooms have numbers on the doors?" Ben asked.

The clerk spun around on the third step.

"Why, yes, of course, sir."

"Tell me the number, and I can find my own way up," Ben said.

The clerk gave a broad mortuary smile.

"Second floor, sir. Room 201. Top of the stairs, sir," he said, holding out the palm of his hand as Ben came up the stairs by him. Ben placed his John Bull hat in the clerk's hand and continued up the stairs.

"Try not to drop it," Ben said.

Anthony's traveling companion, Jarrod, opened the door at Ben's first knock and let him into the parlor of the suite.

Anthony sat in a stuffed wingback chair next to one of the two tall windows showing views of the river. Anthony cradled a folded newspaper on his lap. His left leg was extended and the foot was wrapped in bandages, propped on a padded footstool.

Ben nodded his thanks to Jarrod and crossed the room to Anthony, who made no pretense to rising.

"Gout getting worse?" Ben asked as they shook hands.

"The curse of civilized man," Anthony said.

"Civilized man who doesn't follow his doctor's orders and drinks like a fish," said a man sitting in a chair Ben had passed.

Ben spun around to face the man, automatically reaching to his side where he generally carried his seaman's knife.

The man stuttered. "M-my apologies, sir, if I startled you.

Ben smiled from a reddened face and extended his hand.

"Just unhappy with myself for walking into a room

and not knowing there was a man at my back."

"And perhaps, Benjamin," Anthony said. "You let down your notorious guard because your heart told you that you will always be safe around Jarrod and me."

Ben stood in silence, glancing out the window over Anthony's shoulder.

"Great view of the bay from here. I can easily see *Raven* moored close in," Ben said.

"Close, but not so close as to avail himself of the harbormaster's docking fee, eh?" Anthony said with a smile and raised his brandy glass to Ben.

Jarrod stepped next to Ben offering a silver tray holding a small decanter and two brandy glasses.

"No thank you, Jarrod," Ben said, "But do I smell fresh coffee close by?"

"For me as well, please Jarrod," the other man said.

Anthony pointed his glass at the other man. "My apologies, Ben, this gentleman is Captain Daniel Drayton, a good friend of mine and of the Argyle Corporation."

"A Philadelphia man," Ben said, "by the sound of your accent."

"As is the owner of this fine hotel," Anthony said, "Mr. Matthew Newkirk."

Ben stepped to the window by Anthony's chair.

"Which ship is yours, sir?" Ben asked.

"At present, Captain Pulaski, I am without a ship. Anthony led me to believe you might be of a mind to let me lease your *Raven*."

"Call me Ben," he said.

"Call me Daniel," he said. "What do you think about a lease, Ben?"

Ben blinked his eyes and flashed a glance at Anthony, then returned his attention to Daniel.

"You need to explain to me what you mean by that...what you intend," Ben said, then turned his face toward Anthony, "Both of you."

"Please have a seat, Ben," Anthony said.

Ben folded his arms. "That tone of voice always gets me into trouble, Anthony. *YOU* always get me into trouble."

"Only trouble your conscience allows you to enter, old friend."

Ben sat in the matching chair between Anthony and Daniel, waiting for them to speak.

"Anthony tells me you want to help more..." He lowered his voice. "More slaves to escape, not just one, or two or three at a time, but far more than that."

Ben sighed. "Yes, I do. But I don't understand why the *Raven* needs to be leased, or even what that means to me – or you."

"The Argyle Corporation will fund the lease through Daniel," Anthony said. "This...activity may take months to complete, and we need you to halt your shipping until it is over. I want you to continue to receive an average profit during that time..."

Ben locked eyes with Anthony then Daniel.

"What else?" Ben asked.

"There will be some risk," Dan said, then he traded glances with Anthony.

"Tell it all, or I walk out," Ben said, starting to rise.

"The *Raven* will not be kept from view. She will be seen in a well-known location, and the...slaves we help escape will be noticed by many influential men."

"What location?" Ben asked.

"Washington City is still a slave district, Ben," Daniel said, "We will take them from there, run out into the Atlantic and sail to New Jersey."

"Washington City," Ben said." You want me and the *Raven* to snatch runaway slaves in the nation's capital and sail away with them in front of God and everybody."

"Yes."

"How many?"

There was a moment of silence.

"Fifty. Maybe more," Daniel said.

Jarrod brought two cups of coffee rocking on matching saucers and set them on the stand between Ben and Daniel.

"If you are caught in Washington City," Anthony said. "You could be sent to jail and your ship impounded. And if you are caught in Virginia waters, you could be hung, and your ship confiscated...or burned."

"Then we must not be caught," Ben said with a toothy grin. "Jarrod, let's have a little brandy for our coffee."

An hour later, Ben sauntered down the boardwalk to the dock at the end of St. Clair Street. Walking along St. John Street close by, Isaac spotted his father at the corner.

"Pa," he yelled. "Ben Pulaski!"

Ben stopped and turned toward the voice.

"Isaac, Hello. What are you doing here?"

"I have to leave, Pa. I have to report for duty at Fort Carroll."

"But that isn't until tomorrow, son. Why are you leaving so soon?"

"I have to be there tomorrow, Pa, not on my way there. I need to report to Captain Lee first thing in the morning."

Ben frowned.

"You were in the Army, Pa. You know that."

Ben sighed and placed his arm around his son's shoulder, although he had to reach up to do it. "I just wasn't thinking about that, but I am so glad we ran into each other. Were you hoping I could take you there in *Raven*?"

Isaac glanced around and cleared his throat. "N-no. I am taking the train. I came down hoping you would be here...to tell you goodbye if you were."

"When does your train leave, son?"

Isaac pulled a brass pocket watch from his coat and clicked it open. "Not for a couple hours, yet."

"Good. Can you spend some time with your vagabond father?"

"I would wish for nothing else, Pa," Isaac said, fingering his watch.

Ben noticed engraving on the back and lifted it up to see it in the sunlight.

TO
ISAAC PULASKI
FROM
Harriet KINCAID

"That is quite a gift, son. You must be very proud of it. Her brother once visited us."

"Yes, he told me when I visited there after I got back from Mexico."

"So you were there first. Then came here?"

Isaac's face turned red. "Yes, Pa."

Ben smiled and handed the watch back to him.

"An engraved watch is a special gift, especially when it is from a young woman to a man. I hope you managed to present her with something equally special."

"Yes, I think so...a ring."

"What?" Ben grabbed Isaac by his shoulders. "You gave her a ring? You are engaged? What did your mother say?"

Isaac went silent, pressing his lips together.

"No?" Ben asked. "She doesn't know? You didn't tell her?"

"Isaac is engaged?" Sonja asked, her mouth hanging open and her eyes flashing stormy skies.

"He told me he tried to bring it up to you, but the moment was never right..."

"Never right? That stinker walked around here in a daze half the time he was here and – Oh my Lord. I missed it. I missed it, Ben! I was so concerned with that woman, Ramona, that I never paid enough attention to my son. Oh, Ben, I missed him telling me."

Tears slipped down her cheeks.

Ben wrapped her in his arms.

"He knew I would tell you. He was so proud and happy. It started with his new watch..."

"What new watch?" she asked.

"The brass watch with the engraving from Harriet–"

"He never showed me a new watch. Oh. Ben...Isaac is engaged to a woman I have never met."

He stroked her curls and laid his face against hers.

"You met her brother in this very room. He was respectful and honorable and on his way to his uncle's funeral, who was a Congressman for this nation. I think we can be assured she comes from good stock."

"Yes, well maybe...but, I don't know her."

Ben kissed her forehead. "Our son has good sense, Sonja. He would not pursue a woman no less honorable than his mother, who is an extraordinary woman."

She hugged him tightly and looked up at his face. "Since when do you use a word like extraordinary, Benjamin Pulaski?"

"Since I first heard the word and asked what it meant, and as it was explained to me, your face came to my mind."

She looked into his eyes in silence, and tears flooded

into hers.

That evening Alisha spent the hours in her Papa's lap listening to his stories and bathing in the sound of his voice, until her eyelids were so heavy she could no longer keep them open. Ben and Sonja tucked her into bed together and said her nightly prayers with her, watching her slip away to happy dreams.

In their bedroom alone, Ben described his meeting with Anthony and Daniel. Sonja placed her fingertips gently against his lips and pulled him to her in a deep kiss.

Later, as she lay wrapped in his arms staring at the stars peeking down through the lace curtains, she shifted her position.

"I love you," she said. "Sometimes even that word is not enough. No word is enough for that."

He kissed her again. "I love you more than I ever say. Just the thought that you are here brings me home...always brings me home."

"Ben, if you need to go to Washington without me, do it. Set those people free."

"It is something I can do until the laws are made right. Surely it will happen soon but until then..."

He sighed through her curls, and for a moment they were newlyweds again.

Two weeks later, Ben, Sonja, and Alisha were up and dressed before the sunlight peeked over the eastern hilltops. From across the river in Cecil County, it bathed their front room with golden light. Alisha sat at the kitchen table near the warmth of the iron stove, eating cornmeal mush seasoned with venison sausage. Ben stood at the counter, with his arm wrapped around Sonja's waist.

"When are you coming back, Papa?" Alisha asked.

"Long before Christmas, little one," he said.

"Well before then," Sonja added.

Ben turned to Sonja. "Are you sure you don't need me to speak with George Milton about this Tatum woman?"

"No, Ben. I will deal with this. I need to deal with this. I need to do this. Me."

Ben smiled. "I have seen you take down a grown man with a marlin spike, Sonja Pulaski. If you say you don't need my help, I accept that."

"What's a marlin spike?" Alisha asked.

Ben leaned down and kissed the top of her head. "Your mother will explain all that."

Sonja wagged her fingertip in front of Ben's face and pulled him down to her lips again.

Ben scooped up Alisha and brought her to him in a hug. "You help your mother while I'm gone. You hear?"

"Yes, Papa," she said.

Moments later, Ben stepped onto the deck of a southbound barge, his breath forming small clouds in the cold air. Sonja and Alisha were on their front porch waving good-bye. Ben smiled and waved to them as the mules pulled the barge toward Havre de Grace and the greatest slave escape of his life.

Once in Havre de Grace, Ben met up with Daniel Drayton. Together they made their way to the docks where Alistair waited for them with the *Raven's* rowboat. Alistair rowed them in silence out to the *Raven*. Once on deck, Ben called for the crew, while Drayton stood off to the side. The men formed around Ben, sneaking surreptitious glances at the stranger.

"We all grew up in slave states," Ben said. "It was just the way things were, and we accepted that. Then we woke up, all for different reasons..."

The crew members exchanged questioning glances.

"Someday," Ben said, "this country will come to its senses, maybe soon. Slavery will be swept away by good men, and this nation will find other ways without it."

None of the crewmen made a sound.

"Until that time, I intend for us to help as many escape to the north as we can."

Faces nodded in agreement to Ben, but none spoke.

"You have helped me with those efforts. Each of you has told me you are committed to this undertaking as your part of serving the ship. And you know we are part of a line of people doing this, a growing line, and we are only a small part of the line."

Most of the crew murmured agreement to Ben.

"You may know that I have been asking to be involved in more escapes, greater numbers."

Again, faces nodded in agreement.

"But some of you may wish to be set ashore before this next step..."

There was silence on the deck.

"I plan to sail up the Potomac and free fifty bonded people, from Washington City itself, and take them to New Jersey. The *Raven* will go without the benefit of commercial cargo, and we may be gone a month or two."

Silence remained among the crew. They looked between themselves, then individually turned their faces back to Edward, then Ben.

"Is there more, Ben?" Edward asked.

"I want you to know our risk," Ben said. "If we get caught, we could be arrested. The *Raven* could be burned."

Alistair cleared his throat. "Those of us who have stayed with you, Cap'n, while others left or were put off, understand the purpose of this ship. The cargo pays us, but the purpose completes us."

"Begging your pardon, Cap'n," Wyatt said. "But I don't think we give a damn about the *Raven*, only what she can do to free those people."

A wave of murmuring approval swept among the crew.

Wyatt extended his hand to Ben, who took it in a firm grip. One by one the rest of the crew did the same. Edward added his hand and slapped Ben on his shoulder.

"How could you even think you needed to ask us, Brother? We are with you in this."

"Thank you, Eddie."

"One more thing, gentlemen," Ben said raising his voice and motioning toward Drayton. "The organization that helps arrange things for us will lease the ship as we perform this task. A small sum will be sent monthly to your homes to keep food on the table and fires in your kitchens, since we will work without shares for a while.

Provide names and addresses to Daniel Drayton, here."

Ben turned to Drayton, who displayed a broad smile.

"We are ready to go to Washington," Ben said.

"We've got a problem," said Daniel, the *Raven*'s only black crewman. "We have two Daniels on board, Cap'n."

"We have the solution for that," Ben said.

"Call me by my last name," said Drayton.

They rigged a boom and tackle to shift the small deck cannon down into the bilge as ballast since they would be sailing to Washington City without the usual weight of cargo. Then they sailed to the docks of Annapolis to fill *Raven*'s storeroom, lockers, and galley with all the food and other supplies it could take. Drayton dashed from one supplier to another, handing out lists to clerks and writing bank drafts for store owners. Ben and the crew worked like lines of ants carrying supplies back to the ship, then filing to the next shop. The last order was for fifty bunk mattresses and one hundred wool blankets.

"There will be no convincing visitors to the ship that our outbound cargo will be anything other than people," Drayton said as he checked off items from his list.

"No," Ben said, "but let's hope any visitor is trustworthy."

Ben glanced at Drayton's list. "One hundred blankets?"

"Winter is approaching, Ben. I want our passengers to have two blankets. Depending on the wind, it could take us as much as two weeks to make Cape May."

"Or two days," Ben said with a smile. "But if I am wrong, we can't make those people endure two weeks on winter seas."

The following morning *Raven* faced an easterly wind in Annapolis and had to tack back and forth across it to reach the main channel of the Chesapeake Bay. Once turning south and resetting her sails, *Raven* leaned away from the brisk wind and galloped over the waves making excellent time to Point Lookout and the mouth of the Potomac River. Ben steered her far out from the point, staying in deeper water. The crew adjusted the lay of the sails and pulled the booms across to the other side while Ben spun the wheel to take them north, and the *Raven* flew again across the wind.

Ben allowed the *Raven* to run at her fastest speed, gulping all the power delivered by the wind. Still running up the river, they altered course passed Coles Point on the Virginia side and again fifteen miles farther at Cobb Island on the Maryland side. Once past Morgantown they allowed the ship to slow to a moderate speed as they approached the broken-back turn in the river. There the old Potomac veers southwest before curving begrudgingly back toward the north after a thirty-six-mile loop, and threads along the swamps past Alexandria to Washington City.

Under limited sails, Drayton directed Ben toward lesser-used areas of Washington Wharves. A small steam tug came out to assist docking. Once the *Raven* was tied,

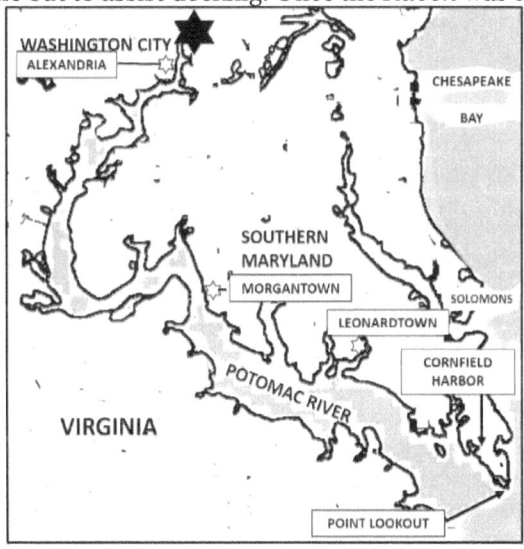

the tug captain came on board to collect his fee.

"You picked a hell of a spot to dock, Cap'n," he said to Ben. "Not close to any of the big warehouses. Mostly just black folk dock here. What are you hauling?"

"We already dropped off our load of lumber in Alexandria, and we have to wait a while for our consignment for Baltimore," Ben said.

"Well, that makes sense. Docking fees down here are fair. But don't think the harbormaster didn't see you come in. That old salt has a mounted spyglass, and he can see every damned inch of the piers. You best make his acquaintance as soon as your feet touch the dock."

"He will be my first visit," Drayton said, as he paid the fee, then added an extra silver dollar. "Thank you for your advice, sir. Kindly have an ale as our gratitude."

The tug captain gave a broad smile. "That I will do," he said and sauntered down the gangplank. As he walked away, Edward called out to him, "Are there taverns nearby?"

"More than you need," he said pointing at the big warehouses at the other end of the wharves. "Other side of them."

"I will go see the harbormaster," Drayton said to Ben, "and then go meet some contacts I have in the city."

"Cap'n suh," said a black man who had walked halfway up the gangplank as soon as the tug captain left.

Ben turned toward the voice. "Yes?"

The man tugged at a copper tag hanging from a leather line around his neck, holding it up so Ben could see it. "Yall need any he'p unloading or carrying anything?"

"Sorry, but we're empty," Ben said and the man turned away. "You hungry?" Ben asked.

He stopped and turned toward Ben. "I's always hungry, suh."

Ben glanced around the deck and spotted their cook. "Warren, please take this gentleman below feed him."

Daniel called out, "I'll do it."

Warren arched his eyebrows and eyed Ben. Ben nodded and motioned for Daniel toward the aft ladderway.

Both men were chatting before they made it to the deck opening.

"Let's get the cargo hatch open and air out the hold, while we're waiting for our passengers," Ben said to the crewmen on deck. "This may not take long after all," he muttered to himself.

Ben gazed into the hold as the crewmen moved the

hatch cover aside.

"Don't think I've ever seen it so empty," he said and noticed Daniel and Edward sitting at the narrow mess table with the black man.

Edward signaled to Ben then made a quick exit from the hold and approached Ben on deck.

"He wants to go with us," Edward said.

"Eddie, I'm not sure it's wise to be telling why we're here – as soon as we get here."

Edward shook his head. "I only asked him if he wanted to go with us when we leave. That's all I've said to him. Ben, I'm not stupid."

Ben blinked his eyes. "No. No, of course, you are not. I've never thought that."

"I am your first mate, Ben, and I run this crew very well–"

"Perfectly, in fact..." Ben said.

"Sometimes you don't act toward me like you believe that," Edward said.

Ben took in a deep breath, and glanced around the deck, not focusing on any particular object, then returned his attention to Edward and smiled.

"I guess we are more brothers than I thought," Ben said, keeping his smile.

"What?" Edward asked.

"I've heard it said that brothers tend to aggravate each other."

Edward compressed his lips, imprisoning the smile trying to escape onto his face.

"Your point is taken, Eddie," Ben said. "I will behave better towards you."

Edward kept his face composed. "Thank you," he said, then released a grin.

Daniel and the rented slave emerged onto the deck and walked down the gangplank together. The slave was carrying a bundle in the rook of his arm. He pointed toward a nearby hillside dotted with shanties and litter, then he and Daniel shook hands.

As Daniel returned to the ship, he eyed Ben. "He's trying to feed a wife and baby off whatever the owner lets him keep, so I gave him some food to take. He also told me where to find a colored tavern".

Drayton scurried up the gangplank behind Daniel.

"We have problems, Ben," he said.

"What kind of problems, Drayton? Are we found out so soon?"

"No. No. No. Nothing as bad as that," Drayton said. "But, it will delay our departure."

"Tell me."

"One of the key passengers is a midwife of sorts. She was loaned out yesterday to another family, an influential family, whose married daughter is ready to deliver her first child."

"How long do we wait?" Ben asked.

"You have children of your own, and you asked such a question?"

"What I am asking is how long do we have in your plan that we can wait here."

"If we sit more than a week, the wrong people will become curious. My views are known among many people in this city. I have spoken publicly here for abolition."

"How widely known is that?" Ben asked.

"Dozens...multiples of dozens...maybe even dozens of dozens, but, but this is a big city."

"And what are we to do about that, Drayton?"

"Ben, I need to make several contacts throughout the city. I think it best if I do not make a circuit back and forth to this ship while I do that..."

Ben folded his arms.

Drayton cleared his throat. "I will go to a house where I am welcome, and from there meet the people I need to, so they can come and go while I stay inside. I will return in a couple days."

Drayton stepped away to the aft ladderway and down into his cabin. Moments later he returned with a small carpet bag and left the ship without further words.

"Doesn't tell us much, does he?" Edward asked.

"No," Ben said, letting out a long sigh. "But it is up to him to quietly let our passengers know where and when to come aboard. He has Anthony's trust, so he must have mine. Let's secure the ship and give the crew two days off."

Edward smiled with a sparkle in his eyes. "Aye, aye, Cap'n."

Ben returned his smile "That includes you too, Eddie. You've earned it. Have the crewmen come see me, for a partial pay. It would be unkind to send them, or you, into Washington City without a few dollars to spend.

Ben brought up a small portable table from the hold and a canvas pouch. He set up near the wheels and counted out five silver dollars for each man, and had them sign for it in the ship's pay ledger. As the first mate, Edward was the last to step to the table. Ben counted out ten dollars for him.

"Try to behave, Eddie. I recall a certain married woman in Havre de Grace..."

Edward held up his hand to halt the comment. "No more, Ben. I am a married man, now. And we both know Belle would take a horsewhip to me if I strayed – not that I would, anymore."

"Just be careful, Eddie," Ben said.

Ben stood at the top of the gangplank as the men made their way toward the city. All but Daniel were headed toward the large warehouses pointed out earlier by the harbormaster. Daniel walked alone toward the shanties on the hill. The sun drifted lower toward the western skyline chased by rolling clouds pulling a charcoal canvas across the sky. The wind increased, bringing a bite of wet winter in its teeth, and the pungent smell of old swamps.

A man dressed in a dark blue uniform hobbled along the wharf toward the *Raven,* his steps were announced by the clack of a walking cane hitting the boardwalk. Ben folded his arms, watching the man. His head was intermittently bathed in smoke coming from a stubby pipe, whipped away by the breeze.

"Yer takin yer damned time, ain't ya?" he said as he approached the gangplank.

Ben stood in silence.

"That other fellah said you'd come pay the docking fees."

"Thought he would do it," Ben said.

"You Yankees always try to git by without paying. Specially when you dock at this end. Thinkin I won't pay you no attention down here."

"I'm from Maryland," Ben said.

The man came to a halt at the foot of the gangplank and leaned with both hands on his cane. "Northern or southern Maryland?"

"Northern."

The man straightened, pulled his pipe from his mouth and spat. "Same as Pennsylvania up there. All of it gone to hell..." he pointed back toward the city with his pipe. "Like most of this place has. Full of Yankees messin' things up."

"How much do you need?" Ben asked.

The man poked the tip of his cane onto the gangplank. "Permission to come aboard?"

Ben motioned with his hand for the man to come.

"It kills my hip to walk all the way down here to collect a fee you shoulda paid right off," he said. "I'm the harbormaster, damn it. You shoulda come to me!"

The harbormaster's face was traced with deep lines around his eyes and mouth.

Ben made a couple passes up and down the empty deck checking riggings, battens and latches, then made his way down to his cabin. After a brief meal of dried meat and biscuit, he lit the lantern above his desk and began a serial letter to Sonja. Such letters were common among seamen, intended to chain together the days and mailed weeks later.

Dear Sonja,

We have arrived at the wharves of Washington City and have a snug mooring site. I have let Edward and the crew out for entertainment in the city for a couple days. Drayton has gone out to make contacts and finalize arrangements to bring our passengers on board. I suspect this may take longer than a few days to bring them all here.

Ben

In the early morning, clumsy boot heels trudged across the deck and Ben rushed up to see who had come aboard. Wyatt was being supported between Alistair and Warren. Wyatt's face was bruised, cut and bloody, and he was dangling by his arms around their shoulders.

"What the hell happened?" Ben asked. "Where's Edward?"

"Jail," said Alistair.

***

Catherine Price knocked frantically on the Pulaski front door.

Sonja opened the door wiping her hands with a kitchen towel. "Hello Catherine, how are you to–"

"That woman has a court order, Sonja."

"What? What do you mean?"

"Jesse heard it from Dan Bartlett on Number 26 just a minute ago."

"Heard what?"

"The judge accepted her claim on Alisha and ordered Deputy Mattingly to pick up someone from the Orphan's Court and come take Alisha."

"Take me where?" Alisha asked from behind Sonja.

Sonja spoke over her shoulder, "Nowhere, dear. That is not going to happen." Then turned back to Catherine, "How does Dan Bartlett know all this?"

"Mattingly told him. Said to tell you he's coming tomorrow."

"Thank you, Catherine. Go home. Ask Jesse to push the swing bridge over the lock. Stay in your house for an hour or so, if you can."

Sonja closed the door, turning around and kneeling before Alisha. "Honey, did you pack the 'Maybe Bag' I gave you?"

"Yes ma'am, everything you said to put in it. Are they going to take me away?"

"No dear. I promise, no one will ever take you away from me. Put on your coat and gloves. We are going on a trip."

Moments later Alisha sat in Ben's stuffed chair, staring at three bulging travel bags placed in the front room, while Sonja wrote a note at the kitchen table.

> *Dearest Ben,*
>
> *I will send you a letter soon telling you what has happened and what I am doing. I can't say anything else in this note, for reasons I will explain. Know that Alisha and I are safe among people that are my friends. Know also that I love you with all my heart.*
>
> *Your wife, Sonja*

Sonja folded the note and placed it on the mantel where Ben kept his pipes. She dashed out of the house to the barn where she hitched their horse to the new buggy Ben bought during the summer. Back in the house, she picked up two of the travel bags and had Alisha carry the third and the old quilt off Sonja's bed, then closed the door behind them. Together, they packed everything on the back of the buggy, mounted the spring seat then drove the horse and buggy to the end of their lane. Sonja halted the buggy and glanced back at their house, then flicked the buggy whip against the rump of the horse. They trotted up Stafford Road to the lockhouse and then crossed the bridge onto the towpath. There Sonja turned the horse north and flicked its rump again. Catherine peeked out of her front window as the buggy rolled north toward Pennsylvania.

Six hours later Sonja stopped the buggy in front of the lockhouse at York Furnace. The horse panted around the spit-covered bridle. The two previous stops she had made to rest the horse on her way had not given him the respite he needed. John Calvert sat on the porch of the lockhouse across the canal. Sonja stepped down next to the buggy and called out for him. He waved and moved forward to swing the bridge into place over the lock.

Alisha sat in the Calverts' kitchen sipping warm broth, while Sonja spoke with Emma Calvert in the front room.

"Where will you go, child?" Emma asked. "You are welcome to stay here, and I know David Booker will be happy to have you up the hill at your father's house."

"No, thank you, Emma. I am going to stay with my family in North Carolina, but I want to leave the buggy and horse at the farm for Ben to find."

"Well, you just sit and rest all you want. I am so sorry for all this calamity that has followed you. After the miracle of regaining your lost daughter, to have that woman try to take her away is horrendous."

Sonja patted her hand and squeezed it in hers. "My father was so lucky to have such good friends here."

"Well, he did a lot for us. Lord, we were never out of apples," she chuckled. "I guess we were the first people he met when he and his wife moved up here from North Carolina in '35."

"He lost her, too," Sonja said. "My momma passed away back in...well it doesn't matter now. He was happy here."

"We were so sorry to hear about him..."

"May I leave a note for Ben with you, Emma? I couldn't tell him much in the note I left at our house. I wasn't sure who would find it."

Emma let Sonja use the little corner desk where John kept his canal ledgers.

Dear Ben,

We arrived safely among friends here

in York Furnace. I will go next to ~~Papa's~~ Aaron's farm and leave the buggy and horse there. Please forgive me for running off like this, but that woman found a way to take Alisha from me. I will never let that happen again. We are going to North Carolina where you and I first met. I plan to stay with my Uncle Jim. He was Papa's closest brother. Please come when it is safe. We will go wherever you say, but never back to Maryland until they accept Alisha as our daughter.

Your loving wife, Sonja

She glanced out of the window. "I should be getting up the hill to the farm, it will be dark soon."

Emma stood with Sonja, "Sonja, dear, we don't have much money, but if you need any..."

"No, no, Emma. I have more than enough but thank you. I've made plans since the moment that woman arrived at my door."

They hugged, and Sonja patted John's arm. Alisha kissed cheeks of both Emma and John. Outside again, John had already watered and wiped down the horse, and adjusted his straps. Within minutes Sonja and Alisha were up the hill in front of the Jundt-Pulaski farm. Helen Booker heard them arrive and came down the steps to meet them.

"David is out in the barn," Helen said. "Your Aaron wanted the barn full of mules to keep the barges moving, and they take a lot of care. I'm just glad to have my husband home for a while... but you know all about canal men."

Sonja smiled and placed her hand on Alisha's shoulder, "Honey you remember Mrs. Booker, don't you?"

Alisha took Helen's hand and curtsied.

Helen's eyes went wide. "Well, aren't you the social one."

"I school her at home," Sonja told Helen. "I try to include manners now and then, although some of it may be out of date, and when she comes home covered in mud, I wonder if it is worth the effort."

Helen laughed with a twinkle in her eyes and smiled at Alisha.

Helen touched Sonja's hand. "Courtesy is never out of date. I think she is precious. So, come inside and meet our growing toddler."

David joined them moments later as they settled around the iron stove in the front room and learned of Sonja's situation.

"Well, Mrs. Pulaski, if you need to run off, what more perfect place than the biggest station on the Underground Railroad in York County, provided by your father and your brother...Have you heard from Aaron recently?"

"Not since he went to California, David," Sonja said.

David nodded. "Please, stay here as long as you need. This big ol' place was intended to be filled with people."

Sonja's eyes drifted from the front room to the door of the back bedroom, where Aaron's wife and daughter had died in childbirth.

Helen finished breastfeeding the baby and turned him around to face Sonja.

"See our little bear," she said, and he promptly spit up.

Sonja chuckled "Leave it to our babies to keep us in our places."

There was a brief knock on the door before it was flung open. A tall elderly man with a long Amish-style gray beard stepped into the front room.

"Well, they're safely away, David," he said.

David stood and motioned toward Sonja. "Pa, this is Sonja and Alisha Pulaski–"

His motions were quick and agile, more like a younger man. "Yes, I've met Mrs. Pulaski before." He shook her hand, "Ma'am." Then gave his attention to Alisha. "But, this young lady I have not, though I've heard much about her from her father."

He smiled and took her hand, pulling her to her feet. Her small hand almost lost in his large calloused one.

"How do you do, Miss Alisha Pulaski? I am Isaiah Booker."

Alisha smiled into his eyes and curtsied.

Isaiah straightened and planted his hands on his hips, then cast about the room.

"Well, now. I've never had such a fine introduction, young lady. You do your Ma and Pa proud."

"They are escaping a harsh edict from a Maryland judge, Pa," David said. "He has decreed that Sonja's daughter is not her daughter and another woman has claimed her."

Storm clouds crossed the old man eyes, and a frown settled over them.

"Any fool can see these two women are related," he said.

He faced Sonja, "What are your plans, Mrs. Pulaski?"

"I will go to my family in North Carolina," she said.

He chuckled. "Well, I've never helped anyone escape south before, but we can start you on your way right now."

Two hours later, in Wrightsville, Isaiah took Sonja and Alisha across the mile-long covered bridge into Columbia. There, Sonja sent a telegram to Anthony Renowitz, Chairman of the Argyle Corporation. Isaiah stayed with them as she purchased two tickets on the Philadelphia and Columbia Railroad on Front Street, and then to Locust Street, where she took a room for the night at the Franklin Hotel.

Sonja gave Isaiah a quick kiss on his cheek, much to his surprise and embarrassment. He backed away, fumbling with his hat in his hands.

"I...I believe you ladies will be quite safe here," he said. "God be with ye." Then he turned and walked away.

Sonja and Alisha exchanged glances and giggled, then went up to their room, following the porter carrying their bags. After dinner, Alisha fell asleep quickly, and Sonja blew out the lamp next to her bed. In the darkened room, still partially lit by the street lamp below, Sonja sat in a chair by the window, looking up at the stars.

"I'm sorry, Ben," she whispered to the sky.

The following morning, they sat next to the window in a railcar as the train whistle shrieked into a steam cloud above. Alisha's eyes danced around the car, taking in all the exciting new sights. She spotted the face of a solemn-looking man, whose eyes pierced the space between them, locking onto her eyes. She spun away from his glare and dropped her attention down between her feet. The engine growled and coughed black smoke from its funnel, their car jerked in its coupling, and the train clawed away from the station. Alisha had her nose pressed against the glass watching the scenery as the train picked up speed in a wobbled dash.

The next afternoon, Deputy Mattingly drove a surrey into Lapidum with Ramona Tatum and a representative of the Orphan's Court along with him. Catherine Price and her husband Jesse watched from the yard as the visitors mounted the Pulaski porch and the deputy pounded on the front door. Mattingly opened the door and stepped in, calling out for Sonja and Alisha. The two women stayed on the porch. Mattingly emerged holding a folded note and faced the Prices.

"Do you know where they are?" Mattingly asked.

They shook their heads 'no' in silence. Ramona glared at the couple.

"I bet they know exactly where she is," she said.

"Well," Mattingly said, "She isn't here."

He walked down the steps and faced the Prices. "You tell her I need to see her when she returns, you hear?"

He handed the note to Catherine.

"I will wait," Ramona said and burst into the Pulaski house.

"Get back out here," Mattingly yelled.

She returned to the porch. "The stove is cold. They were gone yesterday. Knew we were coming. I will wait right here."

Mattingly looked back over his shoulder. "Not without me, you won't. Judge Jessup said you had to be accompanied by both me and Mrs. Holcomb there. I don't want any trouble with this. You'll come back when I do. Come along, ma'am."

He nodded to Jesse, then tipped his hat to Catherine Price and walked back to the surrey.

Ramona sniped from the surrey, glaring at the Prices. "I will get a warrant for her arrest."

October 20th, 1847. Washington City

Ben managed to follow the directions given by the harbormaster and after a brisk hour-walk stood before the blue-gray stuccoed exterior of the City Jail. The harbormaster called it the "Blue Jug." Less than ten years old, some of the stucco had cracked and fallen onto the small weedy area around the building. Ben was directed to a small room off the lobby where a sleepy police sergeant sat behind a high desk.

"I'm told my brother is here."

"Name," the sergeant said with a sigh.

"His name is Edward Leonard."

The sergeant rolled his eyes at Ben. "Yours, mister."

Ben balled his fist at his side. "Benjamin Pulaski."

The sergeant made a note in a ledger. "His," he said.

Ben exhaled a slow breath. "Edward Leonard."

The sergeant made another note, then spun around in his chair and walked away in silence. Moments later he returned with a file in his hand, which he slapped onto the desk surface and then settled back into his chair. He sipped from a coffee cup as he read the single paper in the folder, then leaned forward on his elbows.

"Fifty dollars," he said.

"Fifty dollars?"

"You're lucky we're letting him out at all, mister. Your brother assaulted a police officer."

Ben cautiously withdrew a leather wallet from his coat, emptied it of all the cash he had with him and laid the bills on the desk. The sergeant counted the money, then made a note on the paper in Edward's file. Then he pulled a small piece of paper from a nearby shelf, made several notations on it and handed the paper to Ben.

He took a long drink from his cup "Have a seat out

there in the lobby. He will be brought out to you."

Ben smelled whiskey on his breath as the sergeant spoke. The sergeant scooped up the money and the file, spun around in his chair then stood up and toddled into a back room.

After waiting almost an hour another policeman entered the lobby from a side door, pulling Edward by his arm. Edward's face was bruised and swollen, and he walked with a limp. His wrinkled shirt had dried blood on the front, and his trousers were ripped near one foot. They approached Ben.

"You waiting on Leonard?" the policeman asked.

Ben stood and showed the man his receipt. The policeman sniffed as he looked at the paper.

"He's got a court date in two weeks. November 3rd," he said, still looking at the paper.

Then he focused his attention on Edward. "Pack some clothes and personal effects when you come back, Leonard. You'll be in here a year, for hitting Officer Banyan, unless Judge Flores is in a bad mood – then it could be longer."

The officer turned to Ben. "If he ain't here then and we have to come get him, ninety days will be added to his sentence."

The policeman turned and walked back to where he came.

Edward looked into Ben's eyes and sighed heavily. They stood in silence for a brief moment, then walked out of the lobby without speaking.

Ben paused on the stone steps outside the doorway. "Can you walk back to the ship from here?" he asked.

Edward nodded yes but said nothing.

"I need to send a telegram," Ben said, then he glanced down at the receipt. It was for only twenty dollars. Ben gritted his teeth and jammed the receipt into his pocket.

When Ben returned to the *Raven*, Drayton was on board, waiting.

"I'm running into a lot of scheduling problems, Ben," he said.

Ben ignored him and turned to Alistair. "How is Wyatt?"

Alistair grinned and scratched his chin. "Well, Cap'n, he looks like hell, but it will all heal, I think. He's fit enough to do his job."

Ben asked Drayton to follow him down to this cabin. "How can slaves have a scheduling problem?" Ben asked as he settled into the chair by his desk, then motioned to the other chair for Drayton.

"Ben, schedule is everything. It isn't enough to just get them away from their masters, it must be for long enough to escape before they are missed."

"If we left today, Drayton, how many could we bring with us?"

He hesitated. "Maybe...fifteen."

"And if we wait until you make a schedule?"

"Ben, my current list is around fifty, and it is growing."

Ben's eyes went wide. "When do you think the time will be right for that fifty?"

"March. Maybe, April," Drayton said.

Ben sighed. "I'm taking the ship out of here. Will you go with us, or stay until I return?"

"I will stay. We can communicate through Argyle."

"You will be safe?"

"Yes, Ben. I have friends with whom I can stay."

Edward had changed clothes and washed his face when returned to the deck.

"Is Daniel back?" Ben asked him.

"Yes, Cap'n. All the crew is aboard."

"Prepare the ship to leave," Ben said.

On Edward's direction, the gangplank was withdrawn and the mainsail raised to back the *Raven* away from the pier. Once the ship was free, crewmen raised the jib sails to point her bow downstream on the Potomac River. The foresail ran up in front of the main, and the *Raven* glided silently away from the city. Ben took the windward wheel and Edward relieved Daniel at the twin wheel beside it. They sailed past Alexandria and Fort Washington in silence.

As they turned the *Raven* southwest to begin the long wide hook past Indian Head, Edward spoke to Ben.

"That policeman was drunk and out of his uniform

when he started punching Wyatt."

Ben did not turn his head or speak.

"Wyatt was no match for that man," Edward said.

"You cannot return to Washington City, Edward...I am not even certain the *Raven* can."

Nothing further was said between them until the eastward turn of the river at the bottom of the hook. Even then it was nothing more than "wear ship," so they could tack across the wind.

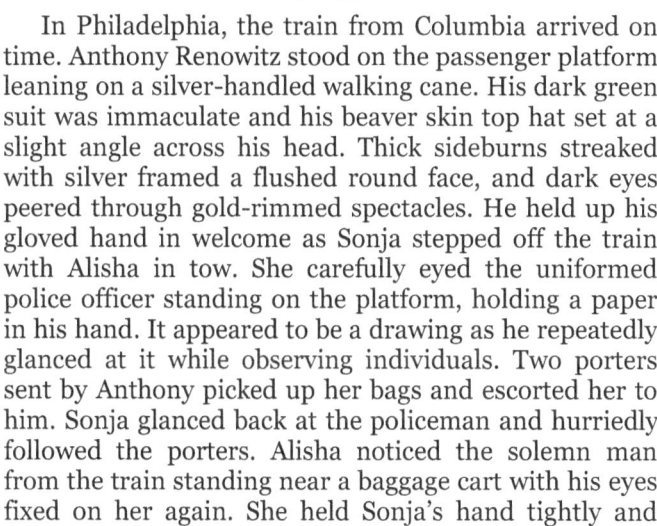

In Philadelphia, the train from Columbia arrived on time. Anthony Renowitz stood on the passenger platform leaning on a silver-handled walking cane. His dark green suit was immaculate and his beaver skin top hat set at a slight angle across his head. Thick sideburns streaked with silver framed a flushed round face, and dark eyes peered through gold-rimmed spectacles. He held up his gloved hand in welcome as Sonja stepped off the train with Alisha in tow. She carefully eyed the uniformed police officer standing on the platform, holding a paper in his hand. It appeared to be a drawing as he repeatedly glanced at it while observing individuals. Two porters sent by Anthony picked up her bags and escorted her to him. Sonja glanced back at the policeman and hurriedly followed the porters. Alisha noticed the solemn man from the train standing near a baggage cart with his eyes fixed on her again. She held Sonja's hand tightly and trotted away with her.

Sonja smiled at Anthony and accepted his embrace and kissed him on his cheek.

"I can't help but remember our first meeting," she said with a faint laugh, "That morning I found you asleep on our front room floor next to Ben with a stray dog in your arms."

Anthony chuckled. "We had far too much to drink that night, Sonja, but it was worth it to celebrate reuniting with my old friend. Even though the swamps of Florida and the prison of China are faded memories–" He glanced among the crowd leaving the train. "Where is Ben?"

She lowered her voice to little more than a whisper. "He is in Washington City, Anthony. You know damned well where he is."

"Oh...I thought, perhaps..."

"No. I am here on my own. And as much as I hate myself for asking, I need your help."

Anthony turned to face Alisha. "I am happy to see you again, young lady. For a little girl who lived most of her life on a tiny fishing island in the Chesapeake Bay, you are certainly getting to travel now."

Alisha accepted his hand and curtsied. "Hello, Mr. Renowitz. I am glad to see you again, too." Then she lowered her voice. "We are running away."

He pressed his lips together and flashed his eyes at Sonja, then bowed to Alisha in return.

He motioned toward the line of carriages waiting nearby. "My landau is this way."

The body of the carriage was painted dark blue. The black leather landau top was up against the afternoon chill. A black-suited man sat erect in the open driver's seat at the front, holding the reins to a matched pair of brushed horses with neatly bobbed tails.

Seated inside, the carriage rolled along cobblestone streets, the steady clopping of the horse's hooves giving a metronome to the motion of the cab.

"I hope you and Alisha will accept the hospitality of my home this evening, Sonja. Camilla is looking forward to seeing you again."

Sonja released a smile. "I haven't seen her since..."

"Not since we took the *Raven*, I think. I had to come alone to Aaron's wedding..."

He fell silent a moment. "I was so sad to hear..."

"Thank you, Anthony. Please forgive me for snapping earlier. Losing Maggie and Sarah like that...None of us have fully recovered, least of all Aaron."

Anthony locked eyes with her, waiting for her to speak further.

"Thank you for passing along the information about him, Anthony. We had no idea where he was."

"It was an easy thing to do...for friends," he said, tapping his fingertips on his cane. "So, tell me, Sonja.

What is happening that drives you from Havre de Grace?"

When they arrived in front of the Renowitz Mansion, Sonja had shared all that had happened with Ramona Tatum. Alisha had slipped her hand into Sonja's during the telling.

The driver opened the door to the carriage.

"Ah, and here we are," Anthony said.

The Renowitz home was a brick mansion of a broad two-story center, anchored by an Octagon-shaped room tower on the right and a one-story addition on the left. The neatly tended front yard began with a white gate in a picket fence from the roadway, then up an intricately designed brick walkway to the front veranda and matched set of front doors. Camilla Renowitz came out onto the veranda with her hands held in front of her, offering a warm smile under soft brown eyes, and auburn hair pulled into a loose net in back.

As Sonja and Alisha came closer to the veranda, Camilla stepped down to the walkway and extended her hands to each of them.

"Welcome to our home," she said and gently drew them into the house.

The foyer was open to a banister on the upper floor and held a brass chandelier of a dozen candles hanging from the ceiling. To the left, a curving staircase of painted wood wound its way to the second floor. Polished floors reflected light in every direction.

"Please come into the parlor and rest," Camilla said.

Anthony stepped close to Camilla and kissed her cheek, then walked ahead of them into the parlor. He opened a dark wooden cabinet and withdrew a cut-glass decanter, then filled a glass with amber liquid.

"Anthony," Camilla said with a tone familiar to all married couples.

He winked back at her and carried the glass to a padded chair where he sat relaxed and sipped from his glass.

"Just one, Camie," he said over the rim of the glass.

Sonja and Alisha sat on a thickly padded settee next to Camilla. Within seconds a well-dressed servant brought in a wooden tray holding glasses of water and sweet tea.

"Thank you, Ralph," Camilla said to the servant. "What is Mary fixing us for dinner?"

Ralph set the tray on a low table in front of the settee and grinned at Camilla.

"She said it's going to be a surprise, but you will like it."

Camilla patted his hand and smiled, then turned to Sonja and Alisha. "I hope you like sweetened tea. Anthony tells me you are from North Carolina, originally."

"Yes. Morganton. That is—"

"I know Morganton," Camilla said with excitement. "I am from Salem, North Carolina."

Sonja brightened and released a beaming smile. "I have not had sweet tea in years."

Alisha tasted her tea and took several gulps, only stopping to gasp for air. "I love this," she said.

"We had no time to get to know each other when Anthony was wounded, Sonja. All I could think of was getting him back to Philadelphia doctors."

Sonja nodded her head. "We only had seconds to say hello and good-bye, when Isaac left with you."

"He was such a dear to have around before his schooling started. Then West Point absolutely consumed his time."

"Dinner is ready, ma'am," the servant said.

"Oh, how rude of me," Camilla said. "I'm sure you ladies need to spend a few moments in the necessary..."

Sonja and Alisha presented blank expressions.

Camilla grinned and leaned close to them and whispered, "Some people refer to them as water closets, though there only a few even in Philadelphia. We don't have an outhouse. Anthony had it installed a few years ago. Go through the white door just under the staircase."

Anthony pretended to not hear the conversation and walked out of the parlor. Ten minutes later Sonja and Alisha came out of the water closet with Alisha smiling and smelling her hands.

Camilla swooped to meet them and put her arm

around Alisha. "Doesn't that French soap smell wonderful?"

She guided them into the dining room, where Anthony sat at the head of a long table that could easily seat a dozen guests. Camilla had them sit on either side of Anthony and then walked to the far end of the table. Sonja and Alisha exchanged quick glances. Then the cook came in carrying a wooden tray covered with a calico cloth and set it in front of Camilla, then sat in the chair next to Camilla. Other servants brought in dishes of fried pork chops, slow-cooked pinto beans, steamed greens, black-eyed peas, and heavy pitchers of sweet tea. They took seats around the table until all the seats were filled, and then each person held the hand of the one next to them. Once the chain was complete, Camilla and everyone bowed their head. Alisha glanced around the table then met Sonja's eyes. Sonja dipped her head and drew Alisha down with her.

"Come, Lord, Jesus, our Guest to be. And bless these gifts bestowed by Thee," Camilla said. "Bless our loved ones everywhere and keep them in Thy loving care."

The momentary quiet erupted into chatter while dishes floated among the guests.

"I am in heaven," Sonja said admiring the table bounty.

"I'm lost," Alisha said.

Camilla smiled and snapped her fingers. "Butter," she commanded.

The butter dish floated to her on eager hands, and as soon as it landed by the wooden tray, with her eyes on Sonja, she flipped off the calico cloth to display a huge steaming cake of cornbread. Ralph cut off a thick wedge and plated it in front of Camilla who slathered it with butter and sent it down the table. Sonja clasped her hands in front of her lips and tears filled her eyes. Camilla sent another piece to Alisha, who looked at it in curiosity.

"It has been so long..." Sonja said, then faced Alisha. "I always meant to have a North Carolina meal for you, but...but..."

"Just enjoy the bounty the Lord provides, Sonja,"

Camilla said.

Anthony raised his glass. "And to Stanislaus Kosciuszko Renowitz, my grandfather who built this house that no one else in the family wanted, and to the estate he left behind, fattened by ruined lives of countless slaves. May this house and his money free a thousand."

Four white hands and eight black ones raised glasses of tea or whiskey, saying, "To Grandfather."

Anthony and Camilla Renowitz stood on the Philadelphia pier in the early morning mist, waving to Alisha and Sonja. The steamship *Herald* pulled away from the harbor into the Delaware River. Once in the deep channel of the river, the side wheel of the *Herald* churned the water into a froth, pushing the ship southward.

Sonja stepped back from the railing. "Let's get settled into our room, Alisha."

"May I please stay out here, Momma? I want to stand right here until we get to Baltimore."

"Sweetheart, that will be many hours from now. You will have all the time in the world to watch the water go by. It will take us all day to get to Baltimore. Then we will walk from this steamship to another that will take us to Norfolk in Virginia—"

"What's the name of that one?" Alisha asked.

"The *City of Richmond*, according to Mr. Renowitz."

"And how long will we be on that one?"

Sonja tapped Alisha's nose with the tip of her finger. "If you had not dozed in the carriage ride from the Renowitz home to the harbor, you would have already heard all this."

Alisha's bright blue eyes remained fixed on her mother's matching eyes, her expectant face smiling.

Sonja sighed and released a wide smile. "That will take another whole day. And then another ship and another day. And then a train. And then another train, and another train. Then a coach...and I do not know the names of any of those things."

"And then we will be in North Carolina, right?"

"Yes, Alisha. Now, let's go to our room. I want you to begin writing notes about your trip in the pretty journal

Mrs. Renowitz gave you."

Alisha began to turn toward their stateroom, then stopped and faced Sonja. "We will go through the C&D canal won't we?"

"Yes dear."

"My other momma would point to the steamships coming out of that canal. We could see them from Momma's island. From Rachel's island."

"Would she, really?"

"Yes, Momma. We were happy on the island. I loved to hear her laugh and listen to all the stories she told me."

Sonja placed her hand on Alisha's shoulder. "She never smiled when I knew her."

"She was sick, then. I think she hurt all the time. She was a good momma until she died."

Sonja pulled Alisha to her in a warm embrace. "I am so glad she found you."

"She pulled me from a tree that washed up on her island."

Sonja's eyes went wide, and she held Alisha out in front of her. "Did she tell you about that?"

"Oh yes. Momma, I mean Rachel, told me about everything. About the ice storm that brought me over the water – that's why she named me 'Moses' – and how she came to the island and her husband, Jason..."

"Her husband?"

"Yes. Jason. He was a slave and didn't have a last name, so he used hers, but he was gone long before I came to her. That's how she came to the island, to live with him, they jumped the broom, but then he drowned, and she couldn't go away, and Mr. Olson said she could stay and take care of the island, and then she was lonely, and then I came."

Sonja stood with her eyes wide and her mouth open.

"Can we eat, Momma?" Alisha asked.

Sonja blinked and let go of Alisha's shoulders. "Yes...yes, of course. Alisha, I had never heard any of that. You have never said anything about that."

Alisha shrugged her little girl shoulders and marched away to their room.

Sonja followed her. Her eyebrows arched, a half smile on her face, shaking her head.

The *Herald* was too late arriving in Baltimore and spent the night near the mouth of the harbor waiting for daylight to dock. The captain sent men in a rowboat to contact the other steamers, and the *Herald*'s passengers were reassured they would not miss their connections.

When the *Herald* moved in the dawn to her mooring site, porters from other ships were waiting on the wharf to carry away passenger luggage. Sonja and Alisha had to walk quickly to keep pace with the porters. Looking behind, Alisha saw the solemn man following them. Passengers on the *Richmond* openly showed frowns to Sonja and Alisha when they came aboard amid hustling of the crew to leave Baltimore. Someone rapped on their cabin door. Sonja caught her breath and brought her hand to her throat, then pointed Alisha to a darkened corner of the room.

"Police?" She questioned herself in a whisper. "Who is it?"

"Ship officer ma'am." He tipped his hat to Sonja in the narrow opening she allowed.

"The captain sends his compliments, madam. He humbly asks that you mention to Mr. Renowitz that he held the *Richmond* past its departure time to accommodate your arrival," he said without a smile, then saluted and walked away.

Alisha stared at Sonja in wide-eyed question.

Sonja sighed. "We made them late."

They shared a nervous giggle.

The *Raven* sailed out from a small protected bay near Point Lookout, Maryland. The natural anchorage was known as Cornfield Harbor to Chesapeake Bay sailors who faced adverse winds leaving the wide mouth of the Potomac River or trying to go into it from the bay. The morning wind was westerly and steady, putting the *Raven* on one of her better points of sailing as she pointed her bow north.

The wind gusted, laying the masts over, and water

splashed over the lee railing. Ben stepped to the leeward wheel to help steer. Edward stood at the windward wheel.

"Loosen the gaffs a little," Edward said to Alistair.

Quickly the tension at the tops of the main and foresails relaxed and the deck returned to a moderate tilt. Ben released his grip on the wheel.

"How are you feeling this morning, Eddie?" Ben asked.

"Much better than poor Wyatt. He can still hardly see from his right eye."

"He took a terrible beating," Ben said.

"He might have been killed if I hadn't stopped that drunk."

They stood together in silence a long moment.

"I probably would have done the same thing," Ben said at last.

Both men kept their attention on the sails and the northern horizon, passing Bloodsworth Island, Hooper's Island and Taylor's Island in almost rapid succession without the need to adjust sails or alter course.

"We're making good time," Edward said.

"Probably eight or nine knots, Eddie."

Black smoke arose to the north.

"Looks like a steamer in a hurry," Ben said. "Burning a lot of coal."

"Do you have plans for another trip down to Georgetown, Ben?" Edward asked.

Ben thought a moment. "I think not, Eddie. I think I will pay off the crew for the winter and just let us all go home for a while."

Edward released a wide smile.

"I thought you might like that," Ben said.

Three of the crew heard the comment and came closer to the wheels. Warren was still down in the galley.

Ben addressed the men. "I would appreciate it if you all stayed on the ship until we moored for the winter in Havre de Grace, then you can head for homes and hearth from there."

Murmurs of approval floated among the men on deck. Daniel stepped down into the hold to tell Warren.

"That steamer is really charging down the main channel," Edward said.

"Let's give her plenty of room. Steer closer to Poplar Island, but watch for shoals," Ben said.

The steamship *Richmond* dashed southward chugging smoke and spewing steam, its side wheels frantically slapping the water and shoving foam in its wake. On the second deck, Alisha and Sonja stood at the railing watching the schooner in the distance lean away from the wind and move toward Poplar Island. Its wind streamer flapped almost straight out in the stiff breeze. The green hull reflected the sunlight of the splashing water as if it were laced with diamonds.

"That's the *Raven*," Sonja said, pointing to the ship. "Look Alisha!"

"Is it Papa?" she asked.

"Of course," Sonja said.

As the two ships drew closer, where individual people could be seen on the decks, Sonja and Alisha began to wave.

"Watch for shoaling," Ben called out. "Let's not get too close to the island."

The ships flew abreast of each other.

"There's someone on the steamer waving," Alistair said.

"Eddie, let's steer back to the north-northwest," Ben said. "That steamer has more than enough room."

"It's Sonja," Alistair yelled.

"What?" Ben asked, turning his attention to Alistair.

Alistair punched the air with his finger, pointing at the steamer passing south. "It's Sonja and Alisha!"

Ben spun to face the stern quarter of the steamer, squinting in the sunlight, searching the deck railings for Sonja.

"Where, where?"

"Can't see her now," Alistair said. "Blonde hair, mother and child alike. Sure looked like Sonja and Alisha."

"No. Not possible. Why would Sonja be on a steamer heading south? No. It wasn't her," Ben said. "Couldn't have been."

"Sure looked like her," Alistair muttered, then walked away.

On the steamship *Richmond,* Sonja turned to Alisha. "I guess they didn't see us."

Alisha gripped the railing and stood on her tiptoes looking back at the sailboat in the distance.

"Probably just as well," Sonja said. "I could not have made him understand anything from here. Only that we're not at home." She released a long sigh and turned back into the cabin. "Come along, Alisha."

"Yes ma'am," Alisha said.

In Havre de Grace, Ramona burst into Lester Watkins' office. "They have run off, Mr. Watkins. Our court order is useless."

Watkins let his shoulders sag, let out a weary sigh, and motioned for her to have a seat. "What may I do for you now, Miss Tatum?"

She held up a gloved finger. "First, we should get the judge to issue an arrest warrant for Sonja Pulaski...for kidnapping."

Watkins reached for a blank piece of paper. "And?"

She held up two fingers. "I want you to begin demanding the release of all my sister's effects and properties."

He scribbled notes on the paper. "She lived on the island north of town, correct?"

"Yes."

"Do you know of any other property she may have owned, perhaps where she came from...Where was that?"

"Baltimore. She was from, well, near Baltimore, but I know she had no property there. Neither of us did."

"I thought you said...never mind. Is there anything else, Miss Tatum?"

"Yes, the hotel is very noisy and full of drunken men wandering the halls. Can you recommend somewhere in town where a lone woman can feel safe?"

"Well, Mrs. Stewart may have a room available. She runs a boarding house on Union Avenue. The one with reddish wood. The locals call it the Pink House."

"Oh yes. I have seen it, but did not know it took in boarders."

An hour later Ramona slipped into the Harford Hotel, where she had been staying since her arrival. She managed to pass the desk without being seen by the clerk and let herself into her room. On the floor, she found a note from the hotel, slipped under the door requiring payment for the room. She crumpled the note and dropped it into the fireplace with the others. Her coal bucket was empty, and there was no more wood for the fireplace. She handled the lamp near her bed, tilting the translucent base to see if any oil was remaining, but it was empty. On her dresser, a candleholder retained a stub not yet burned all the way down to the pewter.

She moved the candle to the table by her single chair next to the darkened fireplace and opened her purse as she sat. Inside, she withdrew the matches she had taken from the Pulaski mantel and the biscuit she found left behind in their kitchen. She lit the candle and the notes in the fireplace, then huddled next to the meager flames while she ate the biscuit. After eating, she withdrew the small flask of rum she had taken from a shelf in the Pulaski kitchen and drank from it.

Ramona stood and carefully removed the only dress she owned and laid it carefully over the back of the chair, then removed all her underclothing and spread it around the room to air out. Naked and shivering in the cold room, she climbed into bed and drew the covers around her as she sat up against the headboard, drinking the rest of the rum.

At dawn, Ramona arose, dressed and slipped out a side door from the hotel. She walked around town several times over the next few hours, careful to use different streets so her loops would not be noticed. At eight-thirty o'clock she knocked on the front door to the Pink House. A sweet-faced mulatto girl answered the door.

"Are you Mrs. Stewart?" Ramona asked.

"No, ma'am, I'm Sissy. I work for her here. Are you looking for a room to rent?"

"Yes I am, but I believe I should discuss that with

Mrs. Stewart," Ramona said.

"Yes ma'am, of course, ma'am, I didn't mean... If you would kindly step into the parlor, I'll run fetch Mrs. Stewart."

Sissy escorted Ramona into the parlor where she noticed a plate left behind by one of the boarders. Two biscuits and several slices of fried bacon remained on the plate. As Sissy reached for the plate Ramona's stomach growled loud enough that both women heard.

Ramona's face blushed. "I have had so many meetings this morning...with my lawyers and such...I completely forgot about breakfast. Perhaps you could leave that plate while you 'fetch' Mrs. Stewart?"

Sissy left the plate then stood, folding her hands. "May I get you a cup of coffee, ma'am? It's still warm in the kitchen and not too old at all."

"Yes. That would be lovely. Thank you, dear."

Sissy returned with the coffee. "Mrs. Stewart is out in the garden. She says now is a good time to hoe the lanes by, so it'll be ready next spring. I'll go fetch her." Then she curtsied and went out through the kitchen.

Minutes later, Mamie Stewart entered the kitchen, wiping her hands, smoothing her hair and her apron. She came into the parlor and extended her hand to her guest. Ramona stood to accept it with a broad smile. Small white flecks of biscuit crumbs drifted down from her black dress on to the floor, and the plate on the table was empty.

Ramona accepted her hand saying, "Good morning, I am Ramona Tatum, visiting Havre de Grace while I settle my departed sister's estate."

"Mamie Stewart, owner of this house, Mrs. Tatum," Mamie said and motioned Ramona back to her seat and sat beside her.

"Mrs. Stewart–"

"Call me Mamie. Do you wish a room?"

"Yes, the hotel is very noisy and full of drunken men wandering the halls. I no longer feel safe there. Attorney Watkins recommended your boarding house."

"Well, I do have an available room on the third floor, shall we have a look at it to see if it would be acceptable to you?"

The landing on the second floor presented a well-decorated parlor that opened on to an uncovered raised porch through glassed doors. Within the parlor were several comfortable looking covered chairs and footstools, arranged around a small iron stove on the left guarded by brass spittoons on either side. Against the right wall was a polished mahogany counter, arrayed with etched glasses, several bottles of whiskey and a carved cigar box set on white linen.

"All our boarders have access to this parlor as well as the one downstairs," Mamie said as they passed it. Then she crooked her finger and drew Ramona up to the third floor.

The third-floor hall was narrow with arched windows at each end and presenting two doors on each side, numbered 5 through 8.

"Each room has a washstand, with bowl, basin and, chamber pot," Mamie said. "If you are neat, the chamber pot is cleaned by the maid and returned. If you are not, the chamber pot is not returned, and you will use the outhouse among the roses at the far edge of the garden."

Ramona's eyes widened and her hand pressed against her throat.

Mamie smiled and patted Ramona's arm with a flourish. "I am confident that you are neat, Ramona."

Moments later Mamie and Ramona stood in the small room near the bed. The peaked window overlooked the garden below.

"Yes this will be satisfactory for my needs," Ramona said.

"Of course it will," she said. "Twenty dollars a month. Half now," she added, holding out her hand. "Supper is precisely at six o'clock. If I am late, you must wait. If you are late, you may not find any food. Biscuits and sliced meat are set out in the kitchen each morning at five-thirty. What's there is there. Leave some for the others," she said, "although they may not leave any for you," she added with a throaty chuckle.

"Well...um...I am afraid I am still waiting for funds from the estate. I was required to advance so much for the hotel and the attorney and the care for my sister's child... Perhaps in a few days, but I do wish to be out of that dreadful hotel..."

Mamie patted her hand. "I understand, Ramona. We can settle that in a few days."

"Thank you," Ramona said.

As they returned down the stairs, Mamie continued with her customary description of her boarding house schedule, speaking over her shoulder.

"I offer bathing privileges weekly, for a small additional fee. There is a special room just off the kitchen, with a bathtub that Sissy will fill with clean hot water for you. I require the room to be scheduled in advance, and baths are no closer together than two hours, so Sissy has time to prepare it for the next boarder."

The two ladies shook hands in the foyer, and Ramona left the Pink House to check out of the hotel and retrieve her luggage. Once outside, Ramona slipped around to a bush at the corner of the house and pulled out her small travel bag, and then sat on a stone seat under the shade of a magnolia tree nearby. When she heard the voices of Mamie and Sissy going into the garden in back, she re-entered the house and went up to her new room.

The *Raven* dropped anchor off the Havre de Grace wharves in the mid-afternoon. Within an hour all was secured for a long anchorage, and the ship's rowboat taxied back and forth taking crewmen to shore. A bay steamer destined for Annapolis sat at the pier waiting for a mailbag. Edward, Alistair, Daniel, and Wyatt boarded the steamer. Ben and Warren were the last to leave the ship.

"My sister lives just over in Aberdeen, Cap'n. I plan to stay with them later, but for now, I'd like to go oystering. I grew up on that, and there's plenty of work like that around here."

"Where will you stay?" Ben asked.

"There's plenty of places to bunk down around here. Cheap, too. There's a black woman named Hattie, took over an old boatwright shop at the edge of town and turned it into a big bunkroom for fishermen."

Ben eyed his cook and gave him a smile. "Yes, I know that shop. It used to be run by an old friend of mine. Actually, it is now, too. I know Hattie. She's a good woman, but stay on her happy side, or you will see stormy seas."

Both men chuckled.

Ben tied up the rowboat near the exit lock of the canal basin, a spot known to canallers, and said goodbye to Warren.

"If you need another place to stay this winter, Warren," Ben said, "You're welcome to bunk on the *Raven*. It will cost you nothing, and I always appreciate a trusted person aboard her over the winter."

"Thank ye, Cap'n." Warren touched his forehead in salute and walked away.

Ben nearly trotted across the grounds past the

lockhouse. The canal superintendent was standing on the porch smoking a cigar and called out to him.

"Welcome home, Ben. One of your barges is about to go upstream. You want to go with them? They shouldn't be long getting the mules out of the barn."

Ben waved back. "No thanks, I need to stretch my legs. A few miles will do me good after just walking the deck for the last few weeks."

Ben fell into a comfortable rhythm making his way along the narrow stretch of towpath, with the placid water of the basin on his left and the turbulent Susquehanna River on his right. Soon the man-made towpath of fill dirt and pounded poles merged into the outer wall of the canal a half mile north of Havre de Grace. There the few trees left near town had grown barely beyond saplings and lined either side of the canal. The towpath remained on the river side of the canal, the other side being the original river shore imprisoned by the towpath, creating the channel for the smooth water of the canal itself. The packed earth of the towpath was firm and wide enough for two teams of mules or two wagons to pass each other going in opposite directions. Both southbound and northbound barges were pulled by mules using the same path, and joining each other in a waltz of practiced moves that amazingly kept tow ropes and mule teams from becoming entangled.

As Ben came to the point on the towpath that sat across the canal from his home, he stopped to admire it. Once a humble log cabin, and then joined with bedrooms on each side covered in battened boards. The house and full-width porch sat safely between the matched pair of huge oak trees standing like sentinels, left untouched when the canal was dug by hundreds of laborers.

Within seconds Ben crossed the swing bridge over the granite lock and turned south again, back toward his home.

Jesse Price, the lock keeper there, called out to him as Ben passed. Ben waved and kept walking, eager to be home to his wife and daughter.

"Ben," Jesse called again, "She's not there."

Ben automatically threw his hand into the air as a

wave, but then stopped dead still.

"She's gone, Ben," Jesse yelled. "She and Alisha left."

Ben spun around in the middle of Stafford Road. "What?"

"Catherine has a note for you. From Sonja."

Ben trotted back down to the lockkeeper's house wearing a frown. Catherine Price emerged onto their porch carrying Sonja's note as Ben approached. She handed it to him as soon as he reached her. Ben stepped off the porch and held the note so the fading sun would shine on it.

He looked into Catherine's eyes. "What the hell happened?"

"A judge ordered Alisha turned over to that woman who was after your child," Jesse said.

"Sonja took Alisha and drove your buggy up north. I think to York Furnace."

Ben turned and trotted down the road to where it turned west, and his lane continued across the little bridge to the farm. Up on the porch he flung open the door and flew through the rooms, calling Sonja and Alisha. He dropped onto one of the porch chairs and caught his breath, re-reading the note. He stood and shoved the note into his pocket, then stepped down to the nearby barn, just off the front slope. The buggy and their horse were gone. The milk cow and two mules were still inside. Of the two mules, only one, Sarah, had ever been ridden.

Ben took down the horse saddle from its rack and strapped it to Sarah. Then he mounted her and trotted back down the road to the lock and crossed onto the towpath heading north.

Long after midnight Ben walked Sarah across the swing bridge at York Furnace. It was a cloudless night, and the meager half-moon had given him enough light to continue, but Sarah was failing. Her breath was ragged, and the vapor from her nostrils in the chilled autumn air rolled weakly toward the ground. As Ben guided her to the base of the hill where the trail went up to the farm, she halted and refused to go further, so he tied her to a tree there. He removed her saddle and set it on the ground, then unfolded the horse blanket from under it and spread it over her back.

John Calvert held up a lantern as he came up the path from the lockhouse. "Thought that was probably you I heard, Ben. She left you a note."

John held the lantern higher as Ben took the note and opened it.

As soon as Ben finished reading the note, he shook hands with John.

"Hope it all turns out well, Ben," John said, then yawned and walked back to his house.

The aroma of fresh coffee lingered in the air near the front porch of the farmhouse when Ben mounted the hill. The place had slipped from Burl Jundt to Aaron Pulaski to David Booker in less than a year, linking tragedies like a melancholy daisy-chain. A voice drifted down from the porch.

"Who is that?" a man asked.

"Ben Pulaski, looking for my wife and daughter."

"They aren't here, son," Isaiah said. "Come in and have some coffee. I was just getting ready to milk the cows."

After a quick turn through the kitchen, Ben followed Isaiah into the barn with a coffee mug in his hand.

"These cows give a lot of milk, Ben, so they get full mighty early and start bellowing if they don't get milked right away."

"You say she sent a telegram from Columbia?" Ben asked. His other hand was in his pocket still fingering the note Sonja had left with the Calverts.

"Yeah. To a Mister Anthony Renowitz in Philadelphia. You going there, too?"

"If I do, I need to make some arrangements first. I need to go back to Havre de Grace, I guess," Ben said. He lifted his hat and scratched his head. "I saw two of my barges in the holding pond above Calvert's lockhouse, and they're riding high in the water, so they're going south."

"How'd you come up?"

"I rode one of my mules from home, and she's not faring well because of it. I don't dare try to ride her again. She and I can ride the barges down the canal back to Lapidum."

"Well, David's their captain. He spent the night here, and he's running those barges down this morning. You might as well come in and have breakfast with us."

After breakfast, Ben and David Booker walked down to the holding pond together and while David signed the lockhouse ledger, Ben tied Sarah at the bow of the lead barge. Ben frowned to himself. The lead barge of the tandem was the *Sarah,* named for Aaron's infant daughter lost at birth on the same day as his wife, Maggie. David mounted the rear barge at its stern and whistled for the mule boy to pull them into the open lock. From Ben's spot at the bow of the *Sarah* to where David stood at the stern of the *Osprey,* was one hundred thirty feet, the length of the *Raven.*

Eight hours later, the *Sarah* nudged against the little dock at the lower edge of the Pulaski front slope. Ben laid two boards from the edge of the barge to the ground on the slope and led the mule down. David waited while Ben put away the mule and went to the house to pack a travel bag. While in the house, Ben took some cash from the money box he and Sonja kept hidden in one of the interior walls. Most of the money usually there was already gone.

"At least she has some money with her," he mumbled to himself.

In the kitchen, he glanced around to ensure nothing was left out that should not be. He noticed his rum flask missing from its customary spot, but made nothing of it. At the mantel, he refilled his tobacco pouch and exchanged the pipe in his coat for one of the fresher ones there, but could not find any matches. Then Ben hurried down the slope to the *Sarah,* pulled up the planks and waved a finger to David. David whistled to the little boy squatting on the towpath, who stood and patted the haunch of the lead mule to begin pulling the barges south again.

In Norfolk, Virginia, the steamship *Richmond* was

busy unloading her passengers and cargo. Following directions from a ship's officer, Sonja and Alisha walked across the dock to the hotel where a ticket office for the Atlantic Steamship Company *Washington* was placed just off the front lobby. The banner above the high clerk's desk read "Steamship Washington, Bremerhaven, Germany."

"Are we going to Germany, Momma?" Alisha asked with surprise in her voice.

Sonja chuckled. "No dear, it will go to Wilmington, in North Carolina and Charleston in South Carolina, picking up passengers for Germany, but we will get off in Wilmington."

They approached the ticket desk. "When will the *Washington* be ready for boarding?" Sonja asked.

"I am sorry, madam," the clerk said. "The *Washington* will not arrive here for two more days. Have you already purchased tickets?"

"They were purchased through my agent," Sonja said.

The clerk opened the passenger ledger. "Your name, please."

She glanced around at the people nearby. "Mrs. Jundt. Sarah Jundt."

Alisha's face snapped up toward Sonja, her eyes wide and her mouth beginning to open. Sonja flashed a frown at her and twitched a fleeting 'no.' Alisha closed her mouth and looked away.

He scanned down the names. "Ah yes. Jundt. Here you are– Oh, there are some things sent ahead for you: a telegram and a note."

He fumbled through loose notes and envelopes at the back of the ledger, then handed her two folded notes. Sonja smiled at the clerk and handed him a small coin, which he accepted without examination or comment. Sonja stepped away from the desk and unfolded the note.

Mrs. Jundt,
I await your arrival in the lobby,
per instructions from Mr. Renowitz.
– Albert Bollard

Sonja frowned at the note, mumbling to herself, "Bollard? I don't know an Albert Bollard."

She opened the telegram and read the words neatly penciled on the lined yellow paper.

> **Have arranged summer home of good friend Thomas Talbot until ship arrives. Talbot Hall empty except staff for you. Albert Bollard to escort you there. He is trustworthy.**
> **– A.R.**

She took Alisha's hand. "Well, let us go see Mr. Bollard."

They walked into the lobby, looking at the men and women sitting in the stuffed chairs within the haze of cigar and pipe smoke. A smiling man with thinning hair rose from his chair at the far end of the room and straightened his coat. Alisha gasped and pulled Sonja back toward the doorway, pointing to a solemn man with piercing eyes sitting close by.

"He has been following us," she said.

The man rose and stepped toward Sonja and Alisha. The balding man observed the movements and rushed across the lobby toward them, reaching inside his coat.

Lester Watkins, Esq, approached the table of Judge Jessup in the Oyster Street Tavern. Nancy Palmer, the tavern's popular table server, stood next to the judge's table giggling as he traced lines in the palm of her hand with his finger.

"And that line says you will have many romances," the judge said.

Watkins cleared his throat. Nancy quickly withdrew her hand and walked back to the kitchen. Jessup sighed heavily and looked at Watkins over the tops of his glasses.

"What do you need, Mr. Watkins?"

"Just a moment of your time, your honor."

The judge straightened his back. "Do you have a case before me, Watkins?"

"No, sir."

"What do you need?"

"I need your advice, sir."

The judge growled the words. "About what?"

"I am told you were the expert in probate and estate settlement when you practiced."

The judge relaxed his spine, offered a brief smile and sighed, then motioned to a chair at his table. "Have a seat, Lester. I'll let you buy me breakfast."

Watkins slipped into the seat. "I have a client who has come from Baltimore to take possession of the child and estate of her late sister. His sister was buried in Lapidum under odd circumstances, and a caretaker of the child has run off with the child."

"That is not probate, Watkins. Surely even you know that."

"Yes. Yes, sir. My client is also requesting we close on the estate so she can afford to take care of the child."

"And?"

"I am preparing to go to the courthouse in Bel Air tomorrow and initiate a title search. I've never pursued the ownership of an island, and any advice or contact persons in Bel Air that you could share will be helpful."

Nancy came by the table delivering coffee to another customer. Jessup reached out and held her gently at the elbow.

"Honey, cancel my other order for breakfast. I'll have a steak, eggs, and biscuits, instead...and bring me a pot of fresh coffee for the table."

As she walked away, Jessup turned back to Watkins with a frown. "Who's the deceased?"

"Rachel Tatum," Watkins said.

"Never heard of her," Jessup said. "Which Island?"

"Shad Island, sir."

Jessup blinked his eyes. "Shad Island. And your client thinks it belonged to this Rachel Tatum? Why does she think that?"

"Her sister lived there with her daughter for the last several years."

"Lived there? Oh hell, Watkins. I know who you're talking about now. That old woman was the caretaker of the old house during the offseason. She was the maid, Watkins."

"What, but Miss Tatum told me–"

"I don't give a damned what your client told you. That island belongs to Otho Scott. THE Otho Scott. State Senator Otho Scott. The fishing company that works out of that island leases it from him."

Watkins stared in silence at the judge.

"Chances are, that dead woman doesn't have an estate. I remember her now. My church used to donate clothing to her and that child. You know she lived with a slave man out there for a while. I'm surprised her girl came out white."

Watkins stared at the calico tablecloth a long moment, then slowly stood and slid his chair neatly against the table and walked away.

"Lester," the judge called. "Don't forget to pay Nancy for my breakfast."

After paying for the judge's breakfast, Watkins walked from the tavern to the Harford House Hotel, where he was told Ramona Tatum had left without paying her bill. Outside the hotel, he stood with his hands in his pockets, letting his eyes wander unfocused over the dirt of St. John Street. Then he yanked one hand from his pocket and snapped his fingers. He spun around and marched over to Union Avenue and turned south toward the Pink House. After crossing Green Street, he met Ramona Tatum and Nadja Lister ambling along the walkway.

"Miss Tatum," he said tipping his hat. "I need to share important information about your sister's estate."

Ramona released a radiant smile.

He leaned close to her and whispered, "She left nothing. She was only the caretaker on that island. She was destitute."

Her smile evaporated, and her face paled. She pulled back from Watkins, bringing her fingers up to her mouth.

"I am sorry, Miss Tatum. Kindly come by my office tomorrow so we can clear all our remaining issues."

"Yes...Yes, of course, sir. I will need to spend some time in the bank first. Shall we say three o'clock?"

"Yes, ma'am. That will be fine." He tipped his hat again and walked away.

"Was it bad news, Ramona?" Nadja asked.

"No. No, not at all. Actually, profoundly good. I had no idea of her holdings."

Nadja offered a toothy grin and looped her arm inside Ramona's. "Well then, dear, let me buy you lunch, and you can tell me all about it."

That evening Ramona was one of the first boarders at the dinner table. She took in a wholesome dinner while sharing colorful tales about her experiences in Europe, and assisted the men at the table emptying three bottles of wine.

At dawn the next morning, Ramona crept down the stairs with her travel bag. She slipped through the front door, leaving it unlatched to avoid further noise, and walked out of Havre de Grace on a foot-path near the railroad tracks.

At three-thirty the following day, Lester Watkins snapped shut his pocket watch, plucked his hat from its hook on the wall, and walked to the end of Washington Street and up the stairs to the office of George Milton, Esquire. Ben Pulaski was sitting in the office when Lester knocked on the door and poked his head inside.

"Oh, my apologies, George. I will wait." He withdrew his head then leaned in again looking at Ben. "You wouldn't happen to be Mr. Pulaski, would you?" he asked.

"Yes," Ben said, exchanging glances with George.

Lester opened the door fully and stepped inside, closing it behind him.

"Please accept my apologies for the rude intrusion, but I have information that I must share with both of you."

Ben and George waited for his comment.

"We have been hoodwinked," he said.

Within minutes, Ben dashed down the stairs and trotted to the telegraph office.

The man stopped before Sonja and Alisha. His small dark eyes holding them. Then he pushed his gnarled hand toward them. At that instant, Albert Bollard threw himself against the man, and they both fell to the floor. Over his shoulder, Albert yelled to Sonja, "Run!"

Sonja grabbed Alisha's hand and pulled her hard out of the lobby doorway and ran to the street. Outside, she frantically looked in every direction, seeking a safe place to run. A ship's officer stood on the corner.

"Help me!" Sonja yelled.

Several men rushed to her.

She pulled Alisha behind her and pointed into the hotel. "A man! In there!"

Two of the men rushed by her into the hotel, adding to a babble of voices echoing in the lobby, which quickly subsided. In the quiet the two men came out smiling, shaking their heads and glancing at Sonja while they muttered between themselves. A hand pressed onto her shoulder. She spun around to see Albert Bollard.

"All is well, Mrs. Jundt," he said.

Behind him stood the solemn man with piercing eyes, holding his woven straw hat before him.

"I fear I have given thee a fright, madam," he said, his English laced heavily with a German accent. "Isaiah will be most displeased with me."

Sonja stepped close to him. "Isaiah? Isaiah Booker?"

"Ja, madam. Isaiah asked that I see that you are safe on your journey."

Tears spread across Sonja's eyes and she touched his arm with her fingertips. "We didn't know. I am so sorry. Were you hurt?"

"No, madam. Mr. Bollard wished only what I did, and we quickly made peace."

"Alles ist gut?" Sonja asked.

"Ja," he gave a wide grin at her German. "Alles ist gut, danke, Frau Jundt."

He bowed his head to her and put on his hat, he offered his hand to Albert then walked away. Albert sighed and motioned to her.

"I have a carriage waiting to take you to Talbot Hall, Mrs. Jundt."

Sonja remained where she stood. "And you are an acquaintance of *Aaron* Renowitz?"

He smiled, and his eyes sparkled as he stepped closer to her. He spoke quietly. "No, Mrs. Pulaski. I know *Anthony* Renowitz. I also know his wife, Camilla – Camilla Bollard Renowitz, since our childhood together. I have been with the Argyle Corporation since the beginning."

Sonja released a long breath, letting her shoulders settle and releasing the grip on Alisha's hand. Alisha wiggled her pale fingers and shook her hand at her side.

"I'm sorry, Momma. I didn't know he was a nice man," said Alisha.

Sonja and Albert both chuckled. "Neither did we," they said.

The morning the *Washington* was scheduled to arrive

in Norfolk, a young man rapped on the front door to Talbot Hall. The butler answered the front door and accepted a folded paper addressed to Sonja Pulaski. He walked into the parlor and stood at the edge of several travel bags aligned as if standing inspection.

His face was emotionless as he announced, "A telegram for a Sonja Pulaski."

Sonja and Albert exchanged frowns as she motioned for the butler.

"Why did he use that name?" she whispered to herself.

Sonja accepted the paper and read the short note.

Do not leave for Wilmington. All claims against you and Alisha are resolved. Tickets await your return trip. Go home, Sonja. – A.R.

Sonja dropped into a chair with a loud sigh and handed the note to Alisha.

"We don't get to go to North Carolina?" she asked, returning the note.

Sonja passed the note to Albert and turned her face to Alisha.

"Not this time, sweetheart," Sonja said. "We are going home."

Alisha pouted.

"Albert," Sonja said, "I cannot tell you how much I appreciate what you have done for us. I know I will be safe here and thank you for arranging to take us to the Norfolk Harbor today, but I would like to just rest a couple days before we dash onto a steamer. Do you think Mr. Talbot would permit that?"

"I am certain of it, Sonja. When shall I return for you?"

Sonja swiveled in her chair and leaned back, propping her feet up on one of the travel bags. "Two days of rest?"

He bowed his head. "I will be back in three days and take you to the harbor."

The butler cleared his throat as Albert left. "If I may say, madam, we are happy to have you and Miss Alisha with us a few more days. Whatever we can do to assist you, we are here."

"Thank you, Mr. Ridley," Sonja said.

He nodded to her and smiled, winking at Alisha as he left the room.

After a delicious lunch, while Alisha took a nap, Sonja settled against the back of a large copper bathtub in her bedroom. A cotton cloth was draped across the tub, its center section floating on the warm water. Next to the tub was a narrow table holding a stemmed glass of wine. Sonja released a long slow sigh as she settled onto the folded cloth at the bottom of the tub.

"Just let me soak a while, Marcie," Sonja said to the maid.

"Yes, ma'am," Marcie said. "Shall I come back in about half an hour with towels?"

Sonja smiled, letting her eyelashes drift closed. "Yes, please come back then, but bring more hot water and maybe another glass of wine."

Marcie curtsied and left the room, closing the door softly.

November 1st, 1847. Baltimore, Maryland

In Baltimore, Ramona Tatum returned to the dirty apartment she shared with three other women near the harbor. She faced a long evening of complaints and snide remarks from her roommates who only accepted her back after she promised to empty and clean their night pails every morning. The following day she returned to the tavern by the pier seeking her abandoned job as a chore woman. The owner refused to have her back unless she agreed to have sex with him whenever he wanted it. After being bent over a crate in the storage room, Ramona spent the rest of the day scrubbing the floors, tables, and chairs in the tavern, and then the tavern's outhouse in the alley beside it. She poured the remaining drops of whiskey and beer from customer glasses into a cracked bottle she had pulled from a trash barrel and took it home that night along with a rag full of food scraps.

The next day, after pulling herself off the crate in the storeroom again, the tavern owner told her he was only going to pay her half what he promised, unless she pleased some of his friends. Between washing mugs and cleaning the tavern, she spent the rest of her day in the storeroom.

On the third day, Ramona limped out of the storeroom at mid-day, as several seamen from an incoming steamer barged into the tavern demanding whiskey. While the tavern owner was busy serving drinks, Ramona slipped into the alleyway and sat on a crate covered in fish scales. A fishmonger had left a filleting knife on the crate, so Ramona picked it up to get it out of her way. She watched the passengers of the nearby steamship waltz down the gangplank, looking for porters and carriages to take them away from the harbor or to their next clean ship.

She fixed her eyes on a blonde woman strolling down the gangplank, holding the hand of a girl who was a miniature of the woman. The woman and the child moved in slow, graceful rhythm as Ramona watched, pressing her thumb against the tip of the fishmonger's knife. Ramona bit her lip watching the woman. Blood dripped from her thumb. Her upper tooth pierced her lip and blood oozed onto her chin. Ramona stood with fists balled at her sides. The skin of her hand holding the knife turned white at the edges of her grip.

The tavern owner stepped up behind her and reached around, grabbing one of her breasts.

"I got a sailor willing to pay three dollars to have you in the storeroom. Get back to work, Ramona," he said.

She spun around exploding with a shrill maniacal rage and drove the knife blade into his eye. The man bellowed, reaching for his face. She stabbed him in his chest then shoved the full length of the narrow blade into his groin. She pulled out the knife and ran screaming from the alley, charging toward the passengers coming off the steamship.

Sonja and Alisha strolled down the gangplank from the steamship *Richmond* taking in the hectic scene of Baltimore Harbor. Businesses were pressed up against the piers elbow to elbow, competing for customers and precious access to the tremendous flow of shipped goods coming and going. Clerks and laborers mingled with well-dressed passengers and seamen, all scurrying in different directions. Warehouses, shipping offices, suppliers, fishmongers, and taverns presented a carnival of sights. Gaudy colored lettering was splashed on both fresh and decaying wood, begging for attention. Shadowed caverns were created over the narrow walkways between the buildings and the tall ships looming overhead. The air was filled with the aromas of fried meat, burning coal, and mildew. The harbor water around the ships shouldered into their berths reeked of oily dead fish and rotting debris dumped overboard.

In the crowd beyond the gangplank, a woman shrieked, and people were pushed or darted away from a disheveled woman running among them. The murmur grew louder among the crowd as the woman worked her way toward the steamship. Hands reached out to pull her down, but she slashed at them with a knife. Sonja and Alisha froze in their steps watching the melee on the pier. The woman shrieked again, shoving an old matron down on the pier and slashing at her companion. The people nearby moved away from her, creating an opening among the passengers at the lower end of the gangplank. A man reached out at her. She sliced his hand. The others backed away. The woman pushed her way onto the gangplank. Her cheeks were smeared with blood, her hair a wiry explosion around her face. Her wide eyes searched the line of people, then fixed on Sonja and Alisha.

"Pulaski!" she screamed. "God damn you! God damn both of you."

Sonja yanked Alisha behind her. She backed against her, pushing them both up the gangplank. A passenger next to Sonja ran away up to the deck, and others cried out.

Ramona stalked up the gangplank, her mouth twisted in a snarl. She crept closer, her eyes glued on Sonja, pointing the knife blade ahead of her as she came.

Sonja dropped her jaw and gasped. "Ramona Tatum? What has happened to you?"

"You! You happened to me."

Sonja turned her head slightly toward Alisha but keeping her eyes on Ramona.

"Run back into the ship," Sonja told Alisha.

Alisha turned and ran. Ramona dodged to the side of Sonja, her eyes following Alisha.

Sonja jumped in front of her and grabbed at her arm and wrist near the knife. Ramona yanked back, slicing Sonja's forearm. Sonja lunged at her. Ramona sidestepped and shoved Sonja down her knees. She raised the knife above Sonja and screamed as she drove it down.

The explosion was just above Sonja, pounding her hearing into fierce ringing echoes, driving away all other sounds. Ramona's forehead shattered into a spray of blood and gray matter, and she flipped onto her back. Albert Bollard stepped closer to the women, the smoke from his gun barrel still rising into the air. He knelt beside Sonja. She looked up at him, watching his lips move, but could not hear his voice, only the crescendo of shrill ringing. She twisted her head to face up the gangplank where Alisha stood wide-eyed. Alisha ran to her. The ringing faded and the voices around Sonja coalesced from muffled groans to spoken words. She was rewarded with the angelic voice of her daughter saying, "Momma, Momma, Momma."

That evening, Ben paced at the end of the long pier reaching out from the Concord Point Lighthouse as the steamship *Herald* finally made its docking in a falling tide. This was farther up the bay than the steamship typically called, but its major shareholder had insisted it make the effort. The captain encouraged his crew to hurry with assisting the lone passenger and her daughter to depart.

"Move along," the captain snapped at his men from the upper deck, even though he tipped his cap to the woman. "Tide's still droppin', and I don't want to spend the night here," he said.

Ben scooped his wife and daughter in a single armful. He kissed Alisha on the top of her head and then melded into Sonja for a long welcome. Alisha huffed in feigned impatience until Ben and Sonja separated, still lingering in each other's eyes.

"What took so long, Sonja? Anthony's telegram said you would be here by– What happened to your arm?"

Ben raised her bandaged forearm and returned to her eyes.

"Stitches," she said.

"Momma got stabbed by the woman that wanted to take me away," Alisha said. "Mr. Albert shot a hole in her head, and a doctor on the ship sewed Momma's arm back on, and we were late getting to that ship," she pointed to the *Herald* moving away in a clamor of bells, hissing steam and splashing water. "And Mr. Anthony sent a telegram to make the ship wait and bring us here and not Philadelphia, but we didn't get to go to North Carolina."

Ben stood there with his mouth open, struggling between a frown and a grin, then showed Sonja a face full of questions.

Sonja opened her mouth to speak.

"I'm hungry," Alisha said.

"Yes," Sonja said. "Let's go eat at a tavern, then go home, and I will tell you all about it. Then you can tell me all about your trip." She lowered her voice. "How many people did you take north?"

"None. It is not finished. I have to go back."

Ben picked up their bags and the three strolled up the pier back to shore. The Pulaski buggy was tied near the lighthouse. The chestnut mare in her traces nuzzled against Alisha's shoulder as the girl patted and stroked the horse.

"Is Stinky going to eat, too?" she asked as she climbed into the back of the buggy.

"We named her Betsy, Alisha. You picked out the name," Ben said helping Sonja into her seat and putting their bags on the seat next to Alisha.

Sonja chuckled. "I do wish you wouldn't call her that."

"She farts all the time, Momma."

Ben tilted his head and smiled. "Yes, she does."

Ben flicked the reins on the horse's rump, and she pulled them up Lafayette Street and then onto Market Street, passing gas as she trotted.

Ben and Sonja shared glances from the corners of their eyes.

"You should have suspected something when you bought a beautiful chestnut mare in her prime for only fifteen dollars," Sonja said.

Ben opened his mouth to respond, but Betsy passed a staccato of sputtering releases forcing him to turn his head away.

At Rodgers Tavern, Ben held up Alisha so she could slip the feed bag over Betsy's head and then went in with Sonja. Steamed oysters were plentiful, and rockfish were still on the menu. Despite Ben's not-so-subtle prodding, Sonja was able to defer discussing her incident in Baltimore until after dinner. Sonja was silent during their slow ride along the lower towpath between the river and the basin. Once the towpath funneled into the eastern side of the canal, she related all of her experiences since the hectic morning Dan Bartlett warned her about the order to give up Alisha. Ben had received three telegrams from Anthony, relaying Sonja's progress, but so much of her travel was unknown to him. When they pulled up in front of the Pulaski home, Sonja was spent from the retelling. Alisha had her arms around Sonja's neck, and Ben stared at her with open mouth.

Ben spoke in a hoarse whisper. "You are amazing, Sonja Pulaski."

Later, after kneeling beside Alisha's bed for evening prayers and watching her fall asleep even as they stood up, Ben and Sonja held hands and strolled into their bedroom. With muted voices and moments of tender silence as they undressed each other, they released their deepest and most cherished feelings, taking each other back to their wedding night.

The next day Delbert Freidman brought two letters up from his general store, where Lapidum's first post office now sat.

He knocked on the frame of the open doorway and leaned into the house.

"Got letters from both Aaron and Isaac," he shouted.

Sonja flew out from the kitchen only seconds before Ben's bootheels hit the top step to the porch behind Delbert.

She ripped open the letter from Aaron, the first since he left. She mumbled random words as she read through the brief letter.

"Well...trapping–" Her head flew up. "Beaver! He's trapping beaver."

"Beaver? Where?" Ben asked, but Sonja slapped his question away with the flip of her hand.

"San Francisco...Sacramento...mountains–" She jerked the paper around to look at the back, then returned her attention to the front. "That's it? Months and months I don't hear from him, and this is what he sends?"

Delbert tried to peek over her shoulder, and Sonja faced him with her chin up.

"W-well, he's my son-in-law," Delbert said.

Ben plucked the letter from Sonja's fingertips.

Dear Ma and Pa,

I hope you and Alisha are well. I have a good job here in San Francisco. We hear a little about the war between America and Mexico, but the people here don't seem to bear us a grudge. I hope Isaac is not in it.

It is time for me to go on from here. I am joining with some other Americanos to go trap beaver in the mountains. There is good money in that, and my new friend Jim Marshall says the beaver are plentiful in there. We are leaving for Sacramento tomorrow and then to the mountains from there. Our last stop will be at a place called Sutter's Store, where I can post another letter. Do not worry. Here, I am free of my agony.

Your Son, Aaron

Tears continued to slip down Sonja's cheeks as she opened the letter from Isaac. She read it quickly and sighed. She smiled as she turned to Ben.

"He will be granted leave from Fort Carroll for Christmas. Two weeks."

She handed the letter to Ben. Ben handed Aaron's letter to Delbert.

Delbert scanned the letter, then glanced over the top of the page. "He doesn't know it's over," he said.

"No treaty or formal surrender down there yet, Delbert. All we know is what Isaac told us," Ben said.

Sonja planted her hands on her hips. "Well that's enough for me," she said.

Ben slipped his arm around Sonja's waist. "And enough for me."

Delbert turned away with the letter and walked down the steps. "Need to show this letter to Mary. It might take away a little of the sting. She's been talking about going to see the grave in York Furnace…"

Sonja and Ben stepped onto the porch to see Delbert leave, his shoulders hanging low. Sonja leaned her head against Ben's chest.

"I am so lucky to still have Aaron and Isaac, even in spite of Aaron's loss of Maggie and Sarah. I can only imagine Mary's pain at losing her daughter and granddaughter."

Ben pulled her shoulders against him and escorted her back into the house.

November flew into December. The canal was drained late, and its water was still a foot deep when the hard winter freeze came. The canal ice formed a roadway for sleds with drivers foolish enough to risk their mule's ankles getting down the treacherous banks, or merchants smart enough to create safe slopes.

Delbert Freidman, Ben's partner, had arranged for their eight barges to be full of coal and close to Lapidum when the water dropped. Now during the harsh winter, with most of the hillside trees cleared years ago, their coal business mushroomed. The barge captains, usually sent home unemployed during the winter, were offered jobs driving the coal sleds with their mule tenders as helpers. Coal burned hotter than wood and people with split wood but no money traded some of their wood for coal. Several coal sleds moved up and down the frozen canal, pulled by sure-footed mules wearing spiked shoes created by 'Mac' McMallery, Lapidum's blacksmith. Other sleds were sent across the river ice to Port Deposit, where Pulaski and Freidman Coal competed successfully with coal brought down by the railroad. Barge coal was always cheaper, a saving grace for the canal.

The approach of Christmas was made exciting in the Pulaski home by the presence of Alisha, anticipating her eighth birthday only six days before the holiday. Isaac arrived the morning of Alisha's birthday, wearing a new uniform and bringing a large box tied with a red ribbon. The Price children arrived soon after, each carrying a simple handmade gift for Alisha and dashing ahead of their parents. Catherine and Jesse ambled up the snow-covered lane laughing over their brood of five. Ben met them at the porch.

"Glad you could join us too, Jesse," Ben said as they shook hands.

"Mac was kind enough to leave his blacksmith furnace a little while and tend to the lock," Jesse said.

Sonja heard the comment and spoke from the

kitchen. "We will send him a piece."

Patty Price, Alisha's closest friend, took her station beside Alisha while Sonja brought out a cake and everyone sang the birthday song that was becoming popular. Patty's twin brother, Jesse Jr., managed to slip a fingertip into the icing before the cake was cut, and smudged it onto Alisha's nose, who promptly punched him in his.

Catherine chuckled and placed her arm around Sonja's waist. "She has her mother's fire."

"Sometimes too much of it," Sonja said, her eyes drifting to Isaac's, whose laugh sounded hollow to her.

Later as the children cavorted on the front slope in the snow, Sonja joined Isaac on the porch to watch.

"What is it?" she asked.

"The box is a Christmas present for Alisha," he said, then paused. "...I was looking for the right time to talk, but I should have known you would beat me to it."

He turned and placed his hands on her shoulders. "Harriet...I mean Harriet and her family...the Kincaids...in New York, have invited me to visit for Christmas."

Sonja's mouth dropped open, then she closed it, fixing him with her eyes. "Is it serious?"

"Yes, Ma. I think it is. We have met several times now. And Wallace, her brother, is a good friend."

A teardrop slipped across her eye.

Isaac spoke. "Harriet has asked that...that I speak with her father..."

The tear slipped down the side of her cheek, even as she allowed a small smile on her lips.

"She has asked?"

"Well, no, Ma...I...I have already asked her. She came with her family to Baltimore last month. We saw each other at a ball..."

"And, you asked her what, Isaac?" Sonja asked, straightening her back and shoulders.

"I have asked her to marry me, Ma."

January 1848. Havre de Grace, Maryland

Ben Pulaski stood at one of the large windows of suite #2 at the Newkirk Hotel, overlooking Washington Street. Below, people bundled in thick wool coats and scarves trudged through the snow with hats pulled low against the wind. Out beyond the end of St. Clair Street, the Havre de Grace Harbor was strangely empty of boats and ships. The water was frozen hard and dotted with horse-drawn sleds and young people on skates. The *Raven* sat out of water on braces thirty miles away at Sparrows Point near Baltimore, where Ben had sent her when the ice began to thicken. Even the steamship *Susquehanna* was sent south, no longer able to break through the ice to carry rail cars to the other side of the river. Engineers were marking a lane between Havre de Grace and Perry Point, where town rumors said they would soon lay tracks.

Ben tugged at his newly trimmed beard. He exhaled heavily, frosting the glass in front of his face, and turned back toward the heat of the fireplace.

"It doesn't sound like you've made much progress, Drayton," Ben said.

"Ben, I do wish you'd use my first name," Daniel Drayton said.

Ben waved the concern away. "I have a crewman named Daniel, and I don't want duplicate names on the ship–"

Anthony Renowitz spoke over his brandy sniffer. "You're not on a ship now, Ben."

"No, but we will be. Now Drayton, tell us what is happening in Washington City."

"There will be sixty or more passengers by spring, but not until then, especially with this hard freeze. We need to wait until April, at least," Drayton said.

Ben fixed his attention on Renowitz. "I want to move more than just two or three slaves, Anthony..."

"You pulled thirty out of Georgetown last year, Ben. We have to help whoever we can, whenever we can."

"This is not a contest, Ben," Drayton said.

"No. No it is not," Ben said, turning back toward Drayton, "but until Congress finally decides to do away with slavery, we should carry away as many as possible."

"You are too optimistic by far, Ben," Anthony said. He wagged his finger and smiled. "You sound like an abolitionist, in spite of your denial."

Ben sighed. "I grew up with slavery. Never thought much about it, but once I did, I also saw many ways to help that I had never noticed, or had the spine to act on."

Anthony smiled. "And it is different now?"

"Yes. It is different now."

"Ben," Drayton said, "As I have explained before, escape plans have to be made for each individual. We need them to be away from their masters a full day without alarm, so we have time to get down the Potomac and into the Chesapeake. Making those plans takes time, and they have to be set in motion when they will work. When they all will work. That means spring."

Anthony coughed. "I readily accept myself as the culprit who lured you into this effort, Benjamin. And, I accept the blame that it almost killed you during our first crossing."

"Yes to both confessions, Anthony."

Ben sighed and sat down on a padded chair facing the fireplace, yellow light painting his face and highlighting his black beard. He pulled out his tobacco pouch and began filling his pipe.

"But, now I am committed to it," Ben said, lighting his pipe.

"But are you committed to the people we free, or the number on your tally?" Drayton asked.

Ben glared at Drayton as blue smoke rose slowly between them.

"Have you heard from Aaron, Ben?" Anthony asked.

"Not since he left for the California mountains...to

trap beaver."

"Beaver skin hats are in high demand, Ben," Drayton said, "and very expensive. He is pursuing a worthy trade."

Ben puffed on his pipe, sending more smoke into the air. "He is pursued more than pursuing. I fear he may find an even more remote pursuit after this."

"You wish him home," Drayton said, staring into the flames.

"Yes. I wish him home."

The clock on the mantel over the fire chimed twice. Ben stood.

"I need to meet with Sonja and Alisha," Ben said. "They are shopping at the new mercantile store, picking out a factory-made dress for our young lady." Ben chuckled. "But, I think it should be a dress made of canvas or iron if it is to withstand the exuberance of my little girl."

Ben met Sonja and Alisha ambling along Market Street. Alisha clutched a large package within her arms and wore a broad smile. He knelt down in front of his daughter.

"And what has your mother bought for you today?"

"A new dress, Papa. Momma says it is as blue as my eyes," she said.

Ben kissed her on her forehead and stood, then kissed Sonja's cheek.

"Are you Momma, now?" he asked.

Sonja smiled. "I am to Alisha. It is what she feels I am. I am still Ma to Isaac and Aaron." She tapped his nose with the fingertip of her glove. "And you are Papa, as well as Pa."

Sonja slipped her arm inside his, and they strolled to Rodgers Tavern.

Inside, while Alisha sipped her oyster stew, Sonja withdrew a letter from her purse and handed it to Ben.

"Another note from Aaron. He is still there," she said.

Ben held the paper to catch the overhead light.

Dear Ma and Pa,

I am well. We are waiting on new traps to come into Sutter's Store. He has a mill and tavern, here. All else is forest and mountains and creeks. We will leave for the mountains soon. Many beaver pelts are being brought out. I will write again when we have our fill of pelts.

    Aaron

"Beaver," she said while shaking her head.

Ben sighed but said nothing for a long moment.

"We will not go to Washington until April," he said.

"And until then, where will you be off to?" she asked.

"Only home, if you can stand me."

She smiled and placed her hand on his. "I can stand a lot of that."

From her collection of packages, she withdrew a small mailed parcel and handed it to him. "From Anthony," she said, "a late birthday gift I suspect."

Ben unwrapped it and found a slim book. He held it to the light.

*Narrative of the Life
of
Frederick Douglass
An American Slave*

He glanced around the room to ensure no one had seen the title of the book, then turned it face down on the table.

"I have heard of this book. I will look forward to reading it at home," he said.

Sonja flashed a broad smile. "A copy was in Talbot Hall. I've already read it. It made me cry, and it made me angry."

Ben glanced over her shoulder, then rolled his eyes at her. "Be angry now," he whispered.

Harold and Nadja Lister stepped by their table.

Harold smiled and nodded to Ben, who returned it. Nadja flashed her eyes in a glaring frown at Sonja, then stopped still in front of her.

"I hear rumors that you had that poor Ramona Tatum shot."

Nadja stood there, waiting for Sonja's reaction. Sonja picked up her coffee cup and sipped from it then set it down calmly.

"If that were true, Nadja," she said. "Wouldn't it be foolish of you to bait the bear?"

Nadja's eyes widened as she was pulled along by her husband who kept his eyes straight ahead.

On the ride home in the Pulaski buggy, Sonja and Alisha were wrapped under layers of wool blankets against the bitter cold. Ben huddled within the new fur-lined winter coat Sonja had given him for Christmas, his wool hat pulled down on his ears, and his hands slipped inside thick shearling gloves. Even the horse was draped in a heavy blanket, tied under her chest.

"Do you remember the sunshine in Bermuda, Ben?" Sonja asked.

Ben smiled. "Yes. That is a wonderful memory to recall."

"I would like to go back there."

"After we take the slaves from Washington City, I would love to do that."

"Maybe we could stay a week or so," she said.

"Maybe two weeks, Sonja, or three."

Early the next month the *Cecil Whig* reported the official ending of the war with Mexico. Ben stood in the front room, holding the paper before the lamplight, reading with bursts of excitement.

"All of Texas, Sonja...and the area called New Mexico...and the Arizona Territory." He stopped to catch his breath, then went on, "And all of California!" He looked hard at Sonja and grinned. "Aaron is in the United States of America, now!"

Sonja sat in her padded chair with her arms folded. "He's no closer, Ben."

Ben huffed and continued to read the paper and

pacing the room, then stopped abruptly after turning a page.

"Gold! They have discovered gold in California—Where is the last letter from Aaron?"

She pulled it from her apron pocket and opened it. Ben snatched it from her, holding it up to the light in one hand, then held up the newspaper in the other.

"He was there!" Ben said. "Sutter's Store. It had a mill, he said. Sutter's Mill, Sonja. He was there."

"But now he is up in the mountains. Trapping Beaver. Trapping Beaver, Benjamin. I wonder if it is as cold there as here."

Ben glanced out of the front window, at the waist-deep snow on the front slope and the barest suggestion of a depression where the canal lay hidden.

"It is probably colder there. Mountains usually are."

"I wish he would send another letter," she said. Her voice made it sound like a prayer.

February finally gave way to March, and the snow remained as dirt-speckled edging along the pathways and roadways. The rails were pulled off the ice between Havre de Grace and Perry Point, and the massive steamship *Susquehanna* returned to shove her iron hull through the thinning ice. It was sweet revenge after a severe winter, and its steam whistle proclaimed warmer weather would soon arrive.

Ben stomped up the steps to the house, making harried attempts to knock muddy ice from his boots and rushed into the front room, tracking mud.

"Sonja, we have a telegram from Isaac," he said.

Sonja stepped out of the kitchen, with her hand to her throat. "Is he not well? Is he injured?"

"In a manner of speaking," Ben said handing her the telegram.

"Oh, good Lord," she said as she read the terse telegram.

She glared at Ben. "He's being transferred to Charleston...getting married to Harriet in Albany...next week! And we are to be there!"

"As you can see, Sonja, he is both injured and unwell."

March 19ᵗʰ, 1848. Albany, New York

Ben tugged at his collar waiting in the vestibule of the Dutch Reformed. His new suit and shirt were not as adjusted to his frame as he had hoped, and he had to force himself not to pull it apart at its all-too-fragile seams. Alisha had been swept away by the bridesmaids and was being prepared for her role as flower girl, Harriet being the only Kincaid daughter. Sonja stood next to him in a gray gown edged with white lace, trim to her figure and showing her beauty at its best. Her golden hair shined in perfect curls. To Ben, she looked like an angel. She smiled patiently and stepped closer to him, whispering.

"I would give anything for a calico dress or canvas trousers."

Ben's heart thrummed with love for her. He also longed for an opportunity to step outside to smoke his pipe, something he could not do. The Kincaids abstained from tobacco and alcohol. His past three days among them gave rise to heavenly praise for the Kincaid's modest home, which allowed him, Sonja and Alisha to take hotel rooms, where he could safely be himself.

Wallace Kincaid approached them in an immaculate uniform and offered his arm to Sonja. Ben stood on the other side of her, and the three marched to the front of the church. As soon as they settled into their seats, the minister raised his hands for the guests to stand and the organ began to play.

The grooms and maids filed in solemnly, with Isaac bringing up the rear. He looked pale in his dark blue uniform and high collar, his rank sewed in gold thread on his shoulders. Next came Alisha, wearing a miniature of Sonja's dress and white shoes – one of them scuffed at the toe. She dropped handfuls of rose petals as she walked down the aisle and took her place at the end of the line of bridesmaids. Then the music rose, and Herbert Kincaid walked his daughter slowly to the front. Her hair cascaded in auburn curls down her shoulders under her veil. Her dress was striking white, tinted pink and yellow by sunbeams coming through stained glass.

Sonja stood in admiration of her child and his bride. Her heart swelled with pride and love and an emptiness she tried to ignore. Isaac was never so handsome as she viewed him through the eyes and comments of the others who knew him only as 'Harriet's soldier.' It was over far too quickly, and the upbeat hymn that crashed from the organ startled her. The reception in the church anteroom was placid compared to the bawdy celebration of Aaron's wedding. She had flashes of Aaron's wife, Maggie, lying in the birthing bed, fading to pale next to her blue baby, but shook it away and smiled.

Between toasts with coffee and fruit punch, there was much talk about unfinished Fort Sumter and the mild winters of Charleston, and the life of an officer's wife. It all flashed by in an instant. Her baby was gone with the cute girl she barely knew. Then they were on the train, jerking over the tracks, dodging the black smoke above the rail car. They raced away from yesterday and drove into tomorrows, where her firstborn son had another family and his own path to follow, without her.

April 5th, 1848. Lapidum, Maryland

Sonja planted her hands on her hips and a scowl on her face.

Ben crossed his arms over his chest. "No."

"I can do anything on that ship that any crewman can," Sonja said. "There is no reason I should not go."

"This effort is a gamble, Sonja. I won't risk you and Alisha."

"Gamble? Ben, you have been saying how gullible slave owners are when they deal with a slave trader. How did that change?"

Ben sighed and placed his hands on her shoulders, but she jerked away from him.

"When Eddie and I can control what happens, it goes smoothly, but it can go wrong when many people are involved."

"Alisha can stay with Catherine Price," Sonja said. "Catherine would love to have her and Alisha will be safe."

"And you think she will be safe when she learns her mother has been killed?"

Sonja poked her finger at his face. "You have not been telling me it will be that dangerous."

Ben huffed. "No, I have not. And it may not. But moving sixty people away from dozens of masters will create problems. I have to recognize that. You have to recognize that."

"So, it is fine for me to be a widow as long as you get a chance to thumb your nose at more masters?"

Ben turned away from her and stepped to the mantel, retrieving his pipe and pouch. He stood packing tobacco into his pipe, staring at her while he did it.

She wagged a finger at his face. "Don't you dare."

He stuffed the pipe stem into his mouth, clamping

down on it with his teeth, then pulled a match from the metal shot glass on the mantel.

"Not in here, Benjamin Pulaski," she said. "I won't have it."

He held the match in front of her face, then struck it on the stove flue, holding it up for her to see the flame. She snatched the lid handle and pried open the front lid to the iron stove, the insides dark and cool, the fire out for days. The flame burned down the wooden matchstick as he held it. Then he smiled around his pipe stem and dropped the match into the iron stove. She smirked and stepped closer as she replaced the burner lid, and gently pulled the pipe from his mouth. He put his arms around her waist and kissed her.

"After this, we will go to Bermuda," he said. "We will take lumber and bring back a load of rum."

"For three weeks, Ben?"

"A month," he said.

<hr>

April 10th, 1848. Sparrows Point, Maryland

Ben stood on the catwalk as the *Raven* slid into the water, finally free of her braces. Her hull had been lovingly re-caulked and painted by the boatwrights of the shipyard. The masts were sealed, new gaffs placed, new running rigging and new sails. It was an expensive stay, but the coal profits of the winter allowed him to pay for her best care. The crew had gathered and were all eager to put to sea.

"She looks brand new," Edward said.

"She does, indeed, Eddie. I had hoped she would carry my son and his new bride to Charleston, but the Army already sent them by steamer."

"So, we go to Washington City?" Edward asked.

Ben flashed a wide grin. "Yes, for a very full load this trip."

"We will be going without Warren, I'm afraid, Ben."

"Is he ill?"

"No, but his wife is. Morning sickness."

Ben and Edward shared knowing smiles.

"When is she due?" Ben asked.

Edward chuckled. "Nine months from his first night home, I believe. He expects an August baby and promised to stay close until then. His cousin wants to sign on."

"Can he cook?"

"Very well, I hear. Warren said the cousin cooks better than he does."

"That is a compliment. I thought Warren's cooking was always satisfying. What's the new cook's name?"

"Chester English."

"Well, if he is acceptable to you, I will sign him in as soon as we get on deck."

The rest of the day was a jumbled overlap of activities with stowing supplies and personal effects, handling new stiff lines and sails, as well as greasing the steering ropes and steering pulleys between the two wheels. By nightfall, after an enjoyable supper cooked by Chester, and a liberal allotment of rum around the crew and captain, the anchored ship vibrated from a chorus of hearty snores.

At dawn the smell of fresh coffee wafted over the deck as the crew raised anchor and set sails to move them out of their protected anchorage and into the mouth of the Patapsco River. There they caught a steady northerly breeze that pushed them out into the Chesapeake Bay for their run to Point Lookout. Ben initially kept the sails closely controlled while he regained the feel of her response to the wind. When they reached past Kent Island to Poplar Island on their east, he had all fair weather sails hoisted. Even the main staysail stretched between the upper lengths of the two masts popped out with a full belly.

Alistair yelled from the stern railing as he reeled in the knotted line. "Nine knots!"

Edward was at the windward wheel, grinning like a schoolboy. Ben shared his grin.

They rounded Point Lookout into the mouth of the Potomac River while the sun was still well above the horizon.

"We have a strong northerly wind, Eddie," Ben said. "I don't care to be tacking back and forth across the

Potomac at sunset. Let's anchor in Cornfield Harbor. We will work our way up the river to Washington tomorrow."

"I hope the wind stays as it is for our run back down," Edward said. "That will give us an excellent speed back to the bay."

April 13th, 1848. Washington City

The sky was overcast. The *Raven* was tied against the wharf at its far end. Rain had fallen intermittently all day, and the cool wind stayed from the north. The musty smell of the city blew across the ship, mildew, fried meat, and burning coal. Ben, Drayton and a black man named Paul Jennings sat at the little desk in the captain's cabin sipping coffee against the damp air.

"Eighty-two?" Ben asked.

"Yes," said Paul. "Can this ship hold that many?"

Ben shrugged his shoulders. "To be honest, I am not sure."

"Some of these people have sailed the bay, Ben. They could serve as crew."

"And what, Drayton? Would you have me abandon my crew here?"

"No. I will arrange passage for them on a steamer."

Ben scratched his beard, then tapped his fingers on the desktop.

"Do you know what kinds of ships they have sailed?" Ben asked Paul.

Paul pointed to the roof. "Like this one, maybe smaller, but two masts, I am told."

"You are told," Ben said, "but no experience yourself?"

"No. I am a house servant."

"He served President Madison, Ben," Drayton said.

"That's fine, but—"

"I mean," Drayton said, "he has connections in this city and knows what he is talking about."

"Daniel and I have met with everyone on the list, Captain Pulaski," Paul said. "We know what they can do, and what they cannot do."

"We may have to leave some behind," Ben said.

"Captain–"

"Call me Ben," he said.

"Ben, some of these people have been waiting over a year to be released. They should already be free. Some have never even served a white master. They live in separate houses with their parents, and go to work each day like paid servants. But all that could change in an instant. We've got to get them out quickly. ALL of them."

Ben sighed, eyeing both Drayton and Paul in turn. "You swear you have men who can crew this ship?"

"Yes," they both answered.

"They will be on this ship for two or three days. I will ask the cook to stay on board."

"We have several cooks," Paul said.

"But none who have worked in this ship's galley," Ben said. "We will free no one if this ship burns to the waterline."

Ben faced Drayton. "When will they come on board?"

"In two days."

"Send four steamer tickets tomorrow for passage to Cape May."

After Paul and Drayton left the ship, Ben called the crew into the hold for a discussion. There he explained the escape plan and informed most of them that they would be leaving the ship the next day.

"No. I am staying with you," Edward said, and his comment was echoed among the rest.

"For each one of you that stays, one of the people on that escape list will be left behind," Ben said.

The group became silent.

"I will go too," Chester said.

"I need you to feed them, Chester, if you will stay. They have cooks among them, but the *Raven* has a unique galley."

He nodded in agreement. The others agreed as well, but all showed stern faces.

Early the next day a black man carrying an envelope asked to come aboard the ship.

"Who are you?" Edward asked him.

"Judson Diggs, suh. I have something for Cap'n

Plaski."

Edward reached out for the envelope, but Diggs maintained his grip. "Mr. Jennings said I give it only to Cap'n Plaski."

Edward called for Ben who accepted the envelope from Diggs. "Thank you," Ben said. "Are you coming with us?"

He hesitated. "May be, suh, may be."

Ben opened the envelope as the man walked down the gangplank and returned to his buggy.

"These tickets are for noon today," he said. "Eddie get them ready to go."

Ben stepped down into the galley. "Chester, the others are leaving for the steamer in a few minutes. Are you still willing to stay with me?"

"Yes, sir."

"Well, thank you. And as I said last night, I will pay you triple when we reach Cape May. I know you will be busy, but again, thank you."

Chester smiled and went back to cleaning the dishes from breakfast.

April 15th, 1848. Washington City

The rain continued sporadically amid gusts of wind still out of the north. Ben wore an oiled coat when on the empty deck. Earlier that morning he had walked the quarter mile to the harbormaster's office to pay for the following week, hoping to keep the nosy old man at bay. Late morning, a buggy pulled up directly in front of the gangplank, and several people scampered on deck. Diggs nodded to Ben then drove the buggy away. Ben escorted the people below. Partitions had been removed throughout the hold to open as much space as possible. Empty rum barrels supported planks for seats along both sides and a double row down the center, on either side of the mess table.

"Enjoy the room you have, for now, folks, it will be damned crowded before this day is through."

Chester came out with platters of biscuits and fried meat and set them on the table, then went back to the galley for coffee and cups. The new passengers relaxed and showed smiles as they settled at the table.

The next three deliveries came in trade wagons, one a bakery, one an ice wagon, and the third a newspaper delivery wagon. Paul Jennings was in the last wagon.

Ben and Paul shook hands on the deck.

"Paul, will you please arrange locations for people below decks? Feel free to use the captain's cabin and crew cabin and anywhere in the hold you see fit."

"Excellent," he said. "There are quite a few young ladies and even a fair sized family of daughters to be settled, the Edmonson girls. My good friend Paul Edmonson, who is free himself and helped make many of the arrangements with Daniel, had tried to buy his family, but the owner wouldn't sell."

"Please keep them all below," Ben said. "We have a nosy harbormaster that has made unplanned visits in the past."

The clouds opened for a few hours and warmed the ship with sunshine. Paul and Ben opened the canvas hatches to allow air to flow into the hold, but soon the rain returned, and the hatches had to be battened again. At noon Ben went below and worked his way through dozens of people, chattering in hushed tones. Paul Jennings pulled along another man and singled Ben out.

"Ben, this is my good friend, Paul Edmonson."

The man smiled as he shook Ben's hand. "Some of these cackling young ladies are of my family," he said. "There is still another yet to come, my daughter, Mary."

Groups of three to seven continued to arrive at different moments during the day. Daniel Drayton arrived in one group. Being white, he was privileged to remain on deck with Ben.

"How many?" he asked.

"Fifty-two by Paul Jennings' count."

"What about Edmonson and his family?"

"He is aboard, and I think all his family except a daughter."

"Mary? I hope she is not convinced to stay."

"Why would she?" Ben asked.

"There is a slave, Judson Diggs, who has been

promised freedom by his master to keep him tethered. The man will never free him."

"Diggs has been bringing passengers to us. I asked if he was coming, but he hesitated."

"The boy's a fool," Drayton said, then went below.

The rain returned, and the wind gusted in spurts, but the clouds overhead appeared to thin. Diggs' buggy returned with a single passenger. A girl stepped down carrying a small travel bag and moved toward the gangplank, her head uncovered in the rain. Diggs jumped down from the buggy and ran to her, grabbing her wrist. He pulled her to him and kissed her, but she broke free and ran onto the ship. He stood there in the rain, speaking after her, but his words were lost. Then he shook his fist at her back and at Ben, then returned to the buggy. He slapped the reins hard on the horse's rump and wheeled away from the wharf.

Paul Edmonson was standing on deck and welcomed the girl, then escorted her below.

Drayton approached Ben.

"I think we should go now. Paul tells me we have seventy-eight passengers on board, and he doesn't think the others can come, according to what he hears below."

Ben ran onto the wharf to free the mooring lines from the bollards then dashed back up the gangplank where he and Drayton pulled it on deck. The sailors among the passengers Ben had spoken with earlier trotted up from below and ran to their tasks. Two men pulled in the mooring lines while Ben gave sail and rigging instructions to the others. Drayton took the wheel. With the main and foresails wing and wing, the ship pulled away from the wharf. Ben then directed the crew to raise the jib sails and swing the booms around to rotate the ship. Within minutes the *Raven* silently pointed her nose downstream in the Potomac and slipped away from Washington. All was still quiet on the wharf. No alarm had been sounded.

The soft wind gently kissed their heads, the clouds parted, and early evening sky was still light blue. The sails flapped in their rigging, and the wind died.

April 15th, 1848. The Potomac River

The wind blew weakly between growing intervening moments of calm. The current carried the *Raven* farther than the wind pushed her and brought them abreast of Alexandria. In the dead air, the mosquitoes swarmed out from the swampland. The hatches were opened, but the trickle of fresh air brought the agony of mosquito bites in the cramped hold. The April air felt like early summer in the calm, and the passengers begged to come on deck.

"We can't chance it," Ben said, then relented, "Maybe two or three at a time, but we dare not show a ship filled with blacks in a slave state."

"I agree," Drayton said.

Paul Jennings, who stood on deck in a seaman's sou'wester went to the ladderway. "I will start a rotation."

The light from shore faded and darkness folded over them. There was enough light to see the shore as a gray smudge. Once past Alexandria, the ship's boat was lowered and tied to the bow. Groups of eight men rotated in the rowboat, barely able to keep the *Raven* from shore as it drifted south. As the temperature dropped during the dark hours after midnight, the mosquitoes drifted away, and the hatches could be shut. There was a constant line of people moving to the seat of ease at the bow. The content of fearful stomachs and bowels floated on the river surface just ahead of the bow. In the jubilation of the arrival day, all the fresh food on board had been prepared and consumed.

Ben stayed on deck through the night, assessing the shoreline, the work of the rowboat, and the appearance of the rotating passengers walking the deck. One of the Edmonson girls came up on deck without a hat and unsure how she should act. Ben gave her a cap and handed her a small coil of rope to carry.

"Just walk around and touch the rigging with it. That will be enough."

Paul Jennings approached him. "Thank you, Captain Pulaski. She is completely lost on a ship."

Ben smiled in the darkness. "So you were with President Madison?"

"Yes, until he died in '39, then I served Miss Dolly until '45."

"Drayton said you were free, is that when she freed you?"

"No...she needed money then and sold me. Senator Webster–"

"Daniel Webster?"

"Yes. He bought me and set me free. I've stayed with him until..." He chuckled. "Until yesterday."

"That girl," Ben said. "One of the Edmonson ladies."

"Mary. The youngest. She has only been barely aware that she is a slave. Never had her hands dirty. She's used to thinking of herself as free, now she will learn what real freedom is like."

"Why did you stay with Webster, when you were free?"

"I was no longer a slave, Captain, but I was still a black man. We either serve the white man or sell to them, begging your pardon. I wanted to go into business."

"And now?" Ben asked.

Paul shrugged his shoulders. "I will start a business somewhere else."

At sunrise, Chester opened a barrel of ship's biscuits, hard salted bread, to feed the rowers climbing back on deck.

At late morning, the *Raven* nudged against a sandbar on the south side of the hook, still only thirty-five miles away from Washington. Anxious murmurs arose from the hold. Ben sent fresh men into the rowboat to try to pull the ship free. Paul Jennings and Drayton began rotating people out of the hold and into the crew quarters and captain's cabin.

"Some of them have been standing for hours in the hold," Drayton said. "We need to give each person a chance to sit a while, maybe even lay down for a few minutes. It's only fair."

"We have a goodly supply of blankets down there," Ben said. "Did you find them?"

"Yes. A goodly supply, but not enough for seventy-eight people to have two each, as I planned."

"And the blankets from my bed and the crew quarters?"

"Hours ago, Ben. All handed out."

Drayton sighed and walked away. Two ministers among the escapees began holding whispered prayer sessions. The men in the rowboat managed to pull the ship off the sandbar, and the slow progress downstream resumed.

In the early afternoon the temperature rose again. A steamboat heading north chugged past the *Raven*. The steamer passengers leaned idly at the rails watching the *Raven* wallow in the calm with her sails hanging limp. The men in the rowboat were poorly rested, grew weary quickly and had to be changed more often. Finally, the ship made the turn at the top of the hook, and faced an almost straight southeast course to the mouth of the Potomac, only forty-five miles away.

The clouds crawled in the sky, too small to give any shade from the sun. The trees in the distance waved lethargic at their tops. A faint breeze slipped across the deck, then sneaked away to the north. Ben had the hatches completely open, but passengers still crowded onto the open deck.

In the home of Mr. Francis Dodge of Washington City, Judson Diggs requested to see the master.

Dodge looked up from his ledger and set his wine glass on the desk. "What is it, Judson?"

"'Scuse me, Massa, but I heard some awful news."

Dodge yawned. "And what news is so awful?"

"They's a abolishuniss taking slaves away in a boat, and they ain't his."

He sat up straight and frowned at Judson. "And whose are they?"

"Some be yours, Massa," he said.

An hour later Judson sat in the buggy at the wharf where the *Raven* had moored the day before. Old man Dodge stood leaning against his cane speaking with the harbormaster leaning against his own.

"No, Mr. Dodge, I never actually looked at the ship. It was moored way down here near nigger town. He signed in as the *Raven* with mercantile goods, and paid for mooring to the end of next week. Said he had goods for all kinds of businesses. Made sense to me. There were trade-good wagons going back and forth all yesterday, even in the rain."

Dodge squinted at him. "How many wagons?"

The harbormaster shrugged his shoulders. "Dozen? Maybe more. Why?"

Dodge jammed his cane tip onto the wharf, splitting it in two.

"Hellfire and damnation!" he yelled.

He limped off to his buggy, leaving the harbormaster staring at the pieces of the expensive cane lying on the wharf.

Dodge dropped onto his seat. "Judson, drive me to the sheriff's office."

<hr>

A faint breeze grew at the mouth of the Potomac River and dashed upstream to find the *Raven*. The warm wind meandered, coming from the south then the east. Ben mustered his crew and instructed the setting of the sails. Soon they sailed across the face of the wind toward the opposite shore of the river, but ever so slightly farther south. He left Drayton to steer while he talked the crew through an evolution of tacking, bringing the ship across the wind in one direction then switching to the opposite direction without losing way. Half of the first turns missed the wind and lost way, but more attempts succeeded as the ungainly crew fell into the rhythm of the maneuver. Soon they were gaining yards southward for each mile run across the wind, then tens of yards and then hundreds of yards. They had traveled the width of the river dozens of times, each time reaching closer toward the mouth. At last, the bay was in sight ahead of them, but the wind was shifting again. The wind came from the east less and less and from the south more and more. After two hours of racing back and forth across the mouth of the river without gaining, they began losing their progress. Ben halted the maneuver and directed Drayton to steer toward the river's eastern shore.

"We are going to have to take shelter in that cove ahead. It is called 'Cornfield Harbor'. We have to wait for the wind to shift again."

"Can't we try it longer?" asked Jennings.

"We're being blown back upstream. We've got to take shelter close to Point Lookout. Tomorrow we can try for the bay again."

The wind gusts from the south grew ominously in strength. The waves slapped against the hull. The upper sails bulged and ship leaned precariously away from the wind. Ben had the upper sails loosened in a jumbled tangle to keep the *Raven* from capsizing. Her hull kissed the bottom at the northern edge of the cove, but her headway carried them across the sandbar and into deeper water. The trees lining the southern edge of the harbor deflected the wind and gave them respite.

"The damned wind is dead against us," Ben said.

April 17th, 1848. Cornfield Harbor

Just before dawn, Ben asked Chester to start cooking breakfast for everyone.

"They already ate all the fresh meat, Cap'n. I can feed 'em fried salt pork and oatmeal."

"I'm sure they will welcome it. I just checked our water barrels, and we have plenty of that."

Ben found Drayton asleep on the deck wrapped in one of the tangled sails. "Drayton, please organize the people to eat in groups. See the crew fed first so we can get the rest of the sails untangled. We will need them in the upper bay.

Drayton sat up, rubbing his eyes. "Maybe we should consider running south, Ben. Down toward Norfolk..."

"Go seaward around the eastern shore and up to the Delaware Bay?"

"It may be our only way, Ben, if the wind doesn't shift to take us away from here."

"We have six tons of people on board, Drayton. We're far too low in the water for that. Atlantic rollers could swamp us."

He sighed and stood up, pulling on Ben's arm to rise. "Yeah, I knew that. I just needed someone else to confirm it."

In the distance, a steam whistle shrieked in the early morning. Over the treetops to the north, black smoke billowed into the sky and dashed north in the wind. Ben and Drayton fixed their eyes on the opening to the little natural harbor. The nose of a modest-sized steamboat shoved itself against the wind into view. A man near the bow of the steamer pointed toward the *Raven*. The man was quickly joined by other men, all carrying rifles.

Paul Jennings stepped next to Ben and Drayton. "Oh my God," he whispered.

Ben turned from the sight and addressed Drayton and Jennings. "Those crates at the bow of this ship hold six-inch cannon if we can get our bow around–"

"No," said Jennings. "I've seen cannon fire. One or two cannon won't stop that steamer. It will only turn those that live into monsters. And they will massacre our people."

Passengers began to climb up from the hold onto *Raven's* deck. The collective moan as they saw the steamer was foreboding.

The steamer pushed into the cove and approached the *Raven*. Ominous in its coming and its hissing steam and black smoke pouring into the air. One of the passengers on the *Raven* had a pistol with him. He ran shrieking to the rail closest to the oncoming steamer. He shouted a string of vile curses and fired at the coming men. One man there grabbed his chest and fell. A chorus of angry rifles answered from the steamer pecking away at the distraught slave. Bits of cloth and blood sprayed into the air behind him, and he fell lifeless into the water.

"That's all," Paul yelled to the others near him. "If you want to live, let them take you."

The steamer bumped hard against the side of the *Raven*. The name *Salem* was painted in gold lettering on the board near the wheelhouse. Men with rifles poured over the railing, pushing the blacks aside and grabbing Ben and Drayton. Others ran down into the hold. Punches from fists and rifle butts pummeled Ben and Drayton in their body and head, driving them onto the deck. Ben spun within the haze of battering, and he lost consciousness.

When he awoke, Ben's hands were tied tightly behind his back, and heavy rope wound around him holding him to the mast behind him. Another heavy rope was looped around his neck. Its other end was held by a young red-faced man to the cheers of others. The aroma of alcohol and chewing tobacco rose from his wet shirt. He felt the shoulder of another body next to his. He turned to see if it was Drayton, but something hard slammed against the side of his head, and he fell into blackness again.

Ben awoke to the rough vibrations of a steam engine in full throttle. He worked to open his eyes, but only his left would obey. His face lay against a hot iron floor. His body was intensely hot on one side. He rolled onto his back, away from the heat, looking up with his eye. A man stood above him holding a rifle.

He spit tobacco juice on Ben. "They shoulda hung you, nigger lover," he said then kicked Ben in his side. Ben heard the crack of his own ribs as he tumbled back into the blackness, wishing he could just stay there until those men went away.

The blackness drifted to gray, but he did not move. Ben forced himself to breathe shallow, to pretend sleep, to avoid another injury. His hands and feet were tied, with his hands behind him. He felt his body from the inside, searching for feeling; twitching to discover areas of pain, wondering what was broken and sorting out the varieties of pain. Then he listened. The thrumming of the steam engine continued at a fever pitch, but it was farther away now. The floor beneath his face was cool; wood maybe. Someone near him made a human sound; a moan. A body rolled against him, but no one spoke. He opened his left eye, his right refused to obey. He was in a storage room, on the steamer he assumed. The body next to his on the floor moaned again.

"Drayton," he said, but it was only a hissing whisper.

He tried to clear his throat, but the dryness was overwhelming. He forced the air out of his lungs again, sharp pains radiating from his broken ribs.

"Drayton?"

The moan turned to a cough. The body rolled on its back. Ben rolled as well and turned toward the body, straining to see in the dim light. It was Drayton. His face was a mass of lumps and bruises. Dried blood tracked from his nose and mouth. The skin around his neck was raw and speckled with blood.

"Did they try to hang you?" Ben asked.

"Hung us both, but someone stopped it. Apparently, you slept through it," Drayton said, then forced out a smile showing the gap of a freshly shattered tooth amid lips caked with blood.

They both grunted and moaned as they worked to sit up, with backs against the bulkhead.

"Where are the slaves?" Ben asked.

"Still on the schooner. Locked down in the hold. Hatches battened. Terrified. I think the steamer is towing it."

"Chester?"

"Don't know, Ben. He was with us a while, taking punches too. He kept telling them he was only the cook. They didn't bring him in here."

"Did that man at the railing die?"

"Think so, but I think no more."

"What makes you think that?"

"One of them gave the old man a head count. Seventy-seven. All of the poor bastards are going back to their owners."

Ben whispered, "Jesus Christ. What have we done to them?"

April 18th, 1848. The Potomac River

"We've passed Alexandria," a man said outside the door, talking to someone else.

Inside the storage room on the steamer *Salem,* Ben and Drayton exchanged glances in the dim light.

"I say we hang 'em now. Let's go to the docks with their god damned bodies hanging at the bow."

"They're going to jail," said another man. "We are a posse, not a lynch mob."

"To hell with you!" yelled another man. "Hang the bastards! God damned abolitionists stealing our niggers.

The sounds of a struggle reverberated through the door. A body was slammed against the door.

Ben tensed and leaned forward. His eyes fixed on the cabin door. A gunshot exploded near the door.

"I said, they're going to jail."

Muttering of several voices faded away from the door. Ben relaxed his shoulders and leaned against the wall, letting out a long slow breath. An hour later the steam engine slowed and then stopped, then the hull thumped hard, and the ship was still. Moments later a key was slid into the door lock and the door swung open. Several men surged in to grab Ben and Drayton.

The early morning sun burned into Ben's eye. He shut it and bent down his head against the brightness.

"Yeah! Hang your head you son of a bitch!" a man yelled.

Several fists pummeled against Ben's face and shoulders as he was dragged through the grabbing mob of men smelling of sweaty wool, burned tobacco, and whiskey. Ben heard the high-pitched yell of a voice not yet broken into manhood and a cold hard object jammed against his skull. Warm blood sprayed behind his left ear and ran down his neck. His knees buckled.

"Hold him up! Hit him again, Bobby."

The pain exploded in his head where he was already hit, and he fell.

Ben felt heat close to his face and opened his eye. A bright flame was held close by a man wearing a round mirror on his forehead. The focused light was painful. Ben pushed it away.

The man with the lantern and strange mirror stepped back, chuckling.

"Thought you were dead for a while there, mister. I was running out of silk thread to sew you up."

Ben reached up to his face and head. Bandages wrapped around his skull and over his left eye. He tried to sit up.

"No. Don't try that, mister," the man said.

Ben managed to get a leg over the side of the cot and rise up on his elbow. His brain spun viciously. Lightning bolts of pain shot through his skull, back, and groin. He vomited in heaving spasms driving him beyond endurance.

"Damn it," the man said, "I told you not to sit up."

"Ben. Ben. Try to open your eyes." The voice sounded muttered from yards away. Ben took in a deep breath, the cool air rushing in as if he was surfacing from a deep swim. Cold water dripped on his right eyelid, tracing down the side of his head. A hand slipped under his head, raising it up. A chilled metal rim touched his lips.

"Try to sip some broth, Ben."

Thin cold broth, greasy and tasteless except for salt dripped into his mouth. His tongue drew it in through dry, cracked lips. He swallowed and opened his mouth for more. He drew in a full swallow, but his stomach cramped as soon as the broth arrived and tried to send it back. Ben rolled on his back, exhausted from the effort. More water trickled down onto his right eye. He managed to open his left.

Drayton sat over him in faint lamplight coming from a distance. He held a battered tin cup to Ben's lips. Ben swallowed three more times, then Drayton pulled the cup away from him and set it on the floor and Ben laid his head back on a lumpy pillow. Drayton brought a wet rag over Ben's face and dripped liquid onto his right eyelid.

"It's badly swollen," Drayton said, "but the solution is clearing the matting that formed in the lashes. You should be able to open it."

"That solution will work," another voice said. "I've patched up many a brawler at my tavern."

Ben's voice barely scraped out of his throat. "Who's that?"

"Eric Little," the voice said.

Drayton helped Ben to sit up. "We're in prison, Ben," he said.

The room walls were made of stone blocks on three sides, slightly more than a man's length between the sides, and half again that far from back to front. Stacked bunk beds stood against each block wall. A small barred window sat high in the rear wall showing a glimpse of a late evening cloudy sky through dirty glass. The front was a wall of iron bars, a portion of its center showing the outline of a doorway ending at a key box four feet from its hinges.

Ben worked to open his right eye, peering into the dimness and the walkway outside the cell where the lamp hung. A desk stood below the light where a uniformed guard sat reading a newspaper, holding it up toward the flame. "Jail?"

Drayton handed Ben the cup. "Prison."

"The Blue Jug, itself," Eric said from the lower bunk on the opposite wall.

"Bailed out Edward from here," Ben said, his voice becoming more fluid.

Drayton stepped to the bars. "Pulaski is conscious now, guard. Can we have some food for him?"

The guard cleared his throat. "Meals are over. He'll get one in the morning."

As Drayton turned back from the bars, the light illuminated his swollen face and lips, and the bandage around his forehead. He limped to the rear bunk and gingerly set himself down.

Ben watched his movements. "Do *I* look that bad?"

Drayton moaned softly as he leaned back against the wall. "Worse. Much worse."

"You both look like walking dead," Eric said. "I heard you were almost hung a couple times. It was all the police could do to get you up here alive. The whole town rioted."

Ben turned to face Eric. "Rioted?"

"For three days, Pulaski. Slave owners broke in and smashed or burned anything that they thought was connected to abolitionists."

Ben held up his hand. "I'm not an abo—"

Drayton leaned forward and pointed at Ben. "Oh, for God's sake, Man. Admit what you are! There's no hiding it now."

Eric chuckled. "Hell, the *Raven* is famous. The angel ship they called her a couple days, but not now."

Ben carefully felt his swollen eyebrow and the bulge around his right eye. "Days? How long has it been...since we were caught?"

"Five days, Ben," Drayton said.

"Five days...five days...what of the slaves? Did any escape?"

"Only the one they killed," Drayton said. "Most of the others are being sold into the deep south. There have been auctions on street corners. Traders from Louisiana and Georgia are buying them almost cheap. Prices for runaways drop."

"I know the Edmonson girls," Eric said. "Like all the masters who had slaves on the *Raven*, they want them sold away cause they don't trust them now, want them punished."

"So why are you in here?" Ben asked.

"Her master stood Mary Edmonson up on the back of his wagon to auction her off, and when the bids came in low, he ripped her clothes off her."

Ben shook his head. "It's all our fault. We caused this. But how does that get you in jail, Eric?"

"I jumped up on the wagon and put my coat around her. I sort of punched her master."

Drayton turned his face toward the darkness.

Tears slipped down Ben's face. "What became of her?"

"A man from a church bought her and her sister Emily. Took them to New York that afternoon, I heard."

"And the rest? Do you know?"

Eric sighed. "Louisiana and Georgia, mostly. Cotton and sugar plantations."

Drayton turned his face back toward the light. "Paul Jennings and Paul Edmonson were released. The slave owners said we talked them into it, and I let them think it. Chester was released, too, since he was just the cook. This is all on you and me Ben. They may hang us yet."

Ben nodded his head and laid back onto his bunk. "Just as well."

The next morning an elderly black man in a tattered uniform coat ladled a meager porridge between the bars dropping it into the prisoners' metal pans.

He whispered to Eric, "Your attorney is getting permission to see you."

"I don't have an attorney," Eric said. "I don't even know an attorney, but let him come."

"I don't do no letting, Mister Little, but I'll do what I can for you. I'm Albert. Regina is my granddaughter."

The old man moved quickly away when the guard returned, smelling of fried meat and fresh coffee. "Get on to your duties, old man."

Eric whispered to Ben and Drayton, "Regina is my cook at the tavern. She is...well...um...she lives with me."

The guard stood in front of the bars. He struck a match on the coarse iron to light his cigar. He stood there a moment blowing smoke into the cell. "Some of those slaves came out of Alexandria. That's Virginia. I hear Virginia law says a man who steals slaves can be hung." He chuckled and sat in his chair at his desk.

Three hours later a man in a tweed suit and matching overcoat walked up to the guard, handing him a slip of paper. "I need to go inside the cell to speak with my clients."

The guard held the paper close to his face under the lamp. "Says you are to speak with your clients, and I am to allow you that. Doesn't say anything about you going inside. Talk through the bars."

The gentleman let out a long slow breath as he stared at the guard who ignored him, then stepped to the bars, with the jailer coming close behind him, and addressed Ben and Drayton. "Good morning. I am Mr. David A. Hall. Some mutual friends have asked me to represent you. Is that satisfactory to you?"

All three men quickly agreed.

Mr. Hall turned to Eric. "Apparently, you do not need representation, Mr. Little. The complainant is amenable to withdrawing his charges. I understand his...manager...frequents your tavern, where he has a sizable account balance. I am informed that if the balance goes away, so do you."

"It is gone as of this moment," Eric said.

"I will pass that message along. Now, Misters Drayton and Pulaski, my first effort on your behalf is to clarify the origin of your passengers. Some originated in Alexandria, but nonetheless, made their way to Washington City, where they boarded your ship."

Hall turned his face toward the jailer. "Unless we are to be wed, sir, kindly back away from my buttocks."

The jailer glared but took two steps back. Hall returned his attention to Ben and Drayton.

"There is a strong difference of opinion regarding the significance of their place of ownership versus the actual point of their departure with you. This will likely take several days to resolve. I will be back after that." He turned to walk away.

Ben gripped the bars. "Is there anything you can do for the slaves being sold?"

Hall stopped. "I dare not touch that issue. It will surely alienate the judge."

Drayton reached between the bars and grabbed his coat. "Don't you need to hear our facts?"

Mr. Hall patted the man's arm and smiled. "Your facts will be your intentions." He pointed at the window. "The facts out there are that you attempted to take away seventy-seven legal slaves without their owners' permission and were caught in the act. Those are the facts I must deal with right now. And my first obligation is to prevent you two from hanging."

April 22nd, 1848. Lapidum, Maryland

Sonja was making up her bed when someone knocked on her front door. She glanced out her bedroom window and saw a horse tied out front and the back of a man in a dark suit standing on the porch looking out at the river.

She spoke as she opened the front door. "No one can ever resist the view from our porch, Anthony." She did not offer a smile, but only cold eyes. "What has happened?"

"Why must you suspect something has happened, Sonja?"

"Because you are here in the morning, and you rode a horse. Your foot must be killing you. Come inside."

"I only rode from Port Deposit, so I could cross Dr. Archer's bridge near the grist mill."

He eased himself into Ben's favorite chair and cleared his throat. Sonja crossed her arms and gave him her focused attention.

"There has been a problem in Washington—"

"What is it, Anthony?"

He released a deep breath. "They have been caught."

Sonja's hand flew up to her mouth.

"They were trapped in a cove in southern Maryland and taken back to Washington City."

"Where are they now, Anthony?"

"Prison."

Tears flooded across her steel eyes and she straightened her back.

"There will be a trial, Sonja. Hopefully, it will not be quick. Unfortunately, it will not be quick."

"We need to go to Washington," she said. "I will get Alisha to help her pack. Will you go with us?"

"No, Sonja. Nor should you. The act triggered three

days of riots in Washington. Two slaves and a free black man were hanged. An abolitionist newspaper office was destroyed, and the editor – a good friend – was badly beaten. Only the police kept him from being murdered."

"So, I can just–"

"You cannot, Sonja. You will endanger yourself and your daughter. You could even present an opportunity to certain men to use you as bait to lure Ben out of prison...and into a mob noose."

"But...but...I must–"

"You must stay here, and watch over your daughter and yourself. The name Pulaski is almost as well-known there as Satan. The word is spreading quickly. The men at the line will soon know. We must warn your canallers. Perhaps halt any more coming back from Pennsylvania for a while. Can they stay at York Furnace?"

"I...I...don't know. Probably."

"One of your barges is in the holding pond down at the lockhouse now. It is waiting below the dock and riding high in the water, so it is empty and waiting to go north. Maybe you should go on it to York Furnace."

"I will stay here, Anthony. If our barges are in danger, so is our house. The slave chasers know we are here, as well."

She walked out onto the porch, looking across the river, wiping her eyes with a handkerchief. Across the canal, four horsemen rode together coming up the towpath. They stopped to stare at the Pulaski home. Anthony stepped beside her.

"They are already here," she said.

Anthony placed his hand gently on her shoulder. "Yes. They are here, but that is as it should be."

She turned on him with fire in her eyes, but he only smiled.

"I knew you would stay. Those men are dedicated to our cause, and they can shoot quite well. With your permission, they will stay in your barn for a while, in the bunkhouse."

She took in a deep breath. "Thank you, Anthony. Would you kindly send one of them on to York Furnace, to let the Bookers know what has happened?"

Anthony waved to the men, who kicked their horses into trots along the towpath to the Lapidum swing bridge. After a quick conversation between Anthony and one of the riders, the man wheeled his horse around and returned to the towpath, heading north. The remaining three tipped their hats in turn at Sonja and lead their horses into the barn.

Catherine Price nearly trotted up the lane to the Pulaski home. Worry etched deeply on her face.

"What is it, Sonja?" she asked.

Mac McMallery had seen the horsemen and left his blacksmith shop, coming only a few paces behind Catherine, wearing the same expression on his face.

"You have good friends," Anthony said.

She gave him a faint smile. "You among them, Anthony. Although I have cursed you many times for being in Ben's life."

He chuckled. "Sometimes Camilla says the same thing about our Ben."

Washington City Prison

"Meat day," Albert said sticking his ladle into the large pot he carried into the walkway.

The jailer craned his head. "Bring that here, boy."

The jailer inspected the contents of the pot, then reached into the pot with his hand and pulled out two pieces of pork and laid them on his desk.

"Go on now. Feed 'em, but not Little. He's leaving shortly. He can get his food outside."

Ben and Drayton held their tin pans out for the ladle while the jailer scrutinized the act.

"Just one scoop each, boy."

Albert filled the ladle with as much gruel as it would hold and dropped it into the waiting pan each time.

The jailer chewed the meat, smacking his lips and licked his fingers. "Go on, boy, you got others to feed." He stood, wiping his fingers on his uniform pants, taking down a ring of keys from a peg on the wall and approached the cell.

"You people got this whole area to yourselves. There

ought to be twenty-four men shoved into these four cells here, but the sheriff is afraid one of the other prisoners would kill one of you – or both of you. Not that I would give a shit if they did."

He pulled a folded paper from his uniform coat and slid one of the keys into the lock on the cell door. "Step back. All of you. Stand in front of your bunks."

He opened the door just far enough for one man to exit. "Come on out, Little. I got your release papers."

A smile flashed on Little's face. "Great! I didn't see them delivered. Must have dozed. When did they come?"

The jailer grinned. "Yesterday morning."

Little froze in his step, facing the jailer. The jailer stood nose to nose with Little and kept grinning.

"Go on. Do something, nigger lover."

The jailer held the papers away at arm's length. Little reached out and plucked the papers as he moved to the center of the walkway.

"I will send you food from the tavern," Little said to Ben and Drayton.

The jailer locked the cell door and spoke to Little's back. "And I will enjoy eating it."

In the early afternoon, a messenger dashed into the area and spoke quietly to the jailer, then walked away. The jailer stood, buttoning his coat and straightening his cap. Seconds later a tall man entered the area, dressed in a perfectly pressed suit and holding a top hat, escorted by a captain of the police who addressed the jailer.

"Bentley, this is Senator Charles Sumner. He is to have complete access to the prisoners."

Bentley saluted the officer, "Yes, sir. Certainly, sir," then bowed to the Senator.

The senator acknowledged Bentley. "Kindly go away for a few minutes and give us some privacy."

Once alone with Ben and Drayton, Sumner spoke to them.

"This has all become a tragedy, gentlemen."

They only nodded their heads in agreement but said nothing.

"There is very little that can be done outside the law. Washington is slave territory and, well, you were caught with the slaves on your ship. There are some of us that wish you released, but we do not have such authority publicly or legally. What we can do we have done. We have arranged for your counsel, Mr. Hall, to be joined by a Mr. Horace Mann, a representative from my state of Massachusetts who comes with excellent legal abilities."

Sumner glanced around the area then continued.

"Gentlemen, we have collected sufficient funds to assure your continued legal representation at the highest level possible. Mr. Drayton, arrangements have been made to see to the support of your family in Philadelphia. A friend known to all three of us is seeing to the safety of your families. Mr. Pulaski, I understand that our mutual friend has personally visited your home in Maryland with well-armed like-minded men."

Ben smiled. "Thank you for telling me that, Senator."

"For me as well," Drayton said. "Do you hear what our chances may be?"

"I'm sorry to have to tell you, Mr. Drayton, but your situation is grim. Your only avenue is proper legal defense. As for us, those who came together at Faneuil Hall, we will make every private entreaty possible – that is where the greatest leverage lies."

He shook their hands, then left.

Ben and Drayton fell into silence, lost in their own thoughts.

Late in the afternoon, the evening meal was brought by a young black man.

Ben held out his tin plate. "Where is Albert?"

The young man only frowned and shook his head, rolling his eyes back toward the watching jailer.

"Go on, boy. You're done here," Bentley said with his eyes on Ben and a smile on his lips.

Two days later, Eric Little arrived in front of the cell carrying two parcels. One he handed to Bentley as they exchanged a short whispered conversation. Bentley stuffed his mouth with food from his parcel and moaned with satisfaction, then nodded toward the cell. Little stepped to the cell and passed the second parcel.

"Open it later. Mr. Hall tells me he is being denied

permission to see you." He glanced back at Bentley then returned his attention to Ben and Drayton. "His captain drinks at my tavern. For now, he drinks for free and his dog Bentley gets fed by Regina's wonderful cooking." He peeked back again and whispered, "She pisses in his sandwich, then drizzles vinegar on it. The bastard loves it."

"What of the slaves?" Drayton asked.

Little hesitated. "Most were sold to the deep south."

Ben whispered, "God forgive us."

Little whispered. "I will send someone back to pick up your trash. Do not leave anything for the jailer."

An hour later, as Bentley dozed in his chair, Ben and Drayton finally opened the parcel. It was a challenge to wait with the smell of fresh bread and fried meat seeping through the paper wrapping. They shoved pieces of food in their mouths and scrambled through the notes and newspapers included below the food. Ben stopped chewing and ripped open a small envelope.

> *Dearest Ben,*
>
> *I wish I could come see you, but Anthony strongly advises me against traveling to Washington. Alisha and I are well here at the house in Lapidum. We are blessed with old and new friends ensuring our safety, but I am not sure it is necessary. The stories of you in the newspapers are frightening. Please send me word about you soon.*
> *— Sonja*

Ben sighed and smiled. Drayton also held a small letter, pressed tightly against his chest. Ben cleared his throat. "Is your family well?"

Drayton smiled. "As much as possible under the circumstances."

He picked up another small envelope and pulled a note from it, then placed his hand over his mouth. He handed the note to Ben and turned away to face the wall, his shoulders shaking.

Alexandria is not the incident origin. Virginia law does not apply. It is not a capital offense. – D.H.

Ben leaned back on his bunk bed and released a long slow breath.

Drayton turned back, wiping his eyes. "There is a pencil there," he said, "And two slips of paper."

Each man scribbled a short note and only minutes later the young man returned with a trash can. The remnants of the parcel were shoved into the can and the man left quickly as Bentley arose from his nap.

"Going to shit. Don't go away." He laughed as he walked out of the area.

While he was gone, Ben and Drayton shared sheets from a Washington newspaper spotted with meat juice.

April slid into May with their only visitor being Eric Little. During one visit while Bentley emptied a small beer jug provided with his meal, Eric whispered to Ben. "I work with Argyle. They come to me in the night. I place them in empty beer barrels and ship them to Harrisburg. I tell all my customers, Harrisburg loves Virginia Beer." He fixed Ben with his eyes. "Do you know the names of the ones you help?"

Ben frowned. "Some, but not most."

"So to you they are still cargo?"

"No..."

"I know the names of everyone, what they want to do and who they love. If you don't know their names, you don't free them, you just pass them on."

"What difference does it make, Eric?"

"All the difference there is, Ben."

Ben said nothing the rest of the day, intermittently staring up at the blue sky through the small window on the back wall.

"I never see the sun anymore," he finally said as the sky darkened.

That night Ben lay on his bunk bed staring up at the few stars visible through the window. He mumbled to himself, chanting names at odd intervals between periods of silence. He could only remember a few that had gone on, and the names of people who had died helping him, and he wept.

June 2nd, 1848. Lapidum, Maryland

> Slave Stealing Case—The correspondent of the Sun, says:
>
> The several cases against Drayton, Pulaski and English for illegally transporting slaves on the schooner Raven, whose capture caused three days of rioting in this city, have been disposed of finally with regard to seventy-seven cases of theft. Mr. English, being only the cook aboard the schooner, was found not guilty and released. Under Virginia Law such theft is punishable by death, however the origin of the crime was declared as the docks of Washington City, rather than Alexandria. As such, the culprits were found guilty of all charges and sentenced to imprisonment in the Washington City Penitentiary for seven years.

Sonja crushed the *Cecil Whig* newspaper and threw it into the blackness of the cold stove. Catherine Price sat nearby with her eyes fixed on Sonja.

"I am so sorry to bring this to you, Sonja, but when I saw it mentioned Ben and the *Raven*..."

Tears streamed down Sonja's cheeks. "Thank you for bringing it, Catherine. I needed to know. Was that this week's paper?"

"No. It came out last week, but was just brought this afternoon by one of the barges."

Sonja rose and stepped out onto the porch, staring beyond the canal and over the river.

"Oh, Ben," she muttered.

Catherine spoke several times behind her, but Sonja

did not respond from her trance. Catherine gently patted her shoulder and walked past her down the steps.

"I will keep Alisha with us a while," she said as she walked away.

Sonja blinked her eyes and called out to Catherine, "No, that isn't necessary. Please send her home. I need to tell her."

Sonja was still standing on the porch when Alisha ran up the Pulaski lane. Alisha's eyes were wide and her face full of questions and concern.

"Are you all right, Momma?"

"Yes, dear. Come up and sit with me."

"What is it?" she asked mounting the steps.

Sonja patted the chair next to the one she had taken. As Alisha sat down, Sonja took her hands and leaned close to her.

"Your father has been caught trying to help slaves escape from Washington City and was put in jail for a while...now he has been sent to prison."

"How long will he be there, Momma?"

"...S-s-s...Seven... years."

"...He won't be home for seven years?"

Alisha stared into Sonja's eyes a long silent moment, then a frown wrinkled her brow and tears filled her eyes. Sonja and Alisha squeezed their hands together, looking at one another but only seeing the blur of their own tears. Minutes passed without speaking, and they finally released their grips, feeling the pins in their fingers returning from numbness.

"Can we visit him in prison?" Alisha asked.

"I would expect we could, dear."

After a cold supper, the two began packing for their trip to Washington.

"Shall I pack like I did when we ran away, Momma?" Alisha asked from her bedroom, her voice echoing through the front room to her mother's room.

Sonja raised her head and spoke to the ceiling. "Take what you can fit into your bag. It will be hot there."

Glass shattered in the front room. Sonja glanced out of her bedroom and spotted a large rock lying on the braided rug, surrounded by glass shards sparkling in the lamplight. A man's voice yelled in the darkness outside. She dashed to her dresser and pulled out the revolver Ben had given her, checked the cylinders by the lamp, then charged to the front door and out onto the porch. The light from the house illuminated two men standing in the front yard. One was close to the porch and the other farther down the slope toward the canal.

"What the hell is wrong with you?" Sonja yelled, holding the pistol at her side within the folds of her skirt.

"You nigger lovers!" the nearest man shouted. His stance was awkward, weaving on his feet.

"You're drunk, mister. Get out of my yard."

"All you Pulaskis are nigger lovers. Hiding them in your barges. I know. I seen that. I seen your drunken son on the barge that burned."

"Shut up, George!" the other man shouted.

George waved away the comment. "Don't worry, Sammy," then he wagged his finger at Sonja. "Your man ain't around, woman. They put his nigger loving ass in prison. Read it in the paper. Everybody knows about it."

"Get the hell off my property," Sonja said.

"A woman don't own property," he sneered. "A woman is property. Maybe I'll come sit with you a spell." He took a sip from a bottle in his hand. "Your man's in prison and your sons are soldiering or drinking somewhere else."

He moved closer to the porch. Sonja pushed the pistol in front of her, pointing it in his direction.

"You stay away, or I'll shoot."

"Now woman, you wouldn't do that to old–"

The night air ripped apart with the flash and explosion from the pistol. Burning gunpowder singed the thighs of his trousers and dirt jumped into the air behind him.

Sonja raised the barrel at his face. "If you come any closer, I will send you to hell!"

"Let's get out of here, George," Sammy pleaded.

George rocked side to side where he stood. "Maybe I'll come back some other night when you are more sociable," he said.

"If you do, I will shoot you on sight, without

warning."

Jesse Price and Mac came trotting up the lane, each carrying a rifle.

"What happened?" Mac yelled.

George turned to face them. "We're leaving. We're leaving. Just a little misunderstanding with the lady of the house."

Both men aimed at George as he walked down the slope where he and Sammy waded across the canal and mounted their horses on the towpath. Still faintly visible in the lamplight from the house, George turned his horse north and waved. Mac pointed his rifle just above the man's head and fired. George's hat jumped from his head. He slapped his hand onto the top of his head and kicked his horse into a gallop as his hat sailed into the river beyond.

Jesse smiled at Mac. "Damn good shot, Mac."

Mac spit in the direction of the canal. "I was aiming lower," he said, then turned to face Sonja, his bushy red hair and beard orange in the lamplight. "I hear rumors those two started the fire on the *Wilhelmina*," he said.

Sonja brought her empty hand up to her mouth and touched her lips. "I am so glad you told me that, Mac. I had been afraid that maybe Aaron had started it."

Alisha ran out from the house and wrapped her arms around Sonja.

"I don't think Aaron would have let that happen," Mac said, "even full of whiskey. He just did what I did when I lost my Sally. Can't imagine losing a child too."

Sonja squeezed Alisha closer to her and shook her head 'no' in silence.

"Would you gentlemen care to come in for some coffee?" Sonja asked.

Both men shrugged a polite 'no.'

"I need to report to the boss," Jesse said. "She'll be worried."

"And I've got a horseshoe that isn't finished," Mac added as both men headed back down the lane.

In the morning, Sonja brought a hammer, tacks and a small piece of canvas to cover the broken window pane. She closed up the house and then she and Alisha placed their traveling bags on the buggy. Jesse Jr. had agreed to ride along to bring the buggy back from the railroad station in Havre de Grace.

They rode in silence until they passed through the canal basin and entered the town.

"You're not old enough to drive a buggy," Alisha blurted out.

"Can too, 'Lisha. Tended mules up to Wrightsville and back six times now. Got paid for it, too."

"Did not."

"Did too."

Sonja let out a heavy sigh. "You two stop arguing."

At the Philadelphia, Wilmington and Baltimore railroad station, Sonja brought down their bags and sent Jesse Jr. away with the buggy. Alisha kept her eyes glued to his back as he left. As he turned the corner onto Adams Street, he looked back and waved. Alisha stuck her tongue out at him and then pirouetted around with her nose up, giving him her back.

Following the recommendation of George Milton, Sonja sent a telegram to the Brown's Indian Queen Hotel in Washington, requesting a room for her and Alisha. Soon after, she and her daughter boarded the train to Baltimore. Three hours later in Baltimore, Sonja hired a porter to carry their bags to the Baltimore and Ohio train to Washington. The air over the train station was filled with steam and coal clouds seeping within the June humidity. Sonja tipped the man ten cents as he wiped the sweat streaming like tears down his face and dripping from his chin. It was another hour sitting in the railcar before the train finally pulled away from the city, creating a faint breeze whispering in through the open windows. The train to Washington made a dozen stops along the forty miles of track before finally arriving nine hours later at the Pennsylvania Avenue Station of the B&O Railroad.

The evening air outside the station was saturated with smells of burnt coal, horse manure, and the fetid aroma of swamps. No breeze stirred. Even in early June, the heat from the daytime radiated from the block buildings, driving rivulets of perspiration down Sonja's back inside her dress. She had a porter call for a cab and gave him a five cent tip. The driver hefted their bags onto the luggage rack and assisted them into the cabin, then climbed up onto his station. Even as the carriage bounced over cobblestones, Alisha's head leaned against Sonja's shoulder in sleep. In only a few minutes the carriage pulled in front of Brown's Hotel farther down Pennsylvania Avenue. The driver pulled down their luggage and then assisted them out of the carriage. He did a quick rotation on the sidewalk pointing north then south, calling out the directions to Congress and the President's home from the hotel.

Inside, another porter accepted her bags as she registered, entering Mr. & Mrs. Jundt and daughter. The desk clerk scanned the lobby then focused his attention on Sonja.

"Will, um, Mr. Jundt be coming in?"

"He has work down the street, and will join us later."

"Yes madam," he said then snapped his fingers and called "Boy."

A middle-aged black man rushed from his seat in a nearby alcove and picked up their bags.

"Room 432," he said and handed the key to Sonja. "I will have another key available for your husband when he arrives," the clerk said.

"He...he may have to work late," she said.

"Yes, madam," he said and turned his attention to other guests.

Sonja and Alisha followed the porter up the wide staircase to the fourth floor and then down a carpeted hall to the ornate door displaying an engraved brass plaque numbered 432. As soon as she unlocked the door, the porter rushed in to set the bags at the foot of the bed then returned quickly to the hall, standing outside the door.

"Do you wish to have a waiter sent up from the dining room, madam?" he asked.

Her shoulders sagged, and she sighed, "Oh yes, please."

"Yes madam," he said bowing at the waist and stepping back. "Chambermaid comes at seven o'clock unless you wish her to come later, madam."

Sonja reached out to hand him a dime. "Thank you," she said.

After she and Alisha had eaten in the room and the cart taken back by the waiter, Alisha washed her face at the basin and slipped into bed. Within seconds she was sound asleep. Sonja sat in one of the two padded chairs placed in front of the empty fireplace and looked at the note given her by George Milton.

Mr. David Hall, Esq.
1200 2nd Avenue, Northwest
Washington City, District of Columbia

Then she pulled her purse close and examined its contents, carefully counting the currency and coins.

"I hope I have brought enough," she said to herself.

She then washed off at the basin, put on a nightgown, then put out the lamp and lay on the bed. She lay there, unable to sleep, while the clock on the mantel struck ten, eleven, and twelve. Shortly after midnight a weak breeze floated through the open window and cooled the room. Sonja drifted off to sleep in a maze of worries.

The next morning, Sonja and Alisha were leaving the room as the chambermaid arrived. As they passed the front desk, the clerk called to her.

"Oh, Mrs. Jundt, the key for your husband is still on its hook. Did he not come in at all?"

Sonja grit her teeth then forced a smile.

"Yes, he did, poor soul, but it was so late he came straight up to the room. I am having lunch with him later and can give him his key then."

She held out her hand.

The clerk hesitated "Um...madam, we generally keep the keys here at the desk and guests ask for them as they return."

"Yes, but my husband is very busy and has only minutes to sleep."

"Is he working for Congress? They have been very

busy lately."

"No..." she said. "He is... with the police."

"Oh, by all means, madam. Here, please pass the key to him for me, my name is Harold Stilwell."

Sonja gave him an empty smile as she accepted the key, and motioned Alisha to join her heading for the dining room.

Alisha stepped close to Sonja and whispered, "Why are we using our runaway name and saying Papa is with the police?"

"Your last name is not respected here, because of your father's actions. Also, I need to keep nosy men from thinking about an unescorted woman and why her husband is invisible."

As they were seated at a linen-covered table beneath an elaborate crystal chandelier, the porter who carried their baggage the night before approached the table. He met Sonja's eyes with intent, then bowed and placed an envelope face down on the edge of the table. He bowed again and walked away. Sonja turned over the envelope to read its addressee:

Mrs. Benjamin Jundt

Sonja glanced around the dining room for the porter or anyone who might have their eyes fixed on her, but saw no one remarkable. She opened the envelope to find a penciled telegram.

> I would have been happy to assist your travel. They will not let you see him. Do not waste your time with Hall. See Mr. Eric Little at the Andrew Jackson Tavern. He is a friend of Argyle. – A.R.

Palmetto Haven, South Carolina

Lydia Binterfield's laughter echoed through the mansion halls, sounding more like barroom guffaws than laughter from a southern lady. Servants in rooms along the hallway exchanged quick glances and doubled their efforts on their tasks.

"Horatio," she yelled, "Come in here at once!"

Horatio Cuttingham dropped the biscuit he was munching in the kitchen and stepped lively to the main drawing room. He found the mistress of the house almost disheveled in her favorite padded wingback chair, tears streaming down her perfect cheeks. Two locks of raven black hair, oddly loosened from her head, dangled in front of her eyes.

She flashed him a genuine smile that crinkled the corners of her eyes, and then released more laughter.

"Look," she said, handing him a newspaper. "Look at the article about slave stealers."

Cuttingham took the newspaper and scanned the front page until he found the notice. Quickly reading it, he then lowered the paper and spoke through a wide grin.

"Good God in heaven, madam. It couldn't have happened to a more deserving scoundrel."

Lydia continued to laugh, pressing one hand against her side and standing up, gasping for air. She stepped to the liquor cabinet and filled a glass with brandy. She drank it down and refilled it.

She held her glass in the air. "To Captain Benjamin kiss-your-ass Pulaski. May you rot in that prison."

She drank the glass empty and laughed again.

Cuttingham grinned at her and kept the paper wadded in his grip as he placed his fists on his hips and performed a quick Irish jig.

Lydia held out her hand. "Give me back the front page. I want to read it again." She held it up to read as Cuttingham scanned other pages for more information.

She spread the page before her. "I shall have this mounted and framed...and nailed over the mantel—"

"Wait, madam. There is more you will want to know."

She looked at him, still smiling, her violet eyes holding the question.

He read to her. "The notorious schooner *Raven*, vessel of the dastardly slave stealers Pulaski and Drayton, has been impounded by the police commissioner of Washington City and will be auctioned off to the highest bidder on Wednesday, the twenty-first instance of this month. Proceeds will be donated to the District's Widows and Orphans Fund."

"Horatio," she said, "go into town and buy us tickets to Washington. Steamship or train makes no difference. Whichever will get us there the quickest. I will have that ship, if for no other reason than to use it as my chamber pot."

⸺⸱ᨈᨑᨑᨑᨑ⸱⸺

The Red House Tavern, Georgetown, South Carolina

Joshua Dunkin walked into the tavern and elbowed his way through a knot of arguing men standing in front of the bar.

"Whiskey," he said to the barkeep.

When the whiskey was poured, Joshua sipped at it then motioned toward the small crowd and asked, "What's all the blather about?"

"Pulaski and the *Raven*. They're slave stealers."

"What?"

"Yep. Got caught at it trying to steal half the slaves out of Washington City itself. Caught him with two hundred slaves."

"They hang him?"

"Nah. The newspaper from Charleston says he was sentenced to seven years in prison."

Joshua slapped his hand on the bar. "Damn the man! He took my nigger on consignment."

The barkeep spoke to the small group of men and motioned toward Joshua. "He lost a slave to that Pulaski, too."

Joshua was handed a beer and patted on the shoulder, then pulled into their group.

"Shoulda hung the man," Joshua said loudly to the cheers of the angry men gathered around him. "And burned that damned ship!"

Renowitz Manor, Philadelphia

Anthony Renowitz folded the newspaper in his lap. "Damn," he said.

"Anthony," Camilla said from the next chair. "Please, watch your language."

Anthony stood and paced the floor.

"What is it dear?" she asked.

"I don't know what else to do. Sonja Pulaski has gone off to Washington, and I already know they will not let her see Ben...and now the Washington police commissioner is having Ben's ship auctioned off to the highest bidder."

"I thought you had already arranged to buy it as scrap?"

"That approach is now water under the bridge, dear. And I do not know what to do."

"You must go to Washington, dear. Speak with your friends there."

"My 'friends' there told me to stay away. Especially after those riots when Ben was first caught."

"It has been almost two months and our friend, Sonja Pulaski, is now walking around that town? How can that be safe?"

"Well, at least she is using her maiden name, Camilla."

"And how will that keep her safe as she pleads to visit Benjamin Pulaski, the notorious slave stealer in a slave city?"

Anthony sighed. "Yes. You are right. I need to go there. I will leave in the morning."

Camilla set aside her sewing and stood next to him,

then kissed his cheek. "I will start your packing."

She smiled and walked away saying, "You always forget something."

<hr>

The Law Office of David Hall, Washington City

"I am sorry, Mrs. Pulaski, but the prison is not allowing any visitors, except law officers and Congressmen. And I urge you to keep your real name secret while you are here in Washington. There has been serious violence since your husband was returned."

"What else can you do?"

"The fact that I was able to convince the judge to recognize Washington as the scene of the crime saved your husband's life. There are appeals in process, but many of the judges hold slaves themselves. They are not warm to any further leniency for your husband."

"How can a country whose states are half free of slavery, condone slavery in its very capital?"

"That is the legal situation, madam. I am sorry, but there is nothing more I can do."

"I should not have come," she said. "I was warned not to come here."

"Someone gave you sage advice madam."

She stood. "Could you arrange a carriage for me?"

"Certainly, madam. To return to your hotel and your daughter?"

She pulled a folded paper from her purse and glanced at it. "To the...Andrew Jackson Tavern."

Hall's eyes went wide, but he quickly recovered. "Yes, of course. You may wait in here until it arrives."

He withdrew, then returned after a few minutes. As he entered, he sidestepped to his desk around the chair where Sonja sat. "If you will permit me, I need to make a few notes on this case."

"Certainly," she said, then began glancing around the room at its sparse decorations. She focused on a small painting of a bearded man with no mustache. The man's nose and eyes were similar to Hall's. Sonja cleared her throat, and when Hall looked up from his papers, she motioned her head toward the painting.

"A relative?" she asked.

He looked at the painting then smiled at Sonja. "My grandfather."

"A lawyer as well?"

"No," he said. "A farmer of profound beliefs."

"A Friend?"

He smiled again. "People use the term Quaker as if that is our sect, but we call ourselves Friends, yes."

"And you work here, in a city; a slave city."

He brought his hands together on his desk. "One can walk among the lions, although the smart man knows when they are feeding and stays away then."

An assistant tapped the office door as he opened it. "The carriage is here, madam."

Sonja stood, then reached across the desk and offered her hand. "Thank you, Mr. Hall. Please do all you can for my husband."

After a short carriage ride, Sonja was delivered to the front of the Andrew Jackson Tavern.

"Please keep the carriage here," she said, "waiting for me...and kindly stay with it."

The driver tipped his hat to her. "Yes, madam. Those were also my instructions from Mr. Hall's assistant."

She smiled as the driver opened the tavern door for her.

"Shall I go in with you?" he asked.

"No, but thank you."

The main room was dimly lit by oil lamps and sparse narrow windows high on the wood-paneled walls. The air was saturated with a haze of tobacco smoke and reeked of burned tobacco, stale beer, and mildew. Men in suits and uniforms nodded to her as she walked to the center of the room and sat at a small table having two chairs. The bartender hustled to her, wiping his hands with a stained cloth.

"I'm sorry, madam," he said.

"Sorry about what, sir?"

"We...we um...don't usually serve ladies here."

"I don't want a drink, sir. I am here to meet with Mr. Eric Little."

He hesitated. "Is this about, um...employment, madam?"

"No. It. Is. Not. Is he here?"

"Yes. Yes, madam. Who may I say is calling?"

"...Mrs. Renowitz," she said.

The man quick-stepped to a door at the back of the room. Seconds later the door was opened by the bartender, followed by another man with silver hair. The bartender returned to his duties as the silver-haired man approached the table, smiling. He stepped beside the other chair and placed his hand on its high back, still smiling.

"I only know one man named Renowitz," he said quietly. "I have met Mrs. Renowitz and you are not her...Who are you?"

"Mrs. Benjamin Pulaski."

He shot a brief glance around the room then sat down.

"Your husband must admire you greatly, Mrs. Pulaski. You are a very brave woman."

"Mr. Renowitz suggested I see you," she said.

"For what purpose?"

"I want to see my husband."

He nodded and sighed. "That is not possible—"

"You can do nothing either?"

"It is not possible for you to visit him. Two men have already tried to see him with the intent of killing him."

Sonja caught her breath in her throat.

"He is safe and was not harmed by either of those men, Mrs. Pulaski. But, if it would satisfy you for now, I could arrange for him to see you."

<hr />

June 6th, 1848. Washington City

Sonja walked leisurely toward the stained granite monument mounted in the center of the block. She wore a new light blue satin dress with matching narrow-brimmed hat and a veil over her face. A weathered bronze plaque was attached to the front of the block engraved with past dates of forgotten deeds and names. The air was sultry, but filled with the songs of several birds in the nearby trees and carried the scent of fresh flowers. Heavy wooden benches stood on either side of the monument. The farther one held a man in a top hat and black suit, engrossed in reading his newspaper, held high in front of his face. Sonja took the closer bench and glanced up at the position of the sun, and then over to the blue tinted stone building across the street. She withdrew a small book from her purse and began reading it.

Inside the blue building, on the third floor, a prisoner moved between cells, emptying the chamber pots. Only two men resided in this section, Drayton and Pulaski. Since the trial, they had been placed in separate cells, but still held in a secluded section away from most of the others. Drayton and Pulaski slid their chamber pots to a small opening in the bars designed for the size. As the assigned prisoner pulled out the chamber pot for Ben's cell, the prisoner let a tiny cylindrical bundle roll from within his hand. Ben spotted the bundle and picked it up when he pulled his chamber pot back inside. When the single guard left the area, Ben quickly untied the bundle to find a small glass vial. Wrapped around the vial was a note.

Drink it all now. Hide the bottle. –
E.L.

Drayton watched him and whispered, "What is it?"

Ben shrugged his shoulders. Footsteps echoed in the hallway signaling the returning guard.

Ben took in a deep breath and swallowed the contents of the vial and placed it and the note in his chamber pot. As the guard resumed his chair at the small desk across the hall, Ben's stomach went into spasms. Wrenching pain shot across his abdomen. He gagged. His stomach cramped and pushed its contents up into his throat. He struggled to retain the vomit, but it spewed from his mouth even as he dashed to his chamber pot. Ben fell to his hands and knees, with his head over the chamber pot, heaving as if a monster squeezed him in a giant hand. Drayton stood at the bars that separated the two cells.

"Guard," he called.

Ben spasmed again emptying the last of his stomach contents into the pot and on the floor. He gagged on an empty throat still trying to vomit. His face turned crimson.

"My God, they've poisoned him!" Drayton cried out.

The guard rushed to the cell.

"Oh shit, what a mess in there," he said. "Orderly!" he called out.

A slave in a tattered white smock ran into the area. "You wants me take him to the infirmary, suh?"

"Where'd you come from?" the guard asked.

The slave motioned toward the direction he came. "'Nother one out there doing this too. Boss said meat poisoned."

"Well, get him out of here to the infirmary, and send someone back to clean this mess up. I'm not doing it."

The orderly escorted Ben down the halls toward the front of the building and into the infirmary. No one was in the room. He lay Ben onto a bed placed next to a low window. He patted Ben's chest.

"It be over in two shakes," he said, then pointed at the window. "When you hear the clock bell you stand at that window and look down at the street. She be in blue." Then he left, closing the door behind him.

The spasms ceased quickly, and his stomach settled. The front of his shirt was saturated. Outside a bell tolled eleven times. Ben forced himself to stand, holding on to the bed, and stepped to the window. He grabbed the bed frame to steady himself and looked out. Down below, across the street near a block monument, a woman in blue stood up and looked in his direction. She yanked off her hat and dropped it at her side, then shook her head letting golden curls cascade onto her shoulders.

"Sonja," he whispered to the glass. "Sonja." He placed his hands over his head and flat against the glass. "Sonja," he said. "Are you well? Are you well?"

The man sitting on the other bench laid down his newspaper and used his cane to step next to Sonja and looked up toward the infirmary.

"Anthony," Ben said. "Is that you, too?"

The blonde woman turned to face the man in the black suit. She slapped him so hard he dropped his cane, and his hat flew to the ground.

"Yes!" Ben yelled. Tears and laughter flowed from him. "Yes. You are well and strong. My Sonja. My Sonja," he laughed.

The door to the infirmary flew open and two guards charged in, grabbing Ben by his arms.

"If you can stand and gawk out the window," one of them said, "You can go back to your cell."

Ben continued to laugh.

"I think he's gone daft," the other guard said.

June 20th, 1858. Washington City

Anthony Renowitz stood before Sonja at the Pennsylvania Avenue train station. The steam and coal smoke drifted away in a rare Washington breeze, and the air was scented with fresh baked bread and coffee from nearby food stalls. Bright sunbeams lanced between the tree leaves outside. The hiss and chug of locomotives reverberated inside the station, like stallions eager to be away.

"A representative made the plea to President Polk, but he refused to pardon them," Anthony said.

"Was that our last hope of getting Ben out?"

"No, Sonja. The Whig Convention has recently selected Zachary Taylor as their candidate for president, and we have people close to him. True, he is from Louisiana and a slave owner himself, but he is also a war hero..."

"And that is good for Ben?"

"Ben served with distinction under Andrew Jackson. That should help our petition if Taylor is elected."

Sonja touched his arm. "You will let me know what is happening, won't you, Anthony?"

"If I hear any news of Ben I will share that with you immediately," he said.

"Do you promise me, Anthony?"

"Of course," he said through a smile. "I don't dare risk another slap."

She pressed her lips together in a reluctant smile and patted his cheek. "Will you always hold that against me?"

"No, Sonja. We both know I have deserved it for years now. I was the one who convinced Ben to sail to China with me in '39, and pulled him into this endeavor for which he now pays our price."

"Enough," she said, "or you will give me the urge to do it again."

They both chuckled as Alisha returned with a pastry from one of the food stalls.

Anthony remained at the station until Sonja's train left for Baltimore, then strolled down Pennsylvania Avenue to his Washington bank. His mute aide Jarrod stood against the bank wall waiting and fell in beside Anthony when he exited moments later. Anthony patted him on his shoulder.

"We may buy us a schooner in the morning, Jarrod, if any luck is with us."

At eight o'clock the next morning, Anthony and Jarrod walked up the ramp to the schooner *Raven*. Bidders were allowed on the ship to view its particulars before the auction. Near one of the twin wheels, an elderly man in a black suit and thin silver hair drooping from under his top hat stood in angry conversation before another suited man. The other man wore a brown suit and sported a mustache that swooped up to meet his side whiskers, but his chin was clean shaven. As Anthony and Jarrod passed the two men, words of the stilted argument drifted to their ears.

"We had an arrangement, Commissioner," the old man said." What possessed you to make a public announcement in the newspaper?"

"It was out of my hands, Mr. Dodge. Senator Hale and Mr. Davis insisted on it. They are..."

Anthony whispered to Jarrod as they walked beyond the conversation, "Looks like that Mr. Dodge thought he had this all sewed up. Hopefully, he is not prepared to pay full price. Let's have a look around Ben's other love."

The deck was spotted in dozens of places with seagull droppings and tobacco spit. The compartments below were all stripped of anything of value and reeked of the sour smell from the bilge. The iron stove and all utensils had been removed from the galley. The captain's cabin was completely bare and empty, as was the crew quarters at the bow. The deck near the bow was gouged in rectangular patterns where something had been bolted, and deep parallel drag marks ran beyond the pattern. The cordage was poor and hung limp from the masts, and the sails were absent.

Coming out of the captain's cabin, Anthony and Jarrod came face to face with a striking woman with violet eyes and black shining hair, wearing a pale green satin dress. A gentleman in a tan suit and wide planter's hat accompanied her. Unwilling to press so close to the woman in such a tight space, Anthony tipped his hat to her then withdrew with Jarrod back into the cabin to allow the couple to enter, then exited around them.

Anthony heard the woman saying, "This is where that bitch doused me with bitter cold water while I was so sick..."

Once on deck again, Anthony whispered to Jarrod, "I believe we have met the nefarious Lydia Binterfield. Mrs. Pulaski spoke quite poorly of her."

At nine o'clock, a man struck his gavel on top of an upright barrel near the stern, beginning the auction. The deck was thickly packed with people, and dozens more stood on the wharf nearby, craning to hear the auctioneer. The bidding began at a paltry one thousand dollars.

"Even in this condition, she's worth ten times that," Anthony said to Jarrod.

Mr. Dodge met each new number with a spritely raised hand until the bidding passed five thousand. Then he glared at the commissioner and shoved his way off the ship. As the bidding approached ten thousand dollars, men began walking away in small groups. At ten thousand dollars, only six men were still bidding. The man in the planter's hat raised his hand at each new number, prodded by the woman in green beside him. At fifteen thousand dollars, two of the bidders walked off the ship, shaking hands with the commissioner as they left. Another bidder left after eighteen thousand, and another after twenty.

Anthony glanced at the woman in green and sighed, then spoke out, "Twenty-five thousand."

The gavel pounded once, twice, then the woman shouted out, "Thirty!"

Anthony locked his attention on the woman's face and spoke without turning toward the auctioneer. "Thirty-five thousand," he said.

The woman glared at Anthony. "Forty thousand," she said.

Anthony frowned at his feet and released a long breath. The gavel pounded once again, paused, then pounded a second time. Anthony closed his eyes tightly, took in a deep breath and began to raise his hand.

"Forty-five thousand dollars!" Lydia shouted.

Anthony's shoulders sagged. He stood motionless for a long moment, as the auctioneer watched his every movement. He dropped his hand to his side. The auctioneer struck the barrel head. Anthony turned toward Lydia and tipped his hat, then walked toward the ramp. The gavel struck a second time. As Anthony and Jarrod walked slowly down the ramp, the gavel struck the third time. The auctioneer's cry of "Sold!" was only a muffled whimper in Anthony's ears as he mounted his carriage.

Lydia made her way down into the captain's cabin, as Horatio Cuttingham signed the promissory papers for the sale as her agent. Lydia locked the door behind her and pirouetted around the small room with her arms folded gracefully over her head. She giggled as she danced to the windows. No other ship, boat, or person had a view into the cabin. She moved to the center of the cabin and pulled up her dress and petticoat, then dropped her bloomers to the floor and stepped out of them.

She giggled again spreading her feet and leaning back facing the ceiling while releasing a great stream of piss onto the floor that lasted several long seconds. When she finished, she released a joyous sigh. Her bloomers were saturated at the edge of her puddle, so she kicked them to a corner of the room.

Minutes later, sequestered within Lydia's enclosed carriage with Horatio, she mounted him in a frenzy, yanking open his fly and bringing them both to a sweaty climax.

"Tell me again how you almost drowned Pulaski when my uncle had him tied up," she said and snickered as he repeated the details.

June 22nd, 1848. The Andrew Jackson Tavern, Washington City

Eric Little poured a dollop of brandy into his coffee and offered the bottle to Anthony who waved it away.

"No. Thank you, Eric. I had too much last night. I need to be clear headed now. Tell me again about your Italian friend."

"New acquaintance, really, Anthony."

Anthony rested his elbow on the corner of the desk. He held his pounding head in one hand and waved away the distinction with the other.

Eric gave a beaming smile. "I met him weeks ago, hiding in the basement of...well, it doesn't matter whose basement. The point is he is hiding to save his own life."

"From whom, Eric?"

"From the family of his dead friend. A friend he accidentally killed in April."

Anthony raised his head and frowned at Eric. "And this helps us how?"

"Well...well. I think first you must meet him. Then all the possibilities will be revealed."

Anthony sighed heavily and rubbed his temple. He sipped from his coffee cup. Eric handed him a sliver of tree bark.

"Here. Chew this."

Anthony squinted at the sliver. "You want me to chew tree bark."

"Yes, exactly, Anthony. It is willow. It will help your aching head to clear."

"Is this voodoo medicine?"

"No. Indian. It works. In my business, I see frequent need of it."

Anthony plucked the piece from Eric's fingertips and stuck it into his mouth.

"So I am chewing tree bark and about to visit your

mystery Italian so that all will be revealed. Eric, you sound more and more like a wizard."

Eric opened his office door and whispered, "Send in Emilio."

Eric stepped back opening the door wide, for the visitor.

Anthony sat bolt upright as he gaped at the man.

"B-b-ben? How in heaven did you get here...?" Anthony stuttered.

"Anthony," Eric said, "it is my honor to introduce Emilio Zenobi, who wishes to disappear but still live."

"He looks exactly like Ben..." Anthony said.

Emilio bowed and stepped before the table, uttering a deluge of frenetic Italian as he clasped his hands in supplication. Anthony could only stare dumbfounded at the man.

"Emilio," Eric snapped, "English, man, English."

"Si...Yes, I can speak English good," Emilio said, addressing Anthony. "Whatever you want, I can do, but I need to be in a place where the Gialanis cannot find me."

Anthony faced Eric, "The Gialanis?"

"The family of his friend. They have sworn a vendetta to kill him. Any member of that family is obligated to hunt him down."

Anthony turned back to Emilio. "And what is it you believe I want you to do?"

Eric grabbed Emilio's chin and turned his face from side to side. "Look at him, Anthony. He is the perfect replacement for Pulaski...and he is happy to serve Ben's time in prison."

Anthony's mouth flew open, and he stared at Emilio.

Eric patted Emilio's shoulder and grinned at Anthony. "This is a perfect time to do it. Emilio will be safe there, the warden and staff are changing since the city elections, and no one will be familiar with Ben."

<hr />

June 28th, 1848. Washington Penitentiary

The guard unlocked the cell door and tossed a bundle of clean clothes to Ben. From behind the guard, a prisoner brought in a bucket of warm water.

"You need to see a judge in two hours," the guard said. "I'll be back in fifteen minutes. God help you if you ain't ready."

"What about me?" Drayton asked from the next cell.

"Shut up," the guard said and walked away.

Ben turned to Drayton. "Whatever this is, I will mention your name for any leniency that may arise."

"Since the city elections some of these new guards are worse than the others," Drayton said.

Ben hurriedly washed off.

"At least Bentley is gone," Ben said as he dressed.

Fifteen minutes later, two guards arrived and shackled his hands and feet, then rushed him down the stairs to a waiting enclosed wagon. They lifted him up into the back of a black delivery wagon and shoved him inside. The door slammed shut and locked, leaving him in nearly complete darkness.

The wagon dashed off behind two trotting horses and bounced for several minutes over rough cobblestones. When the wagon stopped one of the guards yanked open the door, flooding the space with bright sunshine. Ben covered his eyes with his hands until the guards snatched them away from his face to pull him out and up a set of granite steps into a building.

The guards pulled Ben through an interior doorway. The lettering above read 'Criminal Court'. The three hurried down the hall to a large mahogany door displaying a brass plate stating 'Judge Crawford'. They entered and stepped before a reception clerk where the senior guard announced "Prisoner Pulaski for Judge Crawford."

The clerk looked up in surprise and quickly rummaged through his appointment book. He raised his face to them, peering through thick glasses.

"Um...um...you say, Pulaski?" he said. "The slave stealer?"

"Yeah, that's the one."

"He...he is not scheduled for the judge."

"Then you screwed up, sonny. The judge sent for him, and here he is."

"Please. Wait here." The clerk stood and walked to

the door to the judge's private chambers. He cleared his throat, straightened his coat and tapped on the door. When the judge answered, he opened the door and stuck his head inside. There was a mumbled conversation, ending with the judge's emphatic and loud, "No."

The clerk returned to his desk.

"He did not order this prisoner and has no intention of seeing him...or you. You may go," he said.

Once again outside, the guards rushed Ben toward the wagon where it waited down the street. As they approached, two other guards in new uniforms met them.

"You've been fired," one of the new guards said. "We got yer jobs."

The new guards took Ben by his arms and hustled him away as the other guards stood open-mouthed. The new guards pulled him to the back of the wagon, where he was shoved into the darkness. As the wagon pulled away someone near Ben opened the small rear window, flooding the interior with light. Seated on the benches was another man in prison garb with a sack over his head. Eric Little and Anthony Renowitz sat next to the man. Eric smiled at Ben.

"Hello, Ben," Anthony said and tapped the arm of the other prisoner. "This gentleman is in need of your cell for a couple years."

Ben stared in wide-eyed silence as Eric removed the sack from the other prisoner.

"Good God," Ben said. "It's like looking in a mirror."

Emilio smiled at him. "Hello," he said in perfect American.

"This man will return in your place, Ben," Eric said, "at his request."

"What about Drayton?" Ben asked.

"We haven't found a double for him, and he has informed us he wishes to continue his appeals. He says, 'each appeal is another opportunity to address the country to end slavery'."

Eric held up the sack toward Ben. "In you go."

Ben lowered his head, and Eric slipped the sack over his head.

"Drayton is a far better man than I will ever be," Ben said from within the sack.

When the prisoner was returned to Ben's cell, he stepped into the center of the cell and released a heavy sigh. He turned and faced Drayton.

Drayton stared closely at the man. After a moment of silence, he spoke loud enough for the new guard at the desk to hear him.

"Hello, Ben."

The prisoner smiled at Drayton. "Hello, Daniel," he said in perfect American.

Drayton moved to his bed and lay on his back with his hands laced behind his head, and laughed long and hard.

June 28th, Washington City

After leaving Emilio at the prison with the new guards, the wagon driver pulled into the livery stable of a prestigious mansions in Washington. The owner was a friend of Argyle. The driver opened the back door to the wagon to release its occupants. Anthony and Eric stood with wide grins, shaking hands again and gazing at Ben. Ben stood silent and wide-eyed.

"I...I can't believe this has happened," Ben said.

Eric pointed beyond the team of horses. "The driver's quarters are there. Warm water, good shaving soap, and an excellent razor await you. We have to move you out of this city immediately."

Anthony patted Ben on his shoulder. "Go, Ben. You are about to become someone else, so you must get rid of that beard."

Ben fingered his beard and muttered, "Had this twenty-five years...."

"Yes," Anthony said, "and it's a sure thing that no one but Sonja and I know what you look like under that thing."

"Your clean-shaven face will be a perfect disguise," Eric added.

As Ben made his way toward the rear of the livery, Eric whispered to Anthony, "I will let you tell him he has to go away without his family."

Anthony released a heavy breath. "It is the only way this will work, Eric."

Two hours hour later, Anthony, Eric, and Ben sat in Eric's office at the tavern, sharing a bottle of brandy. Ben gently rubbed the pale reddened face that had hidden behind his beard for years. He wore a new white shirt, brown bow tie, a tan wool suit, and a wide planter's hat. His high-top brown shoes were still stiff, and the interior seams rubbed against his ankles.

"One more toast," Anthony suggested, raising his glass.

"No, no, Anthony. I've had enough."

"Just one more," Eric said while eying Anthony.

"O.K. One more," Ben said. "Then you have to tell me what we do next."

Eric filled the glasses to the rim and raised his in salute, "To a clean escape and freedom for you."

Ben frowned. "Only for me, with all those poor people sold away because of me."

Anthony gently lifted the bottom of Ben's glass with his fingertip. "Drink up, Benjamin."

Anthony and Eric merely sipped from their glasses.

Ben put his empty glass down and covered it with his hand. "Now tell me."

"We are going to hide you in Saint Mary's County."

"There is a plantation owner that knows me, down there."

"No. No one knows you there now. The master of Gray Rocks Plantation is dead, and his younger brother who owns it now never met you," Anthony said. "You will use a different name, Ben, and you will become a new resident near Leonardtown...."

Anthony and Eric exchanged meaningful glances.

"You will be a bachelor," Anthony added.

Ben snapped his attention on Anthony. "What? How long?"

"I don't know."

"Will Sonja be told where I am and how to get to me?"

"No."

Eric drew on his cigar and looked away.

Ben sat in silence with a grim expression locked on Anthony.

"We must have everyone think you are still in prison, Ben."

"It will just be another prison without Sonja. How long?"

Anthony shook his head and stared at his drink. "Until we can get you – your double, released from prison."

"How long do you expect me to do this, Anthony?"

"If you go home, Emilio gets his own sentence for impersonating you, and you will be taken back to Washington. If Sonja visits you in southern Maryland, the same thing will happen."

"How long will it take to get my sentence changed?" Ben asked.

There was a long silence.

Anthony sighed. "At least a year."

Ben slammed his hand on the table. "A year?"

Eric pointed his finger at Ben. "You want to spend that year back in prison? Your wife won't see you there, either. You are out of prison, Benjamin, and at no small effort by us, and by people we trust who are willing to help."

"I will look for a way that Sonja can visit you," Anthony said.

Minutes slipped by without another word in the small office, Ben withdrew a pipe and patted his pockets for a tobacco pouch. Anthony pulled the pipe from Ben's mouth.

"No pipe. Nothing to suggest that you are Ben Pulaski."

Ben glared at Anthony.

"At least, not until we get you out of Washington and settled in Saint Mary's County."

"Did you already pick out a name for me?" Ben asked.

"Yes," Anthony said. "In preparation for a time when it is safe for her to travel to you, and since Sonja has already used the name Sarah Jundt when she traveled to Norfolk, I suggest you go by James Jundt."

"James Jundt?"

"And since there is spreading nativism in our cities and growing mistreatment of immigrants, you will use the spelling Y-o-u-n-t. We need to Americanize your name."

Ben frowned. "That name helped win our independence, as did mine. Is it not Americanized enough?"

"Not in these days, Ben. Many people are doing that

with their name."

"Well, the name change doesn't hurt as much as hiding from my family," Ben said.

Anthony rose and motioned for Ben to follow him. They both shook hands with Eric.

"Meeting you was one of my few good experiences, Eric," Ben said.

Anthony tapped him on his shoulder. "We will talk again soon, Eric."

Eric nodded his head and smiled, then escorted them to the door.

They left the tavern and stepped over to Anthony's waiting landau carriage. Ben grimaced and slipped a finger inside his buttoned collar, pulling it away from his neck. Jarrod had folded down the carriage roof and stood by the open door.

"Thank you, Jarrod," Ben said.

Near his feet, Ben found a bulging carpet bag, with the Initials 'JY' engraved on a small brass plaque near the handle.

"That's yours...James," Anthony said as the carriage rocked ahead. "You have three shirts, three trousers, assorted inner garments, a shaving kit – which you must use religiously – and a small flask of whiskey."

Ben smiled at him. "Thanks, Anthony."

As they jiggled over cobblestone avenues toward the wharf, Anthony kept his face turned away from Ben. Nearing the docks, Anthony instructed Jarrod to pull off to the side of the road. He took in a deep breath and slowly blew it out, then turned to face Ben.

"They impounded *Raven*...and sold it at auction."

Ben compressed his lips, but said nothing, his eyes meeting Anthony's without blinking. Anthony worked his jaw in silence.

"What else?" Ben asked.

Anthony sighed. "I bid on it as high as I could pay, but I could not keep her for you."

Ben closed his eyes in silence. Anthony spoke a few words, but they did not reach Ben, so Anthony cleared his throat and spoke again.

"Lydia Binterfield bought it," Anthony said.

Ben's shoulders sagged, and he lowered his chin. After a long moment, Anthony instructed Jarrod to drive on. They soon arrived dockside at the passenger ramp of a modest sidewheel steamer. Ben stepped from the carriage with his bag and glanced up at the nameplate of the little ship, then spun around to face Anthony.

"Are you a damned fool, man? This is–" Ben abruptly lowered his voice and leaned close to Anthony. "This is the *Salem*. The very ship that brought us back from Point Lookout," he said in a hoarse whisper.

Anthony patted Ben's shoulder. "No, old friend, I am not a damned fool. And you need to have faith that you will not be recognized. You will only ride her to Alexandria, then transfer to a larger ship for your trip to Solomons. See the ticket master in Alexandria."

Anthony extended his hand over the edge of the carriage. Ben took it in a firm grip and held it, keeping his eyes on Anthony's, lingering, looking deep into them.

"I know," Anthony said.

Ben nodded briefly then sighed. "Until we meet again."

A small tear slipped down Anthony's cheek, and he turned to face forward. "Let's go," he said to Jarrod, and the team of horses took him away.

Ben walked up the ramp to the main deck and gave his ticket to the man standing there with his hand out. The man stared intently at Ben's face. Ben held his breath. It was one of the men who had beaten him when he was captured near Point Lookout.

"What happened to your face, Mistah?"

Ben stared hard at the man.

"Never make a tavern woman angry, my friend. I don't know what she rubbed on my face, but damned if it don't still burn like a living hell."

The man burst out laughing and gave Ben a friendly pat on his shoulder as Ben walked away.

In Alexandria, Ben boarded the steamship *Pocahontas*. The ticket master had given him the ticket paid in advance for James Yount, and a small envelope addressed to the same name. Inside Ben found an unsigned note.

Mr. Vincent Camalier, Leonardtown

June 30th. Southern Maryland

After changing to another smaller steamboat at Solomons, Ben finally stepped onto the Leonardtown Wharf late in the day. The sun was beginning its evening slide over the trees to the west, and the color of the sky was drifting from lazy blue to gray. Seagulls swept over little Britton Bay looking for fading silver flashes of minnows foolish enough to run near the surface. The air hung damp in the summer heat and was full of hungry mosquitoes, and lightning bugs emerging from their daytime hiding places. Ahead of him the ground rose steeply up the hillside, empty of trees and spotted with old stumps and optimistic saplings.

Ben looked around the wharf area at the few small outbuildings and modest warehouses but saw no human activity except the steamboat pulling away carrying the lone passenger who replaced him. Near the wharf, several working sailboats rocked in the small ripples of the bay's surface. Their busy fishing day finished long ago and their sails tied down for the night. Ben removed his coat and tossed it over his shoulder, then picked up his carpet bag and began the walk up to the town in the distance.

Ben was winded after his walk up the hill. It had taken at least a quarter hour, and his legs complained with aches after his long lazy periods in prison. He took in a deep breath of satisfaction mounting the crest of the hill and turned to take in the view. To his left, a massive two-story block and brick building sat looking down on him in disdain. Before it, sitting at the edge of the yard touching against the dirt street in front of the large building was a smaller one of local rocks, with iron bars in the single window he saw.

"Courthouse and jail, no doubt," he said to himself.

Moving ahead, he saw another substantial brick building sitting at the corner of the street he walked and the side street in front of it. The building appeared to be a bank, with its lower floor darkened for the day, but light in the upper floor and the shadows of several men passing before the windows. The sky was dimming to dusk and to his left his attention was drawn to a wide porch holding two large lamps giving bright light against the coming darkness, and the sound of voices coming from within. He could not fully see the name of the hotel, but the word hotel was well displayed. Walking into the center doorway, he found a busy tavern to his right and a set of stairs before him climbing up to the second floor.

A man approached him wearing a serving apron, wiping his hands with a rag and offering him a broad smile.

"Food, room or both?"

Ben found the smile contagious and released his own for the first time in months.

"Both, sir," Ben said.

"Two dollars a night, supper and breakfast, anything else is on your own. You mind sharing a room?"

"Yes, if it's people I don't know," Ben said.

The smile faded slightly, and the man turned to face a group drinking at a table in the tavern.

"Hey, Smithie. You need to share with Abell tonight. Got someone that needs a loner."

The man he spoke to frowned and leaned over to look at Ben. He said something about a salesman then shared a laugh with the others at the table.

"Three dollars a night, supper and breakfast," the innkeeper said and held out his hand.

Ben reached in his pocket, withdrew three silver dollars and dropped them into the man's hand.

"What'er you sellin?" he asked, eyeing Ben's carpet bag.

"Not selling anything, but I am looking for a man."

"What's his name? I know everyone in town."

"Vincent Camalier," Ben said.

The innkeeper nodded his head returning to his first smile.

"Oh sure. He'll be here in the morning for coffee and eggs." The man pointed his thumb over his left shoulder.

"He's building another house just up the lane from here. Just get down here before six-thirty, or you'll miss him. Who do I tell him is looking for him?"

"Uh...James. James Yount," Ben said.

The innkeeper held out his hand. "Alfred Moore," he said. "Happy to make your acquaintance, James Yount."

Ben shook his hand, then glanced up the staircase. "Which room?"

"In the back on the right. Only got four up there."

Ben hesitated. "Is there a key?"

"Nah, but there's a good oak slide on the inside. Wouldn't go up just yet, though. Sit down and have your supper and an ale first. Smithie will need to go up and shift his stuff out of that room into Abell's."

"Oh, I don't want to force a man out," Ben said.

The innkeeper shook his head. "Nah, he's a regular, and I let him sleep in a loner when it's empty, but he never pays for it." Then he leaned close to Ben. "He's my wife's younger brother," he said and shrugged his shoulders.

June 30th, Lapidum

Sonja mumbled the words of the single sentence in Anthony's letter.

"He is being treated well."

"Is Papa all right?" Alisha asked from her side.

Sonja looked down at her daughter and forced her frown away. "Yes, dear. He is still in that place, but he is being treated well."

She shoved the letter into the pocket of her canvas britches and squinted through the rain splattered window of the *Ugly Boat*'s cramped cabin, then leaned out of the doorway.

"Henry, give it some coal. I think the rain is thinning enough for us to go on."

The boy was tall for a ten-year-old but showed promise. Sonja had him leave the mule tending to younger boys and come on the *Ugly Boat* as her crewman. He learned quickly and was doing a good job. The canvas sail tented over the coal mound behind the steam boiler had been erected as shade for the boy, but it also filled the need for rain coverage. The boiler tinked and began to hiss as steam returned over the rising flames.

Behind the little black steamboat, nine barges tied in three rows of three wallowed among lazy waves spotted with rings punched in the surface by raindrops. A quarter mile to the west, the shoreline was a fuzzy dirty line between the matching grays of water and sky. Sonja pulled the handle on the whistle line and gave two sharp notes to the men on the barges and anyone ahead of her in the mist.

"Steam's up," Henry shouted.

Sonja pulled on the long lever that opened the connection between the piston drive to the rocker arms and the side wheels began to rotate in the water, easing the boat forward. There was a modest jolt as the tow rope to the center barge took the strain of the barge pack. The heavy hemp lines tied between the barges, stern to bow and side to side, had been made properly tight by the three barge captains chaperoning the nine barges.

Generally, each barge had a captain if it traveled the canal singly, or a captain over two barges tied in tandem when the mules pulled them. But free of the canal and on the way to Annapolis, only three captains were necessary to see to the pack of nine. All three captains were trusted Pulaski Shipping employees, even though four of the barges were owned by the Susquehanna and Tidewater Canal Company.

"Those back four ain't very level, Mrs. Pulaski," Henry said.

She glanced out from the doorway then returned her attention ahead. "Those are Canal Company barges, Henry. I'll complain to the superintendent when we get back. I told him we'd take them under contract, but they needed to be balanced before they came out of the basin."

"How come they didn't have that other tug take 'em?" Henry asked.

Sonja grinned. "Because we can do it faster and cheaper. Now, keep the coal going in, Henry. I need all the power this little boat can give. We're pulling over two hundred tons of coal!"

"Oh, it's going in, Mrs. Pulaski. Alisha has the shovel now."

Sonja snapped her attention to the coal pile where Alisha was tossing shovels full into the furnace, her face, hands, and dress spotted with large black smudges.

"Alisha Pulaski! You leave that coal to Henry!" she yelled.

Once near Annapolis in the mouth of the Severn River, the captains re-tied the pack into four rows of two with a single leader in front. Sonja steered the *Ugly Boat* to the back of the pack and then nudged it up the river to Weems Creek. There the barges were pulled in by a steam winch up to the coal warehouse, where they were emptied. Each barge returned to the pack floating high in the water, and as the routine was ready for the last barge, Sonja stepped onto it.

She turned back toward Alisha, pointing her finger. "You behave, young lady."

Inside the warehouse, Sonja met with the manager to collect her payment and sign papers for the Canal Company barges.

"This is far too little, mister," Sonja told him.

"That's the going rate, Mrs. Pulaski."

"The hell it is, Walter. You paid twice this yesterday."

"Things change," he said.

"Not that much. Is this because of Ben?"

Walter scratched his ear and looked around. "Some customers found out Pulaski Shipping brought coal here. Said I shouldn't take it."

Sonja stuffed her fists against her hips. "Walter, if you're not going to buy my coal at a fair rate, then put it back in the damned barges."

"I don't have time to do that," he said.

"Walter, I know it's summer and coal prices drop when it's warm, but if you cheat me today, in cold weather, I won't come back, nor will a lot of other barges."

"Now, Mrs. Pulaski..."

Sonja pointed out the open doorway. "And don't forget, Ben also has good friends in this city who would be willing to purchase coal from another supplier; among the several *other* suppliers in Annapolis."

"Very well. Very well," he said, counting out additional bills. "At least keep this to yourself and allow me to tell my customers I cheated you."

"I will keep it to myself," she said as she counted the money.

Once the barges were reassembled, Sonja moved them to the Annapolis docks at the end of Prince George Street. There she gave her three captains a bonus and sent them off to enjoy themselves in town. She then visited shops where she and Ben usually bought merchandise to refill their barges for the return trips.

The heavy rain returned as she made her way along Duke of Gloucester Street, but she had left her rain slicker on the *Ugly Boat* and was soon soaked with water. She only found one merchant who would still do business with the Pulaskis, but he would only sell to her at full price.

Sonja returned to the barges at dusk without any consignment or manifest for merchandise and made her way to the *Osprey,* where she and Alisha would spend the night. When she stepped down into the cabin, the aroma of crab soup wafted in the air.

"Come sit down and have some supper, Momma," Alisha said and snatched down a towel to help dry her mother's hair.

Sonja kneeled and gave her a long tight hug, then kissed her cheeks.

"It's only crab soup, Momma."

―――――――

"Mister Camalier," Ben said as he approached the table.

The man looked up from his breakfast with a warm smile. "You must be Mr. Yount."

"Y-yes...James Yount," Ben said.

"Sit and join me." He called out to the innkeeper, "Alfred, some fresh coffee here, please."

Vincent extended his hand to Ben as he sat down, then leaned in close to him. "Still getting used to the name?" he asked.

Ben stared at him in silence, but Vincent wiped away the question with the motion of his hand. "Not to worry, my friend. We can talk more freely when I escort you to your new house."

Alfred delivered a pot of coffee and a plate filled with eggs, sausage, and biscuits. "More if you need it," he said as he walked away.

Vincent chuckled at Ben. "Eat up, James. I suspect our mutual friend has been as cryptic as ever. Not always the one for details, is he? He leaves that to us."

Ben assaulted the breakfast and coffee, while Vincent finished his own. Moments later Ben followed Vincent onto the front porch and toward two horses tied nearby.

Vincent pointed his thumb at a saddled chestnut mare standing next to his own horse.

"That one's yours, James," he said.

Once Ben was seated on his horse, Vincent tilted his head and motioned for Ben to follow. "A quick look around your new metropolis, James, then we will trot out to see your new estate."

Out onto the road that Ben had mounted the evening before, Vincent halted and patted his horse's neck. He pointed to the large building Ben had passed the previous day.

"Courthouse. Built in '32. Jail and part-time holding pen in front..."

"Holding pen?" Ben asked.

"Folks around the county don't come into town often. Occasionally one plantation owner may loan a few of his slaves to another on the other side of the county and drops them off at the jail when he's in town. That's part of the sheriff's job. He locks them up for a few days until they're collected by the other owner."

Vincent turned in his saddle to fully face Ben. "Now don't be getting any wild ideas about interfering with that...James. That's not what you are here for. Understood?"

"Yes."

Vincent smiled and wheeled his horse to the left. "This is the bank. Upstairs is a meeting room, used for different things. There is a book society that meets there once a week to discuss books, newspaper articles, and the like."

They rode casually down the center street.

"We are not frivolous with our street names, James. We tend to like calling things what they are. We call our main street Main Street, and the few streets that go off to the side of it, we call Side Streets. Different people also call them by which neighbor or tavern or store they go to there."

Ben nodded his head in understanding and took in the sight of the few buildings along the sandy Main Street. There was another hotel, which housed the newspaper and printer on one side, several homes, mercantile stores and taverns, wheelwright, blacksmith shop, and telegraph office. In the middle of an open field behind the blacksmith's shop stood a line of three wooden structures, each about ten feet high and looking like a lone gate, but without a fence on either side. Each gate stood dozens of yards apart. The ground through the structures appeared well trampled, and a short rope hung down from the center of the beam mounted over each gate.

"What is that for?" Ben asked.

Vincent grinned. "Jousting."

"Jousting? Like the knights of England?"

"Well, ring jousting, actually," Vincent said. "Riders charge through each gate at full speed holding a short steel-tipped lance and try to put it through a small metal ring, less than two inches, dangling in the air. The rider who spears the most rings in the least time wins the joust."

"Hmmm."

Vincent chuckled. "It is a sport, unique mostly to southern Maryland."

Ben tilted his head and frowned at the gate. "I would like to see this ring jousting someday."

"You will, and all things southern Maryland, my new friend. Welcome to Saint Mary's County."

At the north end of town, they paused before a new Catholic church.

"Nothing to see beyond here," Vincent said.

Ben tilted his head toward the church. "That is an impressive church for a small town."

"Saint Aloysius," Vincent said. "I designed it for Father Enders and helped to build it. You would like Father Enders. He handles a hammer and saw better than I do. Parishioners call him the 'Carpenter Priest.' The man loves to fish, too."

He wheeled his horse and headed them back toward Ben's hotel and beyond, along the side street it faced, westward away from town. A half mile from town they came to a fork in the road. Vincent nodded toward the north fork.

"That one goes toward the Main Road. It goes up a

rise, some folks call it Gibbet Hill. In that direction, you can make your way to Waldorf or even Washington."

"No, thank you," Ben said.

"And the other road skirts old Sheep Pen Woods and takes us to your new home."

They took the southern fork, a heavily forested avenue. Ben was not ready to share all his experiences with Vincent, so he continued to ride in silence, and Vincent did not ply him with questions. Gradually the road opened to marshes and fallow fields along a river and then to an open area holding a steep-roofed two-story plank house with a view of the water.

Vincent pointed to the river. "We call that the McIntosh Run."

They rode slowly around the house so Ben could see all sides. The roof projected two dormers both front and back. There were two large windows both front and back on the main floor, with front and back doors set to the right. Two large brick chimneys sat at the same end of the house, projecting above the peak and centering the peak between them. Attached to the left side, snuggled up to the twin chimneys, was a single-story room with its own front door.

"Two rooms upstairs, four in the main house, and that on the left is the kitchen," Vincent said. "It also served as the slave quarter for the previous owner."

Ben slid off his horse. "What became of him?"

"Died. His wife took the children and slave and went to Kentucky. She has kin there. A lot of folks in the county have relatives in Kentucky."

Vincent withdrew some folded papers from his coat and handed them to Ben. "This is your deed. You already have a bank account in town. Everything else is up to you."

He leaned down from the saddle and extended his hand to Ben. "Good luck to you, James Yount. I won't come calling, but we may run into each other in town. You can tell folks there that we knew each other in Washington. I lived there a while, but I grew up here in Leonardtown."

He straightened his back and placed his hands on the

pommel of his saddle then blew out his breath.

"I only know a little about you, James, and do not wish to know more, but I must tell you this: I think highly of the people in this community. Leonardtown is my home. While I will always be a friend to Anthony Renowitz, which is the only reason I am helping you now, he knows better than to test my loyalty to him over my home. If you break Maryland Law and I wind up on your jury, I will let them hang you if the law calls for it."

He tipped his hat and cantered away in the bright sunshine. The silence behind him was soon filled with the shrill songs of cicadas. Ben stood alone while red-winged blackbirds chased dragonflies among the reeds near the water, then walked into his exile.

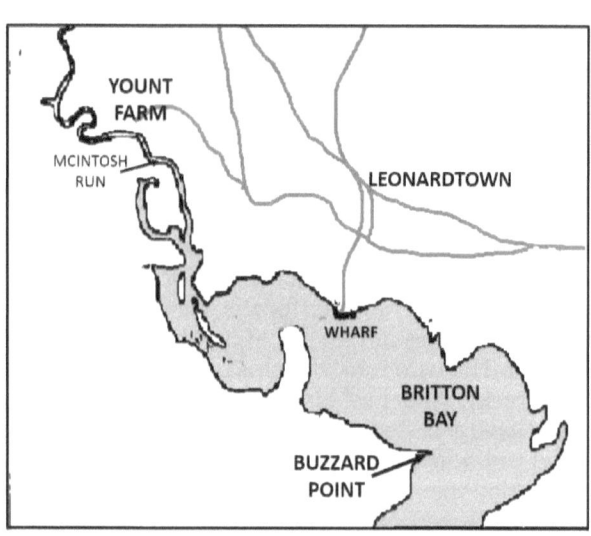

Ben's heels echoed on the pine floor in the house and sunbeams lanced from the windows creating gold squares on the pine. The air was hot and heavy, scented with wood oil, but free of the mustiness of decaying houses. There was furniture sufficient for living. The first room held three wooden chairs, a rocking chair, two small side tables, and a narrow fold-out desk. Through a door to the left, he found a bedroom with bed, side table, washstand, and two rockers placed in front of a large fireplace. A door in the rear of the room opened to a dining room holding a polished table, six matching chairs, and a long narrow table under the back window. The other large fireplace was on the left wall, with a door to the kitchen beside it.

"These rooms will be warm in the winter," he said to himself.

The kitchen was two steps lower than the main house and had a brick floor. There were two cooking fireplaces in the backs of each chimney. The tops of the cooking fireplaces were even with those on the opposite sides, but with separate flues. The lower bottoms at the level of the brick floor created large access for hanging pots on swing-out iron hooks. The walls held several empty shelves but held no cooking or eating ware. There was a heavy work table in the center, and two narrow cots against the far wall. Back inside Ben crossed the dining room to find an empty room in the far back corner. The door to the outside opened inward in that room showing the water across a grassy field and the stairs to the second floor rose across from the door.

"Guess this is the front door," he said.

Upstairs were two more empty rooms, each having windows overlooking both front and rear. The first bedroom opened to the second through a door between them.

Back downstairs he went outside through the kitchen. Thirty steps away, he found a deep rock-walled well with clean water and a sound wooden drop bucket. From there, he entered the barn several yards farther on. Inside were four stalls for horses or mules, a farm wagon in good condition, and a large empty loft above with plenty of room for winter hay. Doves flapped their wings in the loft, and the smell of dried hay lingered in the air, but there were no tools to be seen. Beyond the barn, he located the outhouse which had a smooth seat, a dry shaker roof and stout harness leather hinges for the door.

He walked around to where he had tied his horse and led her back to the barn.

"Gal, we need to take the wagon back into town and get some supplies, if you and I are going to have anything to eat, and anything to eat it with."

In the late afternoon, Ben returned to the farm with a wagon load of supplies and spent two hours placing household and barn items in their places. Afterward, he fed and watered the horse and brushed her down before putting her in her stall for the night. He spread his new blankets on the straw tick mattress in his bedroom and put away the clothes in his travel bag. He brought in the new rifle and revolver and left them in the bedroom. Then he went down into the kitchen and filled his new lamps with fresh whale oil. Finally, the cooked roast bought from the hotel, he set on the work table and placed the loaf of bread from the bakery next to it.

Ben stopped at an open doorway overlooking the back field and the run, feeling a cool breeze on his face. There was a lone broad maple tree centered in the field. He took one of the chairs from the dining room and set it beside the maple tree where he could sit with a view of the run. Then he brought out a mug of rum and sat in the shade smoking his new pipe. Out on the run hungry fish were jumping, snapping up insects buzzing too close to the surface.

"Looks like I'm going to have fish from that run," he said to himself.

Supper waited as he returned to the kitchen for refills to his mug, and he lost track of the number of times he visited the rum cask as the sun sank in the west. As dusk settled, he collected fallen twigs and small branches and built a fire to keep the mosquitoes away. After several mugs of rum, he dozed in the chair.

When he awoke, the fire was nearly out, and the sky had darkened to reveal a dome of bright stars, and the field before him was spotted with blinking lightning bugs. He collected additional wood and stoked the fire until yellow light spread around the maple tree and he could see his way back to the house. There, he lit a lamp in the kitchen and placed another lamp on the narrow table in the dining room and lit that one as well. He ignore the roasted beef and went to the kitchen. Ben filled his mug with rum and then pulled down the new pitcher he had bought for water, filling it with rum as well. He returned to his chair before the fire and set the pitcher on the ground beside him, finished his mug and drifted off to sleep again.

"Ben," the little girl said. "Wake up, Ben."

He stirred in his chair, wiping his mouth and stretching. On the other side of the dying fire stood a little black girl, full-bellied in her pregnancy.

"Hey, Ben," she said.

He squinted at her through the gray smoke.

"Who are you?" he asked.

"It's me, Melissa," she said.

"I don't know you."

"Sho you do. You took me to freedom, Ben. You shook my hand down in that barge."

"What barge? I don't know you."

"It was in the *Wilhelmina*. They was a bunch of us down there in that secret room."

Ben stood up.

"You are not here. All of you ran away from me. I was dying, and you ran away."

"No, Ben. I stayed with you while Miss Mauzey gets the baby from me."

"That was seven years ago," he said. "You can't be here. Your baby was dead."

"Yes. She died, but Mr. Simon buried her in free dirt. You remember me now, don't you?"

"I remember, but you can't be here now. You are not here."

"You held my hand," she said. "You said my name. You said you was pleased to meet me."

"I was. I paid little attention to slaves before that."

"You helped set me free," she said.

He stared at her. "You were the first. You changed my life...and I have not known peace since then."

The figure beyond the fire rippled and changed. She became a black woman, stripped of her blouse. The woman held up her hands, and the chains linking the wrist manacles danced between her arms. She turned within the dim firelight. Her chest and back was laced with fresh whip marks, her blood ran down from the cuts like tree sap.

"Mary Edmonson," he said. Tears welled up in his eyes.

She pointed her finger at his face. The bark of the maple tree split in a dozen places and blood flowed to the ground.

"No! You are not here!"

He moved around the fire, to grab her, but he tripped and fell onto the ground. Dizziness and blackness swept over him.

When Ben awoke, he was still lying on the ground near the cold remains of the fire. The sun was already rising high in the morning sky. His arms and face were covered in mosquito bites. He stumbled to the well and pulled up several buckets of cool water to pour over his head. He pulled up another bucketful of water, unhooked from the well and took it to the kitchen. Inside he found the coffee pot and coffee and started a fire. While the coffee heated, he went to the barn to feed the horse. Then he took her out to the small corral behind the barn, leaving her stall door open so she could go back in from the sun later.

Ben sat at the work table in the kitchen, sipping coffee and uncovering the roast, picking small pieces of meat from the edges, but quickly stopped. His stomach roiled, and he dashed outside to retch. Minutes later he sat again, nibbling some of the bread, which stayed down. His head pounded with sharp pains from each hammer strike, and he forced himself to walk around the field between the house and the run.

At the river bank, he discovered a short pier and a water-filled flat-bottomed boat on the narrow muddy shore below the bank. Once most of the water was removed, he inspected the boat to see if it would still float. The wood inside the boat did not appear as if it had been under water long. He also found oars and a cane fishing pole in the boat.

"Let's see if you will float," he said to the boat.

Using one oar to dig in the mud, Ben found several worms and placed them with their mud in the hollow of a broken oyster shell. He pushed off toward the middle of the run and began to fish. Within minutes he had caught several fat perch. He cleaned the fish at the bank and slipped a stout reed through their gills to carry them back to the kitchen. On his way, his stomach growled, and he smiled.

Ben dredged the fish in cornmeal and fried them in an iron pan over a small fire in the kitchen. The kitchen became unbearably hot as he cooked the fish, so when they were ready, he took his plate and a pitcher of water to the shade of the maple tree near the bank. The breeze drifted up the run and added to the coolness of his shade. As he ate in silence, a beautiful male deer came from the tall grass and brush upstream, wearing a crown of antlers. Ben froze in his position. The buck stepped cautiously to the water, looking from one side to another before putting his nose down. His white-coated tail flicked nervously as he drank. The deer raised his head to look around, but still did not see Ben and returned to drinking. Then the breeze puffed around Ben's clothes and sailed directly to the buck. Instantly, the buck snapped his head up and looked directly at Ben, then bounded away in three lightning jumps.

"Well, we will have venison here, from time to time," he said to himself.

Far to the south where the run emptied into Britton Bay, the rumble of thunder rolled over the tree dashing toward Ben. The leaves at the treetops flashed light and dark green as the fresh wind whipped through them twisting them on their stems. The air cooled and filled with the smell of rain. The darkness rose in the sky as the charcoal clouds charged northward. Ben grabbed his plate and pitcher and headed for the house. The first raindrop pelted his shoulder before he was halfway. The second delivered almost a half-ounce of water against his forehead. The black clouds rolled overhead like stampeding horses, thundering and lightning, fighting among themselves, shoving to be first. The rain came as a wall, charging along the ground, coming out of the tree line from the south, advancing like running soldiers in the heat of a charge. Only two steps from the door to the kitchen, the rain caught him, drenching him before he could escape indoors.

Ben looked back as the thick wall of water filled the space between the barn and the house.

"Glad I left the stall open for the horse," he said.

The gray wall surrounded the house and pounded the roof and walls, rattling the windows with rain and wind. Ben grabbed a kitchen cloth to wipe his head and went upstairs to check for leaks. The drumroll continued on the roof perched just on top of the exposed rafters. Ben walked through the two rooms keeping his eyes up, inspecting for leaks.

"Nothing to worry about here," he said to the rooms and returned downstairs.

In the kitchen, he checked for water coming in on the bricks from the lower kitchen door but found none. Then he went back upstairs to check the windows and returned to check the ones on the main floor.

"Maybe I should go outside and close the shutters."

He placed his hand against the window frames and his fingertips gently against the window panes.

"Wind doesn't feel to be hitting you too hard."

"What are you going to do next? Are you going to

break some of my windows?"

He sighed and headed back toward the kitchen and reached for his slicker, but even as he did so, the rain slackened. He looked out of the kitchen's single front window. The wall of rain moved on, trampling the grass and reeds north of the house. And the sun followed the train of clouds, slipping under their rear ledge. Within minutes, the sky cleared and was filled with sunshine and a blue sky, above a landscape decorated with sparkling wet diamonds on humbled branch and grass. Ben opened the door and stepped outside. The air was fresh and clean. It smelled of honeysuckle and blackberry blooms. He checked on his horse and found her dry and prancing about in the pen.

That night, Ben went to bed without rum as darkness came, and he fell asleep quickly. But the dreams returned bringing the hauntings of slaves who had sought freedom with him and fell deeper into the hell they had tried so desperately to escape; pushed into that hell by his failure. He soon awoke and paced the wet front field on his bare feet, trying to push the thoughts from his head, and trying to chase them away with rum. Dawn found him sitting in the chair under the maple tree. His eyes were red, and the dark pouches under them were growing each day. Gnats and mosquitoes hovered around his face. He swatted at them with ungainly motions and let his free hand flop onto his lap. He drank the last ounce of rum from his mug and dropped it on the grass next to the empty pitcher. Then he lay down and slipped into the blackness that pretended sleep.

July 3rd, 1848. Lapidum, Maryland

Sonja leaned back in her chair in the front room of the Pulaski home and released a deep sigh, laying the letter from Anthony on her lap.

"Is there any news of Papa?" Alisha asked.

"Nothing new, dear. Just more advice to be patient."

Alisha let her shoulders sag and walked back out onto the porch.

Sonja heard Jesse Jr. calling out to Alisha. "There's a beaver in the creek, 'Leesh, c'mon!" he yelled.

"Hold your horses, Junior," Alisha answered as her heels clomped down the wooden steps.

Sonja let Anthony's letter drop to the floor next to the one from Isaac.

"Harriet is with child again," he had written from Texas. "We pray she will be able to carry it full term this time."

There was nothing from or about Aaron. He had disappeared even from Anthony's network.

He is probably dead, she thought, but would never say the words, lest they make the thought real. She frequently pictured him laying broken among the rocks of the California mountains, his face white as the snow seeking to cover him.

She shook her head and reached for the *Cecil Whig,* re-reading the latest article about the Drayton and Pulaski Appeals. "Pulaski remains silent," the article read, "while Drayton waxes fervently for the release of slaves and all who would aid them to freedom. Congressmen Horace Mann of Massachusetts and Garrit Smith of New York propose a cessation of the slave trade in the District of Columbia, while Senator Foote of Mississippi derides the effort as foolhardy 'to put ideas of freedom and emancipation into the heads of the slaves only confuses the natural order as God ordained it.'"

"Mann and Smith are good men," she said. "Bold men, perhaps...perhaps bold enough to help a wife see her husband in prison..."

She went into her bedroom and plucked a few sheets of writing paper from the dresser, then ink and pen from the folded desk and took them to the kitchen table, where the light was best.

Your Honor,
Congressman Horace Mann,

I am the wife of Benjamin Pulaski who is currently held in the Washington Penitentiary. He has been held without the benefit of family visits since his arrest in April.

I am informed by knowledgeable people that other prisoners there are allowed visits from family. I traveled from our home on the Susquehanna River to Washington City in June with the hope of spending a few precious minutes visiting him but was harshly turned away.

Surely, a man who served steadfastly beside Andrew Jackson at the battle of New Orleans as a drummer boy, and bravely under him as a sergeant and lieutenant during the Seminole wars, should have a right to be visited by his family. I beg your assistance in gaining permission for me to visit my husband.

Sincerely,
Mrs. Benjamin Pulaski

She then wrote a similar letter to Mr. Garrit Smith and addressed them both to the House of Representatives, Congress of the United States, Washington City, District of Columbia.

Sonja sealed the envelopes and stepped out onto the porch clutching them in her hand and headed to the barn to saddle a horse. As she reached the barn door, Alisha walked slowly up their lane from the creek. There was a large spot of blood on the front of her pinafore. The lower part of her dress and her shoes were soaking wet.

"Alisha! Are you all right?"

"Yes, Momma," she said and raised her right hand, showing more blood on her knuckles. "Junior pushed me into the water, so I punched him in his nose."

Sonja closed her eyes and let out a heavy breath. "Where is Junior?"

"He went home," Alisha said.

"You can't do that, young lady. Now you march into the house, change clothes and wash that pinafore...and iron it. Then you will dust every inch inside the house until it is perfect. You hear me?"

"Yes, Momma."

"And then you will go to your room and stay there until I get back."

"Where are you going, Momma?"

"Git!"

⸻

July 17th, 1848
Mrs. Benjamin Pulaski,
Lapidum, Maryland

Dear Mrs. Pulaski,
Your letter has touched my heart and those of my peers here in Congress. Mr. Garrit Smith and I have made an official demand of the prison

to allow visitation for the prisoners Daniel Drayton and Benjamin Pulaski. Kindly consider this letter as a response from both myself and Mr. Smith. I will advise you of any response we receive on your behalf.

Sincerely,
Mr. Horace Mann
Representative   of   the Commonwealth of Massachusetts
In Congress
Washington, District of Columbia

Saint Mary's County

Ben stood before the mirror above the water bowl in his bedroom. Thick lather coated his cheeks and chin. His hand trembled slightly as he brought the straight razor near his cheek. It had been two weeks since he shaved, and that long since he bathed. The walk up from the McIntosh in the sunshine had dried him. His hair and body were clean again. The rum cask sat empty in the kitchen as it had for the previous two days, and the last of his coffee sat in the cup sitting on the edge of the washstand. He held the razor by his fingertips and began his first cut down from his sideburns. The slight bite of the blade stung his skin. He pulled his hand away from his face and blew out his breath, shaking his hand to loosen his wrist, then began shaving again. He managed to complete the shave without cutting himself.

On the road into Leonardtown, Ben passed Vincent Camalier going to the north. They stopped a moment to talk.

"Forgive me for being blunt, James, but you look like hell."

"I'm having trouble sleeping in the new house," Ben said.

"That's odd. Others find it restful out there. Oh, Frances Jarboe has been asking about you."

"Who is he and why would he be interested in me?"

"Well, James, he runs the local newspaper, and you are the newest resident of our fair town. So, be prepared to tell him something about yourself."

"Were you headed out to tell me that?"

"Not at all, James. I am off to build a covered bridge over the McIntosh Run some miles north of your place."

Vincent tapped his horse with his heels and trotted on, leaving Ben sitting in the wagon.

Ben shrugged his shoulders and flicked the reins on the horse.

In town, Ben took his wagon to the same mercantile he had visited before, H.W. Yates, Merchandise. As the clerk pulled down the supplies he requested, Ben spent a moment examining tobacco pipes.

"I like the ones with a gentle curve down from the tip," a voice said near his shoulder.

Ben turned to face him. The young man, slightly heavier than Ben, smiled when they made eye contact. He extended his hand.

"You must be our new resident. I am Dr. Andrew Spalding. Actually, Andrew Jackson Spalding, for those that remember him."

Ben accepted his hand in a firm shake.

"I remember him," Ben said. "I stood next to him when the British came from the swamp."

The man's eyes went wide. "Really? You don't look that old, sir," he said with a genuine smile.

"I was only a drummer boy at the time," Ben said, wishing he had not brought up the fact. "I am James Yount."

"Please to meet you, James. Welcome to Leonardtown. Where are you from?"

Ben forced a smile. "Well, Baltimore... and other places I probably shouldn't have been."

"Mmm," he said, looking closely at Ben's face.

Ben tensed when he realized his face was being examined.

Spalding blinked. "Sorry. Forgive my rudeness. It's the new doctor in me, but have you been unwell? The tropics, perhaps?"

"No...well, yes, I have been unwell, but getting stronger by the day. I am here to rest."

"Ah, well...it's just that your forehead is well tanned, but your face is almost beet red and visited by dozens of hungry mosquitoes..."

Spalding's eyes lingered on Ben for a moment longer, then he blinked again.

"Well, if you do need a physician, James, do stop by my new office. It is just up the street. Ask anyone where it is."

Spalding tipped his hat and walked away. Ben returned his attention to the pipes while the clerk finished loading his supplies.

"Is there anything else, Mr. Yount?"

"Yes, I'll have the pipe with the curve in the stem...and a cask of rum and one of whiskey."

The clerk handed Ben the pipe and went off to get the casks. The back of the wagon was filled with barrels of flour and grain, a sack of rice, more household supplies, farm tools, smoked hams, a new rain slicker and finally the two liquor casks. The clerk nervously entered the items in the store ledger, then ran down the tally several times.

"Sir, the total comes to eighteen dollars...and twenty-seven cents, um...um..."

Ben dug into his pocket and pulled out four five-dollar gold coins and handed them to the clerk.

"I will come to this store again, young man. Keep the balance in the till and open an account in my name. Apply it to future purchases, if you would."

"Yes, sir."

As Ben walked out to his wagon, there was a man in a white linen suit standing next to the wagon. Ben nodded to the man as he stepped up onto his wagon seat.

"Looks like you've got a full load," the man said through a smile.

Ben sighed. "It'll do for a couple days," he said.

"You're new here," the man said.

Ben looked directly into the man's face and spoke without expression. "I've lived here twelve years, mister, and damned if you don't come out and ask me the same question every time I come into town."

The man stared at Ben for a long moment, then began to laugh. He held his hand up to Ben. "I suppose I'm not the first amongst us to make the obvious point that you are new here."

Ben showed a grin that he did not feel and took the man's hand. "Nope. I'll bet you are Francis Jarboe."

Francis smiled. His eyes sparkled. "Foretold or warned?" he asked.

"Warned," Ben said, keeping his empty smile.

"Then I would bet that you are James Yount."

"Y-O-U-N-T," Ben spelled.

"Well since the cat is out of the bag, I'll be direct in my nosiness. Why are you here, James?"

Ben kept his grin. "To buy supplies, Francis."

Francis shook his head. "What brings you to Leonardtown? – And please do not tell me 'a steamboat'."

Ben rested his elbows on his knees and sighed. "I have things to put behind me, that are not for the public. And there are things I have before me that I have not yet chosen. But, I will tell you this: I have been to sea in rough weather, hauled coal up and down the Chesapeake, and left people behind that I shouldn't have. When I warn a man, he should take it seriously, and when I tell a man I will help him..."

Francis waited for the rest of the statement...and waited.

After a long silence, Ben spoke with gravel in his voice, "Sometimes a man does not know he is lying when he makes a promise, and he must find a way to live with that."

He flicked the reins on the rump of the horse and drove the wagon away.

Francis reached up and rubbed his earlobe with his finger and thumb. "Sad man," he said to himself.

Mr. Yates had been standing at the doorway and stepped out into the street.

"What'er you going to write about that man?"

"Don't think I know how to write that," Francis said.

Ben drove his wagon into the side road at the corner of Main Street, stopping in front of the tavern where he spent his first night. He turned under the shade of a tree and set the brake on his wagon. Inside, he waved at the innkeeper behind the bar and pulled out a chair at the first table.

"Two ales," Ben said.

Ben snatched up the first mug as soon as Thomas set it down and handed it back empty before Thomas could step away.

"You want a third?" Thomas asked.

Ben shook his head 'no' and sipped from the other mug.

A man sitting at the next table turned to face Ben.

"Good day to you, sir," he said.

Ben glanced at the man and only nodded then turned back to his ale.

"You the man who took the old Scotts' place, on the high ground next to the run?"

Ben released a long slow sigh. "Yes," he said without turning toward the man.

"Great spot to catch fish...just off the little pier..."

Ben took another deep drink of ale, rolled his eyes up to the ceiling and turned to face the man. "Yes, I took several perch there just the other day."

The man stood and moved to Ben's table, pulling out a chair and sitting.

"Oh, that is a heavenly spot to fish, sir. The last of the brackish water never goes beyond there, and the fresh flows down to push it away. The perch are always fat and hungry, but the bass...the bass are magnificent."

The man was unshaven, wore a tattered shirt under a stained canvas vest and smelled of old fish. He offered his hand. "Joseph Enders," he said.

The man's hand was hard and calloused and his grip firm and steadfast.

"James Yount," Ben said. "I've heard of you, priest."

Father Enders smiled. "Ah, the curse of fame." Then he chuckled. "Are you Catholic, Mr. Yount?"

"My grandfather was, when he immigrated from Poland."

"And your father?"

Ben examined the backs of his hands. "His religion was the seas, I think."

"And you?" Father Enders asked.

Ben looked away, toward the light at the doorway. "So...Father Enders...what kind of bait do you use for catching bass."

Father Enders smiled at Ben. "May I come fish on your little pier?"

"Anytime you wish."

He looked around the tavern then leaned closer to Ben and whispered, "Little tree frogs. Shhh."

August 7th. Lapidum, Maryland

Sonja tore open the envelope as she stood before the postal desk in the back of Delbert Freidman's Mercantile store, letting the pieces drift down onto the wood planks.

Dear Mrs. Pulaski,

We are pleased to inform you that the Police Commissioner of the District of Columbia and the Warden of the Washington Penitentiary have granted you permission to visit your husband at the prison, and you may continue to do so as often as once a month, unless such visits cause turmoil to the prison routine, staff or inmates.

Sincerely,

Mr. Horace Mann

Representative of the Commonwealth of Massachusetts

In Congress

Washington, District of Columbia

Sonja dashed out of the store and up the road to the locktender's house.

"Catherine," she yelled, even as she approached the open front door. "I can visit Ben!"

Catherine met her at the door, and they shared hugs over the news.

"Let Alisha stay with us, so you can go alone," Catherine said.

Sonja was almost giddy. "Are you sure Jesse Junior can tolerate that?"

"Your daughter is helping him to learn his manners." She said through a smile.

The next morning, Sonja brought Alisha to stay with the Prices and had Jesse Junior take her into Havre de Grace to catch the train to Baltimore. She had to wait several hours in the Baltimore station for the train to Washington City. It was late in the afternoon when she arrived at the Pennsylvania Avenue train station and hired a cab to take her to the Indian Queen Hotel.

She was fortunate to find the hotel with a few empty rooms. Sonja was escorted to her room on the second floor. All the third-floor rooms were rented by others with more experience with Washington summers, where rare and precious breezes occasionally slipped over the other buildings and into the highest rooms. She spent a sleepless night, pacing the floor in her darkened room where the window curtains hung limp in the sweltering heat.

At ten o'clock the next morning she stepped down from the cab under a glaring sun in front of the Washington Penitentiary. Loose hairs clung to the back of her neck, soaking in the sweat forming there. The lobby was well shaded and walled in cool blocks, the floor was granite, but the air smelled of musty closets. The officer at the reception desk handed her a pass as soon as she identified herself, the form had already been completed. He motioned to a nearby guard standing near a barred door.

"Mrs. Pulaski," he announced.

Through a maze of turns and corridors, the guard brought her before another uniformed man sitting at a desk at the end of a short hallway. Most of the barred cells near his desk were empty, except for two. The guard at the desk took her pass and examined it under the lamp. Without looking up at her, he pointed toward two cells where the men in them sat upon their beds.

Sonja approached the cells as her escort walked out of the area. There was only a bar filled wall between the two cells, and a wall of bars in front of them holding the frame of a door to each cell. The cells were far smaller than her bedroom at home; Ben's bedroom at home. She stepped in front of Ben's cell. The man there rose and faced her with a timid smile.

"Hello," he said.

She blinked several times and glanced over her shoulder at the guard at the desk. She turned back and met the stare of the other prisoner from the next cell and stepped in front of him.

"Are you Daniel Drayton?" she asked.

"Yes, madam," he said.

"Ben spoke highly of you. Many people applaud your stand. I am pleased to meet you."

Drayton only smiled and pushed his eyes toward Emilio.

Sonja stepped back in front of Ben's cell. "Are you not going to kiss your wife, Benjamin?" she asked in a voice she was certain would carry to the guard desk.

Emilio beamed and came toward her. Sonja offered him her lips between the bars. As Emilio neared her lips with his own, she turned her face so he would kiss her cheek. She reached in and grabbed his shirt at his upper arms in both hands, clawing the material into her grip and yanked him against the bars. His face slammed against the iron. She whispered into his ear with a sultry, raspy voice.

"Who the hell are you?"

The Yount Farm

Ben jerked up from yet another bloody dream. "No! No! No!" he screamed, covering his face with his arms, dodging blows that were not there.

He stood up from the rocker and paced the room in the moonlight. He no longer went to bed, unless he collapsed upon it in a drunken stupor. He snatched his mug from the table near his rocker and went into the dining room where the liquor casks were set up on the table. The polish under the spigots were gone where the last drops fell. The water pitcher near the casks was empty and lay on its side. He placed his mug under the rum spigot and twisted the handle. Barely two ounces dribbled into his mug when the flow stopped completely, so he slid the mug under the whiskey spigot and filled it there.

Outside, Ben walked toward his chair under the maple tree, stopping twice on his path to sip from his mug. Mosquitoes buzzed around his face and bit at his bare chest and ankles. Only his filthy britches protected his skin. He no longer swatted away the insects, but they seemed less inclined to feed on his exposed skin. A faint breeze sneaked among the leaves of the tree overhead, opening spaces between them and allowing faint flashes from the full moon in a starry sky.

In the moonlight beyond the charcoal shade of the tree, a figure walked up from the marsh. The metal ringing of the iron chain loops between his wrists gave a cadence to his steps. Ben stood and shook his fist at the apparition.

"I don't know why, God damn it! I tried to help you get away!"

He took another gulp from his mug. "Go away! Leave

me be! Give me peace!"

"I never meant for that to happen," he yelled to the voice in his mind.

Ben turned away from the spirit and stumbled toward the run. He sat on the edge on the little pier, letting his toes create ripples on the surface of the water and making the moon's reflection dance. The apparition stepped onto the reflection of the dancing moon and stood before Ben.

"No!" Ben screamed.

He gulped from his mug until he had emptied it and then lay his head back onto the planks and surrendered to the liquor.

Ben opened his eyes to an early dawn sky filled with crumpled clouds swept forward by a mischievous wind. Father Enders sat nearby, softly humming and teasing his fishing line cautiously across the surface of the water. The little tree frog at the end of the line bobbed in the water at the center of the ripples calling the attention of hungry largemouth bass. Ben sat up and pulled his feet onto the pier. The priest kept his attention on the frog while tracking the dark form in the water under it, working its way toward the frog. Enders eased the frog toward the dark movement.

In a flash, the bass erupted through the surface, its gaping mouth surrounding the frog as it came up and swallowed it whole. The bass leaped out of the water, flinging its tail overhead, then jerking at the first sting of the barbed hook dangling from the loop around the frog's hips. Enders jerked on the line, setting the hook and sealing the fate of the bass. The bass arched and twisted even as it slapped onto the water, fighting to get away but helping the hook to bite deeper. The fishing pole curved at its tapered end, looking as if to snap and splinter at any second. The priest deftly allowed the tip of the pole to slip under the water and follow the pull of the bass, letting its own frenzy wear itself down. The struggle lasted less than a minute.

Enders brought the gasping fish to the side of the pier and tucked his finger under the bass's lip and slipped his thumb into its mouth. He lifted the bass out of the water and held it up to Ben.

"Nearly five pounds," Enders said. His grin wide and his eyes dancing.

Then the priest slipped the fingers of his other hand into the bass's mouth and pulled out the frog. He loosened the loop around the frog's hip and held him out near the water. The frog chirped and jumped from his hand. The priest chuckled and returned his attention to the bass and stood to face Ben.

Holding the fish up, proud as a ten-year-old, the priest grinned. "Let us give our thanks to our God for this bountiful breakfast and share him together."

Ben frowned at him through the pounding in his head and snarled as he turned away. "To hell with you, and your bountiful God. To hell with both of you."

As Ben took a step away from the priest, Enders grabbed him by his belt. He yanked Ben back with muscular shoulders and arms, sending him sailing through the air into the water. Enders jumped into the water after him, landing on his feet in waist deep water and pulling Ben to the surface. Ben coughed and took in a gasping breath. Before Ben could say anything, Enders pushed him under the water again.

"Deus meus, ex toto corde poenitet me omnium meorum peccatorum, eaque detestor, quia peccando, non solum poenas a Te iuste statutas promeritus sum," Enders chanted, then pulled him to the surface. Ben gasped for air, filling his lungs, then Enders pushed him under again.

"Sed praesertim quia offendi Te, summum bonum, ac dignum qui super omnia diligaris!" the priest said and pulled him up again.

Ben tried to stand but could not get his feet under him. His weight was only lifted by the strong arm of Father Enders. Ben hungered for air, and as soon as his head was out of the water, he inhaled all he could. Enders' face was looking down at his.

"Hold that breath," Enders said. "We are not done yet." Then he pushed Ben back under the water. "Ideo firmiter propono, adiuvante gratia Tua, de cetero me non peccaturum   peccandique   occasiones   proximas fugiturum. Amen!"

He yanked Ben up to his feet and slapped him on his back. "Breathe, man, breathe."

Ben coughed, bending over and placing his hands on his knees. "What in the–, what was that?"

Father Enders crossed his arms over his chest. "It is called the Act of Contrition. I said it for both of us. For you, for being stupid; and for me, for letting my anger throw you into the water."

Ben coughed again, spitting up water. "Was the dunking part of the contrition?"

"No, I added that for effect. I see Baptists do it and I always thought it would be fun. I'll have to say another Act of Contrition for that part when I get back to the church; maybe a dozen Hail Marys as well."

Father Enders climbed up the bank and moved to the pier, but the bass was gone. He closed his eyes, clenched his teeth and balled his fists, turning his face to the sky. Then he opened his eyes and let out a long breath. "Serves me right," he said.

He reached out his hand to help Ben out of the water and stood there as Ben lay on his back in the green grass.

"Well, James, at least you smell a little better now, though not much. I would suggest soap as well as prayer. I think you are in great need of both."

He put his hands on his hips and looked down at Ben. "May God help you with the demons you are fighting, my son. Vade ad Deum." Then he made the sign of the cross over Ben and walked away.

Ben lay in the grass, neither angry nor disturbed, then rose up and walked back to the house, back to his whiskey.

Philadelphia

Sonja shoved Jarrod aside as she burst through the front door of the Renowitz house in Philadelphia.

"Anthony! You bastard!"

Camilla dashed into the parlor. "Why, Sonja...why, what?"

"Where is your bastard husband?" Sonja demanded.

Camilla gasped with her eyes wide. "Really! Sonja? What is happening here?"

"Your husband lied—"

Anthony rushed into the room. "Sonja? What the—"

Sonja picked up a vase from a nearby table and threw it at Anthony, where it smashed against the wall. Anthony dodged the vase and ran into the dining room.

"Oh, my word!" Camilla screamed. "Sonja, what has gotten into you?"

"Your husband," she snarled as she elbowed her way past Camilla and charged into the dining room.

Camilla followed after her. "Anthony is your loyal friend, Sonja. We are both your friends," she cried.

Sonja snatched up a teacup from the table and flung it at Anthony, crashing it near his head.

"That scoundrel you call loyal," Sonja said to Camilla, "Has lied to me, saying my Ben was in prison and I had to wait patiently to see him."

"Well, yes, dear, we all know that. It is so awful to have him there—"

Sonja picked up a plate and flung it at Anthony. He batted it away from his face, knocking it to the floor where it exploded in dozens of shards. Anthony dashed to the servants' door but was blocked by Camilla.

"What have you done, Anthony?" Camilla demanded.

Anthony turned to run the other way, but another dish smashed against the wall in front of his face.

"He is hiding Ben, Camilla!" Sonja yelled. "Ben has been out of prison for two months, and your sneaking husband let me think Ben was suffering in prison—"

"What? Anthony! Is that true?"

"Well," he stammered, "well...yes, it is true but—"

"Since when? Since when, Anthony?" Sonja yelled, throwing a plate against his elbow.

"O-ow!!"

"Since when, Anthony?" Camilla called out.

"J-June," Anthony said.

"It's the middle of August, Anthony," Camilla said.

"And you let me think he was in prison. Where is he?" Sonja yelled and smashed a plate on the wall above Anthony's head.

Sonja reached for a large serving bowl, but Camilla took it from her hand.

"That was my mother's," Camilla said, setting it aside and selecting a heavier bowl for Sonja. "Here, throw that one."

Sonja grunted as she propelled the bowl across the room at Anthony then scanned the tabletop for another dish. Camilla snatched another plate and handed it to her. Working in tandem, the two women pummeled Anthony with an unending series of smashing dishes, driving him into a closet in the main hallway. Camilla grabbed the key and locked the door with Anthony trapped inside.

"Where is Ben?" Sonja asked, standing outside the closet door.

There was a long pause, then Anthony's muffled voice drifted out, "Saint Mary's County."

Sonja grit her teeth. "There are people there who may know him."

"Not anymore," Anthony said. "No one but you would be able to recognize him."

"Why do you say that?" Sonja asked.

"When was the last time you saw Ben without his beard?" Anthony asked.

Sonja looked at Camilla, then frowned. Sonja's eyes wandered around the room. She brought a finger to her lips and tapped them as she thought.

"Twenty years ago," she said.

Camilla took Sonja by her arm and led her toward the kitchen. "When is the last time you've eaten, dear?"

"Sometime last night...I am so sorry about the dishes."

"Not to worry, Sonja. My scoundrel is about to buy me many many more." She stopped abruptly and stepped back into the hall just as Jarrod approached the closet door.

"Jarrod. Kindly help clean up all the broken pottery in the dining room, then complete all your other chores – first – before attending to my husband. He is in need of some solitude for the next hour or so."

The Yount Farm

"Leave me alone!" Ben screamed, staring into the darkness at an apparition. Driven from his sleep again by haunting nightmares, he had retreated to his chair under the tree in the front field, but the dream pursued him. It was a black man scarred by the whip beyond recognition. He stood before Ben in a pool of blood that rose to his ankles.

"No more. No more!" Ben yelled.

Ben's eyes fixed on the image. He cocked and uncocked the revolver in his hand; mechanical, without thought, click and click, click and click, click and click.

The figure faded in the growing dawn light. The dark circles under Ben's eyes were another shade closer to black, and red spider webs laced his eyes. The stubble on his face now lay against his skin, sketching the beard he had worn for twenty years, re-covering the scar on his cheek once made by a Seminole lance. His hands trembled. The last of the whiskey sat in the mug by his feet.

A soft footstep rustled the weeds behind Ben. He whirled around and fired the pistol. The explosion of fire from the barrel scorched the hip of a stray dog. The dog had wandered onto the property days ago, seeking a hand to pet his head and feed him a nibble. Now it ran away in terror, yelping in the morning air. Startled birds jumped from the tree overhead slapping their wings in escape as the echo of the shot ran back from the tree line.

He glanced at the spot where the dog had stepped, his attention then drawn to the movement as it ran away.

Ben's jaw was slack, his mouth open, working to form the words to come.

"Didn't mean to," he yelled after the dog, then grit his

teeth and fired again into the ground beside him.

His blood pounded in his head, the headaches were constant now, the hammer blows behind his eyes unrelenting. He brought his hands against his head. The cylinder of the pistol felt cool against his forehead. He scratched his head with the hammer, then lowered the pistol and took up the mug in his other hand. He tilted the mug slightly to catch the morning light, to see how many drinks he had left.

"You don't help me anymore, anyway," Ben said into the mug.

He took two large gulps and returned the mug to the ground. Barely a mouthful remained at the bottom.

He glared at the spot where the figure had been.

"God damn you."

Ben fired the pistol again, staring at the spot, but not seeing it, or even trying to focus his eyes. Then he brought the pistol up to the side of his head, pressing the tip of the barrel to his temple. He closed his eyes and clenched his teeth. He pulled back the hammer with his thumb and pressed the barrel harder. His hand shook. He slipped his finger before the trigger. He groaned, pressing the barrel tighter, pressing the trigger with his finger. He held his breath.

He bellowed like a raging animal.

At the end of the roar, he was still there, still in pain.

He lowered the pistol onto his lap and released a torrent of sobs. He wept for long minutes until the sun rose above the tree line and heated his body. Ben retrieved his mug and drained it, then took in several deep breaths. The pistol was still cocked. Tears filled his eyes. He looked up at the cloudless blue sky through the blur of his tears and opened his mouth. He brought the pistol up to his face and slipped the end of the barrel into his mouth.

Ben pushed in the barrel until he gagged.

He squeezed the trigger.

The gun shook in his hand.

He brought up his other hand to keep the pistol in place.

He squeezed the trigger tighter; ready for the

explosion, the darkness, the nothing to come.

The trigger released the hammer, springing it toward the cap.

Ben loosed a mournful howl.

'Forgive me' echoed in his mind.

The hammer flew.

The hammer slammed down onto a hard-calloused thumb, on the hand of a carpenter.

"Not today, my son," Father Enders said. "Not today."

Havre de Grace, Maryland

The steamboat *Renowitz* made a rare docking at the end of St. Clair Street. At the nearby livery stable, Sonja rented a horse and trotted it quickly to the towpath, then spurred him into a hard run. Within minutes she stopped in front of the lockhouse and walked to the opened doorway.

"Catherine," she called out. "I need to take Alisha away for a while."

Catherine came from the kitchen, wiping her hands, concern on her face.

"Are you all right, Sonja?"

"Catherine, I need to go away. Alisha and I need to go away. Thank you for looking after Alisha—"

"She is not here, Sonja."

"Where is she?"

"We let her and Patty ride with Dan Bartlett on Number 26 to stay with the Bookers in York Furnace a few days."

"When will she be back, Catherine?"

"Well..." she pushed the hair off her forehead with the back of her hand. "They should be back this afternoon, I would think."

Sonja blew out her breath and let her shoulders sag.

"Are there more troubles about your claim on Alisha?"

Sonja smiled and placed her hand on Catherine's arm. "No. No, but I am afraid there is not much else I can tell you. I don't know how long we will be gone, and I can't tell you where we will be...."

"We will be here whenever you need us, Sonja."

Jesse Price entered the house.

"Why, Sonja, I thought that was you dashing up the towpath on that chestnut. Have you heard from Ben?"

"Yes…but, since he has been imprisoned…I will need to take Alisha and go somewhere else for a while."

"Well, Sonja, we'll be glad to look after your place, if that will help."

Sonja fixed him with her eyes and then included Catherine. "You have five children. Why don't you stay in our house until I come back…?"

Jesse scratched his head and turned to Catherine. "I…I don't know…"

Sonja crossed her arms. "I…we may be gone a year, or even more. Take it. Please. Use it, however best suits you, Jesse."

"Well…I'd still need to keep an eye on the lock. I mean, that's what I'm paid to do."

"No, Jesse," Catherine said, "You don't keep your eye on it at night, you keep your ear on it, for the conch shell of coming barges."

"And barges don't come after sundown," Sonja added. "You could just go to work at the lockhouse in the day – like an office – and go home at night."

"We'd be proud to, Sonja," Catherine said. "We've always loved your place."

"Good," Sonja said and extended her hand to Catherine. "It's done. And I will write you if and when it is time for us to come back."

Jesse stood by with a half-smile and half-frown on his face as the two women shook hands and concluded the agreement in front of him.

"I must dash down to the corner to speak with Delbert," Sonja said.

In the mid-afternoon, barge number 26 floated into the holding pond above the Lapidum lock. Within minutes, Alisha was sitting in the carriage next to Sonja as Jesse Sr. drove them up the towpath to Havre de Grace, with the livery stable horse trotting behind. The steamboat *Renowitz* had waited patiently with half steam until Sonja's return and quickly began churning the Susquehanna water with its sidewheels as soon as she boarded. By the time the steamboat passed the Concord Point Lighthouse, the official beginning of the Chesapeake Bay, froth was rolling away from the boat's bow as it charged south at full speed.

The Yount Farm

Ben sat under the shade of the front field maple tree, sipping coffee in spite of the day's heat. Father Enders sat next to him.

"You need to have this field cut and planted, Benjamin."

"Plant it with what?"

"Since you've promised me, and therefore through me, Jesus Christ, that you're not going to have your remains planted here, you should plant corn."

"You take too long to get to an answer, priest."

"Sometimes the better answers require time to see them. You have to let God lead you to them."

Ben frowned. "Like he led us into a dead calm with seventy-eight slaves on board, where we could be caught?"

"No. Like he brought me here with the lure of that bass so I could keep you from making your wife a widow. Like He brought that fellow in Washington that looks like you."

Ben's frown darkened. "Like he yanked freedom out of the hands of slaves and tossed them into a far worse condition than they tried to escape?"

"Benjamin, world events are a storm of pushes and pulls between God, Satan, and the stupidity of man, then add to that the serendipity of weather."

"That's a lousy explanation of the world, Priest."

"Would you die to save your young daughter, Benjamin?"

"Of course I would."

"Because you love her?"

"Of course."

"But you weren't there when she was swept away by the ice gorge, Benjamin. Does that mean you did not love her then?"

"No..."

Father Enders turned to face him and leaned closer.

"Sometimes, my son, an awful event, is simply and painfully, an awful event; not wrought by anyone or anything."

Ben scoffed.

"If you want your demons to forgive you, Benjamin," Father Enders said, "you must first forgive yourself."

They sat together for a long silent hour, accompanied only by the chorus of cicadas in the tree line at the north edge of the field. White clouds tumbled slowly in the sky painting passing shadows on the land beneath them. A breeze occasionally drifted among the leaves of the maple, gently brushing the hair on the back of the men's necks and cooling the sweat on their foreheads. In the middle of the run, just off from the little pier, a fat bass leaped into the air to snatch a dragonfly and fell back into the water with a sparkling splash.

"Do you like fried bass, Benjamin?"

"Yes, I do."

"Let's go see if we can catch that one and maybe a cousin or two."

Father Enders stood and stretched, then reached for his fishing pole.

When he stood, Ben grabbed him in a bear hug. Then Ben released him and stepped back.

"I saw a fishing pole in the barn," Ben said, and walked away, speaking over his shoulder. "I don't want it now, but where did you put my pistol?"

Father Enders laughed. Ben stopped and turned toward him.

Father Enders tilted his head to where the bass had fallen into the water, then sauntered toward the little pier.

Ben sighed and resumed his walk to the barn.

'Just as well.'

———— ༄࿐ ————

Havre de Grace Post Office

The postal clerk and his part-time assistant were busy

sorting the daily pouches dropped off by the contract mail steamer. Mail came three times a week, and on each such day, sorting the mail was a flurry of activity that took almost the entire day. Some envelopes were sealed with wax, some with glue, and some were just folded pages with their ends sealed together. It was not uncommon for the seals to give way, especially in the hot and humid summer months near the Chesapeake Bay.

The postal clerk kept an eye on his assistant, who was known to 'help' the seals open, giving away local secrets and gossip. The assistant lingered suspiciously long with one particular envelope, stained in its travels.

"Keep your nose out of the letters, Jimmie. If I catch you snoopin again…"

"I ain't snoopin, Uncle Bill. It's just that this one came all the way from California."

"California? Let me see that one."

Uncle Bill took it and held it up to the sunlight streaming in through the side window. "What is that stamp…why it's a bear." He looked at his nephew. "Yeah, I heard they took a bear as their symbol out there."

Uncle Bill squinted at the smudged postal stamp. "S…Su…Sutters Mill, California."

"Wonder if it's near where they found all that gold, Uncle Bill," Jimmie said.

"Probably not. Besides, all that talk about gold is probably just hogwash to sell newspapers. Put it in the pouch for Lapidum. It goes to the Pulaskis up there."

August 15th, 1848. Georgetown, South Carolina

Lydia Binterfield stood under a frilled lavender umbrella, held up against a harsh sun. The aroma of low tide mud and old oyster shells scented the air. Beads of perspiration dotted above her smiling upper lip as she gazed at her recent acquisition. The schooner *Raven* was sitting high in the water, imprisoned among dozens of lines holding her hull tight against the dock. Craftsmen scurried back and forth over the ramps between the ship's deck and the pier.

Horatio Cuttingham swept his hand across their view. "She's completely gutted, stem to stern, madam. Only the original upper deck and ladderways remain. She will easily hold a hundred slaves. The canals and channels from here to Charleston are simply begging for more field hands to work the new plantations. Even a buyer from New Orleans has expressed interest–"

"What of the old cannon in her bilge? What is to be done with that?"

"The carpenter assures me that the weight balances the ship perfectly and should be left where it is. He wonders how it was placed there without piercing her hull and warns that we would incur the risk again by attempting to remove it."

"Then, by all means, leave it, Horatio," she said. "Is she ready for her new name?"

"I have contracted with a skilled gold letter painter from Charleston. Um...Madam...will we have two vessels carrying your exquisite name?"

"No. I've decided to rename the steamboat after my dearly departed daughter, Nadine. Have it repainted by the same man who letters the schooner."

Horatio bowed slightly at his waist. "Yes, madam."

"And the owner's cabin?"

"As you ordered, madam. Would you care to view it?"

"No. I will see it for our maiden voyage. You have an experienced man to captain it?"

Horatio gritted his teeth and pressed his lips together, then smiled brightly, "Of course, madam. He comes highly recommended from our contacts in Charleston. He will arrive as soon as the interior is complete, and the new sails are hung."

Lydia spun around and gave her back to Horatio. Twirling her umbrella, she spoke over her shoulder as she walked to her carriage. "Very well, Horatio. Keep them at it."

Horatio blew out a long breath watching her take the hand of her driver as he helped her into the coach.

Horatio muttered under his breath, "Bitch," as he smiled and tipped his hat to her.

The job foreman approached Horatio. "Any new instructions, sir?"

"No. Just keep them at it," Horatio said, then walked away saying, "I need a drink."

In the shade of the tavern, Horatio ordered an ale and lit a cigar. Another man at the bar, unshaven with broad workman shoulders and wearing a soiled shirt frayed at the elbows, stepped next to him.

"So, you're working the *Raven*, are you, sir?" the man asked, pushing the smell of his stale breath toward Horatio.

Horatio gave the man a quick glance, said "Yes," and turned back to the bar.

"I have a quarrel with Pulaski," the man said.

Horatio chuckled and turned back to the man briefly. "Don't we all," he said, then stepped away from him to join other well-dressed gentlemen at the other end of the bar.

"Ah, Cuttingham, join us," said one of the gentlemen. "Unless you desire more intelligent conversation with Dunkin there?"

"Who's Dunkin?" Horatio asked.

The gentleman nodded toward the unshaven man who had spoken to Horatio. "That one there, lighting his cheap cigar. Joshua Dunkin. He's been ranting for months now that Pulaski stole his nigger and owes him three hundred fifty dollars."

Horatio laughed. "Pulaski? Pulaski's in prison." He looked toward Dunkin and laughed again. "That fool will never get his money back, or his nigger."

The gentlemen shared their obvious laugh at Dunkin, then turned to other conversations and more ale. Dunkin scowled at the group, then slammed his mug onto the bar and stormed out without paying for his last ale.

"Hey!" the bartender yelled at his back. "You owe for a drink, Dunkin."

Farther along Front Street, Dunkin entered another tavern where he was still allowed an account.

"Whiskey," he ordered.

As the drink was poured, he snatched the bottle from the bartender. Taking both the glass and the bottle with him he stumbled out onto the docks. He perched himself atop a barrel set on the pier and slowly drank the bottle empty, then threw both glass and bottle into the water. His head slumped forward, and he dozed a few minutes. He awoke with his chin on his chest.

"God damn you, Pulaski," he said to his belly, then struggled to get off the barrel, falling onto the planks of the pier.

A man strolling by attempted to help him stand, but Dunkin pushed him away and cursed him. Dunkin groped for handholds to help him stand, then stumbled farther along the wharf, mumbling another string of oaths against everyone, especially Benjamin Pulaski. Nearing the town market, its bell tower not yet complete, he paused under an oil lamp and dug a piece of paper from his pocket. It was crumpled and crushed from repeated handling with much of the wording smudged by greasy fingers and creases. Under the dim light of the oil lamp, he peered through eyes fogged by whiskey and mumbled the wording he could not see, like chanting a liturgy.

"Three hundred and fifty dollars, less commission," he said with a slur. "To be paid to Mister Joshua Dunkin of Georgetown, South Carolina, for his slave George, taken on consignment, upon sale in Charleston, South Carolina."

He put a fist against his hip, nodding his head and holding the paper up by his other hand as evidence to the imagined crowd around him.

"Signed, Benjamin Pulaski, licensed buyer and seller."

Dunkin nodded to the crowd. "Yes, he cheated me...and he will pay for that deed."

He shoved his hand down to stuff the paper back into his pocket but missed the opening in his pants, letting the crumpled paper drop to the boardwalk. Steadying himself by grabbing the lamp post, he stepped around it and stumbled along the side of the building toward the river. At the corner of the building stood another lamp post, giving light to the wharf, and illuminating the stern of the schooner tied there. Several casks of pitch and turpentine sat neatly stacked on the dock, remains of the sealing and painting work performed earlier in the day.

Dunkin grabbed the lamp post to keep himself from falling into the water and noticed the lettering glittering in the yellow lamplight.

"*Raven*," he said to himself. "*Raven*...of Pulaski."

Then he yelled out, "Pulaski! You son of a bitch, come out of your ship!"

He tottered over the ramp and toward the stern ladderway. "Get up, Pulaski," he yelled. "I know where your damned cabin is."

With his first step on the ladderway, he slipped and tumbled down to the landing before the cabin door. On his knees, he pounded the door and yanked at the handle, but he could not open the door. There was a padlock below the handle. He worked to his feet and pounded the door again.

"Come out, Pulaski, you thief. Face me!"

Silence settled over the ladderway.

Dunkin leaned his forehead against the door, mumbling, "Damn you, Pulaski. I need my money."

He climbed the ladderway to the deck and wobbled off the ship, collapsing to a seat on one of the casks. He took in a deep breath and blew it out, then retched onto his boots. He jerked to his feet and spun around facing the schooner.

"God damn you, Pulaski!" he shouted.

He picked up the cask he had sat on and threw it onto the deck where it bounced once and rolled to the other side. He picked up a second cask and threw it after the first one. Then in a frenzy, he grabbed each cask in turn until he had tossed all eight casks onto the deck. The last cask cracked open at the end and poured turpentine across the deck, down into the ladderway and onto the landing.

"How do you like that, Pulaski?" he screamed.

He went back on deck and picked up the closest cask and smashed it down, splitting it open and pouring pitch. In the night heat, the pitch oozed like honey. He smashed another cask against the main mast, soaking it with turpentine. A cask of pitch he smashed on the dockside wheel, snapping off one of the spokes. Then he pulled out his knife and began slicing holes in the sails tied on the booms.

"Clean this ship up, Pulaski! It's a damned mess," he bellowed and sauntered to the stern ladderway, his pants, and shirt spattered with pitch and turpentine.

Down on the landing he pounded on the cabin door several more times, and stepped down into the hold, looking for something else to damage. The hold was empty except for a small keg of nails and a carpenter's sawhorse. Dunkin blew out his breath and sat on the sawhorse, patting his pockets, looking for the note. Not finding it, he stood and looked down at the deck around the sawhorse.

"Of course. Lost that too," he said, then plopped down on the sawhorse again, still patting his pockets. In his shirt pocket, he found the stub of his cigar and his last two matches. He struck one match along the edge of the sawhorse, but it only broke and fell to the planks. Clenching the cigar between his teeth, he glanced around for a better surface for his other match. Spotting loose bricks piled near the foot of the stern ladderway, he stumbled to them and struck his match. As the flame blossomed at the end of the wooden stick a small tongue of yellow flame hopped onto his shirt where turpentine had spilled.

Dunkin swatted the little yellow fireball, and his shirt burst into blue flames that lunged to his other arm as well. Slapping at himself, he dashed onto the ladderway, slipping on the spilled pitch and turpentine. His head struck the iron padlock on the cabin door. He dropped unconscious and tumbled down into the hold, where the flammable concoction had pooled, his burning body lighting a massive fire. Still unconscious, he was spared the pain as his clothing burned to his skin, flames consuming it in charred flakes and sizzling the fat, muscle and blood that was once an angry human being.

The schooner *Raven* erupted into flames spreading over the flammable decks, spiraling up the newly sealed masts and freshly dried canvas sails and along the freshly pitched running rigging. Her outline blazoned in the night. Flames gnawed between the deck boards, eating their way to fresh air. The fresh paint on her hull caught fire, burning through the planking from inside and dripping fire from above. The roar of the fire shook the nearby buildings and lit up the harbor in a fiery false sunrise.

The ship was fully engulfed when the first fire responders arrived on the dock, with more men running behind. The first man had to hold his arm in front of his face to protect it from the heat. The ship was already far too damaged to save.

"Cut her loose and push her away," he yelled to the others.

Men grabbed hatchets to cut *Raven's* lines. Others brought long poles and oars to push the flaming hull away from the dock and other ships.

"Push her out farther!" someone yelled. "It's low tide. Don't let her settle close."

The flames consumed the ship. Burning spars, rigging, and booms collapsed onto the deck. The tandem wheels turned to cinder and fell into the center as the deck collapsed into the hold. The hull itself was burning toward the water line. The usual damp planking in the bilge burned ferociously, the new pitch between the boards adding more fuel to the flames and joining the inferno. Water poured in through a hundred openings, floating some of the turpentine and molten pitch off the planks. Then the surface of the water itself ignited and burned, and burned.

At dawn, charcoal littered the surface of the water in Georgetown harbor. The air was filled with smoke and the stench of sodden fire.

Sheriff William Postell stood next to Horatio at the edge of the pier above the last sight of the schooner *Raven*. Postell held a crumpled note in his hand.

"There is nothing left of the ship to retrieve, Sheriff," Horatio said. "It is all collapsed into the mud. Nothing is to be seen, even at low tide."

"We found a burned body floating in the harbor this morning," Postell said. "No one could identify it, but we found this consignment note on the walkway. It was likely Joshua Dunkin."

"He had a grudge against Pulaski over the theft of his slave," Horatio said.

"Pulaski is in prison, and Mrs. Binterfield just bought his ship. Why would Dunkin–"

"I don't think he knew," Horatio said. "He probably burned it because it still had the name *Raven* on the stern." Then he laughed.

"Now, why is that funny?" Postell asked.

"Tomorrow it would have shown the name, *Lydia*."

"And you say there was an old cannon in that schooner's bilge."

Horatio nodded his head. "Not that it will ever be brought up again. It is in the mud forever."

"Does Mrs. Binterfield know about this yet?" Postell asked.

Horatio sighed and shook his head 'no.'

"Well, Mr. Cuttingham, I sure as hell don't envy your next duty to Mrs. Binterfield."

September 9th, 1848. Leonardtown, Maryland

Sonja handed her list to the young clerk in Yates' store. "My husband is waiting outside and will help you load it in our wagon."

"Yes ma'am, Mrs. Yount," he said.

Ben had purchased a copy of the weekly *St. Mary's County Beacon* and was sitting in a shaded chair in front of the store.

Sonja tapped Ben on his arm as she walked by.

"Going to the millinery shop, Ben. I need something besides a farmer's straw hat."

She took two steps then stopped and turned around.

"B...James, I saw the new schoolmaster in the store. Would you please speak with him to settle the tuition for Alisha? Free schooling is provided to the poor, but we are not."

Ben entered the store and then returned to his chair. Minutes later, when the clerk came out carrying his first armload, Ben had focused all his attention at a lower corner on the back page of the *Beacon*, reading a brief article.

> Notorious Ship Burned — The correspondent of the Georgetown (S.C.) Gazette, says:
>
> The ship used by the villains Drayton and Pulaski in their brazen attempted theft of seventy-seven slaves from Washington City in April, the schooner *Raven*, was burned to cinders in Georgetown Harbor on the night of August 15th. The remains of the culprit causing the fire were discovered the following morning. Mr. Joshua Dunkin, a local slave owner was known to have suffered theft of his property by Benjamin Pulaski, the previous owner of the schooner, and continued to begrudge his loss. Pulaski and his co-conspirator, Daniel Drayton, were found guilty of all charges and sentenced to imprisonment in the Washington City Penitentiary for seven years.

Ben sighed and folded the paper, then laid it on the chair as he moved to assist loading the wagon. The clerk made several trips back into the store, as Ben rearranged the wagon contents. When they had finished, Ben went into the store to settle his account. Coming out, Ben found Sonja wearing a new hat, sitting in the chair. She looked up from the *Beacon* with tears in her eyes.

"After all we did to save her during the hurricane of '44," she said.

"There is nothing to be done about it, now," he said.

"At least *she* doesn't have it."

Ben helped Sonja onto the wagon and then joined her on the seat, flicking the reins on the horse's haunch he drove the wagon in a lazy loop around the town square. In the field behind the blacksmith shop, a crowd had gathered watching men ride their horses through the gates.

"What is that?" asked Sonja.

"I believe we are about to watch a ring jousting tournament."

"A what?"

Ben pointed to a broad-shouldered farmer mounted on a charging workhorse, bent forward in the saddle with a short stick held out before him.

"The rider has a short metal-tipped lance," Ben said. "He will try to put the tip through a small metal ring hanging in the center of each gate. The more rings he collects in a short time, gain him points of some kind."

At the end of the man's run, he whirled his horse around and charged through the gates again, this time spearing one of the rings, to the applause of the crowd. Again, he turned his horse around and dashed through the gates, after which he brought his horse to rest and handed his ring to a judge.

"Apparently they get three tries," Ben said.

A gentleman on a thoroughbred ran the course next. He stopped after two runs, having skewered all three rings. Ben and Sonja added their applause. A man in a black robe standing at the edge of the watching crowd turned toward Ben and Sonja.

New rings were attached to the gates, and another man took his mark at the far end of the field. A judge whipped down a small flag in his hand, and the rider spurred his horse. The horseman leaned far forward with his elbows close at his side and the lance tip floating steadily above the horse's head, seeming to stay at an exact height over the charging horse. The crowd grew silent. Ben and Sonja could hear the horse's hooves pound and a ringing clink as he took the first ring. The horse's speed increased through the second gate, and the second clink echoed in the air. Hushed voices among the spectators shushed one another, and in almost dead silence, except for the pounding hooves, the third clink resounded and was followed by a roar of applause. Sonja jumped to her feet. Ben and Sonja applauded.

"It is good to see you, James," Father Enders said, with his hand on the bridle to Ben's horse, stroking its nose.

Ben glanced down and smiled, then jumped down

and shook hands with the priest. Sonja remained in her seat and gave her attention to the priest as Ben motioned his hand toward her.

"Father Enders, this is my wife...Sarah."

Ben fixed his eyes on Sonja's face. "Sarah...this is Father Enders of St. Aloysius Catholic Church. He was one of my first friends here, and I am honored to introduce you to him."

Sonja's eyes flickered between the two faces and settled on Father Enders' smile.

"It is a pleasure to meet you...Father."

"I hope you two are doing well out there," he said.

She returned his smile. "Actually, we three are doing well out there."

"Three?"

"Yes, our daughter is with us, well, when we can coax her out of her little boat and away from her fishing."

Father Enders' face filled with light, "Ah, she likes to fish, does she? Is she leaving any of those fat bass for me?"

"You have to come see, Father," Ben said. "You haven't been out to see me since...in a while."

"Now that I hear of this – daughter. What is her name?"

"Alisha. Alisha...Yount," Sonja said.

"A lovely name," he said. "I must come out and meet Alisha."

"You are always welcome," Ben said.

"Perhaps in the middle of next week, if that would be tolerable," he said, then turned his face to Sonja. "I love to drop a frog at dawn."

Sonja glanced between Ben and the priest, a quizzical expression on her face.

Ben and Enders shared smiles, then the priest walked back to the crowd.

Sonja pointed her wide eyes at Ben. "You're good friends with a Catholic priest?"

"You object?"

"N-no. I am just surprised. Especially since you have not even mentioned his name since I arrived."

"He and I like to fish for bass in our run," Ben said,

then flicked the reins on the horse.

She kept her eyes pinned to the side of his face for a moment, then frowned. "He fishes by dropping frogs?"

"Just the one," Ben said.

Havre de Grace, Maryland

A gentleman in a stylish well-fitting suit sauntered along the extended walkway from the large weekly steamer to the shore near Concord Point Lighthouse. His silver-topped cane tapped on the boardwalk, matching his stride and the heel strikes of his shiny high-topped shoes. Below his felt Cahill hat, set at a jaunty angle, he wore long black side whiskers, a thick mustache dangling below the sides of his mouth, and chin whiskers combed neatly to a point. Behind him, two porters carried an assortment of matched leather luggage and packages. He trouped to the nearest livery stable and rented a coach and four. There, he stood aside as the four horses were attached and the porters loaded his baggage, then tipped the porters handsomely, under the keen eye of the driver.

The driver tipped his hat. "Where shall I take you, sir?"

"Lapidum," he said.

The driver blinked his wide eyes and tipped his hat again. "Yes, sir."

"And, do not dally," the gentleman said.

The driver mounted the coach and snapped the reins on the horses. The coach soon crossed the swing bridge at the lockhouse, then dashed north along the canal towpath. Arriving at Lapidum, the driver waited while Jesse Price swung the bridge around to him. Then the driver worked his horse team with finesse to make the sharp left turn and pull the coach across the narrow bridge. The driver pulled up in front of Freidman's Mercantile and Post Office, then jumped down and opened the coach door.

"This is Lapidum, sir."

"Very good," he said. Then he stepped down and adjusted his coat. "Wait here. We will go elsewhere as soon as my business is finished inside."

Once inside the store, the driver heard loud voices for several moments, then the gentleman returned to the coach in a somber mood. He pointed toward the uphill turn in Stafford Road and the narrow lane continuing off it into the trees.

"Straight as an arrow, across the little bridge, to the log house beneath the big oaks in the distance," he said.

The instant the coach pulled in front of the Pulaski home, the driver hopped down and opened the door for the gentleman, tipping his hat. A woman stepped out onto the porch wiping her hands and staring at the sight as the gentleman approached.

"What to do you want?" Catherine Price asked.

The gentleman punched his hands onto his hips. "Who are you?" he asked.

Catherine straightened her spine and raised her chin. "And who are you?"

He relaxed his shoulders and gave her a broad smile, then removed his hat.

"I am Aaron Pulaski."

Palmetto Haven, South Carolina

Lydia Binterfield sat in her deceased uncle's padded leather chair, resting her elbows on the large mahogany desk shipped to her from Havre de Grace, where she once lived. The desk had been her late husband's, its top still stained on the right from his mortal wound, delivered by her lover. Another stain at the center was from the fatal shot to her half-brother's head by her hired assassin, after her brother exiled her to South Carolina. She slid her fingertips delicately over the two stains, admiring the sheen of the colors in the evening lamplight.

One of the house servants escorted Reed Jefferson, the plantation overseer, to the doorway of Lydia's study, then left them alone. Jefferson tapped lightly on the doorway.

Lydia studied a document she had read several times, pretending not to hear him until the timid third set of knocks.

She looked up and smiled at him. "Ah, Mr. Jefferson, thank you so much for leaving your duties to meet with me. How are the hands?"

"Performing well, madam," he said coming before the desk, "without backtalk from any of them."

"Excellent, Mr. Jefferson. Since we came to our agreement on expectations of the house servants and field hands, I have been very pleased with your accomplishments."

He bowed slightly. "Th-thank you, ma'am. I am eager to serve you."

"Yes...yes, I see that."

There was a noticeable moment of silence.

"And now I wish to offer you even greater responsibility."

"Yes, ma'am. Whatever you need of me."

"Mr. Jefferson...I need you to add additional duties to your role as overseer. I need you to serve me as the plantation manager."

"Ma'am? As overseer and manager?"

"We will call you by your new title of plantation manager, and you will perform both overseer and management duties as I assign them."

"Thank you very much, ma'am."

"And...we will increase your salary in recognition of your promotion. Is that satisfactory, Mr. Jefferson?"

"Oh, yes ma'am, that is most satisfactory. Thank you."

"That will include signing orders, invoices, shipment and purchasing documents," she said.

"Oh...well...ma'am...I..."

"You need not worry about sums and business details, Mr. Jefferson, but businesses do run smoother when there is a man to sign the correct papers. I will ensure everything is in order with them."

Jefferson's chest expanded, and his spine straightened. "Very good. Ma'am. Very good. Is there anything I can do for you at this moment, to...start off cracking, as Mr. Cuttingham might say? And, oh, is he assuming new duties as well?"

"Well, Mr. Jefferson, his duties will take him elsewhere. I wish you to discharge him immediately and have him removed from the plantation before the night is through."

Jefferson's mouth fell open, then he immediately closed it. "Yes, ma'am."

"Very well, use whatever steps you feel are required," she said as her smile faded. "See me in the morning to confirm that Mr. Cuttingham is gone, and we will confirm your new title then." She motioned him away and returned to reading the document.

Outside the mansion, Jefferson walked quickly to the bunkhouse where his assistants slept and relaxed at night when not on duty. He entered without knocking and glanced around the open area. He pointed at two men he trusted most and knew neither had love lost for Cuttingham.

"Murphy, Smith, come with me. Bring your rifles."

He paused on the front porch for the two men to step out, then spoke again.

"We have enjoyable work to do, boys. Mr. high-and-mighty-Brit Cuttingham just got his walking orders from the lady, and we get to deliver them."

The three shared broad grins.

"She wants him gone before sunrise," Jefferson said, "but I says we throw his British ass out right now."

"Did she say not to bruise him?" Murphy asked.

Jefferson's eyes sparkled. "I don't think she'd want the man dead – for all the trouble that would cause – but I figure anything else is fair game."

Thirty minutes later, a badly bruised and soiled Horatio Cuttingham was tossed into an aging flat-bottomed bateau with a single oar and no luggage, then shoved away from the plantation's loading dock on the river.

"Maybe Pulaski will find you," Jefferson yelled.

"Yeah, and cut your damned throat like he promised!" Murphy yelled.

Jefferson stood with his arms crossed watching the boat drift away from the dock lights, then turned to his assistants.

"I'm taking his quarters, boys. I'm making both of you my senior assistant overseers so you can share my quarters between you if you can get along. There's room for you both. That place is comfortable and has bedrooms for me and my nigger girl, but I'm taking her with me. I'm used to her, and she does everything I tell her; day and night."

The other two chuckled and followed Jefferson back to the white quarters.

"Can we get our own girls now, Mr. Jefferson?" Smith asked.

"Long as it don't rile any of the servants working around the mistress."

He stopped and turned on them, pointing his finger. "But you do something that causes that kind of trouble, and you won't be alive when you go into the river."

October 17th, 1848. Leonardtown, Maryland

Ben sat comfortably among the stuffed chairs arranged in an oval on the upper floor of the bank building. The Leonardtown Reading and Debating Society met there monthly to discuss current events, local gossip, and recent books. Ben sat at the far end from the discussion master, which was proper for a newcomer, and even surprising that he was invited at all, especially to Vincent Camalier who sat next to him.

Ben's invitation came from Dr. Spalding, an admirer of mystery stories, who had loaned Ben his copy of "The Purloined Letter" by Edgar Allan Poe. Even though Ben stumbled into the invitation accidentally by appearing interested in the story during a conversation with the doctor, with the help of Sonja, he did read and enjoy it. Ben came to reading late in life, having missed so much schooling as a youth, but he had mastered reading business ledgers and was learning to read newspapers and stories in journals. Ben and Sonja both read it and discussed the story in the evenings, drawn into solving the mystery of the letter. Days later, when Ben chanced upon the doctor in town and spoke of the story, Spalding suggested Ben join the next meeting of the society to hear the group discuss it.

At the beginning of the meeting, while the men collected drinks from the refreshment table in the corner, the conversation went directly and heatedly to the coming presidential election. "The Purloined Letter" quickly faded from group interest.

"...but the Whig party was against the war with Mexico," said a heavyset bearded man in a dark brown suit, wagging his finger at another member.

"Yes, true, but Zachary Taylor is the candidate, for

God's sake," said the other. "The hero of the war."

"And the Democrats led us during that war, George," said Camalier.

"And it was the Democrats who led our country into the financial panic of '37," said another.

"But look at their candidate, Andrew," George said. "Lewis Cass is from Michigan. How can we expect him to speak for us?"

"Yes," added another, "but Taylor is a Kentuckian, and has slaves of his own. He will do the right things."

"Don't forget about the new Free Soil Party," said Spalding. "Van Buren is going to pull some Democrats away."

"Hogwash," sputtered another.

A cacophony of conversations bubbled around the room, proposing a variety of complaints and actions. Spalding turned to Ben.

"James, what do you think?"

Ben sighed and looked down at his hands.

"Well, sir, I stood next to Andrew Jackson as a drummer boy at New Orleans in '15. And then served under him in Georgia as private, corporal, sergeant, and lieutenant, until I was wounded...."

Silence swept around the room, and all eyes turned to the quiet man holding a borrowed copy of "The Purloined Letter."

"...General Jackson always said General Taylor was an honorable man, even if beyond his prime. I would like to think that a man who could be trusted to lead the entire army of the United States of America into battle, could be trusted to do the right thing in Washington."

Several men clapped, a few calling out "Huzzah. Huzzah." The rest were quiet, but without scornful expressions in his direction. Camalier leaned over and patted him on his shoulder, holding his drink toward him in salute and smiling.

After much more heated discussions, the group rose to go home, shaking hands and welcoming their ladies in from the outer room. Several ladies accompanied their husbands but generally met by themselves to discuss their own issues. The retreat from the debating society allowed a few brief minutes of social mingling and tempered the heated rhetoric that had arisen in the previous half hour. A tall man with a thick mustache and long side whiskers, who had said little during the meeting, approached Ben and shook his hand.

"I was in Georgia under Jackson, as well. In which unit did you serve?"

Ben hesitated. "Colonel Clinch's Regiment."

"Ah yes, Henderson and Renowitz's 'Cotton Mouth' soldiers were in that regiment. Fine fighting men. Did you know any?"

Ben bit his lip then let out a long slow breath and took the gamble. "I served directly under Lieutenant Renowitz."

The man's eyes went wide. "Good God, man. You were a Cotton Mouth." Then he frowned. "I was Colonel Clinch's Adjutant. I don't recall an officer among the Cotton Mouths named Yount."

A fat bead of sweat trickled down behind Ben's ear and meandered down the side of his neck. He swallowed.

"It was a battlefield commission, sir. Captain Henderson was dead, as were most of the other officers. Lieutenant Renowitz was newly arrived, and I was his sergeant at the time. I was wounded soon after, but General Jackson confirmed my rank when I was discharged."

"Ah, yes, I see. Well, Lieutenant James Yount, I am pleased and honored to meet a fellow veteran of that nasty war in Spanish Florida. Welcome to Leonardtown, sir."

The man walked away smiling and nodding to the others, apparently assuming Ben knew who he was.

Sonja stepped next to Ben and slipped her arm under his. "Who was that?"

"Someone who knows far too much about a part of my real life," he whispered. "Now, what did you ladies discuss? Sewing, cooking, and babies?"

Sonja turned her face to him with ice in her eyes.

"You men. You assume we are mindless flesh bags to be squeezed and jumped upon so we can push out babies and clean the house."

Ben jerked his head back and widened his eyes. He met hers with a keen focus for a brief pause. A wrestled smile emerged on his lips.

"So, other than discussing how your husbands are pigs, what other topics arose?"

"The election, Ben. What else? Just because we don't yell at each other like you men do, doesn't mean we don't harbor the same concerns."

He took her hand as they walked down the stairs. Once outside, Camalier and Spalding were having an animated conversation under the lone street lamp on the corner.

Spalding smiled at Ben and Sonja. "Sorry we didn't get to that story tonight, James."

A moan arose from the nearby jail window. Spalding turned toward the sound and frowned. "The sheriff is out of town, and no one has fed those poor slaves today."

"I thought old man Wilby was supposed to take care of that when the sheriff is not around," said Camalier.

"Are they waiting for someone to pick them up?" Ben asked.

"Yes, Josiah Bond was supposed to collect them yesterday, but he's down with yellow fever, and I told him to keep his family at home until he recovers," Spalding said.

Ben turned toward the jail as another moan drifted across the road. "Who has the key?"

"Anyone," said Camalier. "It hangs on a spike inside the jail office, and the door to the office is never locked."

"Yes, that's how old Wilby gets in. I need to see if someone knows what has become of him," said Spalding.

After a short chat, Spalding and Camalier tipped their hats again and returned to other friends in the crowd.

Ben fixed his attention on the jail.

Sonja leaned closer to Ben whispered to him. "What are you thinking, Ben?"

"Nothing. There is nothing I can do about it."

They said goodnight to the two men and stepped away. Moving toward their wagon, beyond the meager light from the lamp post, Ben slipped his arm around her waist and pulled her closer to him.

"I must confess, Mrs. Yount," he whispered. "I do enjoy a good squeeze now and then."

She punched her elbow into his side.

"Not tonight, you won't."

Late that night, the quarter moon peeked between sliding clouds, painting near deserted Leonardtown with momentary bands of dim silver light. In the shadow of Moore's Tavern and Hotel, a man skulked along walls without windows and windows without light. He flitted from the shadow of the hotel to that of the large oak tree near the courthouse. A clump of heavy clouds drifted ponderously in front of the moon, draping the road in darkness, hiding the silhouette of the man. Moments later, there was a faint squeak as the jail office door opened and the man entered. He stood still in the darkness, breathing short breaths, waiting, waiting.

Ben calmed himself and put out his hand against the wall, searching in the darkness for the spike that held the keys. Dangling from his other hand the sack of food for the slaves scented the stale air with the aroma of fried ham and fresh biscuits. His free hand touched against a spike, but nothing hung from it. He felt further along the wall but found no other spike. He sighed and moved farther along the wall. Metal chimed close to his face. The unmistakable feel of a cold steel gun barrel pressed firmly against his cheek.

"You tryin ta steal my slaves, mistah?"

Ben froze. "J-just going to feed them."

"You lyin. You don't needs a key to pass food inta them niggas upstairs."

"I was just going to feed them."

The sack of food was snatched from Ben's hand. The gunman kept the pistol barrel against Ben's head but handed the bag to someone else.

"Here, Wallace. Take this food and lead our passengers down the hill."

Ben relaxed his shoulders. "I spent too many days in darkness with a man not to know his voice."

The gunman chuckled and lowered the pistol. "I'll be damned."

They embraced in a brotherly hug.

Ben held his hands on the other man's shoulders. "How in this world—"

"Let's get down the hill and then we can talk, Ben."

An hour later, his head still spinning in curiosity, Ben climbed into a rowboat and sat near the stern as the boat made its second trip out to the fishing sloop anchored in Britton Bay. The clouds had herded together and filled the sky in darkness, blocking the light from the moon. A weak wind played across the surface of the water. Only a dim light on the sloop gave them direction to follow. When he neared the sloop and stood up in the boat, a large bulky figure stepped between Ben and the light, and a strong hand pulled Ben up onto the deck.

"Come below," the man said.

In the hold, under the covered hatch, two burning oil lamps hung from hooks. Ben squeezed his eyes shut to the glare of the light, at first only seeing silhouettes encircling him. He blinked several times as his eyes struggled to adapt to the meager light that felt like bright sunshine after the hours of darkness. The first face to finally come into focus brought a wide grin on Ben's face.

"Simon Bond. Why in God's name did you leave Canada?"

Simon spun Ben around to face the men around him.

"Gentlemen, this is my greatest friend, Benjamin Pulaski." Then he slapped Ben's shoulders. "And these magnificent men around you are free negroes, just recently resigned from Gray Rocks Plantation."

All the faces around Ben were black and laughing. One man stepped forward wagging his finger. "Not all of us are recently resigned."

Ben grabbed his hand and shook it vigorously. "Bartrum, it is good to see you again, although I never imagined you and Simon would ever leave Canada."

"I am a Canadian citizen now, Ben," he said

Ben looked at the others. "What are your names?"

He extending his hand to each man as they introduced themselves. When Ben had greeted them all, he turned back to Simon.

"So, this sloop has a black crew and captain," Ben said.

"Black crew," Simon said, "except for one white boy pretending to be captain. We don't dare sail down around here without a white face."

Ben glanced all around the hold, smiling and looking at the faces.

"I don't see a white boy, Simon, and I don't see your wife, Lettie, either. I'm glad you were sensible enough to leave her safely in Canada."

Simon displayed a toothy grin. "Well, she had to stay at home with our son"

"You have a son?"

Simon turned away, speaking over his shoulder. "Let's go introduce you to the captain. He agreed to stay out of sight until we had the passengers settled," Simon said. "I figured these new freemen would be more comfortable coming on board to a black crew. Blacks are still kidnapped and taken farther down south. Big money in that."

The captain's cabin was just beyond the rear bulkhead from the hold, so they had to climb out of the hold. The quarter moon gave them meager light. Simon gestured toward the cabin top sitting barely above deck and the heavy tiller aft of that.

"No wheel on this boat," Simon said. "Just pull or push, but she responds quickly enough."

They rounded the cabin and stepped into the narrow well before the single door. Simon knocked on the door.

"Visitor to see you, Cap'n," Simon said.

"Enter."

Simon pulled the door open. "Too small for three people in there," he said and pushed Ben inside, closing the door behind him.

The captain sat behind a small desk at the rear of the cabin with his back to Ben. Ben glanced around the small room. A bright oil lamp hung over the desk. The right wall was filled with a single narrow bed. The left wall held a narrow shelf, shoulder high with a peg railing. A compass and sextant sat among several books and a small spyglass.

Ben frowned and cleared his throat. "Captain..."

The captain slowly turned around. His neatly combed

black hair shone in the lamplight, flowing onto thick side whiskers that ended below at the edge of his jaw and then joined a heavy mustache. His chin was shaven clean. He was surprisingly young looking. His eyes sparkled with amusement, but he said nothing.

The captain smiled and rose to his feet, extending his hand and opened his mouth to speak. Ben gazed at the details of his face and his eyes flew wide open. Ben reached forward and grabbed the captain, pulling him over the little desk in bear hug.

"Aaron!"

Aaron pulled away and dashed around the desk, returning to his father's arms.

"How?" It was all Ben could say.

Still embraced, Aaron spoke into his father's shoulder. "So much to tell you, Pa. So much I want to know."

Ben pushed Aaron out to arm's length. "You look wonderful, son. You must come see your mother. Let's take a rowboat up the run."

"I want to see her with all my heart, Pa, but I must finish this task first."

Ben hugged him again, then released him and wiped his eyes. "What do you need to do?"

"Just a quick run down to the Potomac and meet a steamship at Saint Clement's Island. Come with me. We will be back by sunrise."

They stepped up onto deck together where men were already loosening ties on the sails in the cool dark air and pulling up the anchor. Simon moved quietly among the other men on deck, whispering to each one.

Aaron leaned close to Ben. "Simon is the real captain. All I could add is some money and a white face, but it was so good to see him again – and to be a part of this."

They stepped to the tiller. Aaron chuckled softly. "He lets me steer as long as I show my face to passing boats."

The light breeze was sufficient to move the sloop once the sails were up. The ship glided gently toward the east, then caught fresher wind beyond Buzzard Point for their southerly run to the Potomac. With most of the stars covered by clouds, the slender beaches on either side showed as faint ash colored lines in the distance.

"I came home to Lapidum in early September," Aaron said. "When I discovered Ma had left with Alisha, I went to York Furnace to see David at Grandpa Jundt's farm. It was the first time I had been back since Maggie and Sarah died."

Aaron took in a deep breath in a moment of silence. Ben looked straight ahead, waiting for Aaron to continue.

"Ma had told the Bookers about you being in prison

and that awful woman who had tried to take Alisha away. So, I went to see Anthony in Philadelphia."

"What did he tell you?"

"I think everything, Pa. Ma's trips to Norfolk, then Washington. Your capture and imprisonment. Grandpa's death. Your escape from prison. The *Raven* burning. And, finally, where you were hiding."

Ben swept his arm over the deck. "And all this, you put together since then."

Aaron laughed. "No. No, Pa. Anthony and Simon were already working on this. Simon was going down to help anyone from Gray Rocks he could. He needed a white face that could steer a ship when I came to Philadelphia, and I needed a way to find Ma and Alisha...and you when I learned of your escape."

"I am so glad you came, Aaron." Ben patted his back. "You do look well, son. Very well. Apparently, beaver trapping agreed with you, in spite of our worries about you in the California mountains."

Aaron laughed out loud.

"Shhhhh!" whispered Simon standing before the mast.

Aaron returned to a low voice. "I never did get to go beaver trapping, Pa."

"You didn't? What have you been doing?"

"Well...Pa...I...we...we...discovered gold not far from that store where I sent my last letter, Sutter's."

"Gold? Enough to get you back to Maryland, huh?"

"No. A lot of gold. Hundreds of pounds."

"What? Surely not hundreds of pounds."

"Surely so, Pa. My share was actually over two hundred pounds."

"Good God, son. That is a fortune."

"There were three of us that found it together in the stream, and we each staked a claim of about an acre on either side of the stream. When I thought I had enough to last my lifetime, I started thinking about going home. I sold my claim and went back to San Francisco to catch a ship."

"That's where I hear every loose man in the country wants to go to," Ben said.

"Yes. It was a hundred times more crowded when I got back there. I tried to get passage on a ship, but most ships were losing their crews as soon as they moored. San Francisco Bay was filling up with abandoned ships. Some had been run aground and broken up for firewood. So, I started buying those ships for next to nothing."

"You own ships?"

"Only one now, but I bought dozens. I hired men to take them apart and stack the wood."

"For firewood? Is there much money in that?"

Aaron laughed softly. "No. The men needed more money to afford supplies to go after the gold, so I had all the workers I could use. And the gold claims needed lumber for shacks and water slews to work the gravel for gold."

Ben looked at his son in the dawning light, his face full of pride and admiration.

"Pa, I bought sound seagoing ships for a hundred dollars and sold their lumber for thousands. I kept the best one for my return and gathered a crew."

Aaron smiled. "I told them if they would get me to New York, I would make them all equal partners in it. That would give them more money than they ever made. So they stayed with the ship, elected their captain and were filling the ship with men eager to go to California."

"Why New York, Son?"

"Pa, I had always heard there were a lot of rich people in New York, so I figured they would have good banks."

"That was sound thinking, son. I am really proud of you. But you should know that your mother and I would be proud of you if you came home poor, as long as you came home to us."

"Pa..."

"Yes, son?"

"Pa...I have more than four hundred thousand dollars..."

Ben's eyes went wide, and Aaron's filled with tears.

"...and no wife or child to care for."

Ben put his arm around Aaron's shoulders. Aaron pulled a handkerchief from his coat and wiped his eyes.

"But I know what to do with that money, Pa.... The

same thing Anthony Renowitz is doing with his. Every man, woman, and child I can take out of slavery will be a part of my family."

Ben looked out over the water at the growing line of light above the eastern shore and sighed.

"I have learned an important lesson through my failure in Washington, son. I was counting freed slaves for my own ego, and because of that, I damned most of those from the Capitol to a far worse life than they ever imagined enduring. I hope you never have to experience that kind of shame."

Ben folded his arms and took in a deep breath. "Each person we help has a name...is a human due our respect...is a loved one to someone. We can't just help them get away from where they are. We have to help them get to where they can have a life without slavery or slave chasers hounding them. Even if we are only a step in that journey, we have a responsibility to move them in the right direction."

Just beyond the southern tip of Saint Clement's Island, the sloop dropped anchor as the sun rose above the tree line and the crew busied themselves with setting out fishing lines. The Virginia shore was a slender thread of pale trees three miles in the distance.

Simon raised a narrow light blue pennant to the top of the mast. He locked eyes with Aaron and motioned his head toward the bow. Aaron stepped toward the center of the deck, with Ben following him.

"I need to show a white face, Pa. That's my arrangement with Simon."

Ben smiled and knuckled his forehead like an old sailor respecting his captain. Aaron released a chuckle. Simon approached them and pulled off his hat and bobbed his head to Aaron.

"Massah, massah, tell me whats ta do, suh. Yassah, yassah."

The crew chuckled at Simon's speech but kept their heads bowed while they worked.

Aaron turned away from the island and grinned. "You're putting it on thick, Simon."

"People like me have to speak like that every day,

Aaron, but I enjoyed playing the fool for the crew's amusement."

"So, what do I need to do next?" Aaron asked.

"Just keep showing that pine colored face of yours, young'un." Then he turned to Ben and bobbed his head again. "I look forward to a long chat with you, old friend, when we get back to your little bay."

"I want to hear about your plans and your family...Pa," Ben said.

Simon shook his head no as he smiled. "My son calls me Father, not Pa, and he is going to have a little sister or brother in the spring."

Ben grinned and moved to extend his hand to Simon, but Aaron grabbed it.

"Oh, yes, of course," Ben said, "people may be watching."

From far out in the river, a passenger steamboat gave two short blasts of its horn and then moved toward the sloop. As the steamer came near, she stopped her side paddles, and her crew tumbled out canvas fenders along her side. The sloop's crew pulled up the anchor, setting her adrift and then grabbed onto the steamer's railings with boat hooks. A steamer crewman opened the railing and stood by holding a ledger up with officious pomp, then winked at Aaron. The escaping slaves were brought up from the hold and sent single file onto the steamer. The crewman with the ledger made a great show of counting the slaves and making marks in the book, then after the last one stepped aboard, he offered the ledger to Aaron for signature.

On the page before Aaron, were some misspelled obscenities and a stick picture of a man with an enormous penis standing behind a cow. Aaron made a show of accepting the count and signed the ledger with additional obscenities. The crewman winked again and saluted him. He closed the railing as the sloop's crew released their hold with the boat hooks. The steamer added power to her wheels, speeding on her way south to the Chesapeake Bay.

Ben smiled at Simon. "Very smooth operation, Simon."

Simon smiled and turned to Aaron. "Please point to the masthead, Mon Capitaine."

Simon called out to the crew to set sails, then turned back toward Aaron and bowed.

"And now young Mister Pulaski, if it won't dirty your lily-white hands, please steer the *Jester* back up to Leonardtown without running her aground."

"Appropriate name for your sloop," Ben said. "I didn't notice it when I first came on board."

"Named her myself," Simon said.

The sun was well up into the late morning sky when the *Jester's* rowboat moved up the McIntosh Run toward the little pier at the edge of the Yount Farm. Sonja was out by the barn after feeding their horses. She turned toward the water at the sound of men's voices yelling her name. She held her hand above her eyes to shield them from the autumn sun as the boat neared. One man stood up in the middle of the boat and waved at her. She frowned, at first concerned since Ben had been gone all night, but then saw his face in the boat as he rowed. The standing man yelled again, and again, as she stepped cautiously toward the water.

"Ma! Ma!"

She stopped and placed her hand against her chest. "Oh...oh..."

"Ma! Ma! It's me, Ma!"

"Oh...my...God. Oh my God," she mumbled stepping faster and faster, running toward the pier, tears welling up in her eyes. Then she screamed, "Aaron!"

She pulled her skirt above her knees and ran as fast as she could toward them.

"Ma!"

"Aaron!" Sonja called to him. Turning her head back toward the house, she yelled. "Alisha come out. Aaron is here!"

The door to the house burst open as Alisha charged toward Sonja, then seeing Aaron, she changed her run toward him. Alisha was faster than Sonja, getting to the pier a split second ahead of her. Alisha threw herself into his arms, wrapping herself around her brother, and tipping them both backward. Sonja ran to them, grabbing them in her arms as Aaron fell backward. Aaron roared. Alisha screamed. Sonja screamed. All three tumbled from the pier into the water. Simon grabbed an oar to extend to them, but Ben pushed it aside.

"It's only waist deep here," he said. "Learned that from Father Enders." Then he jumped into the water with them, pulling them to their feet.

The four of them shared hugs and talked in a gibberish of broken words and unfinished comments that no one could else could understand. At that moment what was said was far less important than holding on to each other. Simon watched them with a broad smile on his lips and tied the bowline to the pier, then stood in the boat.

"I am not getting my boots wet," he said, then stepped up onto the pier.

Later with dried bodies and damp hair, except Simon, the five shared a long and generous supper ending with the retelling of Aaron's story while he held his mother's hand and his sister sat at his knee. Ben brought a second chair as he and Simon carried two mugs of rum out to the maple tree in the front field.

"So, what will you do next, Simon?"

"I will stay down near Solomons, where I can get messages from my friends near Gray Rocks. Anytime one of those folks can slip away I will come collect them and send them north."

"You hope to do damage to that plantation?"

"I hope to rob them of every slave there."

"Won't they buy more?"

"Ben, I imagine you know what's happening to slave prices as well as I do. Every time they lose a four-hundred-dollar slave, it will cost them a thousand dollars to replace him. I learned a lot about economics in Canada."

"That plantation family has a lot of money," Ben said.

"I think they used to," Simon said, "but from what I learned from Lettie, old man Williamson lost a lot on gambling and bad business investments. If I steal twenty of their slaves, it will cost them thirty thousand dollars to replace them. In Mississippi and Georgia, good field hands are fetching fifteen hundred dollars each. The prices are bound to go up like that around here. Aaron has offered to have an agent buy ten local slaves at that price, just to drive it up quicker. The seven men we took away from here last night could cost them as much as ten thousand dollars to replace."

"Will Aaron stay with you on the *Jester*?" Ben asked.

"No. It worked out for both of us this trip, but he has other things in mind. I'll let him tell you what those are. Besides, I have another family member of yours willing to come work with me."

Ben frowned. "Who?"

"Your brother."

"Edward?"

"He is free to come and go anywhere, Mister Yount. While you cannot. Odd, isn't it?"

Ben chuckled. "Odd, for now, but Anthony thinks he can get me pardoned after the election."

Simon composed his face. "I hope that is so, old friend. In the meantime, stay away from stealing slaves."

"I was just going to feed them.... Now tell me about your family."

"Benny was born six months after we settled in Canada," Simon said through a broad smile.

"Benny?"

"Benjamin Miles Bond."

"Thank you, Simon," Ben said. "I am honored."

Simon faced Ben and his smile faded. "He is named after Benjamin Franklin."

"Oh...oh, well that is a fine thing...that..."

Simon burst into laughter, slapping Ben on the shoulder. "Of course he is named after you. You are the closest thing to a brother I have ever had – even if you are too pale by far." He laughed again. "Lettie and I decided that since neither of us had known our fathers, we would name our son after our brothers."

"And does Miles live close to you?"

Simon's laughter stopped. "No. He went down to New York before Benny was born, and we have heard nothing of him since then."

"Never a letter?" Ben asked.

"He never learned to read and write, Ben."

"He would have learned much from you, Simon, as I did."

Simon gazed up at the first stars showing themselves in the evening sky.

"I will need your son one more trip, Ben, then after I pick up Edward in Solomons, I will bring Aaron back here – or he will make his own way back. We have yet to discuss that."

"I will make my own way back," Aaron said as he approached them carrying a chair.

From the house, bathed in yellow lamp light in the open doorway, Sonja called out to them. "Bring my chairs back in here when you men are through."

<hr />

November 7th, 1848. Leonardtown, Maryland

A crowd milled about on the brown grass yard in front of the county courthouse. Just beyond the edge of the property, ale stands were set up under banners on opposite corners; one for Taylor and Fillmore, the other for Cass and Butler. Some men, who had not yet gone into the courthouse to cast their vote, enjoyed being escorted from one stand to the other by supporters. Dr. Spalding approached Ben, Sonja, and Alisha. His cheeks were red in the chilled air, his smile broad and he rubbed his hands together.

Spalding removed his hat and gave Alisha a showman's bow stirring her giggles. He gave Ben and Sonja a friendly nod as he replaced his hat.

"Just think, my friends, on this very day, in every town all across our huge country, we are all voting for president at the same time. What an amazing feat. The entire country all on a single day."

Vincent Camalier stepped from the crowd and joined Spalding. He tipped his hat to Alisha and Sonja.

"Your daughter could be a younger twin, Mrs. Yount," he said, then turned his attention to Ben. "This time we will know the results much sooner than before, James."

"I hope this new law continues," Spalding added. "We should hear the results as early as February when Congress counts the votes."

Ben brought his hand to her elbow, and steered her away, taking Alisha by the hand. The Pulaskis ambled farther into town.

"Anything new from Aaron in his letter?" Ben asked.

"I set it on the table for you to read yesterday," she said.

"I meant to, but then had to go after that damned horse again. Dolly does not like to stay in our barn. It's no wonder we got her for such a low price."

"Well, I would still rather have her than...what is the name Alisha gave her...Betsy, the farter," she said and chuckled.

"She called her 'Stinky.' So...anything new from Aaron?"

"No. He is still planning to have that Hughes man in Havre de Grace make spikes at his factory and ship them to his lumber business in California," she said. "He will visit us next week."

Ben smiled, then grew silent for several steps.

"I would like to see Zachary Taylor win the election. I know he is a slaver, but Anthony said in his letter that Taylor is our best hope for a pardon," Ben said.

Sonja frowned. "I would think Lewis Cass would be more likely to do that, Ben, since he is from Michigan," she said.

Ben's face snapped up, then swiveled in both

directions, but no one was nearby.

He whispered hoarsely, "James."

Sonja let her shoulders sag and blew out her breath. "I'm sorry...James."

Alisha looked down at her shoes. "Yount, Yount, Yount."

A boy sauntered by, sticking out his tongue at Alisha, and walked on.

She stooped down and plucked a stone from the road and spun around, launching the stone at the boy with a fast overhand throw. It hit him hard in the center of his back. He winced and stiffened his back, then turned his face to her over his shoulder.

"Didn't hurt," he said with a clipped breath.

"Alisha!" Sonja said. "Why did you do that?"

"He did it to me, but the schoolmaster didn't see him."

"Who was that?" Ben asked.

"Jimmy Moore," she said.

"I think he likes you," Ben said.

Alisha whirled around to grab another stone, but Sonja snatched her up by her curls and pulled her close.

"That is enough, young lady."

Ben smiled and kept his attention straight ahead.

As they passed the bank, the tall Major Ben had spoken with at the debating society stood talking to another man near the entrance. The man dressed in a brown suit, his hat down low on his forehead. Their eyes met, and Ben nodded to him and smiled. The major watched Ben keenly, not acknowledging him, just watching. He said something to the other man with him who turned and looked boldly in Ben's direction.

Ben glanced at the man but did not recognize him. He tapped Sonja's arm and inclined his head toward the man.

"Do you know him?"

Sonja regarded the man then shook her head no.

"He seems to have a keen interest in me," Ben said.

Sonja turned her face to Ben. "And of course, if he is looking at us, he is looking at you and never your pretty wife."

Ben whispered, "Maybe he heard you call me Ben."

Her eyes widened. "Certainly not...I hope."

Ben stopped and took in a deep breath. He blew it out, then turned and walked toward the man, his arms swinging as he stepped.

"May I be of assistance?" Ben said to the man as he stood in front of him.

The man's gray eyes were intense, and his clean shaven face showed no emotion. "Well...um...why yes, yes you may if you are the husband of Sarah Yount."

"I am, sir."

"I am Detective Brandon Alexander from Baltimore City, and I wish to interview Mrs. Yount."

"Why?"

"I understand she was the targeted victim of a deranged woman in Baltimore Harbor who was shot by a Mr. Albert Bollard, a private security investigator."

"She explained all that to me. I was in another city at the time. Did she not submit herself to interview then?"

"That was only cursory, Mr. Yount, and filled with misunderstandings by the initial officer. We now have evidence that this Ramona Tatum knew your wife previously and there was already bad blood between them."

Ben held his hand out in question. "I have only been in Leonardtown a few months, recovering from...my...trips abroad. How is it you knew to come to this lovely town to interview my wife?"

"Ah yes. She had been on my inquiry list for some months. My mother's sister lives in Leonardtown, and she sends me copies of the *Saint Mary's County Beacon*. There was a recent article about the Leonardtown Reading and Debating Society, listing you and Mrs. Yount in attendance, and of course Major Carmichael. Now, sir, may I call on your home tomorrow and interview your wife?"

"We live a mile or so out of town–"

"Yes. So Major Carmichael was telling me. He is quite impressed with your war record, back in...'15 was it?"

"Long before your time, I believe, Mr. Alexander."

"Well, I am 35 years old, so I was only two years old

then, but I did see service in Mexico. May I visit your home tomorrow, Mr. Yount?"

"Yes...you may...Two o'clock."

"Thank you, sir." The man tipped his hat and walked away.

Ben turned to Carmichael, who had stood there listening to the conversation.

"Good day, Mr. Carmichael," Ben said.

Carmichael smiled. "Good day to you, Mr. Yount. By the way, I have been reviewing my personal papers of our days in Florida, and still have not come across the name Yount among the Cotton Mouths."

Ben returned his smile. "Have you come across the name of Bond, Sergeant Simon Bond?"

"I do not recognize the name, sir."

Ben kept his smile, but there was no light in his brown eyes. "He was with me in the swamps. Apparently, your papers may be incomplete, sir. Good day."

Ben returned to Sonja and Alisha. "The man was indeed oogling my wife."

"Nonsense," Sonja said, but without rancor.

Ben gave her a warm smile and placed his hand gently on her arm.

"Actually, Sonja, he is a detective from Baltimore, and wishes to question you about Ramona Tatum."

Sonja frowned and glanced at the back of the detective as he walked up the street.

"I thought I was through with all that. I don't want to have to discuss it again."

"I believe it is unavoidable, Sonja. And you have to give it very careful thought." He lowered his voice. "She attacked Sarah Yount, but it appears that her grudge was against a Sonja Pulaski."

Noon, November 8th, 1848. The Andrew Jackson Tavern, Washington City

Wilson Landry swallowed the last of his whiskey and ordered another. The bartender frowned and pulled out a small ledger from a shelf under the bar. Then he stepped close to Landry and spoke in a hushed tone.

"I am sorry, Mr. Landry, but you have reached your limit in my credit book."

"That is not a problem, Freddy. When the election is counted, I will be flush in money for years to come."

"Still, sir, without approval from Mr. Little, I can't serve you anything more."

"You do realize that I work for the attorney general of the United States, don't you? I could hold great power over your freedom."

"Mr. Landry, I realize that you are a clerk for the attorney general—"

Landry's voice grew slightly louder. "I am an assistant supervisor, sir."

"Yes sir, Mr. Landry, I'm sure you carry a heavy responsibility."

He raised his voice again. "I'll have you know that I am working directly for Mr. Isaac Toucey, himself, helping to write the pardon list for President Polk. There are many people depending upon me to spell their names correctly so they may walk in freedom's air again. That, Freddy, is power."

"Yes, it certainly is. I will need a moment to discuss this with Mr. Little. In the meantime, allow me to provide you another whiskey, on the house."

Landry smiled and sipped his drink as Freddy walked to the back room. Seconds later, Freddy returned to escort Landry to the tavern's office. Eric smiled and shook his hand as Landry took a seat before the small desk while Freddy returned to the bar. There were several small pieces of paper laid side-by-side on the top of the desk.

"Mr. Landry, I need to share some information with you, do you mind?"

Landry made a grandiose gesture with his hand and then folded his arms.

"Let's see here, Mr. Landry, you owe my tavern ninety-nine dollars and seventy-five cents."

Landry opened his mouth to speak, but Eric waved his comment away with a finger, which he tapped on the second note.

"You owe eighty-four dollars to the Lucky Chance Tavern," then he tapped the third note, "one hundred forty-two dollars to the Whist Parlor on 7th Street," and tapped another note, "one hundred eighty-six dollars to a bordello...well, let's just say you have several hundred dollars in debt, Mr. Landry."

Landry focused his attention on the notes.

"And your salary is two hundred forty-five dollars a month, correct?" Eric asked.

Landry released a long slow breath that ruffled the papers on the desk. "Yes."

"And you will never get out from under that debt?"

"...Probably not."

"What if I could make all that debt disappear?"

"How?" Landry asked, staring at the notes.

"Does it matter, as long as no one gets hurt, and you do not get in trouble over it?"

"As long as no one gets hurt and I don't get in trouble. Yes," he said, raising his eyes to Eric. "But what will I have to do for you, Mr. Little?"

"Nothing now, Mr. Landry, but someday I will need a small favor, and I will expect you to do that favor for me."

"Will it be dangerous?"

"No, Mr. Landry, it will be an insignificant act in the grand scheme of things, and completely within your routine work."

"And what do I do now, to make this deal? Do I have

to sign something incriminating?"

"No, Mr. Landry. All you have to do now is shake my hand, and all of these notes will go into a dark drawer, never to see the light again as long as you keep your word. Do I have it, sir?"

Landry lowered his eyes and sat in silence a long moment.

"Yes," Landry said and held out his hand to Eric.

As they stood, Eric swept the notes into a drawer and stepped around the desk to walk with Landry.

"As of this moment, Wilson, you have no debt, and not only that, but you have an unlimited tab at this tavern for you and a few friends."

"Now?" he asked, showing a broad grin on his face and straightening his back.

Eric escorted him back to the bar and assisted him in his seat.

"Freddy," Eric said, "Mr. Landry is one of our most cherished customers. He is to be served whatever he requests, as long as he can still stand. On the house."

Eric glanced around the tavern, meeting the eyes of the other customers. "Loyal customers like Mr. Landry here, are to be rewarded."

When Eric returned to his office, Anthony sat at the chair next to the desk, sipping brandy poured from a dusty but expensive bottle once owned by a King of France. The door to the liquor pantry where Anthony had watched stood open. Landry's debt notes were spread over the desktop.

"Anthony, you owe me nine hundred and sixty-seven dollars," Eric said.

"The way you handled Landry was a pleasure to watch," Anthony said, then tapped the notes and frowned. "But these debts total eight hundred seventeen."

"And that bottle of brandy cost me, and now you, one hundred fifty."

Anthony smiled, then reached to a nearby side table and pulled a second brandy glass onto the desk.

"I suggest we split it."

1:00 o'clock in the afternoon. The Yount Farm

Ben, Sonja, and Alisha sat at the dining room table with their new farmhand, Albert, finishing a large mid-day meal.

"Albert," Ben said. "You handle those plow mules like they were obedient puppies."

"Thank you, Mr. Yount. We're real lucky to still have soft ground at this time of year. This is late to be turning it over," Albert said. He was near middle age and showed the hard years he had spent working other people's farms. His thinning hair on a freckled head above soft green eyes and a nearly constant smile made him easy to approach and quick to like.

"We are glad to have you with us, Albert," Sonja said. "I hope your new bed down in the kitchen was comfortable for you last night."

"Yes, ma'am. I'm going to have a nice warm winter." Then he stood from the table. "I never ate with the owners before, but I surely thank you for this wonderful meal."

"You are always welcome at our table," Sonja said through a smile.

He gently tweaked Alisha's nose and was rewarded with her giggle. "I'll get back to my chores, now," he said then nodded his head to Ben and went out through the kitchen.

Sonja watched him leave, then turned toward Ben. "He just showed up here yesterday?"

"Yes, as I told you, Father Enders sent him here with that note—"

"Note? You didn't tell me about a note. What did it say?"

Ben dug into his vest and pulled out a crumpled piece of paper, handing it to Sonja.

"I wanna see too," Alisha said and stood behind Sonja, peeking over her shoulder.

Sonja glanced up as Ben stood to leave.

"The priest certainly has a pretty handwriting," she said.

Ben stretched and pulled out his pipe, then headed for the door. "I'll be out at the maple," he said over his shoulder as Sonja read the note.

Dear James,
This is to introduce Albert Mattingly, a parishioner of Saint Aloysius. He is a kind man and a hard worker. I told him you had no farm hand.
– Fr. Enders

"That doesn't say much," Sonja said.

"Does that mean Father Enders likes Albert?" asked Alisha.

Sonja smiled at her. "Yes. I'm sure that's what it means...and maybe that Albert needs us as much as we need him."

Alisha leaned her chin on Sonja's shoulders. "Mmm. It told us all that without words," she said.

Sonja turned in her chair and held Alisha's cheeks in her hands, then gazed at her eyes. "You are a smart young lady, Alisha Pulaski."

"Alisha Yount, Momma," she said.

Outside, a horse neighed. Sonja stepped to a window and saw Mr. Alexander stepping down and tying the reins to the front post.

"Go get your father, Alisha Yount," she said.

Moments later, Ben and Sonja sat with Detective Alexander in the sitting room. A cup of coffee sat on the side table near the detective's chair, and a small notebook was open in his lap. He referred to a couple pages, then turned his attention to Sonja.

"You are Sarah Yount, a passenger of the steamer *Richmond*, arriving in Baltimore Harbor from Norfolk on November 1st of 1847. This is correct?"

"Yes."

He took a sip of coffee.

"As you were leaving the ship, you were attacked by Ramona Tatum, an apparently deranged woman who charged you with a fishing knife?"

Sonja pulled up her sleeve exposing the skin of her forearm and the red scar. "Yes."

"Why you, Mrs. Yount?"

"...I do not know. She was crazy."

He looked down at the notebook.

"She pushed past other passengers to confront you. You had never met that woman before?"

"...No."

He closed the notebook and slid it into his coat pocket, then withdrew another notebook. And opened it onto his lap.

"A witness I interviewed two days after the incident..." He glanced up at Sonja. "Said that you exchanged heated words with her before she lunged at you."

"...She was deranged. I told her to stay away from my daughter and me."

"And you had never met her before? Anywhere else, Mrs. Yount?"

Sonja swallowed. "...No."

He made a note in the book, then took in a deep breath and turned the page to view other notes.

"Her roommates said she had recently returned from upper Maryland after visiting for a period of time due to the death of her sister," he referred to his notes again. "In Havre de Grace. Have you ever been to Havre de Grace, Mrs. Yount?"

His eyes locked on hers.

Sonja touched her throat. "...No."

He referred to his notes again. "As soon as the police officer interviewed you, you then boarded the steamship *Herald* ?"

"Yes."

"Where did you go, then?"

Sonja swallowed again. "To my stateroom to lie down. My daughter and I were very upset over the incident."

"I can only imagine how difficult that must have been, but where did the steamship take you?"

Sonja was silent, her eyes fixed on his. Drops of sweat dripped down the back of her neck under her hair and wandered down her spine. The palms of her hands perspired.

"I apologize if my questions disturb you, Mrs. Yount, but I must insist—"

"She came to Philadelphia," Ben said as he stood up. "You can check the ships logs, I am sure."

He smiled at Ben. "I have already, Mr. Yount."

"Where I borrowed money from friends to buy this farm. You can check with the local bank in Leonardtown, which receives bank drafts from Philadelphia."

"Oh, I shall," Alexander said.

Ben stepped to the door and opened it.

"You have disturbed my wife pursuing lines of questioning that are outrageous and insulting to a woman who was an intended victim of a deranged stranger. You should leave."

"I have more questions," the detective said.

"They are of no consequence to me, my family, or Saint Mary's County. You are far away from your area of authority, Mr. Alexander. Now, leave my house and do not return unless you can obtain a legal warrant compelling my cooperation."

Alexander stood up. "You invited me here, sir."

"No. You insisted on interviewing my wife, pretending to be acquainted with Mr. Carmichael. You have abused both his and my good will. Now leave."

Alexander snatched his hat from the side table, spilling the coffee cup, then glared at Ben and left the house.

"Do not return," Ben said as the detective mounted his horse and trotted away.

***

Steam Tug *Hannah*, Georgetown, South Carolina

Horatio Cuttingham stepped off the *Hannah* as the sun drifted low on the horizon. He carried a long coil of hemp rope across his shoulder and dropped it next to a rusting bollard. The tug captain called to him from the pilot house.

"Just leave the line there tonight, Horatio. You can tie it 'round the bollard after you paint it in the morning."

Then the captain retreated into his cabin.

Horatio stood and stretched his back, twisting it from side to side and rubbing just below his ribs. Then he straightened himself, shook his shoulders and headed for a tavern on the wharf. Not a place he would have gone when he worked for Lydia Binterfield, but one of the few he could afford and with patrons who now accepted him. As he neared the tavern, a well-dressed young man approached him.

"Good evening, Mr. Cuttingham," he said cheerfully.

"What is so bloody good about it, and who the hell are you?" Horatio asked.

"I could be a friend, Mr. Cuttingham, and I believe you could use one."

"Then buy me a drink. What is your name?"

The man offered his hand. "Abraham Wallen, at your service."

"Good for you. About that drink?"

"Certainly, Mr. Cuttingham, but not here. Come with me to the Red House Tavern."

Horatio drank in silence until the second ale arrived at the table. He smiled and flipped his finger toward the empty table surrounding them at the far end of the tavern.

"So, my fine young gentleman, why are we here sitting away from the others and why are you buying me drinks?"

"I want to offer you a job, sir."

Horatio took a long drink from his mug and picked at a smudge on his frayed shirt sleeve.

"Doing what?"

"I want you to captain a schooner."

Horatio laughed and drank more ale.

"Who has put you up to this?" Horatio asked.

"A friend of a friend who means you no ill will."

He drained his mug and set it hard on the table. "And why the hell would this friend wish me anything?"

Abraham glanced around the tavern. "Because you know this harbor, and the Waccamaw River, and the plantations along it. Also, because there is no love lost between you and the owner of Palmetto Haven."

Abraham raised his hand to attract the attention of the bartender, then held up two fingers. As soon as the fresh mugs were set on the table and the barkeep was gone, Abraham leaned forward. "Does that appeal to you, Mr. Cuttingham?"

"Absolutely, Abraham."

"Good. There will be a passenger steamer in Georgetown tomorrow, and the captain will hold a ticket for you to go to Charleston."

Abraham reached into his coat and withdrew twenty dollars. He laid the money on the table and tapped it with his fingertips. You can use that to drink yourself into a stupor, or get a good bath, a decent shave, and a new set of clothes for your trip. Good luck to you, sir."

December 19th, 1848. The Yount Farm

Smiling faces sang 'Happy Birthday' to Alisha as Sonja carried a cake bearing ten burning candles to the dining room table. Ben, Aaron, Edward, Simon, and Albert formed a flush-faced off-key chorus that offered the harmony of a British cannonade. Alisha giggled at the bright candle lights on a cold, overcast day. The yellow lamplight cast golden yellow squares from the windows onto the snow outside, and the maple tree stood bare in the front field, abandoned by its usual companions, Sonja's chairs. Alisha stood in her chair clapping her hands as Sonja set the cake before her. Sonja slipped her arm around Alisha's waist as the little girl jumped to her feet in the chair to blow out the candles.

Ben shifted the cake aside, and gifts were stacked in its place. With screams of delight, Alisha opened her gifts and hugged the necks of each giver. The last gift had been set aside in the kitchen and only brought in after the others. Adorned with a green velvet bow, Aaron retrieved the gift and carried it laboriously into the dining room, setting it on the table with a thump.

"For me?" Alisha yelled and jumped up to Aaron's chest, hugging him tightly.

"Thank you! Thank you! Thank you!" she said.

Lamplight shone in glowing spots on the curves of the beautiful hand tooled leather saddle. Engravings of bows and flowering vines snaked around the saddle seat, and the seat itself was engraved 'ALISHA.' Alisha jumped up on the table and perched on her saddle. Edward began slicing the cake and serving, Alisha remaining on her saddle while she ate.

"Now I will look at my gifts," Sonja said as she picked up the canvas bag from the side table, mail collected in

Lapidum by Aaron. She poured all the envelopes onto the side table and scratched through them plucking out first those addressed in Isaac's neat handwriting. Then she sorted them by date, so she could read them in order but stopped with the one in the middle bearing a large heart drawn on the back. She ripped open the envelope and read it quickly, then gasped, throwing her hand over her mouth. She glanced wide-eyed toward Ben and began reading the letter again, tears streaming down her cheeks.

Ben moved toward her, but as he approached, she stood up screaming and threw herself into his arms.

"Twins!" she yelled, "Twins! A girl and a boy."

"And Harriet?" Ben asked, reaching for the letter.

"All are well, Ben. All are well."

Ben snatched the letter and held it up to the light.

"Sonja Anne and Herbert Benjamin," he read.

Aaron threw his arms around his parents. "I am so happy for Isaac and Harriet."

Hours later as Sonja put a still-excited Alisha to bed upstairs, Ben sat with the other men before the fireplace in the front room. The curtains were drawn against the night cold, and the fire had burned down to a bed of bright red coals. Ben was leaning back in his chair with his crossed feet extended toward the fire, and his rum cradled between his hands resting on his stomach. His eyes were half closed. Albert stood and stretched.

"Thank you so much for including me this evening, Ben," he said.

"You are part of the family, Albert," Ben said.

Albert bid them all good night and went to his bed in the kitchen.

Ben spoke quietly. "What are your next plans, Simon?"

"I'm going to kill John Madison."

Ben sat up and placed his drink on the table beside him. The others opened their eyes fully and sat up as well.

"What? Who is that?" Ben asked.

"He is the overseer at Gray Rocks. I have learned where he goes every Sunday afternoon."

"I thought your plan is to drive Gray Rocks into the ground," Aaron said. "To make them destitute."

"This will push them there."

"No," Edward said. "They will only hire another, and probably at less pay. Someone even more ready with the whip, likely," Edward said.

"Where is your economics in that, Simon?" Ben asked.

Simon glared at Ben. "It needs to be done."

"I could see how that could be satisfying," Ben said, "but it will also stir up concerns among the local slave owners. A murdered overseer will point to a slave – whether that is the truth or not."

"So, this overseer goes to the same place every Sunday afternoon?" Edward asked.

"Yes."

"How long has he done that?"

"Months. Years, maybe."

"Then he will likely continue to do it?" Edward asked.

"I would assume so," Simon said.

"Then we have time to consider some other action to hurt Gray Rocks through him," Edward said.

"Maybe we should look for a better way to use him," Ben said.

<hr>

December 20th, 1848. Washington City

Wilson Landry sat in the office of the Andrew Jackson Tavern, sipping the last drops of brandy once destined for the table of King Louis-Auguste.

"So, how goes this list project you are burdened with, Wilson?" Eric asked.

"Oh, Eric, I fear the damned thing will never end!"

"It must be such an aggravation."

"A drudgery, my friend, an utter drudgery. There are eighty names on it now."

Eric stepped into the liquor pantry and brought out another bottle, this one from a case sent to a Georgia Senator. He opened the bottle and refilled Landry's glass.

Landry regarded the bottle. "Oh, is there no more of

that French brandy? I do like it."

"Alas, Wilson, there are no more French kings, and thus, no more French king's brandy. However, it is French, and the elite of New York like it."

"Very well, Eric, I thank you."

"So the list grows, does it?"

"It grows, and it shrinks, then it grows, and it shrinks. I stay up half the night re-writing it after his majesty King Polk scratches out and scribbles in. Toucey does not even look at it. He just takes the new list to the President. Then Polk sends it back with more scratches and scribbles."

"Maybe you need more clerks."

"Yes. Yes, I do, but the President will hear nothing of the sort. But the nightmare will not last much longer."

"Why is that, Wilson?"

"His Majesty told Toucey, the list must be finalized and on his desk for signature no later than December 28th, so there will be no question as to which president gave the pardons. He wants it gone before Congress identifies the next president."

"So, it is likely that the next list you are given will be the final version to be copied."

"Yes. Then the damned thing will be done for this year."

"In that case, my friend, now is the time that I ask you for that favor you promised me."

Landry focused his eyes on Eric's face. Eric opened his desk drawer and withdrew a small folded paper and handed it to Landry, who opened it near the lamp. His eyes widened, and he turned his gaze on Eric.

"You want me to add these names to the presidential pardon list?"

"Yes."

"What if I am caught? You said I would have no danger?"

"You will not be caught. You will tell Toucey it is finished. He doesn't even look at it. He is tired of handling it, as are you. He will tell the President it is finished. The President is tired of handling it and getting ready to go home. He will sign it without re-reading a list he has gawked at for months."

"But if he does..."

"You will blame it on a clerk. He will be fired. You will hire a new clerk. You will keep your job. You will remain debt-free, and drink here for free for the rest of your life, because you are my friend."

Landry drank down the rest of his brandy, took in a deep breath, then blew it out. "Very well, Eric. It will be done."

He slipped the note into his pocket, picked up his hat and marched out of the office.

At six o'clock that evening a man in a black suit knocked on the door to the home of the Washington City police commissioner. When the butler opened the door, the man handed him an engraved social card stating only his name.

"I must see the commissioner on an urgent matter."

The butler admitted the man into a well-decorated parlor and asked him to wait. Seconds later, the butler returned and escorted the man to the commissioner's study. As the butler withdrew closing the door, the commissioner put on his spectacles and glared at the visitor. He flipped the card at the man.

"You are not he. You are a fraud sir, get out."

"I am neither he nor a fraud. I have an urgent message to you from President Polk."

The commissioner gave his full attention.

"Among the people being pardoned by the president are several men convicted of slave trading with newly imported Africans..."

"Yes..."

"Two men convicted of mutiny..."

"And?"

"Two men convicted of stealing slaves."

"So?"

"Benjamin Pulaski and Daniel Drayton."

"Good God, no! That is insane. There will be riots."

The man stood in silence for a moment. "Probably...if it is known."

"Of course it will be known," the commissioner said.

"Not if you tell the warden it will cost him his job if he discloses it. Not if you order your warden to tell his people Drayton and Pulaski are being moved to another prison out of the District."

"And why would I do that?"

"Because it will be a personal favor to the president of the United States, who could ensure you that you will be re-appointed to your position under the next president."

"Mmm. I am not certain he has the remaining political power to do that."

"Oh, be certain of it, sir. Also be certain that he is willing to provide you a personal pardon for the graft you have been involved in during your commission."

"What is your name?"

"It is not important, Commissioner, but understand that I have performed similar duties for the last four presidents. And I expect to perform for the incoming one as well. We all have secrets that should be kept in the dark, sir."

"I will consider it."

"Consider it until December 27th. If I do not receive your word by then, Drayton and Pulaski will still be among the pardons, but you will not, and the prison warden will become the next commissioner."

The commissioner glared at the stranger.

"I will see myself out," the man said, then he put on his hat and left the room.

"How do I reach you?" the commissioner called after him.

December 23rd, 1848. The Yount Farm

"Come with me, Pa," Aaron said.

"There is still no ice on the river?" Ben asked.

"Only plates of thin sheet ice. I want to show you something."

Can you not just tell me, Aaron?"

"No. It is an early birthday present, but I don't want to wait until January 1st. I will have to be gone, and it may be much colder then."

"That is only nine days away, Aaron."

Simon nudged Ben from behind. "Come on, old man, go see your present from your son."

"I am far from old, Simon Bond," Ben said.

"You're almost fifty!"

"Not for another year and nine days."

"Don't be so vain," Sonja said as she shoved his coat and gloves into his hand and helped push him out the door of their house.

The group kept behind him nudging him through the thinning snow toward the pier. Edward stood waiting in a small sailboat.

"What is that?" Ben asked.

"It is called a daysailer," Aaron answered.

"Is that my present?" Ben asked.

"No, Pa. We need to go just beyond Buzzard Point, but it would be silly to row all the way down the McIntosh to get to the *Jester*, and then climb on her just to sail around the point."

Everyone except Albert got into the sailboat, including Sonja and Alisha.

"It's awfully crowded," Ben said.

"She's twenty-two feet, Ben," Aaron said. "She will hold us safely, and still run before the wind across Britton Bay."

Ten minutes later they sailed out of the mouth of the McIntosh Run. The sky was steel gray without texture, the breeze modest but biting, and the short waves had white caps. The surface was garnished with laces of ice, undulating between the waves. The passengers snugged deeper into their winter coats with their collars turned up, their fogged breath drifting away like smoke from dark teepees. The little sailboat leaned away from the wind and dashed past the wharf to Buzzard Point.

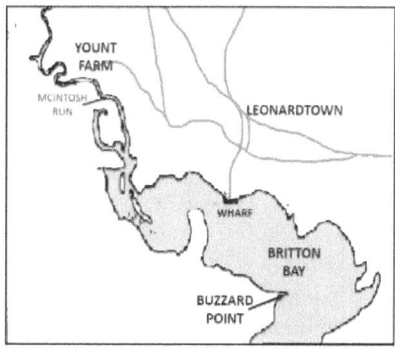

There they tacked and ran south only a few hundred yards, where Simon and Edward lowered the sails.

"Look ahead, Pa," Aaron said.

"Look at what, son?"

"Look down the bay, Pa."

"I can't see all the way down the bay, son, that damned ship is in the way."

"What ship, pa?"

"What ship? Have you gone blind? That three-masted schooner dead ahead."

Aaron made an effort to squint in the direction of the schooner, then pointed at it.

"You mean that three-master schooner right there?"

"Yes."

"The one with the dark green hull? The one that's a hundred and twenty-five feet long at the deck, and a pudgy twenty-eight feet abeam that only draws eight feet when she's fully loaded? That one, Pa?"

"Well, it's the only one, son…"

Aaron's eyes sparkled, and he grinned like a ten-year-old, as did Simon and Edward.

"Happy Birthday, Pa."

"Oh my God!" Sonja screamed and laughed.

"Is that ours?" asked Alisha.

Ben eyed Aaron. "Surely you are joking."

"Pa, I could buy ten of those, if there was a need."

Ben's mouth dropped open and he turned his eyes back to the ship.

"Good God in heaven," he said.

Ben kept his eyes on the ship a long moment, then turned his face toward Aaron and Simon. He wore a broad grin and his brown eyes danced with light.

"Now we have a much better way to use the overseer...and it is time I do what I am supposed to be doing."

December 26th, 1848. The Andrew Jackson Tavern. 4:00 O'clock

"Well, Jonathan, how did you like your role here in Washington?" Eric asked.

"My best one ever, Eric, and only an audience of one to appreciate it."

"So, the Commissioner agreed to give the orders to the warden?"

"He told me he had already done it. The prisoners will be at a side door at dawn tomorrow."

"Thank you for helping me, Jonathan."

"I am so tired of playing King Louie on stage, under all that white makeup and the wig. It was a true pleasure to pretend to be someone ominous with my own face. I shall pursue such a stage role when I return to New York."

"How can I repay you, old friend?"

"Only the return ticket, as I requested, and your promise that you will visit me, the next time."

They shook hands. "Done."

Eric handed Jonathan the train ticket to New York City and escorted him out of the tavern into the growing darkness. Coming back into the tavern, Eric caught the attention of the bartender.

"We have some work to do, Freddy."

***

The Office of the President, Washington City. 5:00 O'clock

Vice President George M. Dallas walked into the office without knocking, the president's secretary hovering over his shoulder in the background. President Polk waved away the secretary and sighed.

"George, it's late in the day...."

Dallas wore a smirk as he dropped a stack of papers onto the president's desk. The top paper was the neatly penned pardon list delivered earlier by the attorney general. The papers below it were the individual pardons for each person. All the forms had been signed by Dallas.

"Mr. President, are you satisfied with this list of pardons?"

"I have seen it until I am sick of it. I will sign those damned papers and then be done with it."

"That is a unique collection of people, Mr. President. There could be complaints."

"There are always complaints. Do you object to any of them, George?"

"I am still a Philadelphian, Mr. President. I applaud your list."

Polk eyed him a moment, then stood and offered his hand. "Why, thank you, George. We haven't always agreed on my decisions, and I am happy to know this last set of pardons sits well with you."

"It sits very well, sir." Dallas smiled and gave a slight shake to his head, then left the room.

President Polk took in a deep breath then blew it out.

"Irving," he called at the door, and it immediately opened. "I knew you were close out there. Let's get these things signed and then go home."

Irving brought an inkwell for the sideboard and several pens. Polk sat at the desk, turned the stack of papers at an angle so it would be easier to position his arm while signing, then held out his hand. Irving dipped the pen into the ink, shook the drop hanging on the steel tip and handed it to the president. He lifted the lower edge of the list with one hand to expose his signature and brought the pen down to sign it. He handed Irving the pen and accepted the next one offered, raised the lower edge of the next paper and signed again. The mechanical motion continued until at last, he signed the bottom of the final form.

The president leaned back in his chair and sighed, rubbing his wrist. "Keep the ones I need to hand out personally and send the others to the attorney general in the morning."

"His secretary is in the outer office waiting to pick them up."

Polk smiled. "Good man, that Mr. Toucey. He knows how to put his staff to work."

"As do you, Mr. President."

"Quit kissing my ass, Irving. I'm going upstairs to change for another social. You go home as soon as you give Toucey's man the rest of those pardons."

In the outer office, Irving selected the special pardons and placed the others in a large envelope for Wilson Landry. Irving was busy closing up his desk as Landry left.

Landry headed straight for the attorney general's office. There he withdrew the pardons for Drayton and Pulaski, folded them and slipped them inside his coat, then he placed the others on Mr. Toucey's desk. He removed the final list from the top and replaced it with another. The replacement looked exactly the same, except the names of Pulaski and Drayton were not included.

Home of the Washington Police Commissioner. 5:30 O'clock

The police commissioner inspected himself in his bedroom mirror, straightened his tie, then tugged his tuxedo coat firmly against his chest.

"Hurry, my dear," he said into the air. "We cannot be late to this party. The president will be there, and we shall talk."

"Yes, dear." Her voice drifted in from the next room carried on an undisguised tone of aggravation.

He stepped out of his room, meeting her in the hall and rushed them down the stairs, passed the butler at the front door and then into their waiting carriage.

"Really, Walter, must you push me so?" she said.

A Private Mansion, Southeast Washington City. 6:00 O'clock

The Commissioner and his wife nearly threw their coats into the arms of the doorman. As soon as they entered the huge salon, already filled with guests chatting amiably and brightly lit by three huge crystal chandeliers holding dozens of candles, the commissioner approached the host for a quick handshake.

"Has the president arrived?" he asked.

"He is by the piano, sir."

Leaving his wife standing alone, he made his way to the far end of the salon. At that instant, the president stood alone sipping his glass. The commissioner made his bold move. He approached President Polk, grasped his hand in a firm handshake and leaned close to the president's ear.

"It is done sir," he whispered. "I have already given the order. They will be out of the city the first thing in the morning and no one the wiser."

Polk frowned and stepped back, pulling his hand away from the commissioner. "Who...ah commissioner. What are you babbling about?"

"The secret pardons, sir...for Drayton and Pulaski."

"Pardons, those are not – Drayton? Drayton and Pulaski? I signed no such pardons for those men."

"But, but...your man sir, he came to my house...orders from you...

"I sent no man to your house," Polk said, a scowl descending on his face. "What have you done, Commissioner? What orders have you given and to whom?"

"To, to the prison warden, Mr. President. To release them."

"You ordered the release of Drayton and Pulaski? Are you insane?"

Polk scanned around the room, focusing on a large man in a poorly fitting tuxedo standing alone in the corner. He signaled to the man, who came toward him. The President tapped the commissioner's chest.

"Are these men out of prison?"

"No. No, not yet, sir, not until in the morning."

"Then you get to the prison, now. And stop that release."

The president turned to the large man. "Ashton, go with the commissioner. Make certain that the orders he

gives are followed immediately, then report back to me –
regardless of the time."

Washington Penitentiary. 6:00 O'clock

Eric and Freddy, dressed in heavy dark blue coats and
fur hats, brought the panel wagon through fresh snow
near a side door of the Washington Penitentiary and
waited. They walked to an iron door and knocked on it
three times with a rock. The lock mechanism in the iron
door clanked and the door swung open, bathing the side
yard in yellow light through a light snowfall.

"We are here for the prisoner transfers," Eric said.

The guard peered out at the wagon then to either side
of the doorway.

"That's not supposed to happen until the morning."

"We need to get 'em out of the city. We can't chance
someone seeing them."

"Wait here," the guard said, then slammed the door.

Two guards stepped out, each pushing a handcuffed
prisoner before them. The prisoners' hands were secured
behind them, and each clutched a meager canvas bag
that slapped the backs of their legs. Eric and Freddy
jumped down from the driver's seat and opened the
wagon's back doors.

The lead guard jerked his prisoner to an abrupt halt
before the open doors.

"Don't you got something for me to sign?" he asked.

"Not a fookin' thing, man," Eric said. "We just do
what we're told, same as you."

"At least tell me where yer taking them," the guard
said.

"To the fookin' train. Then we shove 'em into a freight
car, and we're done. You wanna go with 'em?"

"Hell no," the guard said. "I'm sick of sitting in that
damned chair twelve hours a day, watching these two
piss ants read newspapers and write letters."

The guards chuckled and removed the handcuffs.
Together with Eric and Freddy, they shoved the
prisoners into the wagon.

"Where are you taking me?" Drayton asked.

"Someplace you ain't gonna like," Freddy said, adding a growl to his voice. "Someplace deep in the south."

Freddy pushed Eric in after them. "Lock 'em down tight," he said. "And watch 'em like a hawk."

Eric picked up a chain from the floor and began to rattle it as Freddy closed the back door, leaving the little window open.

"Good riddance," one guard said, then they both laughed and went back to the yellow light and warmth inside.

A Private Mansion, Washington City. 6:20 O'clock

The commissioner and Ashton took horses from the host's carriage house and rode through the city. Breath rushing out from the horses' nostrils like escaping steam. The snowfall thickened. Blocks away they galloped into an intersection, just as a man stepped off the sidewalk. The commissioner yanked on his reins to avoid hitting the man. The horse's hoof slipped on the snow, and he plummeted onto his side. The commissioner flew from his saddle, sliding slid several yards in the snow, but without injury. The horse whinnied in pain. Ashton ran to the horse to examine it.

"Leg's broke, Damn," he said. "Commissioner, take my horse and keep going."

Leaving Ashton with the injured horse, the Commissioner mounted the other horse and continued to the penitentiary.

Washington Penitentiary. 6:40 O'clock

The Commissioner mounted the front steps and pounded on the door.

"Open the door, Damn you, this is the police commissioner!"

A sleepy-eyed guard opened the door and let him in.

"Where is the warden?"

"He's at home, sir."

"Take me to the cells of Drayton and Pulaski," he said.

Another guard, sitting in the lobby reading a paper,

stood as the commissioner spoke. The commissioner pointed at him.

"You. Come with me."

Pounding the steps to the next floor, they entered the lonely hallway to the secluded cells. The desk was empty, and both cell doors were opened. A guard lay sleeping on one of the cots. The commissioner kicked the cot.

"Wake up, damn you!"

The guard pulled himself up, half asleep but standing. The commissioner grabbed his coat collars.

"Where are Drayton and Pulaski?"

"Gone, sir. Transferred as ordered."

"Ordered by whom? When? To where?"

"By the warden, sir. They were transferred to another prison. Farther down south the other guards said."

"Which other guards?"

"The ones that took 'em, sir. 'Bout a half hour ago."

Marching back to the lobby, the commissioner found Ashton waiting with his hat in his hand. His knees were wet from kneeling in the snow.

"We have to get some men together," the commissioner said. "We need to call out the police to search for them."

Ashton frowned and approached the commissioner. "No sir," he whispered. "I think that would bring far too much attention to what has happened."

"But...but the president told you to ensure my orders are followed."

"Yes, sir, he did, but I have other orders from him that I must follow now. In this situation, the best orders are to keep things quiet. I have a carriage outside to take you home."

⚬⚬⚬⚬⚬

Washington City. A wagon rushing north. 7:00 O'clock

The darkness within the panel wagon was occasionally broken by moonbeams slipping through the small open window in the back door.

"Surely you can now tell me where we are going," said Drayton.

"Yes, I can Mr. Drayton," Eric said, kicking aside the loose chain on the floor. "You are going home."

Drayton stared silently into Eric's face.

"You are Mr. Little," Emilio said. "And what of me?"

"You will stay in the back of the tavern for a couple days, until you decide where you want to go, and our mutual friend brings you the money to get you to where ever that is."

"I would like to walk in the sunshine," Drayton said. "Is that possible?"

Eric placed his hand gently on Drayton's arm. "Of course, Mr. Drayton. As soon as we get out of Washington. In the meantime..."

He reached down to snatch up a blanket covering a basket and two suitcases. He opened the basket and began pulling out smoked sausages, baked bread, cheese, and bottles of wine.

"On the way, we will have a picnic, and you will change clothes."

An hour later they pulled away from the road and stopped within a stand of trees next to a creek. An enclosed carriage sat in a small clearing. Drayton stripped off his prison clothes and stepped into the creek to wash. His body covered itself in goosebumps, and his breath came like steam from his mouth as he splashed himself with ice cold water. Eric built a fire and tossed their prison garb into the flames as both men changed into new clothes, while Freddy took the horses from the wagon and attached them to the carriage. When the other three were settled into the carriage, Freddy withdrew a bottle of whale oil from the boot of the carriage and splashed it in and on the wagon. Then he took a burning stick from the fire and tossed it into the wagon. The wagon burst into flames as the carriage team trotted farther north.

Within another hour they drew up to a modest train station on the edge of a small town. Eric pointed to the east. "That track will carry you around Washington, then to Baltimore and on to Philadelphia and New York."

He pointed west. "That track will take you to Pittsburgh, then to New York where you can get a ticket to Massachusetts."

"I do not wish to travel in a slave state for one second longer than I must. I would like to take the train to Pittsburgh."

Eric reached into his coat and withdrew a thick envelope.

"This will allow you to go anywhere you wish."

"Thank you, sir. I only wish to go home to my wife and family. Please tell me, how has Ben faired?"

"He has been in hiding in southern Maryland under another name."

Drayton smiled, but there was no light in his eyes. "Then it is time for both of us to go home."

He drew Eric into a long hug, then did the same to Freddy. "Thank you. Thank you."

"Please use a name other than your own for now, Mr. Drayton," Eric said. "We expect a pardon from the president—"

"The president is pardoning me?"

Eric smiled. "He is, but he is unaware of it. You will be contacted by a Mr. Renowitz when the deed is official."

Daniel Drayton put on his hat, pulled his overcoat close and picked up his suitcase.

"Goodbye, then," he said and turned toward the train station.

"Mr. Drayton," Eric said. "Was it all worth what you endured, when we could have taken you out a year ago?"

Drayton sighed and faced Eric. "It was my protest against the infamous and atrocious doctrine that there can be any such thing as property in man!"

He glanced up at the sky, then turned away.

Eric watched him walk away, then gave his attention to Emilio and pointed at his face. "You need to shave. Then we will return to my tavern."

***

The Andrew Jackson Tavern. 8:00 O'clock

Landry snickered as he laid the pardons on Eric's desk and picked up the tall glass of brandy waiting on him.

"No one saw the names," he said with a giggle.

"Mr. Landry, you are an artist," he said, and opened his desk drawer, taking out the debt notes on Landry.

He removed the glass from the oil lamp on his desk, exposing the flame, then handed one of the notes to Landry. Landry stared at it a moment then smiled and grabbed it, holding it over the flame. Eric picked up a nearby brass spittoon and set it on the desk. As the note was consumed by the flame, Landry dropped it into the spittoon. One by one, they burned all the notes and dropped them into the brass cauldron.

"Go have Freddy open a fresh bottle and set it on a table just for you," Eric said.

Landry danced out of the room. Eric slipped his hand into the desk drawer and withdrew another folded note. It was the note from the bordello, showing Landry's debt there, now paid by Eric.

"Just in case," he said, returning the note to the drawer.

Eric rose from his desk and stepped to the back door of his office. He opened it into his storage room and went to the back of the building overlooking alley. Emilio was sound asleep on his cot at the rear of the storeroom. Three empty wine bottles lay on the floor close by. Through the back window, faint moonlight dropped in, painting Emilio Zenobi's clean cheeks in faded pewter.

Freddy burst into the storeroom.

"The police commissioner is out here, and he just punched Landry in the face!"

Eric dashed from his office to find two men wrapped in a gouging embrace, each trying to protect his own face even as he tried to poke an eye of the other. Muffled grunts and curses erupted from each man.

"Oh no," Eric said in a whisper. "These two men should not know one another."

He and Freddy pulled them apart.

"What is this about?" asked Eric.

"He took my seat," Landry whined.

"There are no reserved seats in a public tavern," the other said.

Both men showed red eyes and gave slurred speech while they struggled to stand.

"Gentlemen, you should go home and forget about this," Eric said.

"Do you know who I am?" the commissioner said raising his chin, oblivious to the spittle on his lips.

"No," said Freddy, "and we don't want to, and tomorrow you won't want that either."

"I will provide you a carriage home, sir," Eric said to the commissioner. Then he patted Landry's shoulder. "Please wait in my office, and I will get you home soon."

Landry huffed and walked away toward the back of the tavern. The commissioner grasped his own lapels and wobbled precariously on his feet.

"I'll get the carriage," Freddy said.

Later, Freddy returned to the tavern after delivering each man to his home. Dawn was well advanced, and a thin yellow strip glimmered behind the crest of the trees on the avenue. The gray clouds were drifting apart, and light blue hinted between them. Freddy fell into the chair in front of Eric's desk.

"Hell of a night, boss," Freddy said.

Eric blew out his breath. "Did either man ever say

they knew each other?"

Freddy shook his head and rolled his eyes toward the ceiling. "No. Just two drunks fighting over a chair."

"Go home, Freddy. Stay a couple days. Come back fresh for New Year's Eve."

⁓⊙⊙⊙⁓

December 27th, 1848. The Office of the President

Irving escorted Mr. Toucey into the office.

"You sent for me, Mr. President?"

"Did you bring the papers I requested?" he asked, holding out his hand.

As Polk took them, he eyed Mr. Toucey. "These are all of them? You are certain?"

"Yes, sir. Except those held out by Mr. Irving."

"Irving," the President called.

The door opened, and Irving placed the other pardons on the President's desk. "May I assist you, sir?"

"No. I need to do this for myself."

He looked up at both of the men. "Sit."

Polk pulled the top sheet off the pardons from Toucey and placed the list to the side. He read the first pardon and then lined out the corresponding name on the list. When he had finished the stack from Mr. Toucey, he set them aside and went through the bundle brought in by Irving. When he completed the list all the pardons had been set aside. He scowled at both men.

"You swear to me these are all the pardons I signed?"

They both assured him, then he leaned back in his chair, resting his hands on his stomach and interlacing his fingers.

"Mr. Toucey, is the police commissioner position elected or appointed?" Polk asked.

"Appointed, sir."

"By whom?"

"By...by you, sir."

The president nodded his head. "Mr. Toucey, get me a new name for that position before the end of the day."

The president regarded Mr. Irving. "I believe you once told me that your brother-in-law had been fired from his position as an officer at the prison? Why did that happen?"

"It was after your election, sir."

"Ah...Is he a good man? A Democrat?"

"Yes, sir, to both questions."

"Have him come see me this afternoon."

⋯⋯⋯

December 31st, 1848. Great Mills, Maryland

The small rural village held a blacksmith shop, where the owner served as farrier and wheelwright as well as a bender of iron. On the opposite side of the dirt road that went north to Washington and south to Point Lookout, stood the mercantile store, which also served as the village tavern. Sunday services were over at both the Protestant and Catholic churches, so men gathered at the tavern to discuss the winter weather and spring planting, and drink ale. John Madison sat at his customary table near the fireplace, drinking his third ale.

Ben Pulaski entered the tavern, bought an ale and exchanged a few brief words with the owner, then stepped beside Madison's table.

"Excuse me, sir," Ben said, "I understand you are the manager of Gray Rocks Plantation."

"Overseer," he said into his mug, not looking up.

"I understand your employer wishes to purchase additional slaves?"

"Not at a thousand damned dollars a head, if that's what you're looking to do."

"Not at all sir, but...may I sit and join you?"

Madison looked up at Ben. "Buy me an ale," he said.

Ben motioned to the owner then sat down. "Far less than a thousand dollars, far far less."

Madison glared at Ben. "How far less?"

"Here's the thing, sir—"

"Who are you?"

"Ashton Miller, sir. I am a licensed slave trader sent here to deliver twenty prime slaves to a plantation in Delaware."

"So, what's that got to do with me?"

"Well, sir, the purchaser has died, and his wife refuses to accept them. She says she is returning to

Philadelphia..."

"So?"

"Well sir, they have already been paid for, and I've no place to deliver them."

"Give them to me," Madison said, then chuckled.

"Sir, I wish to sell them...again."

"Why are you telling me all this?"

"I think we can help each other. I do not want it known that I re-sold a dead man's property for my own benefit, so I am not looking for an official sale, just a modest exchange of money for the slaves."

Madison glanced around and then paid keen attention to Ben. "Go on."

"Mr. Madison, I make a three-hundred-dollars commission on each sale. I wish to double that. But, I need assistance from you to sell them without papers."

"And why would I do that for a stranger?"

Ben dropped his voice almost to a whisper. "Because if you help me sell these twenty slaves at only six hundred each, which is a bargain, you will keep half of that. That would mean six thousand dollars for each of us."

Madison's eyes went wide, then he glanced around again and leaned close to Ben. "Where are the slaves now?"

"In a ship moored at Solomons."

"When would I get that money?"

"The moment your employer pays me."

"What exactly do you need me to do?"

"First: Tell your employer you can get twenty slaves at only six hundred dollars each, but it must be for cash, and there will be no papers. Second: Bring your employer to my ship on Solomons two days from now and help me make the sale."

Madison emptied his mug and nodded his head, ignoring the second full mug already sitting near his elbow. "What's the name of your ship, so I come to the right one?"

"It is the only three-masted schooner at the pier."

January 2nd, 1849. Solomons, Maryland

Simon and Ben addressed the collection of men in the hold of the ship. Three were crewmen from the *Jester*, four were new crewman hired onto the schooner, and thirteen were local freemen hired for the day.

"This is a ruse to fool a greedy plantation owner into thinking you are for sale. The owner is Jason Williamson of Gray Rocks Plantation. Have any of you met him before?"

There was silence among the men.

"Good. You will each get twenty-five dollars for today. We will bring you up on deck five at a time in ankle shackles," Ben said.

Several men shared anxious glances.

"The shackles will not be locked, just hooked," Simon said. "So you will have to walk carefully. As soon as the buyer looks you over, you will be brought back down into the hold and pass the shackles onto the next five. Don't say anything to the buyer, and don't do anything that might make the buyer remember you in the future."

"He will stay in this area, a very angry man," Ben said. "Do not give him any reason to remember you."

"White folks don't remember black folks, beggin' your pardon, sir," said a man in the back.

"They do if you make'em mad," said another.

"When do we get paid?" one man asked.

"A soon as the buyer pays us and leaves. You will have your money with you tonight," Ben said.

"Do you understand?" Simon asked.

"Are you going to do this?" Ben asked.

The men traded smiles and nodded their heads in agreement.

Edward Leonard, Ben's half-brother, leaned on a barrel near the stern of the ship. Ben came to him smiling.

"It is good to see you again, Eddie."

"You are insane, Ben, but I think it will work. Any man who can walk out of Washington Penitentiary can pull off this stunt."

"I had tremendous help, Eddie. I will be years thanking all who helped."

"The others are coming back, Ben. Most the crew from the *Raven* are coming."

Ben squeezed his arm. "Just remember, for today I am Ashton Miller. After today, I am James Yount. My wife is Sarah Yount. And my daughter..."

"Yes. Yes. Yes. I understand, B'...James...Ashton."

"Good," Ben said. "I am glad you have it so clearly. Now, please hang a work canvas over the name at the stern and wrap the bow design with burlap."

The smell of fish stew and baking bread wafted through the ship.

"It smells wonderful, Warren," Ben said as he passed the galley.

At two o'clock, a rowboat bumped against the wharf. Jason Williamson and John Madison climbed up and sauntered across the gangplank onto the *Raven*. Ben sent Edward into the hold to inform Simon to stay below since Jason had seen Simon before. Ben approached Jason.

"I am Mr. Ashton Miller, and you are, sir?"

"I am Jason Williamson," he motioned to Madison, "and this is my overseer John Madison."

Ben swept his eyes over Jason and sniffed. "You appear rather young to master a plantation, if you don't mind my saying so, sir. Are you prepared to purchase slaves of high quality?"

"I am the rightful heir of Gray Rocks and own it, sir. And, yes, I do mind your haughty tone."

Ben gave a short bow. "Very well sir, you have brought specie? Coin?"

Jason frowned. "I have brought bank drafts, which I can fill out and sign if I like what I see."

Ben sighed and withdrew his watch from his vest. "Sir, I am only accepting coin. There are other potential buyers due here in one hour. If you do not wish to purchase on my terms, good day to you." Ben turned away and motioned for Edward.

"Wait," Jason said. "Yes, I brought coin, although I am not accustomed to doing so when buying slaves."

"This is a unique situation, Mr. Williamson, as evidenced by the humble price I am asking for my seller.

Six hundred each, only if the entire lot is purchased and paid for in coin."

"Very well, I will look at them."

Ben checked his watch again then sighed.

"Indeed." He turned to Edward. "Bring up the first set, Edward, if you will." Then he turned back to Jason. "These are a spritely lot, full of vigor, but a little unruly at times, so we will show them in groups of five and keep the others tethered below until time to show them."

"Sounds like I will need an overseer with a firm hand," Jason said. "I have that." He nodded to Madison.

The first five were lined up in front of the main mast. Jason ordered them to remove their coats. He went to each one, checking teeth, squeezing arms, and pushing against their abdomen. He stopped at Warren.

"This one is a bit flabby," he leaned close and sniffed, "and smells like food, but I can use him in the kitchen if he doesn't perform well in the field."

He wiped his hands on his handkerchief and stepped back to Ben. "Let's see the next group."

The next two groups came and went receiving only minor comments from Jason and none were rejected. Madison remarked favorably about their condition. The last group was entirely crewmen of the two ships. Jason lingered in front of the third black man, Daniel, from the *Raven*'s crew who came from Boston and spoke with an Irish accent. Ben held his breath. Jason reached down and pressed against Daniel's penis, then glanced at Ben.

"This one might do well as a breeder," Jason said, then returned to Ben. Daniel wore a broad grin but looked straight ahead.

"Very well. I'll take the lot," Jason said.

Ben gave a short bow.

"I will pay you when you deliver them to my plantation tomorrow," he said.

"No," Ben said. "If you wish me to tell the other buyers they have been sold, then they must be purchased now. Otherwise, we are wasting each other's time." Ben motioned to Edward. "Take them down and lock them in the holding pens."

"I can pay you half now, Mr. Miller, as a good faith

deposit and come back tomorrow with the rest of it, and enough men to get them to my plantation."

Ben paced the deck for a full minute, then checked his watch again.

"Here's what I will do, young Mr. Williamson," Ben said. "I will hold on to your six thousand in coin and to all of the slaves. Tomorrow morning you will be here by ten o'clock. If you are not here then, I will sell all the slaves to another buyer and leave with his money and yours. Do not dally, Mr. Williamson, and do not play on my good nature."

Jason turned to Madison. "Go get the chest from the boat."

Madison delivered the chest and Jason shook hands with Ben, then the two men seated themselves in the boat and rowed across the Patuxent River.

"You satisfied with half the price, Ben?" Edward asked.

Ben smiled. "I never wanted any more than this. I honestly intended the other half to go to Madison."

"Why?"

"Because he would be found out, and most likely killed on the order of Jason."

Simon stepped close to Ben and placed his hand on Ben's shoulder. "I like the irony of that, Ben."

"So, what will happen now?" Edward asked.

"Jason just lost six thousand dollars in gold coin. Chances are he will have to borrow some to make up the money he brings in the morning. All he will have left is debt and land."

"And his remaining slaves," Ben said.

"He has seventeen now, and I will have them all in Pennsylvania before the end of January."

"It is almost sad," Edward said. "He has lost his father, his brother, his half-sister, and now he will lose his home."

Simon poked Edward in the side with his finger. "And yet, that is far more than those seventeen slaves have ever had."

"Yes," Edward said.

"Alright, gentlemen," Ben said. "Let's get this ship

ready to sail. We can't be here in the morning."

Ben went down into the hold, set the chest on a barrel and opened it. "It's payday," he called out.

Looking through the chest he discovered it was filled with twenty-dollar gold pieces, but only twenty-dollar gold pieces. He glanced at the faces around him.

"Gentlemen, it looks like you won't be getting the twenty-five dollars for your work today." He could only hold it back a few seconds and then said, "You will have to be satisfied with forty."

"Don't spend that gold too soon," Simon called out. "There will be a very angry and dangerous white man out here in the morning looking for it. This harbor will not be a safe place tomorrow."

January 3rd, 1849. Solomons, Maryland

The morning sky threatened snow and thin ice laced the water near the pier. Madison rowed the boat slowly around the area where the ship had been moored. Their other boat, with men to handle the new slaves, was still rowing across the Patuxent River. Williamson sat pulled tightly within his coat with the collar turned up and the money chest wedged between his feet.

"Where did it go?" Jason said. "Where did the ship go?"

A local man stood on the wharf looking down at them. "I don't know, Mr. Williamson. It was here last night, but it was gone this morning. He told me last night he had to run over to the Eastern Shore this morning but would be back before nightfall."

"How did he register?" asked Jason. "What name for the ship?"

"Well, he never actually did that, sir. But said his name was Ashton Miller...and he had a big black with him, Simon. I had seen him before. Simon Bond, it was..."

"Simon Bond? Big black? Damn it to hell, that man shot my father!"

Madison stopped rowing. "Let's go on shore, Mr. Williamson."

Jason glared at Madison. "This is all your fault! You convinced me to come here yesterday to see the slaves."

"They were at a good price, sir."

"Good price? Madison, you imbecile. I paid six thousand dollars for nothing! For nothing, you son of a bitch. You stupid son of a bitch!"

"He paid up last night," said the man on the wharf. "Said he'd fill out the ledger before he leaves tomorrow. Paid me a twenty-dollar gold piece last night."

"What?" Jason stood shrieking. "That was my money. My money!"

"Calm down, please sir. You're rocking the boat," Madison said.

"Shut up, you stupid son of a bitch!"

Jason slapped Madison with his hat, then repeatedly hit him with it again. Madison yanked it out of his hands and threw it into the water.

"You got to quit that, sir,'" Madison said.

Jason struck at Madison with a flurry of slaps. Madison slipped off his seat into the bilge at the bow. Jason leaned forward over him to slap him again. Madison kicked his boot into Jason's face, splitting his lip and breaking his nose. Jason plopped down on the stern seat, his eyes wide open in shock, blood streaming down from his nose and mouth.

"Well, shit," Madison said. "It's all done for now."

He pulled his boot back then drove it against Jason's chest, propelling him out of the boat.

Jason plummeted into the frigid water, splashing and gasping.

Madison called out to Williamson as the boat drifted away. "You're only a few feet from shore, sir. You can probably even stand up there."

Madison regained his seat and drew the money chest close. He pulled on the oars, moving the rowboat out toward the bay.

Jason stood up sputtering and screaming. "You get back here! I will have you whipped until there is no skin left on your back!"

Madison strained against the oars, sending the boat farther and farther from shore as the other boat arrived.

"Yeah, I figured you'd want to do that, you little snot."

Madison kept rowing far out into the main channel, where he stopped to rest his arms.

The other boat had pulled Williamson out of the water.

Madison smiled. "You boys are too tired from crossing the river to catch me, now."

He could still hear Jason screaming, but could no longer hear the actual words.

Madison took in a deep breath. "Well, John, you're on your own. Where the hell are you going?"

He rowed another ten minutes then sat there drifting.

"I still got a cousin on Smith Island. Maybe he'd put me up a while...maybe he'd turn me in...nah, nobody out there turns nobody in...I'd give him a hundred dollars...he'd like that."

Madison glanced at the western shoreline. He could no longer make out Jason and only barely made out the pier. The other boat was not coming out.

"I'll bet that little shit is giving you hell," he said.

He turned in his seat and looked eastward.

"Wind's mild. Cold, but not hard to row through...I can make it to Smith Island easy...more south then east...maybe go somewhere else from there...yeah, that would be smart."

He looked down at the chest of gold near his feet and patted it affectionately.

"Let's go to Smith Island," he said to it. "Then tomorrow we'll decide what's next."

January 8th, 1849. Havre de Grace, Maryland

Detective Alexander sat in Deputy Sheriff Mattingly's office in the early afternoon. Alexander had pulled up close to the little iron stove in the corner, holding his hands out to the heat.

"So, you are chasing after Sonja Pulaski?" Mattingly asked.

"Not chasing, just an inquiry, regarding Ramona Tatum."

"Ramona Tatum? She was a pain in my ass. Trying to take away the Pulaski girl."

Alexander pulled out his notebook and scribbled in it. "I thought she came here to collect her sister's abandoned child."

Mattingly sighed and refreshed his coffee cup from the pot on the stove. He offered the pot to the detective, who waved it away.

"Ramona's sister, Rachel, was caretaker out on Shad Island. A baby washed up there in '39, and she kept it as her own. Turned out the child, a girl – Alisha – was the missing Pulaski baby everyone thought dead–".

"Pulaski? The Tatum child was the Pulaski child?"

"Yes. When Rachel came down with consumption she told the real mother, Sonja Pulaski, the child was her lost baby."

Alexander scribbled furiously in his notebook.

"So, when this Ramona showed up," Mattingly said, "She tried to take the child as a Tatum. Turns out she only did that to get the island, thinking it belonged to her dead sister."

"Ramona tried to take away the found Pulaski baby?" Alexander asked.

"Yes – well it, I mean she wasn't no baby then. Five, I think, by then–"

"How did you know the child was really this Pulaski woman's?"

"Easy, young man. All a person had to do was look at 'em with their own eyes. The child was the spitting image of the real mother, Sonja Pulaski. Golden blonde hair, fair skin, and eyes bluer than blue. Both of them."

"Blonde hair and blue eyes?"

"Yes. Her husband is Benjamin Pulaski, one of the slave stealers they caught in Washington and put in prison there."

Alexander spoke, rising from his chair. "I have met them! Sarah Yount is Sonja Pulaski. That's the connection."

He ran out of the office, leaving the door open.

"Close the damned door!" Mattingly yelled.

January 9th, 1849. Washington Penitentiary

The new warden crossed the lobby to the man in a brown suit sitting in the visitor's chairs. Late morning sunbeams pierced the tall room from high windows, and the warden's footsteps echoed off the granite floor and walls. He held the visitor's business card in his hand.

"What can I do for you, detective?"

"I am investigating a shooting, that I believe was a murder."

"A murder…in Baltimore, I understand."

"Yes sir, but I think this is a very complicated murder that involves the Pulaski family."

"A Maryland family named Pulaski," the warden said.

Alexander held up a finger. "Yes, sir, but the Pulaski you have here is part of that family. A Polish family."

The warden chuckled. "I keep hearing that, but the guards tell me he was Italian. I think you have your facts wrong, besides the prisoner is no longer here."

"What? Where is he?"

"Transferred to another prison farther south," the warden said then looked away.

"Where, Warden?"

The warden sighed, glanced around then whispered, "I don't know."

"Well, where do you think he went?"

The warden would not look at the detective. "That prisoner is not to be discussed," he said. Alexander left the lobby, stepping out into the falling snow.

<hr/>

Morning. January 10th, 1849. Leonardtown, Maryland

Ben stood with Aaron in front of the post office across from the courthouse, bundled in heavy woolen coats. He pulled open an envelope addressed to him in a familiar handwriting.

You have your pardon. Do not discuss. Go home. – A.R.

Ben smiled and handed the note to Aaron. Aaron slapped him on his back, and they both returned to the wagon. Ben snapped the reins on the horse's haunch and trotted out of town past the Moore Hotel.

Minutes later, the stagecoach from Waldorf stopped in front of the hotel, and Detective Alexander stepped down. He walked briskly to the home of retired major Richard Carmichael and knocked on the front door.

"Who is James Yount?" Alexander asked.

Carmichael released a grim smile. "That is a question I keep struggling with. Come in, detective."

As soon as he stepped inside, the detective whirled around to face Carmichael. "The woman is Sonja Pulaski. I think she, or someone close to her, killed a distraught spinster in Baltimore."

"Why? How does that connect to James?"

"They fought over custody of a daughter. I believe Sarah and Alisha Yount are in fact Sonja and Alisha Pulaski, wife and daughter of the slave stealer Benjamin Pulaski."

"That could explain it," Carmichael said. "In all my notes, everything Yount has told me about his military experience points to a Benjamin Pulaski. But, are we truly talking about the same man?"

Alexander pulled out his notebook and flipped through several pages.

"The clerk at the Indian Queen Hotel described Sonja Pulaski perfectly, but the register named her as Sarah Yount. An application placed at the Washington Penitentiary requesting visitation with Benjamin Pulaski by Sonja Pulaski listed her temporary residence as the Indian Queen Hotel."

"And James Yount knows much about Benjamin Pulaski, but still..."

"James Yount and Benjamin Pulaski are described with similar features but one, a beard."

"The scar!" Carmichael said. "Pulaski was cut in the face by a Seminole lance. It is in the records. Yount carries a slender scar on his left cheek. Of course! That man should be in prison!"

"And yet, Major, there is no Benjamin Pulaski at the prison in Washington City. I believe he has bribed his way out."

"The lying bastard," Carmichael said. "We must see the sheriff."

At the Yount farm, Sonja, Ben and Alisha danced in a circle in the front room.

"I don't want to stay here another second," Sonja said, then frowned. "We have met some wonderful people here, Ben, and I have hated lying to them. The lying became too easy. I don't know if I can face them, now."

"We should just go away," Alisha said.

Ben blew out his breath. "This will be very difficult."

"It is the perfect time to leave," Aaron said. "You came in mystery. Leave that way. We had already planned to spend a couple days sailing on the *Heron*–"

"The *Heron*?" Sonja asked. "Is that what you named her Aaron?"

"No, Pa did."

"I thought it would give us a fresh start, as well as more room."

"And what of the farm? Of Albert? Of the animals? We can't just leave," Sonja said.

Ben and Aaron exchanged glances.

"We have already thought of that," Ben said.

"Without even discussing it with me?" Sonja asked, folding her arms.

Ben smiled. "We are giving it all to Albert."

"We signed the papers days ago, just in case," Aaron said.

Sonja grinned. "Well, I agree to that.'

That afternoon, the Saint Mary's County Sheriff frowned at Carmichael and the detective. Both visitors wore holstered pistols at their side.

"At the very least, Sheriff, the man is a fake and a liar," Carmichael said. "God knows how he may have already used his lies in private around here; what damages he may have inflicted that have yet to surface. That's what people like that do. They cheat and are gone in the wind before they are caught."

"I stake my reputation on this, Sheriff," Alexander said. "I have tracked his trail, and that of his devious wife, all over the state and into Washington. The man you know as James Yount is the slave stealer Benjamin Pulaski, a fugitive."

"Thought he was in prison," the sheriff said.

"Somehow his is out and no one can answer why," Alexander said.

"Very well," the sheriff said. "Let's go to the Yount Farm and sort this out."

He opened his desk drawer and withdrew his new revolver and checked the cylinder for loads. The three men mounted horses and trotted out of town past the Moore Hotel. Within twenty minutes they arrived at the Yount Farm.

"Hello in the house," the sheriff yelled.

Albert Mattingly stepped out, holding a paper in his hand.

"Can I help you, Sheriff?"

"We are here to see the owner," Carmichael said.

Albert chuckled. "Well, sir, that'd be me, I believe. They just gave it to me."

Detective Alexander jumped from his horse, barged past Albert and shoved the door open.

"They just went off and left their house to their farm hand?" Carmichael said.

"Yes, sir. Wasn't that a wonderful thing to do. They gave me a signed paper."

"Pulaski!" Alexander's voice echoed within the house.

Albert twisted his head toward the house and then up at the sheriff. "They ain't here. Left about a half hour ago. Had a little sailboat out on the run."

At that moment, the daysailer rounded Buzzard Point and dashed to the *Heron*. With few possessions, the four Pulaskis climbed onto the ship. Daniel welcomed them, had the sailboat tied at the stern then escorted them to the cabins. In the parlor of the master cabins, Aaron pointed to the one on the right.

"That is yours," he said to Ben and Sonja. "Alisha and I will sleep in the forward cabins tonight."

"What about that one?" Ben asked pointing to the cabin door on the left.

"That's for the Captain, Pa. You are the owner. You don't have to run the ship details, just manage the operation. Sometimes you won't even have to go to sea. Your captain will do that."

Ben blinked his eyes. "And who will be the captain? You?"

"No, I have other things to be doing on land, Pa."

"So, who is the damned Captain?"

"Time for you to meet him," Aaron said, then knocked on the door to the captain's cabin.

The door opened and Horatio Cuttingham stepped out into the parlor.

"Hell no!" Ben said. "Oh, hell no!"

CONFESSIONS OF THE AUTHOR

Thank you for reading "Brazen Deceit."

1. This novel is inspired significantly by a historical event known as the "Pearl Incident," which occurred in April of 1848. A devoted abolitionist, Daniel Drayton, and his co-conspirator, Edward Sayres, brought the schooner Pearl to Washington D.C. At that time, the capitol still allowed slavery and held over 70,000 slaves in the city. Drayton and Sayres attempted to take away 77 slaves, sail down the Potomac River and ultimately deliver the slaves to freedom in New Jersey. The schooner was becalmed for crucial hours and only sailed as far as the mouth of the Potomac River before slave owners, using a steamboat, caught them near Point Lookout. All the escaping slaves were recaptured, and most sold at auction in retribution by their owners to hard labor plantations in the deep south. Drayton and Sayres were captured and sentenced to long prison terms. President Millard Fillmore granted them pardons four years later in 1852. Drayton wrote his memoir of the incident and his imprisonment, which was published in 1855. Long-suffering over the disastrous fate of the slaves he attempted to take to freedom, Drayton committed suicide in 1857, at a hotel in New Bedford Massachusetts.

Drayton's final dialogue with the character Eric Little in the scene near the train station in Chapter 35 is an actual quote from Drayton's memoir.

You can find the memoir at the Library of Congress website:

Drayton, Daniel, and American And Foreign Anti-Slavery Society. Personal memoir of Daniel Drayton, for four years and four months a prisoner for charity's sake in Washington jail. Including a narrative of the voyage and capture of the schooner Pearl. Boston, B. Marsh; New York, American and foreign anti-slavery

society, 1855. Pdf.
https://www.loc.gov/item/14019577/.

I encourage you with all my heart to read it. If you have tears to share after reading it, shed them for Daniel Drayton and the nearly four million slaves our country held in 1857.

2. In 1848 today's Breton Bay near Leonardtown was known as Britton Bay.

Please also go to www.rflackeybooks.com for a bibliography of all the Pulaski Saga (click on "Pulaski's World"). While fiction does not demand a bibliography, I think it useful to share the books I read as I developed and wrote this series. The website also contains both actual and representative photographs of images that were in my mind as I wrote.

Thank you for coming along on this journey with me.

– Robert F. Lackey
www.rflackeybooks.com
https://www.facebook.com/RFLackey.author

Share your thoughts about this novel with Robert at Rflackey.author@gmail.com

Coming in Spring 2019
The next Pulaski adventure

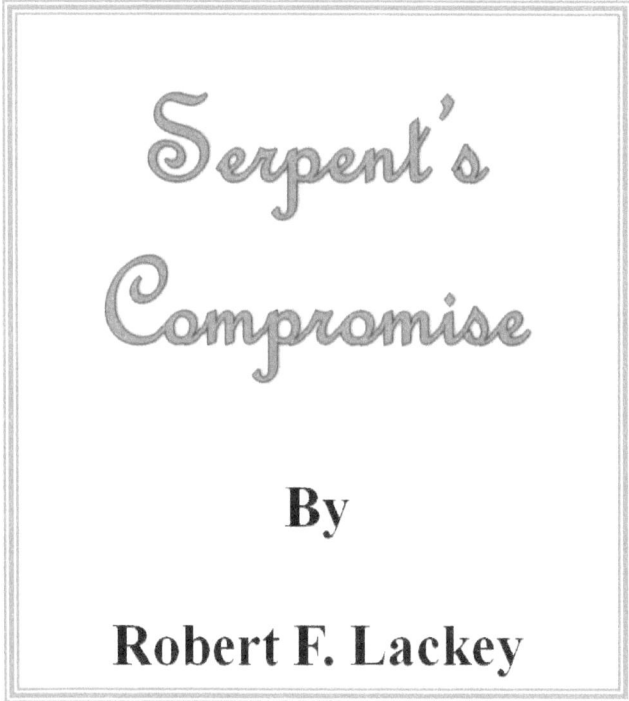

The Pulaski saga continues with the 6th volume, into the years 1849-1859. Ben and Sonja face the devastating impacts on the underground railroad, brought by a serpent placed among the agreements of the Missouri Compromise of 1850 — The Fugitive Slave Act.

Dear Reader,

I hope you are enjoying the Pulaski Saga. Reader contact is valuable to me, and in light of that, I've included a few maps in this novel, to help you visualize the easts and wests the Pulaski's travel, and I will continue to do so.

The next story, Serpents Compromise, will encompass ten years in the Pulaski lives, 1849-1859. It is a much broader timeline than previous Pulaski novels. While these novels are fiction, I work hard to keep the characters defined by the history of the time periods. The Pulaski Saga delves into historical themes, but represents them through the eyes and experiences of the Pulaskis, to personalize that history in a vibrant story.

The theme of the next story centers around the Fugitive Slave Act, and it is presented from the Pulaski's perspective. Since they have grown from acceptance of Maryland Slavery to growing actions helping slaves escape north, the Pulaski experience under the act needs to be told within a broader arc. As I begin writing the manuscript, I realize it needs to be developed under four great shadows of the act, which will be divisions of the next book:

Before the Compromise
The Compromise
The Impact of the Compromise
The Legacy of the Compromise.

Fear not friends, this will not be a dry history lesson. It will contain all the action and personal relationships of a Pulaski story, as they adjust to the new realities that test their determination. So, hang onto your seats and get ready for the next ride! There are still more books about the Pulaskis to write. We have miles and years yet to go together.

EXCERPT FROM SERPENT'S COMPROMISE

"The gray clouds overhead had drifted away in the autumn breeze exposing a bright blue sky. Ben Pulaski crouched on the deck behind the low cabin in the middle of his barge. His ears were ringing. The echoes of the firing had been almost deafening within the granite walls of the canal lock. The water in the lock wasn't completely up when the slave chasers came at them, and the lock tender abandoned the gate. That had kept the barge low within the granite chamber. The top of the cabin was even with the upper edge of the wall, just a stubby smokestack and a slender line of pock-marked wood showing above the stone blocks.

"I'm out of bullets, Ben, " Lyle Mattingly said next to him. The wound in his arm had saturated his sleeve with blood that had begun to trickle onto the deck in the cool sunshine. "I still got some powder, though, and some caps. You got any more lead?"

Ben shoved his hand into his bullet pack on his belt, and shook his head no, then held up his revolver. "I've got three loads left in the cylinder."

"Pulaski!" The shout came from the treeline, thirty yards away from the lock. "You've got to stop, Pulaski."

"Sounds like Sheriff Nayers," Lyle said. "He and I used to have drinks together once in a while when I still had a badge myself."

Ben peeked over the edge of the cabin roof. No one else had come out from the trees. Three bodies lay twisted on the dirt near of the lock, spattered with blood where the bullets had ripped into them. Ben rolled onto his back against the cabin, settling onto the deck and blew out his breath.

"Damn it to Hell. This was supposed to be an easy trip, Lyle. Just a trot up to Wrightsville and then back down to Lapidum for Alisha's wedding."

"Well, it sure went to Hell in a hurry, didn't it, Ben."

Ben cocked the hammer of his pistol. "No, Lyle. It's been going to Hell for a long time." "

Please visit Robert's website and Facebook(TM) page to learn about his current and future projects:
www.rflackeybooks.com
https://www.facebook.com/RFLackey.author

Books by Robert F. Lackey and his alter ego, Pug Greenwood, are available at his website, and through Amazon.com, BarnesandNoble.com, Booksamillion.com, and other booksellers. Kindle versions are available through Amazon.com.

Share your thoughts about this novel with Robert at
Rflackey.author@gmail.com

Future Pulaski Novels Planned

DESPOT'S HEEL
(1859-1862) Due out Fall 2019

BLOODY GROUND, SHALLOW GRAVES
(1862-1865) Due out Spring 2020

BRUTAL PEACE
(1865-1870) Due out Fall 2020

PULASKI'S REDEMPTION
Due out Spring 2021